❧ Touched ❧

Touched

Carolyn Haines

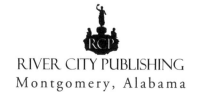

RIVER CITY PUBLISHING
Montgomery, Alabama

River City Publishing, 1719 Mulberry St., Montgomery, Al 36106

Second paperback edition ISBN 1-57966-006-1
10 9 8 7 6 5 4 3 2 1

Copyright © Carolyn Haines, 1996
First published by Dutton, an imprint of Dutton Signet, a division of Penguin Books USA Inc.

LIBRARY OF CONGRESS CATALOGING-IN-PUBLICATION DATA:
Haines, Carolyn.
    Touched / Carolyn Haines.
    p.   cm.
    ISBN 0-525-94160-6
    1. Girls—Southern States—Fiction. 2. Man-woman relationships—Southern States—Fiction.
3. Drowning victims—Southern States—Fiction. 4. Forecasting—Southern States—Fiction.
I. Title.
    PS3558.A329T68   1996
    813'.54—dc20
                                            96-679
                                          CIP

Printed in the United States of America
Set in Goudy
Designed by Eve L. Kirch

PUBLISHER'S NOTE
This is a work of fiction. Names, characters, places, and incidents either are the products of the au-thor's imagination or are used fictitiously, and any resemblance to actual persons, living or dead, events, or locales is entirely coincidental.

*For Diana Hobby Knight—a child of the
Singing River and a long-dead town.
"Sense of place" shapes her way of life.*

Acts 28: 3–6

3: And when Paul had gathered a bundle of sticks and laid them on the fire, there came a viper out of the heat, and fastened on his hand.

4: And when the barbarians saw the venomous beast hang on his hand, they said among themselves, No doubt this man is a murderer . . .

5: And he shook off the beast into the fire, and felt no harm.

6: Howbeit they looked when he should have swollen, or fallen down dead suddenly: but after they had looked a great while and saw no harm come to him, they changed their minds, and said that he was a god.

One

IN that airless zone of southeast Mississippi, July is only the promise of things to come. The last comfort of June's cool nights are gone, and August is building, building slowly in the shimmer of the sun. The days grow long and hot with no relief in sight. Mosquitoes and copperheads lurk in the coolest shade of the piney woods. It is only dawn and dusk that are bearable.

I can still feel the touch of a July morning on my skin, when the grass is soaked in silver pellets of dew and the first slanted white rays of the sun burn the green pine horizon into a dark, grainy day. Even now, some twenty years later, I remember exactly.

The date was July 1, 1926. By midday the sun was riding high in a sky bleached as pale as old lace. The air was as much water as gas. Standing in my kitchen, I could hardly draw a breath.

I folded the box of taffy closed and tied it with a red string Elikah had brought me from the barbershop. From his seat at the kitchen table, he watched. He'd finished his lunch and pushed the plate back, satisfied with the zipper peas and okra and the corn bread I'd made. In a week of marriage, he'd found no fault with my cooking.

"Tell Miss Annabelle I said 'Happy Birthday,' " he said as he pulled up his suspenders, snapped them into place on his muscled chest, and reached for his coat.

"You look nice." I was shy with him, still trying to find where I fit in his life. He was the handsomest man I'd ever seen. It hurt to look at him, and I couldn't bear it for more than a few seconds running.

"Go on." He nodded toward the door. "It's time."

Dressed in my hot, gray flannel dress, I stepped off the porch and into the heat of the one o'clock sun. It was a birthday party for Annabelle Lee Leatherwood, a nine-year-old chinless wonder who had the misfortune to take after her mother in physical appearance and personal conduct.

July 1, 1926. It was a new month. A new life for me, and I was late for the birthday party. Chas Leatherwood, a man of influence, ran the Jexville Feed and Seed. An invitation to his daughter's party was a summons, and Elikah had made it perfectly clear that I would attend, properly dressed and with a gift.

The sun was blinding, but the afternoon storm clouds had already begun to mount in the distant west. They came disguised as castles and dragons of fleecy white, but they were edged in angry gray. I knew they'd build, their deceptive masses catching colliding winds to crash and mingle, until, after a half hour or so of magnificent late-afternoon collisions, the rain would fall down in a straight sheet. But I figured I had at least three hours of swelter to endure before the momentary relief of the rain. And I was late.

I had made taffy for a present, but it hadn't set up properly, and I could feel it beginning to ooze through the pretty papers and the box as I hurried to the Leatherwood house. The stickiness of the box was disgusting. Warm. Like blood.

The clouds to the west were building quickly, a wall of fanciful shapes. They were almost motionless, trapped by the heat, waiting for the wind. Just before the storm broke, there would be the blessed relief of a breeze. But that was still hours away.

Two mockingbirds argued and shrilled in the big magnolia tree in Jeb Fairley's front yard, and I stopped to listen and to give my burning feet a rest. Some folks didn't care for the birds, but I liked them. In the spring when their young are in jeopardy, they're bold, even aggressive. Once a mockingbird had come out of a crepe myrtle tree where she had three fledglings in her nest and pecked my stepfather smack in the forehead. The bird didn't live to tell about it. Jojo Edwards wasn't a man who let even a bird get anything over on him. He killed the mother and the babies and chopped the tree down for good measure.

That's an image I carry in my head, and not even the long passage of time can dull it. I see Jojo's angry, sweating face. Hatred sparks blue from the eye slits in his fat. I can hear the ax blade biting into the smooth, barkless skin of the crepe myrtle. The sound is punishment. The blade doesn't grab in the way it does on a tree with bark. I see the raw chunk when the blade comes away, the useless flutter of leaves dropping to mingle with the feathers of the dead birds.

The memory made me hotter, afraid, and I started to run. As I turned the corner of Canaan onto Paradise Street, I heard the music. Tinny, wobbling, it seemed to come from a long way away. From all I'd learned of Jexville in my five days there as the wife of Elikah Mills, the music more likely came from the moon. The forbidden sound entered my ears and went straight to my blood. Who in Jexville owned a gramophone? Who dared to play one on the afternoon of Annabelle Lee Leatherwood's birthday party? The sticky plight of the candy, Jojo's cruel eyes, were forgotten as I started to run toward the music.

The red dust spurted up around my black shoes and coated the hem of my dress, but I didn't care. A fine red grit was settling over the bottom of the taffy-soaked box. At the white picket fence of Elmer Hinton's yard I ran out of breath and slowed. It was unseemly for a married woman to be seen running in the streets, but the music made me want to run more. I didn't know the song, but it was fast and naughty. Forbidden.

With each step the music grew louder, and when I turned right on Revelation Road, I saw her, a nine-year-old flapper who was dancing with abandon. Duncan McVay.

I would have recognized her anywhere.

Standing out on that hot street with that sticky candy, I was struck dumb by my first sight of her. She was wearing a yellow sleeveless dress that hung straight from her shoulders to her narrow hips, which were banded by a wide yellow ribbon. From there, a short skirt barely covered possible. She was tall for her age, and her long, thin legs were a blur of motion.

She was riveting as she stepped forward, then back, eyes rolling for effect and then crinkling shut with laughter. She danced alone, aware of everyone staring at her but not the least put out. Around her sat a dozen other children. Some looked terrified, others jealous. No matter what their reaction, none of them ignored her. Duncan McVay was the center of everyone's attention, including the women who stood in a disapproving group beside the back steps. They watched, too, unable to stop themselves from looking even as they disapproved.

One other woman stood at the handle of the gramophone, cranking it tight so the record spun fast and the little girl danced all the harder. Although she tried not to, this woman smiled. She glanced from the dancing girl to the knot of unhappy women, and her smile widened slightly, her own blue eyes crinkling in just the same way as the girl's.

With a cry of delight the child finished the dance and threw her hands up in the air. Her black patent leather shoes were covered orange with the dust she'd stirred dancing in the only grassless patch of ground in the Leatherwoods' backyard. She'd virtually wallowed out a hole in the ground.

"Doesn't anybody want to Charleston?" Duncan looked at a tall, skinny boy. He looked down at the grass and plucked a handful.

"Robert? Do you want to dance?" Duncan persisted. "It's fun. And easy. Mama can start the record over and I can show you."

Robert kept looking at the grass. The other children were silent, until one girl giggled.

Without turning around, Robert stood up. He shot a quick look at Duncan and saw that she was still waiting, but this time with some impatience.

"I can't," Robert whispered. "We're not allowed to dance." He turned and walked away, going right past me with his face a flaming red.

I still held the dust-soaked taffy box, which was getting soggier by the minute. My shoulders and the top of my head were beginning to bake in the relentless afternoon sun, but I didn't want to step into the yard. I'd heard enough about JoHanna and her daughter to know who they were. To be honest, I'd expected something else—horns, at the very least.

"I think it's time for ice cream," Agnes Leatherwood announced loudly. Only one child responded, a portly little girl whose unfortunate face slid into her neck without benefit of a chin. She directed an angry look at the girl in yellow.

"I want my ice cream," the plump girl said, her voice a challenge for anyone to contradict her wishes. When none of the other children got up, she put her hands on her hips. "If y'all don't come in the house now, you won't get any ice cream."

Two of the girls got up and went to stand beside her. They waited, just as their mothers waited at the steps. Agnes, a skinny version of her daughter, looked at Duncan as if she might cry.

"Put on another record, please, Mama." Duncan put one hand on her little hip and looked out. "Anyone here not a fraidy-cat?"

Two other girls got up and went to stand beside Agnes and Annabelle Lee and the mothers. Then two boys followed, then another.

The music spun out across the yard, a lively tune that set Duncan's feet flying. JoHanna McVay leaned one hand on the gramophone and watched her daughter dance. The women, transfixed, failed to go inside until the song ended.

Duncan was sweating and her black hair, cut in a sleek bob that framed her face and made her dark eyes more noticeable, was damp with sweat.

"One more song, then come inside and have some ice cream," Jo-Hanna said, cranking the machine and putting on a slower record. By her tone and actions, JoHanna McVay acted as if nothing unusual had happened in the yard. If the other women and children had intended to exclude her and Duncan, she didn't appear to notice the slight. She adjusted the needle on the record and turned away to go inside. It wasn't until she moved that I took real notice of her. She was defined by movement. Her steps were long, a contradiction of the mincing feminine steps I'd been warned to execute, yet they marked her as a woman.

In contrast to the white blouses and drab skirts of the other women, JoHanna wore a soft coppery dress with golden flowers mingled as if the colors had bled slightly. Her pale arms were daringly bare. There wasn't a collar to her dress, but a loose gathering of material that fell in a soft fold across a generous bosom. Her entire neck and a portion of her chest were revealed by the loose construction. The skirt hung straight to her calves and was dangerously slit to allow for those long strides. I had the fancy that she was some force of nature. Wind. The cool, teasing breeze of dusk or evening. Her hair, a reddish chestnut, was piled on her head in a mass that hinted at disarray. It captured the light in a dance all its own.

At the edge of the steps she caught sight of me, still standing at the corner of the yard. Several dribbles of melted taffy had oozed out of the box and drawn the interest of some passing ants. The small insects were gathering rapidly, as tantalized by the taffy as I had been by the sight of Duncan dancing.

"You must be Elikah Mills's new bride." JoHanna came forward, her hand extended. "I'm JoHanna McVay. Welcome to Jexville."

Her blue eyes assessed me, but I didn't feel judged, as I had by the other women. She saw the places where my gray dress had been let out. It had belonged to my younger sister Callie, and I'd had to take it for traveling down to Jexville for my wedding. It still didn't fit exactly right, binding me around my chest and arms.

"I see you made taffy for Annabelle. That was thoughtful." She noticed the sticky drizzle that fell at my feet. "If you don't move fast, those ants are going to be all over you."

She took my arm and moved me toward the house.

"How is it possible that no one in town mentioned that you were mute?" She looked me directly in the eye as she asked.

I smiled, then grinned. "I'm not mute."

She nodded. "I didn't think so. A tidbit like that would be gnawed and licked over to the point that even I would have heard about it."

I looked over at the child who was still dancing. A fine sheen of sweat now covered her face and arms, but she had no intention of stopping. She'd forgotten where she was or who was with her; she was taken with the pleasure of the music and executing the intricate steps.

"My daughter, Duncan," JoHanna said as she led me toward the steps. "I'm sure you've heard about us. Just believe about a tenth of what you hear and then sift through that with a malice comb. What you'll be left with is some very boring facts."

I cast a look at her, noticing for the first time that she was older than I'd thought. The fine lines around her eyes were visible only when she stopped smiling. Her chestnut hair was livened with reddish highlights, but there was also silver there, especially at the temples. I looked back at Duncan.

"She's nine and I'm forty-eight." JoHanna spoke without turning around. "I was sinfully old when I conceived and tragically old when she was born. The biggest disappointment in town was that my old body didn't give out and allow me to die in childbirth."

She was smiling, but there was a strange energy behind her words.

"You look fit enough." The words popped out of my mouth before I thought them through. Speaking before thinking was a habit that had gotten me in trouble more than once. I'd vowed to curb it, but so far had only dulled it back some.

JoHanna put her hands on my shoulders and laughed. "Fit enough for what?" she asked. "Getting pregnant or having the baby?"

I could feel the blush move up my face, and I could see that only delighted JoHanna the more. Still laughing, she shook her head and pointed me toward the kitchen, where Agnes Leatherwood was pulling the dasher out of the gallon of ice cream she'd made.

"Mrs. Mills has brought a gift," JoHanna said, ushering me into the room.

Agnes took one look at the ruined box and dropped the ice cream dasher. "Thank you, Mattie." She took the box and put it in the sink. "That was very thoughtful of you." Out of the corner of her eye she glanced at JoHanna.

"The taffy didn't set too well." I realized I should have thrown the box away. All of the women were staring at me, at the dribble of taffy on the floor where I'd held the box away from me.

"Too humid for candy to set, but it was a sweet thing to think of." JoHanna went to the sink and got the dishcloth. In a moment she had the sticky candy off the floor.

When she looked up, she saw that all of the women were still staring at me. She tossed the dishcloth across the room into the sink. "You know, Agnes, it's a shame that you won't let Annabelle dance. The girl is fat. Some exercise might do her good."

I saw the glint of humor in JoHanna's face as she winked at me, then turned to face the fury of Annabelle Lee's mama.

"Annabelle is not fat. She's highly sensitive. And dancing is a sin."

"So is gluttony, but that hasn't stopped a good number of people in Jexville." JoHanna looked completely innocent, not as if she wasn't pointing out that half the women in the room were on the portly side.

"You are a scandal, JoHanna McVay. You're going to be the ruination of Will's good name and his business." The woman who spoke was big, and her face had gotten red.

"I dare say Will can take care of his own reputation and his own business." JoHanna went to the sink. "Now are we going to serve up this ice cream or not?"

Outside the gramophone had wound down. There was the scratch of the needle across the record, and then the sound of Duncan winding the handle. The record got off to a slow, dragging start, then picked up speed and was soon racing at a fast clip.

"Serve the ice cream," Agnes said. She was still angry, but she didn't have the courage to confront JoHanna directly.

JoHanna dipped the big spoon into the metal container and lifted out the ice cream, complete with big chunks of peaches. "This looks delicious, Agnes." She transferred it to a bowl, then handed it to me.

"Duncan looks hot. I'll take this to her." I didn't wait to see the reaction to my words. I walked out into the hot sun letting the screen door slam behind me. I should have taken the bowl to one of the children waiting in the next room, but JoHanna had stood up for me.

Duncan waved but didn't break her dancing.

I held up the ice cream, the condensation on the bowl leaking over my fingers and dripping twice into the dust. Duncan grinned at me, and I signaled her to come into the shade and get the ice cream. She was so hot. Dust had begun to stick to her legs.

The sun was still shining in that white-hot way of July, which meant no storms were immediate. The air was perfectly still, so still that the scratches in the record were suddenly magnified. The song was a ragtime. I don't remember which one, but I held the bowl, glad to be out of the company of those women and fascinated by the intricate steps Duncan was only too pleased to perform for me.

There was no warning. The bolt of lightning came out of the hazy blue sky. It was a double fork. One prong hit the pine tree and the other Duncan. A blue-white light flared over the entire yard, and a ball of fire ran down the pine tree and exploded against the side of the house.

When I looked back at Duncan, she was on the ground with smoke coming off her and big holes burned in the yellow dress.

The bowl of ice cream fell to the ground, but my fingers were still bent in the shape of holding it. I remember that I thought I couldn't inhale. The dress was already too tight, and the air was suddenly sucked dry of oxygen. It seemed like an hour that I stood there, trying to run toward Duncan, trying to breathe, trying to scream.

JoHanna came out the back door not even bothering with the steps. She ran like a gazelle, her skirt flying up over her legs. She fell to her knees beside Duncan and lifted her into her arms.

Duncan's head flopped back, and I could see her eyes were rolled up in her head. Smoke came from her hair, which had fallen out in great clumps. I could smell the burning hair and cloth and flesh, and I felt the tears sliding over my face.

Some of the other women had come outside, and the children were peeping through the screen door. No one made a sound. There was just the music, and finally the needle made its way to the end of the record and set to shushing against the label.

"Get a doctor." I spoke but didn't believe I had. When I turned and no one had moved I pointed to the boy named Robert. "Run and get the doctor."

He took off fast, his eyes too large for his pale face.

JoHanna sat in the dirt, Duncan crushed against her, and she rocked back and forth. Small sounds came from her, murmurings that I couldn't understand.

No one went to her, so I did. It was impossible to look into Duncan's rolled up eyes and not know that she was gone. The bolt had knocked the life out of her in one powerful blast.

I was standing just at JoHanna's shoulder, wondering what to do, when the clouds began to roll out of the west. They were the same clouds that had been hovering on the horizon since noon, growing darker and angrier with each passing hour. But they'd hovered in the distance, far away from the red clay streets of Jexville. Now they were on the move. They came toward us, thunder rumbling louder with each tick of the clock. Lightning shot out from the low-lying clouds in nasty forks.

I knelt down and put my hand on JoHanna's shoulder. "Let's take her inside," I said.

She ignored me, murmuring softly to her dead baby in that strange, lilting pattern. I didn't know then, but it's the same noises a mother cat makes when she's trying to lick life into a kitten. Cows and dogs and horses have their same version of the noise. All animals do, I suppose.

"Mrs. McVay, let's take her inside. It's going to storm." I lowered my grip to her arm, trying to move her gently away from the corpse. When I looked behind me, no one else had moved. They were watching us as if we were some strange creatures imported from an exotic land doing things they'd never seen before.

"Will someone help me get them inside?" I tried not to sound angry, but I hated their cowlike faces, the stupid way they stood, slack jawed.

"She's not dead." JoHanna whispered the words, but I knew they were meant for me. In that moment, I swear I thought I'd die from pity.

How could she look at that burned body that had been flung halfway across the yard and not realize that the life had gone?

Finally, Nell Anderson stepped forward. "The doctor is on his way, JoHanna. Let's take Duncan in the house, where he can examine her." She spoke with gentleness.

"She's not dead." JoHanna shrugged away from both of us. "Just leave us alone. Go away and leave us alone." She bent down lower, shielding Duncan from our sight.

Behind me, Rachel Carpenter started to cry softly. "Somebody get Reverend Bates," she said. I heard another of the children slam out of the house and run. I never turned around to look. All I could think of was Duncan, alive one minute and dancing her heart out. Now she was gone.

I knelt beside JoHanna just as the first big drops of rain began to fall. They struck the dust where Duncan had been dancing, causing little flares of orange to jump up, as if the ground were alive and pulsing. The stump of the pine tree sizzled.

"Mrs. McVay, let's take her inside. It's going to rain."

"She's isn't dead." JoHanna never stopped rocking. "She can't be."

I could hear the rain in the magnolia tree beside the gramophone. It hit the slick green leaves with snaps and pops. It hit me, too, but I didn't feel it. I could see it striking JoHanna's shoulders, fat drops soaking into her coppery dress.

Nell Anderson knelt beside JoHanna on her right. "We need to send for Will. Where is he this week?" She reached out to straighten one of Duncan's little socks. Her shoe was missing. It had been blown clean off her foot.

"He's in Natchez."

"We'll send a telegram."

"Try the Claremont House. He'll be in there sometime today."

Nell was crying, and I was crying. Only JoHanna didn't cry. Nell got up to send the telegram, but I stayed, watching the rain soak into Jo-Hanna McVay as she keened softly to her dead girl.

When I looked up, the other children and mothers had left or gone inside. Agnes and Annabelle Lee were standing at the door, watching. They were both crying, too.

The ground had begun to puddle with water, but JoHanna refused to consider going inside. Dr. Westfall arrived, his white hair flying around his head and his black bag in his hand. He tried to lift JoHanna, but she hunkered down over the body and cried out to be left alone. I saw his hand move out to Duncan's neck and rest there for a moment, and then he reached up and closed her eyes. When he stood, he shook his head at Agnes and walked to the back door.

They spoke in low whispers for a moment, and then he went inside.

"JoHanna, we have to move out of the rain." I knew if she didn't get up and move, they were going to come back outside and force her. I could imagine what they were doing. They'd send for the undertaker. They'd give JoHanna a shot. Then they'd tear them apart. I put my hand on her arm. "We have to go inside if you want to keep her a little longer."

"Make them leave me alone." She finally looked at me, and she was crying. "She isn't dead. I can feel her. Make them leave us alone for just a little while."

"Move under the magnolia tree." It didn't offer much protection, but it was better than nothing. The rain had leveled off to where it was a steady drum on the leaves. Together we picked up Duncan and carried her the few feet to the tree. JoHanna sat with her back to the trunk, cradling her child.

"Make them leave us alone." She didn't beg or plead. She asked.

"Just for a while." I didn't know how long I could hold them off. I didn't know why I felt like I needed to. All I knew was that once they took her baby, she'd never get her back. A little time wasn't much to ask.

I walked across the yard, my gray dress sopping. Inside the house I heard the murmur of low voices. They were already planning what to do, how to do it. The undertaker was on the way, and Dr. Westfall was filling a glass syringe with something. It certainly wasn't for Duncan.

"Leave her alone."

Everyone in the room turned to look at me. I could see from their faces that I gave them a fright.

"She's in shock. The girl is dead, and we can't leave her out there in the rain." Agnes wrung her hands as she spoke. She wasn't hard-hearted, just unable to think beyond what appeared proper.

"Leave her alone. It's her child. There's nothing to be done for Duncan. Let Mrs. McVay have the time."

No one had ever paid the least attention to anything I'd ever said before. Maybe they didn't know what to do, so what I said was better than nothing. But we stood there for fifteen or twenty minutes, looking at one another and listening to the rain. Agnes made a pot of coffee and gave us all a cup, and we took seats around the kitchen table, where the unfinished bowls of ice cream had melted and begun to draw flies.

The undertaker came in the front door, along with the Methodist minister. We were a sorry group, but no one wanted to go to the back door and look out in the yard.

Sitting there in that hot kitchen, I knew that JoHanna was not liked, but no one could have possibly wished that tragedy off on her. No woman is capable of wishing the death of a child on another. At least that's what I believed.

Finally the rain stopped. It had been thirty minutes or more. I knew there wasn't much longer to wait. I could see on their faces that they feared for JoHanna's sanity. They were repulsed by the idea that she could embrace a dead body. To their way of thinking, it was best to get it over with.

"Let me talk to her." I stood up and waited, but no one else volunteered. Walking across the kitchen and out the door, I saw things with a clarity that was painful. The leaves of the magnolia had been washed a deep hunter green. Part of the red dirt from the road had flooded into the yard, creating muddy red miniature rivers that cut around the magnolia, as if Duncan and JoHanna were stranded on an island. Up above, the sky was a perfect blue, deeper in color than it had been all summer.

JoHanna was as I'd left her, all energy and attention focused on her child. She was brushing Duncan's face with her fingertips, talking so softly I couldn't make out the words. Her hair had come down from the bun she wore and it was longer than I'd expected, and wet now, so that it was darker. It clung to her neck and shoulders and molded to her breasts beneath the wet dress.

I walked across the yard, slowly, dreading every step. I wanted to cry but I didn't. About ten feet away, I stopped. "It's time to go inside now, JoHanna."

She looked up but said nothing.

I heard the screen door close behind me and I turned to find nine-year-old Mary Lincoln and Annabelle Lee coming toward me. They stopped.

"Is she dead?" Mary asked. "I've never seen a dead person."

"I have." Annabelle Lee looked at the ground. "Lots of times."

"Go back inside." I tried not to snap at them but couldn't help myself. "Git! Right now."

Mary darted around me and ran up to the tree. At the sight of Duncan she froze.

I wanted to scalp her on the spot, and I was just reaching out to do that when Duncan's eyes opened. She stared directly at Mary.

"Don't sing with your mouth open, Mary, or you'll drown," she said.

Ꮿ Two Ꮿ

JOHANNA closed her eyes briefly, then opened them. That was the only movement, until Mary went squalling back into the house with Annabelle Lee on her heels. They acted as if they'd seen Satan. Duncan *was* a frightful sight. She looked like Job after the Lord had sent down His plagues, only worse. The smell of her burned flesh was indescribable, but she was alive.

She stared after Mary and Annabelle, but she didn't move. It was JoHanna who finally straightened her back and eased Duncan into a sitting position.

"We have to clean those burns," JoHanna said as she lifted Duncan's leg and looked at a spot as big as my hand that was real bad. "Is Dr. Westfall still in the house?"

She was talking to me, but I could only swallow. I still didn't believe Duncan was alive, but she was looking at me. Only by now there were great dark circles beneath her eyes. The rain had mostly put out all the little smoldering fires in her clothes and hair. Great clumps were missing, and she looked just awful. It occurred to me that I was caught in a nightmare. No one could survive lightning. Duncan was dead. I was in shock.

"Mattie, could you get the doctor out here?" JoHanna cradled Duncan against her chest. Her eyes, edged with white, darted in the direction of the house.

I didn't have time to budge from the spot. Dr. Westfall and his black bag came flying out of the house, sent no doubt by Mary and Annabelle

Lee. Agnes was in the doorway, along with the remnants of the party. They were as awed as I was—and about as useful.

Dr. Westfall stopped dead in his tracks when he saw Duncan, but then he came on over and began to look at her arms and legs. He knelt in the wet grass, ignoring the damage to his suit pants. The discoloration in Duncan's face was bad, but there were no burns there. Her scalp was singed, but the damage wasn't that bad. Dr. Westfall went for the more serious wounds on her legs.

"Second degree here, JoHanna." He talked as he worked, but he kept lifting a furtive glance at Duncan. Even as he touched her, felt the warmth of her flesh, he didn't believe she was alive.

No one did. Except JoHanna, who'd refused to believe that she was dead.

"Let's move her in the house." Dr. Westfall rose to one knee.

"No." JoHanna's voice stopped him in his tracks.

"I need water, disinfectant, a place to work. The burns are serious." He held his anger barely in check.

"No. We're not going in that house. We're going home."

"JoHanna . . ."

"Do it here, Doc. It's her legs and her back. I can feel the heat."

"It's a matter of sterile . . ."

"Duncan is not going in that house." JoHanna looked up at the building not thirty yards away. There wasn't anger or hatred or fear in her gaze. It was like a person who sees a snake in the road ahead and decides to take a detour.

"Go get some water and some rags." The doctor addressed me even though he didn't look my way. "Be quick about it."

I took off like a scalded cat and was back with Agnes's best crockery bowl filled with hot water and a stack of her white dishcloths.

Shaking his head at JoHanna's stubbornness, Dr. Westfall bandaged the worst of Duncan's burns, brusquely warning JoHanna about the ones on her back and how they were to be washed and dressed and what would happen if infection set in. He worked with great efficiency and without ever speaking directly to Duncan. For her part, she never cried out though her eyes were clouded with pain. She stared into JoHanna's eyes, taking her comfort there.

With the bloody washbowl and empty bottles of disinfectant at his feet, the doctor finally looked Duncan directly in the eyes.

"Do you know who you are?" he asked. He was puzzled by her silence. She was a child, and the wounds had to be hideously painful. Why hadn't she cried out?

Duncan looked at him, comprehension plain on her face, but she didn't answer.

"Duncan, can you hear me?" he asked.

She nodded.

"Do you hurt anywhere?"

She shook her head.

"Can she talk?" he asked JoHanna.

"She did. To Mary." JoHanna placed her fingers on Duncan's throat. "Talk to me," she said softly.

Duncan swallowed but said nothing.

"It could be shock. It could be something that'll wear off in a day or two." Dr. Westfall didn't look at all certain. His fingers raked through his nimbus of white hair. "Bring her to see me tomorrow, JoHanna. I've done all I can for now. Tomorrow we'll be able to tell more."

"I will. Thank you, Doc. You've been good to us."

He grunted and stood, snapping his case shut and shaking his legs so that the wet knees of his britches didn't stick to his skin.

JoHanna continued to hold Duncan on her lap until Dr. Westfall was gone. I noticed that he went around the house and down the street, obviously unwilling to answer the questions that the women inside the house would bombard him with.

"Let's go, Duncan," JoHanna pushed herself up and then turned to give Duncan her hand. The child took it but didn't stand.

Without being asked I went behind her and caught her under the arms, taking care not to touch her back. She was tall but thin. I'd lifted plenty of sacks of feed and watermelons. Duncan weighed about the same as two big Shouting Methodists. She was just lankier. When I finally got her feet under her, I eased her weight back down.

I'm not certain if her legs shifted or her knees buckled, but she wouldn't take the weight. JoHanna came to help me, but after a few tries it became clear that Duncan either couldn't or wouldn't stand.

JoHanna knelt down and straightened Duncan's legs, pressing the tops of her feet and her ankles. "Can you feel that?" she asked, looking up.

I was standing behind Duncan, holding her up. For the first time that day I saw fear in JoHanna's eyes. She'd known all along that Duncan was alive. But she couldn't guarantee that the child would be normal.

Duncan shook her head no.

JoHanna pressed her knees. "How about here?"

The quick shake.

JoHanna's hands moved higher, to her thighs. "Here?"

Duncan began to understand. She reached down with her own hands to capture her mother's, pressing the fingers deep into her legs in a moment of panic. She shook her head, fast, then more wildly as she began to look first at JoHanna and then at me. Her mouth opened, but no words came out.

"Let's put her in the wagon," JoHanna said, indicating the red wagon that was parked behind the magnolia tree. We lifted her, JoHanna with the legs and me with the shoulders, and carried her to the wagon. As soon as she was settled, JoHanna took the handle and turned toward Peterson Lane. They lived a mile out of town in an isolated area.

"Aren't you going to the doctor?" I couldn't believe she was going the opposite way. Duncan couldn't walk. Her legs were like dead things.

"There's no point." JoHanna took a long look down the way the doctor had gone. "He's done all he can do."

I couldn't believe what she was saying. Maybe they didn't have enough money for the doctor to come back. "He'll put it on credit." I spoke without thinking, horrified the instant the words left my mouth.

"It's not a matter of money," JoHanna said, starting to walk toward home. "Old Doc's done what he can." She had managed to get the wagon out of the yard and close to the edge of the road.

"Shall I walk with you?" I was already walking beside them. I didn't want to go back to the party, and I didn't want to go home.

"No. We're fine. Will will be home if he gets word." She was walking fast, the wagon leaving narrow ruts in the soft red earth.

"Can I do anything?" I stopped at the corner of Redemption, wanting to go but not certain. Elikah would be waiting for me.

"Yes, you can." JoHanna stopped walking long enough to turn to me. "Take the gramophone home with you and keep it safe for Duncan. Ask Agnes to loan you a wagon. She'll be glad to do it just to keep the gramophone out of her house."

"I'll take good care of it." I'd have to figure out how to get it home and hide it from Elikah. He didn't hold with such contraptions.

As if she sensed my worries, JoHanna stopped. "Are you sure?"

Looking into her blue eyes, I was sure. "I can manage that for you, Mrs. McVay."

"JoHanna," she corrected, taking five seconds longer to stare into my eyes and make certain that I could do what she'd asked. "Bring it out to the house tomorrow, and I'll give you some squash and beans and potatoes for your husband's supper."

"I hope Duncan is okay."

JoHanna didn't answer. She started walking again, a ground-covering stride that meant business. I'd never seen a woman walk with such determination, and I felt a chill. She was going out to that isolated house, all by herself, with her daughter nearly dead from a lightning bolt.

I didn't tell Elikah about the lightning. Didn't have to. It was the talk of the town before JoHanna and Duncan had made it to the turnoff for Peterson Lane. When I first got to Jexville I was amazed at the speed with which tales got carried from one end of town to another. I learned in a few days that good gossip was enough for a man to get up from a haircut and a shave and hurry over to the café for a cup of coffee and a leandown. While the women met over kitchen tables and clotheslines, the men hunkered over coffee and talk at the café, or in the barber's chair.

By the time I got home, three men had already been by the barbershop to give Elikah the news, and he'd been over to the boot stop to tell Axim. By the time I got home that afternoon, it was already settled that the hand of God had smote Duncan McVay for her waywardness and for her mother's wild and wanton ways. It was God's punishment on a nest of sinners, or at least those were the sentiments of most of the townspeople. If there was any sympathy at all, it was for Will, a man surrounded by willful women.

It had taken me longer to get home because I had to hide the gramophone. I'd borrowed a wagon from Agnes, but I knew better than to try taking the player home. Elikah had strong views on music and dancing. Since I was new in town, it took a little thinking, but I finally managed to wedge the wagon and gramophone up beside the haystack at the livery stables. It was safe and dry, and there was little chance that anyone would stumble over it. At least for a night. Then I hurried home to start dinner.

One of my favorite things to do after dinner was to sit out on the porch and swing. The creak of those old chains gave me a sense of peace, even on the hottest nights.

It was at night that Jexville revealed its true beauty. It reminded me of a dog that strayed up to our house when I was fourteen. Suke was an ugly, yellow animal with small eyes and mange. At night, though, after the dishes were done and the younger children put in bed, I'd sit on the stoop and Suke would come up and push her nose into my hand. There, in the darkness, we could both be beautiful.

When the stars came out at night and the wind whispered through the pine needles rich with the smell of resin, Jexville had a kind of allure. There were areas where oaks and magnolias made lush groves. Some of the new settlers had planted pecan trees, which would grow into groves of big gray trunks with slender, intricate branches. When the rawness and redness of the new main street and the smell of new lumber for some of the stores finally wore away some, it would not be as bleakly ugly. My own little house, the yard scratched barer than a scaly chicken's head, would have flowers in the next spring. With a little care, a little effort, Jexville would improve. Hard work could turn a lot of things around.

With the day finished and the night ahead, I could slip into my old daydreams. They were silly things, gleaned from the pages of penny magazines and glimpses of the traveling shows that sometimes played at the Meridian Opera House. I knew they were false, but they gave me intense pleasure. It was years later before I began to wonder how a human heart can know something to be false and still try so desperately to believe in it.

The night passed, and the hot, pink kiss of the morning sun found me dressed and pacing the kitchen floor. Elikah was a handsome man back then. He took great pride in his mustache. While I made breakfast, he made sure that each hair was in place. In his starched white shirt and black suspenders, he did look the part of the town surgeon, much more so than Dr. Westfall, who always looked as if he'd been stampeded. Elikah was fond of saying that in a town without the good fortune to have a doc, the barber often served that purpose. It always gave me a little chill, which made him smile.

As soon as he was finished with his eggs and grits and the dishes were done, I hurried out to retrieve the gramophone. I had thought out a route that would skirt the edges of town and, most important, Janelle

Baxley. On my first day in Jexville, Janelle had made it her business to tend to my business. Getting off the train in Jexville, I had been frightened and worried. My first emotion at Janelle's warm hug and piercing blue eyes was delight. With her lace blouse and fitted skirt, she seemed so grown and capable. That was before she told me how everyone in town wanted to help me forget the fact that Elikah had been voicing his misgivings about me in the café. She said it was only normal for a bridegroom to be nervous, but that Elikah had gone to the station to meet me with enough money in an envelope to send me back home if I didn't look tractable and decent.

Janelle was one person I didn't want to meet as I was pulling the gramophone down the road to Peterson Lane.

I'd picked a good time of day and managed to get across the railroad tracks without even sighting so much as a rabbit. Once I was away from the town, I walked a little slower, letting my arm rest from the pull of the wagon. It was a hot day. Too hot for my ugly navy dress, but I had nothing else to wear. It seemed only overnight that I'd given up my cool cotton shifts for grown-up clothes. The trade was distinctly not in my favor. I didn't dwell on the disappointments of growing up as I walked along. A blue jay marked my progress with warning cries, and there were stirrings in the high Johnson grass that tufted the road. Alone, I could let my imagination fly. I could pretend that down the road was a wagon of Gypsies who would take me in and teach me to tell fortunes and sing. We'd travel the world, and I would become famous for my dreams and visions. We'd sail across to Europe, where the king and queen would ask me to visit them for tea. It would be a spectacular life, and it shimmered just around the next curve in the heat.

Peterson Lane curled in and out beside the banks of Little Red Creek, a crystal amber and gold creek that took its sweet time shifting through pastures and woodlands and finally down to the swamp on the east side of Jexville. At places, Little Red was shallow enough to wade across, with a pure sand bottom that was as close as I thought I'd ever get to white sand beaches and blue waves. There were holes, though, where a tree had fallen and a natural dam piled up, making the water deep enough to swim. I didn't know those places. Not yet. It was JoHanna and Duncan who would teach me such pleasures in my new home.

When I first came up on their place, I stopped and took some time. The first thing that caught my eye were clothes on the line, among them the remains of Duncan's yellow dress. JoHanna had been up early to wash.

Six oak trees shaded the front yard, far enough away from the house that they gave some shade but didn't smother it. On the east side of the house was a screened porch with a swing. It was completely shaded by two towering trees, a magnolia and a cedar. The side yard on the west was sunny. That's where the clothes hung as still as slats of wood in the windless morning. Farther back from the house was an old chinaberry tree. Parked behind it was a beautiful red car.

There had been plenty of cars in Meridian. Jojo had bought one once, but it didn't last. One day it was gone, and Mama never knew if he'd wrecked it or lost it or if the bank had come to take it away. And no one dared to ask. It had been black and ugly, smelling of grease and trouble. I didn't care when it was gone, except the noise always gave us some warning when Jojo was back.

This car, though, hidden somewhat by the clothes and the tree, was like something from one of the magazines I loved to read. A movie star would have ridden in it. Someone exactly like JoHanna.

The hot sun scorching the part on my head finally brought me back to the dirt road I was standing in. It hadn't been a long walk, but I was already sweating in the July heat. Part of it was the dress. It wasn't really a summer dress, but as a married woman I had to have long sleeves and sufficient folds of skirt. Until I'd married, even though I was too old, I'd worn the dresses of a young girl. We didn't have the money for extras, and I'd never felt bad about being cool and comfortable in the summers. This blue dress was strained at the waist where Mama had gotten pregnant with Lena Rae. She hadn't worn it in years. She said after four children, her waist had never gone back. Then four more had stretched everything to the point that not even a corset could help. So when I accepted Elikah's offer, I got the blue dress.

I was lost somewhere between the past and the present when I saw a furtive movement out by the last oak tree in the front of the house. The yard was raked clean of all leaves, with beautiful flowers blooming in clumps of reds and yellows and purples and a pink as electric as the sky at sunset. Among all that color there had been the shifting of red on brown.

A dog?

I hadn't heard any barking, but some dogs didn't. Some liked to sneak around from behind. I wasn't afraid of dogs; in fact I got on with them pretty good. I'd learned, though, that a sneaky dog was like a sneaky person. You turned your back at your own peril. Still pulling the wagon, I eased down among the trees. If the dog didn't come out barking, maybe it would just slink away.

I wasn't prepared for the sudden flurry of feathers just at face level, nor the strange, torn cry that came along with it. I fell back, crying out loud as I put up my hands.

I felt the center of my palm sliced open as the air around me beat with the confusion of dust, feathers, and talons. I screamed again as I tried to get away from the creature, but I tripped over the handle of the wagon and fell backward. The bird came right after me, thrusting its claws forward as it beat the air with wings. I thought immediately of a hawk or eagle, but I managed to catch a look at it as I yelled for help. It was a brown rooster.

There was the sound of the screen door slamming. "Pecos! Get off her!" Footsteps sounded on the porch and then across the yard.

I had pulled the heavy skirt over my head to protect my face. Groping around behind me, I was shocked to make contact with a big foot attached to a strong leg. I knew that it was Will McVay, JoHanna's husband.

Before I could right myself, he lifted me, shaking my skirt down around me as he brought me up into the sunshine and air filled with small chicken feathers.

"Are you hurt?"

He had one side of his suspenders up and one down over a cotton undershirt. There was lather on one side of his face, and in the dirt at his bare feet was the razor. He eased me to my feet and released his grip on my armpits.

Looking in his eyes, I saw old Suke looking back at me. I was in as sorry a shape as that poor dog had ever been. Will McVay had seen my drawers made of a flour sack. Shame burned my cheeks and made my scalp tingle as if it were being bitten by ants. "I brought Duncan's machine." I mumbled because I could talk but couldn't look at him.

When he didn't answer and didn't move, I had to look up. Instead of staring at me, he was looking at the ground, just to my side. I looked down there, too, and saw the blood. It was dripping from all four of my fingers and just a little slower from my thumb.

"Pecos caught you with a spur." He reached over and lifted my left hand. The palm was sliced clean open. From his back pocket he pulled a starched white handkerchief and wrapped it around my palm, drawing the knot tight. "The fingers require a lot of blood. Looks like Pecos laid open some arteries."

It didn't matter what he said. I watched his lips move, the soap lather already dried on his face. He had dark brown eyes the color of Lizzie Maples's chocolate pound cake and black hair combed back from his strong face.

He was not handsome, not like Elikah. There was not a dimple in his cheek or the quick ability to show pleasure or anger. There was a distance from his feelings that he guarded closely. Neither anger nor pleasure would be his master.

His hand went under my elbow as he steadied me while at the same time he bent to pick up the wagon handle. Together we walked to the porch, where he let the wagon stop and guided me up the steps.

"Hannah, baby, we've had a little accident." He opened the screen door for me, then nudged me inside.

He wore a scent like rain falling through sunshine and beating on wide green leaves, of grass fresh cut. Clean. Stepping from the harsh sun outside into the cool dimness of the hallway, I thought I'd faint. His grip on my elbow tightened just enough to support me, and in a few seconds I was across the floor and seated on a green sofa with strange, carved legs and a back that arched and scrolled like a dragon's. I was in a dream.

The carpet was a red as dark as drying blood, but it was swirled with a pattern of colors and design that made me want to cry it was so beautiful. The chair across from me had a high back and fringe that dangled to the floor. Instead of a doorway to the dining room, there were curtains, thick and heavy and tied back with more tassels, these thick as ropes and made of gold. The light filtered into the room through soft white curtains at the windows that seemed to be made of gossamer lace.

I was aware of his eyes on me, watching with that guarded look that betrayed nothing. I knew that he pitied me, but it was not the hard pity of the women of Jexville.

"Has marriage to Elikah been so terrible that you've forgotten how to speak?"

His question sent the blood thundering to my cheeks and ears, and I looked down at the carpet, finding comfort in the vivid colors.

"Mattie speaks when it's necessary. She did a fine job of taking up for me and Duncan yesterday."

At JoHanna's voice I looked up, relieved to see her. She was standing by the strange curtains, her arms lifted above her head as she twisted her thick chestnut hair into a bun. She held the pins in her mouth and still managed to talk around them with perfect clarity. It took only a minute for her to have her hair in order, and she lowered her hands and came into the room.

"How bad did Pecos get you?" She reached for my hand and I gave it to her. The handkerchief was soaked with blood.

"Get the turpentine, Will." She cast a look at him.

"Needle?"

My gut turned quickly. Would they have to sew it up? I'd never had stitches, but Jane, the girl after me, had cut her foot open one summer. Jojo had held her down while she screamed and thrashed and Pres Watkins had put five ugly stitches in her foot. Mama and I had sat on the back steps, crying.

Untying the knot, she revealed the gash. Her fingers poked at it with the same gentle touch she'd used on Duncan. "Just the turpentine," she called out to him, "and a clean cloth." She turned back to me. "This will burn like hellfire, but it won't get infected and you won't have to have it stitched."

Unable to verbally agree, I nodded. I'd had turpentine poured into a wound before. But it was better than stitches.

We went out on the front porch, and Will held me while JoHanna stepped in front of me, holding my hand.

It was liquid fire, but then it was over. I found myself back in the house, seated at the kitchen table with a fresh, clean cloth wrapped around my hand and a cup of coffee steaming before me.

"Pecos has never attacked anyone before." JoHanna looked at Will, who stood in the doorway, his shave forgotten, then down at me. "He's been insane since she was hurt."

"The rooster?" I watched the way the light from the kitchen window made her skin transparent. Her blue eyes were icy, and they seemed to swallow the light and give it back with a blue frost. She'd said she was forty-eight. My own mama was seventeen years younger, but she was an older woman than JoHanna.

"Pecos is Duncan's pet. We had a dog, but someone poisoned it. Duncan wouldn't have another. Not right now. She found that rooster up at the feed store." JoHanna sat at the table, signaling Will to join us.

"His leg was broken." Will straddled the chair. He rubbed at the dried soap. "JoHanna splinted his leg, and Duncan took care of him." He lifted a shoulder, his dark eyes showing a sudden warmth. "Pecos is one helluva watchdog, even if he did get carried away."

"He's upset because Duncan's so sick," JoHanna explained. "He's trying to protect her."

I looked from one to the other. They seemed to think it was perfectly okay that a rooster had attacked me with a viciousness I'd never seen even in a wild hog. The rooster was protecting their daughter, so that made everything hunky-dory.

"He could have blinded me." My hand was still on fire.

"He could have," Will agreed, "but he didn't." He stood up. "I have to finish dressing." The look he gave JoHanna held meaning only for her.

She rose, too. "If that's what you think you have to do, Will." There was a warning in her tone, but I didn't understand it. I only knew that they were speaking one conversation but having another.

They stared at each other, a long moment of exchange that left me breathless. Will turned away and JoHanna looked at me. "Duncan would like to see you."

I followed her across an enclosed porch that was crammed with plants I'd never seen before, and we returned to the main portion of the house. Duncan's bedroom was to the left, a big room with two windows that opened on the sunny side of the yard. Sheer curtains that were the golden pink of a ripe peach hung at the window and gave the room a soft, magic kind of glow.

At first I tried not to look at Duncan. I was afraid. She'd been so badly hurt, I couldn't make myself look again and confirm what I'd seen.

"She hasn't talked yet, and she can't walk, but she isn't in horrible pain." JoHanna was at my elbow and encouraging me into the room. With her behind me I walked up to the bed. There was no place to look except at Duncan.

Once our eyes connected I couldn't look away. She was frightful, the bruising worse and the burns more clearly defined along her scalp and arms. A light, yellow chenille bedspread was across her legs, but I could see the places where thick bandages had been applied. Strangely enough, though, Duncan didn't seem to be aware of her appearance. Or her injuries. Her eyes were the same chocolate brown of Will's, and they were just as steady.

"I brought your gramophone home," I told her.

She nodded but didn't smile.

"Pecos took out after Mattie and sliced her hand open."

Duncan turned to look at the open window. The bird was sitting there. It gave me a start because it hadn't been there before. I'd looked straight at those pretty curtains and seen only the sun. The rooster had crept up there without making a sound.

"Pecos is sneaky," JoHanna said, but there was fondness in her voice. "We used to let him sleep behind the stove in the kitchen, but he kept sneaking out and pecking me when I bent over to get something out of the oven." She laughed, and Duncan smiled with her. "He's always been bad, but he'd fight the devil to protect my baby."

Pecos flapped off the sill and disappeared.

All the strange gossip about JoHanna and Duncan came back to me with a force that banded around my lungs. I was already dizzy from the smell of the turpentine and the heat. I put my hand on the iron rail of Duncan's bed and braced.

"Will has to head out to Memphis today." JoHanna spoke to Duncan, and there was no emotion in her voice.

"He's leaving today?" I opened my mouth before I thought. I had to grip the bedstead to keep from putting my hand over my face. Why was I constantly talking before I thought? It was the one thing Jojo punished me for that I never resented.

"He left Natchez yesterday with a shipment of crystal sitting on the dock waiting for the train to Memphis. He's responsible for it, and he wants to be sure it's moved carefully to the warehouse."

Memphis, Tennessee, was up at the top of Mississippi, but to me it was in a distant land. I'd seen pictures of women in elegant, sparkly dresses lounging in hotel lobbies beside men dressed in black—black suits and white shirts that made them look like dangerous characters from some Hollywood fantasy. Will stayed in those hotels. He went to the lobby and sat, the strange lights from the bar caught in the crystal glass he held.

JoHanna straightened the covers over Duncan's legs. Her hand drifted upward, touching her daughter's hand, then her cheek, then her hair. It made my chest ache.

"Tell me about your mama," JoHanna said, her fingers still caressing Duncan's ruined hair. "Tell us about your family." She indicated a chair by Duncan's bed while she took another. There was a book folded open on the nightstand.

What could I tell them? My mother had been born Lydia Belle Carter. When she was fourteen her father had run off and abandoned the family. At fifteen she was pregnant with me and accepting the proposal of John Kimball. Daddy worked for the BM&O railroad in Meridian as yard supervisor. We had a small house, and I had two sisters and a brother before Daddy got caught between two cars and crushed. Mama never told me, but I heard them talking, saying he'd been pinched nearly in two. From there it was a slow fall into deeper and deeper misery, with the ultimate bad mistake coming in the form of Jojo Edwards and four more children.

"Mama can sing," I finally answered her. "She used to sing a lot, but she doesn't much anymore."

❧ *Three* ❧

JOHANNA loaded the wagon with potatoes that we dug from the
rich brown dirt of her garden. She worked with an ear to Duncan's
window, but her hands explored the dirt as if it were familiar skin. She
drew up clumps of green onions and carrots. From beneath thick, dark
leaves she cut the yellow squash and the prickly okra. She talked of
places I'd only read about, making them seem real and somehow
attainable. When the wagon was full, she walked me to the road.
With the sun still in my face, I walked home, plotting how I would
come back.

It was three days later, on the Fourth of July, before I saw them again. I
had hunted through the dry goods store to no avail in my search for material that looked anything like the curtains JoHanna had hung in Duncan's room. I wanted the light that sifted through them, softer than the
harsh July sun, light that was alive with its own color. But the store didn't
carry anything close. I could not explain what I wanted, so I let it go. I
had my reason to go back to Peterson's Lane and the McVay house. Jo-
Hanna could tell me where to get the curtain material. I would go as
soon as the Independence Day party was over.

The two biggest churches of Jexville were both having dinner on the
grounds to celebrate the day. It was a rivalry posed in the smiles of
friendliness, but there were sharp overtones that spoke of status and loyalty. Each church competed to see which would have the finer and more
elaborate feast, which would have more congregants in attendance.

The sun was hot, and the town still buzzed with the gossip of Duncan's lightning strike. Elikah had gotten up at dawn to start his preparations with the pig pit they had been digging since the day before. I made jars of sweet tea and followed him to the churchyard. I had been put to cutting the chickens that Elikah and two other men were cooking over a huge fire pit. A whole pig was sizzling in the pit on the east side of the church, giving off a tantalizing odor if I didn't look at it.

Ignoring the heat, a dozen children were running and screaming, checking the tables that gradually filled with cakes and pies and pickles and breads. Otto Kretzler, the man who built the railroad, had brought the pig to our church, and also one to the Baptist church, which stood catty-corner from us, close enough for the children to run back and forth, reporting on each new developing dish or bit of decoration.

Elikah had told me that Will McVay had left town the day after the lightning and had not returned. Elikah said Will wasn't coming back, that JoHanna had finally driven him away. I knew better, but I didn't say. It wasn't just Elikah who said such things. It was the whole town.

I cut the chickens, the sweat rolling down my back and staining the navy of my dress a darker hue. My hair was hot, and I had pinned it up, trying to imitate the twist that JoHanna wore with such ease. Too fine and slightly curly, my own hair slipped from the pins to torment me by dangling down my neck and in my eyes. I knew the women watched me, thinking that a handsome man like Elikah could have done better than me. He had courted some of the girls who now stood in the shade of a big oak, fanning themselves with cardboard scenes from the local funeral home and laughing as they dipped their heads together. They wore pale-colored dresses with ribbons in their neat hair. Instead of cooking, they had been given the chore of sticking red, white, and blue bunting around the tables and pinning ribbons on the lapels of the men's suits. I hated them, and myself.

I hated the chickens, their pale skin yellow with fat, and the ugly puckers where feathers had been. Looking down at a half-cut carcass, I thought of Pecos. My own hand was stiff and painful, and I had told Elikah that I cut it trying to carve a joint of beef. He'd looked at it, nodding when I told him I'd poured turpentine in it, and said that it would heal. He told me to be more careful, and later that night he'd poured more turpentine into it for good measure. It had hurt more the second time.

I severed a thigh and drumstick and stopped to wipe the sweat from my brow with the back of my hand. The bloody knife lifted in my raised arm, I heard the motor car. In that same instant, I saw JoHanna. She was wearing a big hat that cast a shadow all down her bosom, a straw hat with a cluster of red flowers in the front where the brim was pinned.

She was sitting in the front of the big red Auburn Touring Car with Will driving. Duncan was in the rear seat with Pecos riding on the back. They slowed for Duncan to look out at the scene. JoHanna pointed to me and smiled. Then they went on down Main Street, disappearing in a cloud of orange dust.

"They're going to the doctor in Mobile," Janelle Baxley said as she came over to me, her eye critically examining my dissection of the chickens. She pointed at a half, "Don't leave it like that. Too thick to cook."

"How do you know?" I stabbed with the knife, sinking the tip of the blade a good inch into the wooden table.

Janelle flinched, but she didn't step back. "The men are too impatient. They won't let a big piece cook."

"How do you know they're going to the doctor?" My sleeve was soaked with sweat, but I had nothing else to wipe my face on.

"Duncan hasn't walked or talked since the lightning. Doc Westfall says she won't."

I didn't believe Doc Westfall was making predictions, but I didn't say so.

"There was brain damage," she said, nodding wisely. "She'll probably be like a big old cabbage the rest of her life."

I'd seen Duncan's eyes. They were distinctly uncabbagelike.

"Agnes said the girl was dead." Janelle dropped her voice to a whisper. "She said you were there, standing right beside her. Was she?"

"Yes."

Janelle stepped closer. "Was she really dead? You know Agnes exaggerates so that I didn't want to believe her. Was Duncan really dead?"

"Yes." I couldn't help it. My reward was the widening of her eyes, the flutter of her lids, as if she'd just been smote by the Holy Spirit or a really bad whiff of something rotten.

"My goodness." She huffed a little in excitement. "So it's true."

There were still a dozen chickens to cut, and my hand was hurting. I looked at it and saw that the wound had reopened. Blood had soaked the bandage I'd tied around it. Janelle looked down and saw it, too, but she ignored it. In her new print dress she didn't want any part of the bloody gore of cutting chickens.

"You know they say that not even the devil would have that child, so he sent her back." She wasn't smiling.

I drew the knife out of the wood, running my fingers along the blade in an absent gesture. "I heard it was God that sent her back."

Janelle stepped away from me. "God?"

I nodded solemnly. "God."

"Well, he wouldn't have her either."

"Not exactly. He gave her a chore to do." Without warning I brought the knife down hard on the half chicken she'd been discussing. The blow cleaved it. I looked up from the chicken directly into her eyes. "Duncan is his chosen one."

"I have to see to the tea." Janelle hurried away, looking back once with her eyes wide.

By the time the table was finished and the food ready to eat, the heat and the blood of the chickens had made me sick. Elikah brought me a glass of tea under the shade of the oak. The other girls had gone off with their families or their beaus, and I had the strong support of the tree trunk and the cool shade all to myself.

"You need to go home," Elikah said, looking at my ruined dress and my hair, at the blood on my hand. There was whiskey on his breath, and I knew that in the dawn hours when the pig roasting had begun, Tommy Ladnier had been by with his jars of clear liquor.

Liquor was the nectar of Satan, and Tommy Ladnier was the devil's own spawn. But he had the finest clothes and the best car, and I'd heard in my short stay in Jexville three times about his house on the Mississippi Gulf Coast with a brick gallery that was terraced straight down to the waters of the Mississippi Sound. Each weekend Negro musicians played their dark music and men and women danced, drunk on whiskey and moonlight and the promise of sex.

The way I heard it, Tommy Ladnier spent money by snapping his fingers and giving an order. Someone rushed to carry out his most outlandish whim. But Tommy worked six days a week delivering his goods. Personally delivering. The trademark of a fine salesman, Elikah always said. My husband, and most of the men of Jexville, were regular customers of Tommy Ladnier.

I gave Elikah back the unfinished glass of tea and started home, wanting nothing more than to strip my old dress off and throw it away. I wanted to take the scissors and cut the dress into bits so small that not even my mama could make it go back together again. And then I wanted to cut my hair. I wanted to hear the sharp tear of the blades beside my ear. It was a clean, crisp sound that declared independence. I'd been by the barbershop two or three times and stood in the doorway as Elikah relieved a customer of his troublesome locks.

"Screetch!" The hair would fall, revealing white scalp or a loppy ear. "Screetch!" And the neck would be revealed for the cool breeze.

My good hand itched for the weight of the scissors. It was a dangerous desire.

Instead, I took off my dress and put it to soak in a pan of water. Elikah had drawn up another pan, and I stood in the washtub and poured it over my head as slowly as I could. The water was heavy, and my arms trembled and made me spill some of it, but as it fell over me, my arms steadied.

When I got out, I dried. Elikah would not be home until much later. There would be singing in the afternoon, and bonfires as the night fell. I had heard all the plans, couched as they were in quiet disguise. While the children faded into sleep in the hot afternoon and the women began to clean up, the men would continue to drink. Late at night, when the bonfires had gone dead from lack of wood, the men would stumble home, where their wives and children already slept. It was the way that Elikah and many of the men had always celebrated the Fourth of July.

I rubbed myself with the delicious roughness of a towel dried stiff in the hot sun. Even though I worked harder, I was beginning to put on weight. There was more food in Elikah's house and fewer mouths to feed. Clutched by my worst fear, I probed my belly. More than anything in the world I dreaded being pregnant. Pregnancy meant a lifetime of slavery. Pregnancy was the death of all hope. Pregnancy was the terror of a hungry child and no means to get food for it.

Stiff and frightened, I crept into bed and hid beneath the clean cotton sheets, my hair heavy and damp and still around my face and at last in a condition where I could like it, at least a little.

I dreamed of Pecos. At first he drove Will's beautiful red car, his gobbles swinging crazily in the wind as he steered with the tips of his feathered wings. Then he was dancing in the bare yard of JoHanna's house with the carcasses of the chickens I'd prepared to cook. Though they had no heads or feathers, they had feet and could dance the Charleston. It was a strange dream but not troubling, and I awoke to the stillness of late night and an empty bed.

I had never been alone a night in my entire life, and I stretched, finding a cooler place on Elikah's side of the bed. A slight breeze came through the window I had left open, and I realized I was naked. Elikah would be scandalized. The thought pleased me, but I got up and put on one of his clean shirts that I had not yet ironed. He would never know that I'd worn it.

Barefoot, I went to the swing on the porch. The night was dark but the stars were very bright. I wasn't certain, but I thought I could see the smoldering embers of the bonfire. Elikah would be home soon, and it would behoove me to be dressed in a gown and asleep in the bed when he returned. It was unseemly for a young bride to wear her husband's shirt and nothing else on the front porch of her new home. But the cool night air on my bare thighs made me remember the strange freedom of my childhood. When Jojo wasn't home, I often slipped out on the porch of the old house to dream and think. I slept in old shirts of my brothers, and because I was still a child, no one objected. It was a good memory.

As I started to sit down, my hand brushed the top of a strange object, a box, that had been left on the swing. It hadn't been there when I came home and went to bed. It was a large box.

At first I couldn't think what to do except stand there with my hand on it. What could it mean, a box on the swing? I took it inside and went to the bedroom to light a lamp. It took only a moment to find the card. "To Mattie. Thanks for helping Duncan and JoHanna. Will."

In all of my life I'd never gotten an unexpected gift. I tore it open, thinking that I was dreaming once again, and this one much more pleasant than the one about Pecos.

Inside the soft tissue were a white blouse and a pale green skirt. The material was buttery, it was so soft. I knew it would be cool. A white blouse and a skirt. The blouse had tucks and tiny buttons. Not severe but very elegant. Hardly daring to touch it, I folded it back exactly as it had been and put the lid on the box, then shoved it up under the bed until I could think what to do.

Elikah would make me return it. And he would be furious with me. I had lied to him about the vegetables, saying that I had traded some of the taffy I'd made for them from an old man pulling a wagon through town. He'd lifted the lid on the pot where the potatoes were boiling and watched the smooth, white tubers shift and roll in the bubble of the pot. We decided that in the fall I would plant the turnips and onions and winter squash that did well in Jexville. There was no need to barter for vegetables when I knew how to garden.

He hadn't asked many questions, and I hadn't elaborated on my lies. But how was I going to explain the skirt and blouse? If I told him they were from the McVays, then he'd ask why they'd sent me a present. The complications of the gift spiraled out of my head and around the bed, making the room spin with dire possibilities.

The note had been signed by Will. I clearly remembered the way the soap had dried on one side of his face, interrupted in his shave by the rooster's attack on me. I had no memory of the rooster slashing my hand, but if I closed my eyes, I could still smell Will's soapy face, still see the small scar on his right hand as he held a compress against my wound. His eyes were the color of chocolate pound cake, lighter in the center with a dark rim. Duncan had his eyes, with a glint of challenge that came from her mother.

The gift had to be returned. There was no way to avoid it. But even as I tried to force myself to accept that decision, I shrank from the image of standing on their front porch, box in hand, lifting it slowly over the threshold and into JoHanna's hands. Never in my life had I wanted an article of clothing more. As my fingers brushed the coarser cotton of my sheets, I could feel the glide of the material. Like a whisper, a lover's whisper on my skin. The feel of the skirt about my legs would be like tiny small strokes of pleasure with each step. I could not give it up. Yet I knew that I had to.

In the gray light of dawn, Elikah's face was red and bloated, his mustache unbearably askew on the pillow as he slept. I was uncertain whether to wake him for work or allow him to sleep since he looked ill. I made his coffee and woke him with a cup when he just had time to dress and eat before the barbershop opened at seven. He worked long hours and made decent money. Unlike most of the men I'd known, he didn't drink every day.

To my complete surprise, he took the cup of coffee and propped the pillows behind his head. "Mattie, you need some new dresses. Go down to the dry goods and pick something out. But make sure you can take it back if I don't like it." He sipped the coffee from the mug. "Something green. To go with your eyes."

I thought the floor had shifted beneath my feet. My own guilt almost gagged me, but when I turned to stare at him, he was examining a toenail that was giving him trouble. As the town barber, he felt obliged to give a demonstration of cutting it out of the quick and had planned to do so that day. It was part of his rivalry with Doc Westfall. Elikah had a need to uphold the "traditional" role of barber as surgeon and healer, even if he had to perform his operations on himself.

"I'll get you some hot saltwater to soak that," I offered.

He put his feet on the floor and handed the coffee cup to me. "No time. Just put my eggs on."

He was gone with a brush of his mustache, once again neatly groomed, across my cheek and a reminder to "find something pretty for yourself."

Perhaps I had dreamed the skirt and blouse, an omen of Elikah's sudden generosity. A store-bought dress. Something I had never owned until that very night. And something I certainly had never considered walking into a store and buying. A dress cut out and made up in a shop.

I sat at the table and finished my coffee, knowing that the first order of business was to take the skirt and blouse back to JoHanna's. What had the doctor in Mobile said about Duncan? I could ask that and hope that Will was not at home when I returned the package. The thought of looking at him as I handed back his gift was too terrifying.

I was struck so numb by my next thought that I almost dropped the coffee cup. What if JoHanna didn't know Will had left that gift for me? Surely that was impossible. But what if he was gone and I went there, gift in hand, only to open the door on a situation that looked bad, for both Will and myself?

A mockingbird fluttered into the chinaberry tree by the kitchen window. It watched me with sharp black eyes, head shifting from side to side, as if assessing the purity of my thoughts. I did not want to give up the skirt and blouse; had I found an excuse to keep it?

I put water on the stove to heat and dragged out the bathtub and dumped the cold water from the night before into the yard. The cool water last night had washed away the heat, but I wanted to soak in hot water. Once clean, I pulled the box out from under the bed and slipped into the blouse. The skirt drifted over my head like a mossy green wave. I buttoned it around my waist and knew I would not give it back. I could not make myself, no matter the cost.

❧ *Four* ❧

"**Y**OU'RE as flushed as a new bride, but then you are right new at it." Olivia McAdams pulled a pale yellow dress from the rack where it hung. "It's a day dress. Cool. Folks around here need to make some concessions to the heat." She looked at the gray flannel I was wearing with a sympathetic eye.

She wore a white blouse and dark skirt with dark shoes, a look some of the magazines advertised as "business girl." She also wore lipstick and dark stockings.

"Elikah said green." I spoke before I thought, so I had to finish it. "And I have to be able to bring it back if it doesn't suit him."

Olivia laughed out loud. "Well, he's paying for it, I guess. Look around and I'll see what we have right here in the sale rack. Maybe get you a good price so there's something left over for some shoes." She pointedly did not look down at my feet but turned her attention to some dresses hanging far against the wall.

Gordon's Dry Goods was a big wooden building divided roughly in half. On the west side were hardware and staples, overalls and long johns, candy and guns, dressmaker patterns, bolts of material and ribbons. There was always the smell of metal and the acrid bite of new lumber, the fatty pine resin still weeping on some of the boards that were dry-stored in the back. Men sweaty from the fields came in to buy a piece of harness or oil for a tool. They lingered as they did at the barbershop, not for long, but enough to pass the time and glean a tip about who was buying what. Or if the women came in, they bought their clothespins and bluing for their laundry and discovered that Mrs. Johnson had a new recipe for seven-egg pound cake that required one of the "just arrived from Mobile or New Orleans" heavier baking pans.

Ready-made clothes were sold out of a separate register on the east side of the building. Here, light filtered in through a big glass window where displays had been set up to show off the smartest clothes. No wall divided the store, but there were two separate doors so that a customer could signal his or her intent upon entering, as if the whiff of perfumed powder or aftershave wasn't enough to mark the difference of intent.

With the yellow dress draped over her arm, Olivia watched me as I stood, held captive by the array of choices, by the pale light that slanted in through the big pane and gave everything a blond look.

"I'll put this one at the counter. Go on and look around," she urged, waving me on like a mother to a timid child. I suppose it was plain to anyone that I'd never shopped for myself before. I'd been in big stores in Meridian and in Gordon's a time or two, but never with the idea that I could have something that I picked out. Something just for me.

"Thanks." I moved into the center of the store and turned around. There were racks of dresses and skirts and blouses, and even a stand of little hats for ladies. Going-to-church hats, nothing like the big straw picture hat that JoHanna wore. I'd never have the nerve to wear such a hat, but I might wear one of the little felt ones with a sprig of foliage or a pretty feather I could find in the woods. I went by them without touching.

Lined against the wall were dresser-type shelves with drawers where beautiful lace panties resided in cool tissue-paper boxes. I'd looked at them once before when Janelle had dragged me in to shop with her for the Fourth of July picnic dress. She hadn't bought any of the things either, but she'd made Olivia McAdams open every drawer and lift out each pair of panties, each brassiere, even some of the very expensive silk stockings that floated over my hand like water whipped with foam.

On the same side of the store, but in the back, were clothes for men. The dark suit coats hung along one wall while the pants hung in the center of the floor on big wooden cylinders. There was a round rack filled with belts measured in waist sizes, and another, bigger rack with the only item of men's apparel with pretty colors, the neckties. There were boxes of suspenders and bow ties, and the wonderful straw hats that Will wore at such a rakish angle.

Olivia was shifting through dresses at another rack. After discarding five or six dresses, she lifted out a green print. "How about this calico? It should fit. We can make the alterations if you need them." She motioned to the back of the store. "There's a dressing room back there, behind the curtain."

I froze, hand reaching for a pretty red and yellow scarf that I couldn't have but wanted to touch.

"You want to try them on?" Olivia asked, her gaze following mine around the store. "There's nobody here now but us."

It hadn't occurred to me that I would have to take off my clothes in the back of the store. Olivia watched the realization dawn on me and then laughed again, patting my shoulder. "You can take them home and try them on if it makes you feel better. Old man Gordon don't have to know."

"No, I'll try them on here. No point in taking them home and bringing them back." The truth of the matter was that at home I'd have no one with whom to share the experience of my first store-bought dress. Will's secret dress was for trying on at home alone. For this dress, I wanted another viewpoint, another female say-so.

Olivia's grin was spritely. For the first time I realized she wasn't really a woman. She was large-busted and stout, a fact that made her seem grown. But she wasn't married, and she helped support her mother's brood of nine children in the rambling wood house they owned on Canaan Street. Janelle had told me all of this in a whisper the day we'd gone to look for her celebration dress. I'd been afraid Olivia would overhear.

"Take them both," Olivia directed as she got the yellow dress from the counter. "That way you won't have to come out and get the other."

What could it hurt to try on the yellow? I took them and went back to the little closet that had been outfitted with hooks on one side for the dresses. It was hardly big enough to cuss a cat in, but it would do to change clothes.

Peeling out of the gray flannel was like shedding the past. I thought of my sister and was stabbed by a twinge of fear. What would become of her now that I was gone? Would Jojo find some man to buy her off his hands the same way he'd done me? I was married, true enough, but Jojo had seen to that part.

I tried the yellow first. It was cotton, and the sleeves were short and cuffed with lace and a hem that rose a good four inches above my ankles. I was too old for a sash, but the dress had a white belt that called attention to my waist.

"Come on out," Olivia ordered. "There's a mirror out here so you can take a gander at yourself."

I didn't want to put on my ugly shoes, so I stepped out barefoot, head-first, to make sure no one had come in while I'd changed. On the other side of the store, old Mrs. Tisdale was selling dried beans to a little boy I didn't know. I could hear the hard beans pinging into the scales as she weighed them out by the pound.

Olivia took a look at my bare feet and put her hands on her hips. "Well, well, if it ain't little Cinderella."

My image in the mirror transfixed me. Instinctively I reached up to pin up my straggly hair, anything to make me look older.

"Try the green," she said, never shifting from the worn pine floor.

The green was not nearly as pretty, but it did serve to make me look married. It also made me feel less nervous. The yellow was as if I was exposed, showing something indecent, even though it was a perfectly decent dress.

"I like this one," I told Olivia.

"I expect your husband will, too." There was something dark in her eyes that was the opposite of her hearty laughter. "You want to wear it home?"

I did, but I couldn't. "I have to let Elikah see it before I buy it."

"You could wear it on down to his shop. I can't see that he wouldn't like it."

I shook my head. He wouldn't like it if I put him on the spot like that in public. He liked to make his decisions at home, after he'd had some time to think. Wearing the dress down the street was as good as saying it was mine. I went back in the closet and unbuttoned it, letting it fall around my feet to step out of it.

There was a quick tap. Then the door swung open, and Olivia stood there with another dress in her hand. "Here, try this one. It was hanging in the . . ." She stopped as she looked at the backs of my bare legs.

I turned around quickly.

"Ah, hanging in the front," she finished, all life gone from her voice. "It might suit you better than the green print." She stood there holding the dress as I stared at the floor, unable even to reach up and take the dress from her.

"How old are you, really?" she finally asked.

"Sixteen." I had just turned the last week in June. The day I had been married, in fact.

"Are you okay?" She just stood there.

I nodded. "I, uh, broke Elikah's favorite cup." I tried to explain the marks.

"You look a little young for marriage and a little old for a strappin'." She handed the dress in to me and closed the door.

I took the solid green dress with the white collar. It was cotton and cool, but not as carefree as the yellow one. Olivia hadn't said so, but the yellow made me look my age. Young. But there were plenty of girls sixteen who were married and starting families. My own mama had married at fifteen, then given birth to me just after she turned sixteen. She was young, but she said she never regretted those years with Daddy. I remembered him some, sitting at the table in his engineer's cap and his large hands seamed by coal. I was seven when he was killed. The next year Mama took up with Jojo. The railroad was going to put us out of the house, and even though she did washing and ironing for some of the railroad officials, she couldn't make enough to pay the rent and feed four kids. It was Jojo or starvation, she said, and she made the choice.

When Elikah came home for dinner, I showed him the dress. He made me turn around and pin my hair up and then he grinned. He told me to go back and get some decent shoes that didn't make me look like I lived on a pig farm and had to wade through mud every day. He also told me to buy some underthings and described what he wanted. He was still grinning when he asked if I wanted him to write down a list.

Instead of going back to Gordon's after I washed the dishes, I slipped out the back and cut across the train yard to go to the McVays'. It was hotter than blue blazes on the hard-packed dirt road, but my mind was whirling along as fast as my feet.

What had the doctor said about Duncan? They had come back sometime during the night to leave the gift on the swing. The more I thought about it, the more I was certain JoHanna had put Will up to doing it. He wouldn't have thought to buy something like that on his own. No man did. It was too much what I would have picked out myself, and men never thought that way. JoHanna had done it and then put Will up to signing his name so that I'd . . . what? Keep it? I hadn't been able to think anymore along those lines because I didn't know how to pursue it. In my experience, grown-ups did things to get something they wanted. But what could JoHanna and Will want from me? I had nothing to give them.

The homestead came into view. I stopped to look for two things— Will's red car and that damned rooster. My hand still burned when I washed dishes, the lye soap eating at the open area. It was healing without any infection, but I didn't want to risk another encounter with Pecos.

The red car was gone, but JoHanna was at the clothesline, bringing in the wash before the afternoon thunderstorm could arrive. She was folding the towels and dropping them down into her laundry basket, her back to the road. Pecos strutted back and forth beside her, his quick little rooster head darting this way and that as if he were boxing someone.

"Mrs. McVay! JoHanna!" I called, ready to run if Pecos should move in my direction.

JoHanna turned, her hand still on the line. When she saw me, she smiled and waved me over. My hesitation was obvious. "Pecos is fine as long as I'm here." For good measure she reached down and tucked the rooster up under her arm.

His beady black eyes drilled into me like pencil leads, but he didn't make a squawk or ruffle a feather as I walked into the yard.

"How's Duncan?" I could see that JoHanna had aged in the past few days.

She lifted her straw sunbonnet off her head and started to answer. I didn't hear a word she said. Someone had butchered her hair. I knew I was standing there like a mouth-breather, but I couldn't help it. There were places on her head where the shears had come so close it looked as though her scalp were burned, then other places where the growth was half an inch or more. Her beautiful chestnut hair was completely gone.

JoHanna dropped the hat and ran her hand over her head. "It's that bad, huh?"

"What happened?"

She stooped to get her hat, put it on her head, gave the rooster a toss out into the grass, and turned back to the clothesline. "Duncan." It was all she said.

I could almost feel the stiff bristles of hair beneath my hand, though I had not moved in her direction. "JoHanna." I spoke her name on a whisper.

"My lord, Mattie, you're acting a total fool. It's hair. It'll grow back." She folded another towel, her motions fluid and mechanical.

"It was so beautiful."

"It'll grow back." Her voice was impatient, but when she turned to me she stopped folding her towel and smiled. "I made Duncan a braid of my hair to play with. We'll grow out together."

At last I was able to focus my attention on something other than her ruined head. I looked at the window where Duncan's beautiful peach curtains undulated in a tiny breeze. "What did the doctor in Mobile say?"

"So the gossip is out." JoHanna turned back to the clothesline and her work. Instead of putting the pins in a little sack, she left hers stuck on the line. "I suppose it was all over the picnic."

"Janelle." It was all I needed to say.

"Well, Dr. Liebermann—he's a specialist in neurology—said that it was possible something in Duncan's brain had been damaged by the lightning." The only indication of her pain and fear was the tremble in her hands as she missed the clothesline trying to put a pin back. "There's no way to tell. She may regain the use of her legs and her speech." She shrugged. "She may never walk or talk again." She took down one of Will's shirts. Her hands moved over the collar, a gesture she wasn't even aware of. It was as if she were trying to draw the essence of her husband from the cloth.

I reached out and took her hand, holding it in mine.

"I can't cry out here. Duncan might see." She let me take the shirt from her and she moved on to another, unpinning and folding it to drop down in the wicker basket that she pushed along in front of her with one foot.

"The gossip is that Duncan died." I don't know where those words came from, but I let fly with them before I even considered what they meant.

JoHanna never missed a tick as she took down the clothes, her gestures once again perfectly fluid and mechanical. "I know."

"What should I say? I told Janelle it was true, because . . ."

JoHanna stopped and looked at me, her eyes like some strange, fractured gem that caught the light and shattered it into blue chips.

". . . Because they said that not even Satan would have her, and that he sent her back. So I said no, that it was God who sent her back because He'd given her a chore." I was on fire with the need to confess what I'd said. What if I'd made it worse for Duncan?

JoHanna's laughter rang across the yard, causing Pecos to streak over toward us, his wings lifted in the preamble to attack.

"Stop it, Pecos." She flapped a shirttail at the bird before she whirled around and hugged me to her. "Mattie Mills, you are too good to be true." She started laughing again, this time a conclusion, a softer sound. At last she wiped her eyes and hugged me again. "I'll bet that old biddy is still trying to get that out of her craw."

"You aren't mad?" I couldn't believe it.

"Why would I be mad? It was the perfect answer to gag that old witch. How can she wag her tongue about that without giving Duncan credit for being blessed?" An idea lit her eyes. "You know, there's a big baptism next Sunday down at Cedar Creek. Some of the girls Duncan's age are going to be 'washed in the Spirit.' " Her smile widened, and the worry of the last few days lifted. "I think maybe we should go watch. Me and you and Duncan."

"Okay." I agreed, knowing I would do whatever necessary to get away. "And Will?"

"He's gone off to Washington to deliver some goods to a few old politicians."

I was so astounded by that news that I couldn't even answer. Will needed to be home instead of halfway around the world.

"Sunday. I'll come by to get you about nine o'clock. I can pack us a little picnic."

"How?" I looked around. The car was gone.

"Oh, Duncan and I have been working on this." She folded the last towel, picked up the basket, and started walking toward a shed in the back. I followed along with Pecos trailing me, his wings held up and out and his movements a sideways skitter as he kept watch over me, just in case I made a desperate move that he needed to punish me for.

When we got to the shed, JoHanna motioned with her head toward the old red wagon she'd used to haul the gramophone. In it now was a cowhide rocker that had been strapped into the bed of the wagon with two good leather belts. JoHanna put the clothes down and touched the chair, putting it into motion. The straps allowed a bit of rocking, but not much.

"It's Duncan's litter; we will be her bearers." JoHanna's smile was delighted and mocking. "We've already tried it out, and she finds it quite comfortable. I can pull her in that and have plenty of room for the picnic basket."

"Okay." I believed that JoHanna could do anything. If she had pulled out an embroidered carpet and said we would fly on it to Cedar Creek, I would have agreed.

"Then it's settled. Come on in the house and have a glass of tea." She hefted the laundry basket up on her hip and started walking toward the house. I had to stretch my legs to keep up with her. JoHanna didn't waste a movement. She was direct, purposeful. In my hot gray dress, I followed like a willing sheep.

Five

I WAS waiting in the swing in my Elikah dress when I caught sight of JoHanna. Even though I was looking for her, at first I didn't believe what I saw. She was wearing her big straw picture hat with a mixture of black-eyed Susans and reddish-brown rooster tail feathers around the rim. Her sleeveless yellow dress actually had a band of swinging fringe along the hem. She would have caught the attention of a blind man in a hurricane.

She strode with her hands behind her back, her chest cutting the air in front of her like the figure on the prow of some gallant sailboat. Behind her came the wagon with Duncan and the rocking chair tipping forward and back. Riding on the back of the wagon was Pecos, his wings constantly shifting up to preattack mode as he scanned left and right for any threats to his beloved human.

I flew off the swing and went to meet them at the corner. Elikah had gone down to the shop, even though it was Sunday. Once a month, Tommy Ladnier made Sunday deliveries to Chickasaw County. It wasn't his best territory, but he was unwilling to give it up to the Dillard boys in Greene County, so he made his regular deliveries and enforced the perimeters of his territory. I had deduced that the barbershop was his drop-off point. The men all went down to the barbershop for a few nips and to investigate Tommy's wares. Elikah said the men liked the barber chairs, but I thought it was because the shop was long and narrow, and if the blinds were closed on the front window, it was a private place. There was also a folding table in the back with chairs for five.

The one time I'd gone to clean the shop, I'd found decks of cards and the multicolored chips that gamblers used for money. It wasn't the only illegal card game in Jexville, just one of the more regular. And one of the more protected. Sheriff Quincy Grissham was one of the men who went in the back door of the barbershop on those Sunday mornings.

Elikah liked for me to go to church. He said it was a woman's duty to keep up that end of the household for her family. When I'd told him I was going to the baptism at Cedar Creek, he was happy as a one-eyed dog on a butcher wagon. It didn't matter that the service was Baptist. Elikah was a Methodist because that's where he happened to light when he moved to Jexville. He said there wasn't a penny's worth of difference between the two, so it was no big shake if I went to the Baptist service. Lots of people from the Methodist church would be there.

"Hi." I ran up to the corner, sort of breathless. It was better for me to meet them on the street than to have them seen at the house. "Hi, Duncan." She stared at me with that direct, pefectly composed look. A lot of the bruising was gone, but she still looked pretty bad. Her legs were wrapped in clean bandages where the burns were worst, and her hair was still a terrible mess.

"Been watching for us?" JoHanna asked as I fell into step beside her.

"Yeah."

"Elikah wouldn't want you going with us."

She spoke a statement. I didn't feel compelled to lie, so I didn't say anything.

"He's a handsome man."

"Yes, he is." A flush touched my cheeks. I looked at her, a quick glance to see if she was being polite or sincere. She was sincere. "Why didn't he marry a local girl? I saw them at the Fourth of July picnic. They would have married him. Why didn't he marry one of them?"

JoHanna looked back to smile at Duncan. They didn't speak a word, but there was something that passed between them.

"I suspect Elikah didn't want to be bothered with a wife who had family right around him."

I nodded. Elikah had never offered a question about my family or about how they were doing. He'd given me money to mail a letter to them, but even when Mama wrote back he handed me the letter and didn't even ask what they'd said. If he had family, he didn't say. He was a man who just didn't have much need for other connections.

"How is Elikah?"

"Fine." I looked down at my new shoes. "He bought me a dress and some shoes, but it wasn't as nice as the one y'all sent."

JoHanna kept pulling the wagon. We'd passed the last building on the road until we got to the Hancock farm, about half a mile out of town. Cedar Creek was another mile. It was going to be a long, hot walk.

"Will has excellent taste in women's clothes. He picked that out for you." She smiled at my shocked expression. "My only concern was that it might cause trouble for you, but Will said you were smart enough to handle it."

"I haven't shown Elikah the dress."

"Handle it however you see fit."

We walked along in near silence; the only sound was the creak of the rocker or an occasional flap from Pecos. The rooster made me nervous at first, but it became apparent he had no intention of leaving Duncan's side.

"Why are you going to the baptism?" I'd been to the Mississippi Methodist Church twice since I'd come to Jexville, and none of the Mc-Vays had been in attendance. "Are you Baptist?"

"No." She gave me a look. "Why are you going? Are you religious?"

That question set me back on my heels. I was going to be with her. So far as I'd seen, God hadn't made any great interventions in my life for the better. But church was a woman's duty, and it was a place to go. "I'm going 'cause you asked me," I finally answered. "Do you believe God might heal Duncan?" That had been at the back of my mind, too. I was wondering if JoHanna was hoping for a miracle.

JoHanna walked on a bit, her face calm, serene. "What I believe is hard to say," she said, her pace steady, the sun hot on both of our shoulders. "I believe 'god' is in all living things, even grass and trees. It's a tough belief in a sawmill town." She was mocking herself.

"You think trees have God in them?" I looked around. The huge pine trees along the roadway had already been harvested. In a nearby field, the raw stumps still bled resin, the scent as pungent as any other death. On the other side of the road, the stumps had been burned or pulled out and pasture allowed to grow. Half a mile back, the huge trunks of the unharvested trees made a leafless wall of brown.

"I think every thing alive has something of a soul." She cut a look at me. "Even men."

I knew she was teasing me, but the idea was so fanciful I couldn't let it go. "Who else believes this?"

She shrugged. "Not many around here, that's for sure. But it's an old religion. I certainly didn't make it up."

"Did you get baptized?"

She laughed. "If you count swimming naked in a cold creek and glorying in the beauty of the water a baptism, then I've been immersed. But as far as I know, people who believe like me don't even have church buildings or any kind of formal rituals."

I watched her face and saw the humor and spark of mischief that I'd seen duplicated in Duncan's face the day she'd danced. Now I understood better why the men of Jexville disliked her so. She talked wild. Her words were tiny darts of freedom that stung the men, even when she spoke of nothing but trees and creeks. Her awareness of things struck at the root of men's lives. Why it should threaten them so, I didn't understand, but I knew it did.

"Why are we going to this baptism, then? It's the Jexville Baptist Church."

"I know." Her blue eyes were shot with light and gave back to me the vista of the pine forest and the blue sky. "Since you've been spreading the word that Duncan has been sent back from the dead to complete a mission for God, I thought we'd show up and just watch."

"JoHanna!"

"No harm in watching." She still held the wagon handle behind her back, and she turned to face the road once again. She started walking, knowing I'd fall back into step with her.

It was my first indication that she actively sought to start talk about herself. She stirred the fires of speculation with deliberate actions. "And Duncan?" I looked over my shoulder at her and met her dark gaze. It was impossible to read the expression on her face, but I thought for a moment that a shadow of sorrow touched her eyes and drew her dark eyebrows together. Then it was gone, and she looked at her mother's back. It was as if she touched JoHanna, who turned back to look at her. That silent communication passed between them.

"It's okay, Duncan," she said. "You'll be dancing on their graves in a matter of no time."

"JoHanna!"

She laughed, and if I had closed my eyes, I would have seen her as a girl. She was such a contradiction.

"Tell me about growing up," she said. "What's your best memory?"

My new shoes were still stiff, but they were getting a good breaking in as we moved along the road. There was no traffic, and I hadn't felt so safe and content in weeks. The memory she requested wasn't hard to grab hold of. In her company, I felt bold enough to tell it.

"My sister Callie and I snuck into the Meridian Opera House one afternoon."

"Ah, the spice of trespassing." She nodded. "And an opera house, the perfect place for adventure. Do you like opera?"

I looked down the road. The trees were tall and thick in this area, shading the road. There had been talk of the state sending in heavy equipment to improve the highway to Pascagoula. "I don't know," I admitted. "I never got to hear one. The place was empty. It was afternoon, and Callie and I wanted to look at the costumes." Even from such a distance, the memory made me smile. "The dresses were beautiful. They were slick and had those glittery things sewn into them, like fairy brides."

JoHanna smiled. "Fairy brides, no less. And were you afraid?"

"Yes. Callie and I were terrified we would be found out. We had no business there. Mama didn't have money for us to attend a real performance. We only wanted to see what it was like in that building where the people came out late at night all dressed up and laughing."

"I have some records of operas. Will buys them for me when he goes to some of the bigger cities. He says it sounds like cats in a fight, but I like some of them."

"Records?" I couldn't hide my amazement. "Of operas?"

"It isn't the same as a show, but you could at least learn the music if you wanted. Maybe Will and I would act them out for you."

I laughed at the idea. Would they really do such a thing? "Okay."

"When he gets home," she promised. "Maybe by then Duncan will be well enough to play a part. We'll do costumes and the whole thing."

I looked back at Duncan. Pecos had moved up to ride on the arm of her rocker. He heard something in the distance, and he swiveled his head all the way around without turning his body. It made me real nervous.

"Here's the turn." JoHanna pulled the wagon down a steep drop that ended in a six-inch bed of sand. It took both of us to heave the wagon through.

From the woods the sound of singing came like sunshine through thick leaves, just a phrase here and there. It was an old hymn, one Mama used to sing at the kitchen sink when she cut up the turnip roots that were the staple of our fall diet. She said the song gave her comfort, but it only made me afraid. It was about going home, across the River Jordan. That meant dying and going to heaven. I didn't like the song.

Coming through the trees, the pure, true voice of the woman singing had power. We eased along, being as quiet as we could, until we came out at the top of an incline that swept all the way down to the amber creek.

The Baptist choir was standing on the sandy slope in the beautiful robes they wore each Sunday: crimson red on the whitest sand I'd ever seen. Farther back on the grassy part of the slope just above and behind the choir were the spectators with their picnic baskets. After the service there would be food.

In between both groups was a cluster of young girls, all in white dresses. They'd come to be washed in the blood and accepted in the church as members. Even as we stopped the wagon, undid the belts, and lifted Duncan and her chair out onto the sand, the minister was walking down into the amber swirl of water. The baptism had begun.

He was a tall man with dark hair slicked back neat against his head, his lean body cutting the current of the water as he waded in until he was waist deep. Turning to the bank, he lifted his hands. The choir finished off the song they were singing about coming to the Lord. The young girls clumped together; then one stepped out and began to wade into the water.

"It's Lily Anderson," JoHanna said. She pulled a blanket out of the wagon and threw it on the ground for us to sit on beside Duncan. Up on the slope just in the shade of the small scrub oak trees, we had a good view but we weren't actually a part of the event. A strip of white sand separated us from the others, like a barrier neither wanted to cross.

The day was bright and hot, and the water of the creek looked tempting. I remembered what JoHanna had said about swimming around naked. It was scandalous but also tempting. Did she really do such things? I looked at Duncan, but she was leaning forward in her chair, watching the girls who were about her age. They were all singing away, their young voices piercing but thin. Annabelle Lee had the best voice, and she knew it.

Her mama was on the edge of the crowd, so proud she was about to pop. There were a couple of men there, but Elikah said religion was women's business and most of the men seemed to feel the same way. They just made themselves scarce when it was time for a service.

Little Lily Anderson gave a squawk of fright when the preacher lifted her up and dunked her backward in the water. She came up squirting a gusher out of her mouth and drew a few giggles from the congregation and a smile from JoHanna. Duncan, though, didn't look amused. What worried me was that Pecos seemed to pick up on his mistress's attitude. The bird was bristling as he sat on the back of her rocking chair.

"Hush, Pecos." JoHanna reached into the picnic basket and brought out a handful of dried corn. She scattered it at Duncan's feet, but the bird ignored her. His little head ducked and darted, beady eyes fixed on the proceedings at the creek.

"I had a dog, once, a long time ago." I thought of Suke and the loss of her was just as fresh as it had been when Jojo took her off and shot her. "I never thought of having a pet rooster."

JoHanna leaned back on one arm and let her other touch Duncan's foot. Duncan had on socks and shoes, her little feet ready for action, even though she couldn't walk.

Down in the creek Annabelle Lee was wading in. The preacher was talking, but I wasn't paying attention to what he was saying. It was like a chant, familiar yet dulled and unclear. The sun made the sand dazzling, and I was beginning to drift off into one of my island fantasies when JoHanna leaned forward.

"Annabelle looks a far sight better dry than she does wet," she said.

She did in fact. But for the first time the child looked genuinely pleased. Had she found something special beneath the cold water of Cedar Creek? "Do you think they really feel something?" I asked.

JoHanna shook her head. "I don't know. Maybe some of them do."

I wiped a sheen of perspiration from my forehead. It might be worth the trouble just to get in the creek. "If those girls died right now, would they go to heaven?"

JoHanna chuckled in a soft way. "I wouldn't lay any bets one way or another. There goes Mary."

It was the girl who'd come outside to see Duncan dead. She waded right into the water without the hesitation of the other girls. The preacher said his chant and reached behind her to support her back. Over she went.

Instead of coming back up grinning and dripping, Mary started to fight. Her legs thrashed in the water; the amber current was turned to white foam. Mingled in there somewhere was her dress, which floated out around her.

The preacher stepped back, startled. Mary was just beneath the surface, her outline visible to us up at the top of the slope. I could see her, but I couldn't see what she was fighting against.

The preacher grabbed a leg and pulled, but he just got tugged forward, nearly losing his footing in the sandy bottom. Fear widened his eyes, and he reached down in the water. Mary's hands came up and caught at his neck, circling with a strength that panicked him. With a hoarse cry he broke free and ran toward the bank. Behind him, white girl legs kicked harder, churning the water.

"Mary!"

That single cry tore the sky.

"Damnation." JoHanna got to her feet. "She's drowning." She started forward, but so did several members of the congregation and the choir. It was a small stampede into the water.

"Mary!"

I put my hands over my ears, but I couldn't force my eyes away from the creek. There were so many people in the water I couldn't tell what was really happening. The preacher was sprawled in the sand at the edge of the water, and a couple of women were tending to him. He was safe, but Mary had not emerged.

I couldn't rid myself of the sight of her legs, thrashing and kicking, as though some big monster had risen up from the dark pools of water and gotten hold of her head.

"Mary!" Brenda Lincoln tried to run into the water, but several women grabbed her, pulling her back on her butt and holding her down in the sand.

The only men in the congregation were down in the water. Now even Mary's legs were gone. There was no trace of her, but the men kept going underwater, then coming back up and making gestures.

"Oh, no." Johanna sank back into the sand. Her face was white, but perspiration glistened on her skin. "No," she whispered again. Then she looked at me. "They let her drown."

Duncan rocked slightly forward in her chair. Her expression angry, her clear voice carrying on the intensity of her emotion. "I told her not to sing with her mouth open."

Six

WE loaded up the wagon as fast as we could. Down below us, one of the men had finally managed to bring up Mary Lincoln's body. He carried her out of the creek and laid her in the pure white sand. Brenda Lincoln sat in the sand beside her, rocking and keening as Nell Anderson and Agnes Leatherwood tried to console her.

One of the young boys had been sent sprinting up the slope to the nearest house that had a phone, to call Doc Westfall and get him out to the creek. The boy passed us with a curious look but didn't linger to ask any questions about the rocking chair or the rooster. He ran on by.

JoHanna was white. Even her blue eyes had paled until they seemed completely translucent. I couldn't look at her, the same way I sometimes couldn't look at Elikah. She didn't ask Duncan a single question or even express any shock that the girl had opened her mouth and talked as normally as she had the day she had been forked by the bolt of lightning. No, she just flipped the blanket together, sand and all, put it in the wagon with the basket, and signaled fast for me to help her lift Duncan and the chair.

"Can you walk?" I asked Duncan. If she could talk, maybe she could walk, and JoHanna wouldn't have to pull the wagon all the way up the hill.

Duncan shook her head.

"Can you still talk?"

She gave me a sideways look. "Of course." Her attention was focused down the hill. "I told her not to . . ."

"Hush up!"

It was the first time I'd heard JoHanna speak harshly to anyone, especially Duncan. She was terrified, but I couldn't understand why. Duncan could talk. It was a miracle.

"Lift," JoHanna said as we picked up the chair and put it in the wagon. JoHanna buckled the belts and picked up the handle. "Would you push from behind?" she asked, starting forward without waiting for me. She was going home no matter what I chose to do.

I bent down and heaved. The heavy sand trapped the wheels, and Pecos fluttered his wings at me, pecking down as if he wanted a taste of my eyes. Ignoring him, I gritted my teeth and pushed.

"JoHanna McVay!"

I turned back to look at the woman yelling. Brenda Lincoln was standing at the feet of her dead child, but she was looking up at us.

"JoHanna McVay! Bring that young-un down here!"

JoHanna gave the wagon a vicious tug. "Push, Mattie," she whispered without acknowledging Brenda. "Push hard. We have to get out of here."

Instead of pushing, I turned to look back at the creek. Brenda Lincoln was pointing a finger at us as everyone else looked up the hill at us, transfixed. The crimson red robes of the choir fluttered in a sudden breeze. There was a rumble of thunder, far away and distant.

"Stop her!" Brenda turned to the people around her. "Stop her!" Her voice rose hysterically. "That little monster. She cursed Mary. She caused her to drown."

Beneath Brenda Lincoln's hysterical voice was the sound of JoHanna panting. The quick, panicked breaths were close, intimate, and more frightening than the hysteria down at the bottom of the sand slope. One of my new shoes came loose in the deep sand and I finally caught a good purchase with my toes. I gave the wagon everything I had, and we made it out of the sand and onto the more solid ground of the path.

"Go!" I ordered JoHanna. "Go!"

Behind us the congregation had begun to shift, their voices growing louder. Surely they would not come after a helpless child and her mother. Surely not. But I'd seen fear and anger in action more than once. Jojo was never as mean as when he was scared.

The sounds below were blocked out by my own labored breathing as JoHanna and I fought to move Duncan to safety. The pattern of the sun in the tree limbs was like a blur of motion as we rushed along the path, JoHanna pulling the wagon and me bent down pushing. I kicked my other shoe off and gained the use of my toes. A low branch caught Jo-Hanna's hat and knocked it off her head, revealing the shocking lack of hair, the glimpses of a cool white scalp beneath the chestnut bristle where she'd cut too close.

"Leave it," she said of the hat.

I went back for it. If they saw her now, coming on us in a frightened fury, the sight of her head might be the final straw. I grabbed it and plopped it on Duncan's head as we set off again.

By the time we reached the main road, we were winded and shaky. No one had tried to stop us. No one had given pursuit. But I had had time to consider what would happen when Elikah heard about my activities for the day. I would rather have faced the crowd of angry Baptists than to have to confront Elikah at night, especially after his visit from Tommy Ladnier.

"I'm sorry, Mattie. I had no intention of dragging you into this." Jo-Hanna signaled for me to move up beside her. The road was solid, and the wagon rolled easily enough for her to pull it without me pushing.

"He's going to be mad." What was the point of trying to pretend I wasn't afraid? I was, and it showed.

"Come to my house. Will will be home Tuesday, and he can try to explain to Elikah. They've always gotten on."

I shook my head. Hiding would only feed his anger. There was a fine line to walk between cringing and standing up for myself. It was my marriage, and I had to learn to work it out. Mama had taught me that much. Outside interference only made matters worse.

"Oh, Mattie." She dropped the wagon handle and pulled me into an embrace.

Like two fools we stood on the side of the road and cried. Duncan and Pecos watched us, and I had about as much sense of what the bird was thinking as I did Duncan. Those black eyes gave up nothing. In that regard she was like her daddy.

When we were through with our cry, JoHanna looked down at my feet and started to laugh. "Your shoes."

I'd thought of that, too. They were brand-new, and I'd lost them. Maybe someone from the creek would pick them up and bring them to me. I wasn't going back to get them now.

We walked on in silence. At the edge of town, JoHanna motioned that she was going to cut over on Jerusalem Road to hit Peterson Lane without going into town. I don't know if she was trying to spare me or if she wanted to be alone, but I was glad. She took my hand.

"You're welcome to come with us."

"No, I need to get supper going."

"Go over to Jeb Fairley's and use his phone to call me if you need me," she said.

"Okay." I just wanted to be on the way home.

She released my hand and stepped back. I was turning to go when Duncan called out to me.

"When my legs get well, I'll teach you to dance the Charleston," she said.

I hadn't forgotten the fact that while one girl had drowned, a miracle had occurred for Duncan. I hadn't talked about it because it upset me, but now it was staring me square in the eye. "How did you know Mary Lincoln was going to drown?" I asked her.

Duncan shifted so that Pecos could move onto the arm of the rocking chair. "I saw it."

"Just like it happened?"

Duncan cocked her head, and the damn rooster imitated her. "Not exactly like today. I heard the singing, and I saw the girls in their white dresses. There was the choir in their red robes and Reverend Bates down in the water. I saw Mary walking down into the water, and I saw her trying to come up for air. Under the water, her mouth was opening and closing, like she was singing." She wiped her forehead with the back of her hand. "Mama, pull the wagon over to the shade, please."

Fear nipped at my heart. Had Satan brushed his hand across the child? "Have you seen anything else?"

JoHanna stepped beside Duncan, and Pecos hiked his wings an inch.

"I see things sometimes, but they aren't clear, not like Mary. They don't go together to tell a story right." Duncan's face was serious and completely composed. "I wasn't certain it would really happen to Mary. It was like pictures in my head." She looked up at JoHanna. "I tried to tell Mary, didn't I, Mama? I told her not to sing with her mouth open."

JoHanna took her hat off Duncan's head and put it back on her own head. We had left behind the isolation of the old road. This close to town, someone could come up on us. She knelt down. "Duncan, have you seen anything else? Any other pictures in your head?"

Duncan's eyes came alive with mischief. "I saw my friend Floyd from the boot shop come to supper tonight to tell me a story."

JoHanna reached up to touch Duncan's face. "You'd like that, wouldn't you? You haven't seen Floyd since you were hurt."

Duncan laughed. It seemed she grew stronger and more alive with each passing moment. "I would. He was telling me about the river and how Fitler came to be. It was a wonderful story."

"I'll give him a call." JoHanna stood up. "Did you really see him come to dinner, like you saw Mary drown?"

"No!" Duncan laughed. "But he will if you ask him."

"Yes, he will." JoHanna went to pick up the wagon handle.

"That's not the man who thinks he's a cowboy?" I'd seen him hulking around the streets. He wore a holster, and some fool had whittled him a gun. He was in the habit of stopping right in front of a person and drawing down on them, pretending that he could shoot them with his wooden gun. I'd seen him a couple of times, but always at a distance. I always crossed the street to avoid him.

"That's Floyd. He's Duncan's best friend."

"He's a loon." I spoke, once again, without thinking.

"He is not! He's a storyteller." Duncan was bristling with sudden anger. She pointed her finger at me. "Take it back. He's not a loon. He's just different."

"I take it back." I turned away. "I'd better get on home."

Like most things in Jexville, word of what happened at Cedar Creek made it back to Elikah before I could even get home good. I changed back into my old clothes and shoes and started some cucumbers and peeled tomatoes in vinegar for supper. Elikah had gotten a block of ice, and the cool vegetables would be good on such a hot day.

Potato salad with mustard and red onions was one of Elikah's favorites. We had a bin in the kitchen that was cool and dark, and I got several taters out of there and started peeling them. I was about halfway through when he came in.

"Hello, Elikah." I put the knife down and turned to greet him. I met his gaze without flinching.

He held my new shoes out to me. "Didn't you forget something at the creek? I hear you left in a mighty big hurry." He let loose, and they dropped to the kitchen floor with a clatter.

"Thanks. I'm glad someone brought them back."

The shoes lay between us like a sin. Elikah nudged one with his toe. "That little girl, Mary Lincoln, her dress got caught on a tree trunk. That's how come she drowned. You know, in all the times they've had baptisms right down at that creek, no one has ever drowned before. Preacher Bates, he never saw or felt that old dead tree. It was like it was waiting out in the water, just waiting for Mary Lincoln to come along, and then it slipped along the sandy bottom and caught hold of her dress. Can you imagine?"

The more he talked, the more afraid he made me. "No, it was a terrible tragedy."

"You saw the whole thing?"

I nodded. "I'd better get these potatoes peeled. I thought some salad would be good with the pork chops."

"Fuck those potatoes." He was suddenly excited. "I want to know what you saw. My own wife an eyewitness to a drownin', and she wants to peel potatoes."

I swallowed. "I just saw her walk into the water, and the preacher sort of dunked her backward. Then her legs went to thrashing, and she didn't come up."

"Just like that." He held up his hands, palms facing me, a gesture of surrender that wasn't surrender at all.

"That's what I saw. Then people ran in the water to help her, and I couldn't see anymore."

"I see." He turned his hands over as if he studied the palms. "That's what you saw. Nothing more."

"It all happened so fast."

"And then you ran?"

It was a statement-question that didn't require any real answer, except I had to answer something. "It was awful. We decided to head home."

"So fast you lost your shoes?"

"The wagon got stuck in the sand and—" I wasn't going to tell him that JoHanna was afraid.

"And you ran off 'cause you knew you were doing something you shouldn't have been." He walked around the kitchen, slow, stopping to look out the window over the sink, as if he pondered something seriously. He came back to stand in front of me. "Innocent people don't run. Now what exactly did that little McVay girl do to Mary Lincoln? What kind of curse did she put on her?"

"Elikah, there wasn't any kind of curse." I tried to sound reasonable.

"True or not? True or not! When Duncan McVay was struck by lightning, the only words she spoke were that Mary would drown?"

"Elikah, she'd been struck by li—"

He slapped the table so hard it made the salt cellar jump and topple. Salt spilled over the table and onto the floor.

"True or not?" he demanded.

I didn't answer. I focused on my shoes on the floor. They'd fallen on their side, revealing the nearly new soles. For some reason the sight of them, lying the way they were, made me want to cry.

"Mattie, I think you'd better answer me."

"Not," I said without looking at him.

I didn't see his hand, but I bent down to pick up the shoes and caught the blow on the top of my head. Even so, it knocked me off balance and I fell to my knees. He pushed me the rest of the way over with his foot.

"Stay away from that woman. Everyone in town knows she's a slut. That husband of hers knows it. I know it. Now you know it. Stay clear of them. And if I ever hear of you going anywhere with them again, you'll be more sorry than you ever want to believe."

Looking up at him from the floor, I could see the redness of his face, the hardness of his eyes. I kept perfectly still. To move would have been to invite another punishment. No fear, but no foolish bravado. He could hurt me and no one would say a word. I was his wife, and I had embarrassed him by my behavior.

"You hear me?"

"Yes, Elikah."

He stepped to my head, his foot on my hair. "Belt or switch?"

I couldn't get up, and I couldn't move. His toe was right beside my ear. I had to look up at him. "I think I can remember without a whipping."

He knelt down and pulled me to a sitting position. His breath was harsh with whiskey and tobacco. "I think you remember better when you can't sit down for a day or two."

"Elikah, please . . ." I stopped myself. Begging excited him. Then it would be more than a beating. "Belt."

"My daddy never gave me a choice," he said, going into the bedroom and coming back with the strap he used to sharpen his razor at the barbershop. "No, he never gave me a choice. Now pull up that skirt."

ᥩ Seven ᥩ

THE month of July passed. August brought its own lethargy and the paralyzing fear that I was pregnant. I had heard that JoHanna and Duncan had gone up to Fitler to stay with one of her relatives. At first I was glad they were gone. That day, after we got back from the creek, I'd felt as if something bad had touched me, just a brush across my skin, but a taint. Mary Lincoln's death, Duncan suddenly talking, then Elikah, it had all been too much. I had my own life to manage, and I had to concentrate on that.

It was a Wednesday morning when I woke up too hot and sick. Elikah was still asleep, his hand on my thigh. I didn't want to move, didn't want to wake him. But I had to get to the outhouse or mess the bed. Inching away from his hand, I finally slipped free and hurried outside.

The still August morning was close, suffocating, but I sat on the swing in the gray light and tried not to think about nausea in the morning. How many times had I seen it? Seven, to be exact. Seven brothers and sisters. Seven more mouths to feed. With a child, I could never escape.

The sun crested the horizon with a hot golden kiss. The nausea passed and I went in and started breakfast, praying the smell of bacon wouldn't set me off again. I had only to get Elikah out the door to the barbershop. If I could manage that, I'd survive. One step at a time. Then I was going over to Jeb Fairley's.

"You're mighty quiet." Elikah watched me as he ate his breakfast. "The toast is perfect."

"Good." I buttered a piece for myself and risked a small bite.

"Vernell is driving over to Mobile and catching the train to New Orleans Saturday. I thought maybe we'd go with him and Janelle."

The bite of toast got stuck to the roof of my mouth. "New Orleans?" I managed. "What for?"

"Just to go. It's a real old city. A hundred years ago Andrew Jackson and his men rode all over this place on their way to the Battle of New Orleans. Vernell said there are cannons and battlefields." He held his fork in midair as he talked, as if he wanted to convince me, but also didn't want to lose a minute of the morning. "We might ride one of those riverboats."

JoHanna had told me about the riverboats that once moved up and down the Pascagoula River to Fitler with their cargos. Fitler had been a boom town with gamblers, whores, and a French restaurant with a chef from New Orleans. On one of my visits JoHanna had talked some about New Orleans, and just the way she'd said the name made me want to go there. There was music and dancing and an entire city of colored folks with white blood known as high yellows. The streets were made of brick, and Napoleon had stayed there, as well as Andy Jackson and Jean Laffite, the pirate. There was voodoo and cemeteries with graves on top of the ground, and markets where exotic vegetables and clothes could be examined and bought.

"This Saturday?" My excitement had far outstripped the drawback that Janelle Baxley was going along.

"We'll have to go early. Hell, maybe we could go on over to Mobile Friday night. Stay in one of those fancy hotels by the river. Then spend Saturday night in New Orleans. Would you like that, Mattie?"

Elikah could be both kind and generous, seemingly without reason. This trip was his gift to me, like the dress and shoes. Something he realized I lacked. I would have danced with Satan for the chance to go somewhere. "Yes, I'd like it a lot."

He grinned and reached across the table to catch my hand. "I made the right decision when I married you. You're a good girl."

He got up, snapped his suspenders up, put on his coat, and then bent down to kiss me on the cheek.

"Have a good day." My smile was genuine.

"How about some snap beans tonight?"

"I'll see what Bruner has on his wagon." He was the old man who drove into town each morning about ten o'clock with the vegetables he harvested from his farm.

"Next summer we'll have our own garden," Elikah said. "Your daddy said you had a green thumb."

I wanted to tell him Jojo wasn't my daddy, but I'd already told him that enough times that he knew it. Jojo would have told him I had wings and could fly if he'd thought Elikah would pay more, but the truth was I could generally make anything flourish. Just as long as it wasn't a child.

The screen door slammed and he was gone, walking the few blocks to the barbershop. We didn't have a car, just one old horse, Mable, who was mostly retired. Since we lived in town we could get everything we needed on foot or have it delivered. I never minded walking up to Royhill's Market and Mara Nyman's bakery. I'd determined to go over to Jeb's as soon as Elikah was out the door, but his little surprise about New Orleans had changed things. He wanted snap beans for supper, and he also had a real taste for the hot, light yeast rolls that Mara made fresh each day. I'd been saving pennies from leftover bills and had nearly ten cents, more than enough for some fresh rolls for Elikah's supper, but I had to get the order in early. Mara's goods didn't last long, and it was a first come, first served basis.

In my haste I forgot my concern about babies or anything else. I felt fine. The sickness had passed, and it was surely something I'd eaten the night before. I took off my apron and ran out the door without even washing the breakfast dishes. New Orleans! New Orleans! The name of the magic city exploded with each of my pounding feet. On a train! I was going to New Orleans!

I was so excited that I absolutely forgot about running in public and was speeding along the street, my hair having long since given up its hold on the pins and fallen about my shoulders. I was halfway to Mara's when I heard the laughter. It was a thick, rich sound like cane syrup on a cold winter day. Suddenly, I was the fly, trapped in that amber haze of syrup. If Elikah heard that I was running down the street, my hair all down my back like a wild thing, he'd decide I wasn't grown enough to go to New Orleans. I stopped like I'd hit a wall, then turned slowly to see who was laughing at me.

Floyd was a hulking young man, thick through the shoulders and with big, bulging muscles. Had it not been for the slow smile of a child and the gray eyes that held both wonder and sorrow, he would have been the most ideal specimen of a male in town. As it was, he was a loon with the face and body of a god. He'd been leaning in the doorway of the telephone exchange, and he walked over to me. Without thinking a thing about it, he reached out and picked up a strand of my hair, admiring it in the early sunlight.

"Pretty," he said, smiling right into my face. "You looked like a princess running in the sun."

"Floyd." I backed away. I'd avoided him since I got to town, afraid of my own pity and then ashamed of my fear. Daddy had taught me that mother animals in the wild destroy their own babies when they aren't healthy. Floyd had been given life, then abandoned on the doorstep of the Baptist church. Now he lived on the salary Axim Moses paid him in the boot shop and the handouts of different people in town. Maybe it was how close I came to his circumstances that made me fear him so.

"Mattie." He grinned wider. "You're Duncan's friend. So am I."

"Yes." I smiled back at him, warmed by the total lack of malice in his own gaze.

"Duncan and JoHanna are gone to Fitler. They'll be back today. Duncan's coming so I can finish the story of the woman who lives under the bridge by Courting Creek. She's dead, you know, but she lives there and waits for her love to return. He went off to the big war and never came home. So she drowned herself by jumping off the bridge. And now she waits for him to come home."

He started to reach out for my hair again, but I held up my hand and he stopped instantly.

"I wasn't goin' to hurt you." His face grew solemn. "I'm big but I'm not stupid."

"I know." I quickly twisted my hair back into a bun and tried to knot it so it wouldn't come down. I looked up and down Redemption, glad that the streets were empty. Only a few patrons had been seated in the café when I went by. Chances are no one had seen Floyd touch my hair. He was a harmless man-child, but I wasn't so certain Elikah would see it that way.

"Tell me about this woman who lives under the bridge." Courting Bridge was only ten feet above the flow of the shallow stream. Hardly far enough for a fatal fall, and the water certainly wasn't deep enough for a full-grown woman to drown unless she stuck her head in a sand wallow. I wondered where Floyd had gotten this morbid flight of fancy.

"Her name was Klancy, with a *K,* and she was Otto Kretzler's niece. She'd come here from a place called T-r-i-s-t-e over in Germany before the war got so bad. She and her family didn't believe the Germans were right, so they left all of their stuff and came here. When her folks took sick and died coming down the Mississippi, she came on to her uncle's and finished school here. The man she fell in love with was a teacher, Harvey Finch. And he went off to fight and got killed in one of the big battles. She—"

"Wait a minute, Floyd." His wealth of detail had me flustered. "Is this true?"

He nodded. "Every word."

"Even the part about the woman living under the bridge?"

"That, too. That's the best part."

"But she's dead."

He shrugged his shoulders. "So? She's a ghost. That's the best part of the story, and you can see her on a clear night when the stars are shining. She's standing on the side of the bridge, looking down into the swollen creek. Horses won't cross the bridge at night sometimes, 'cause they can sense her even when a human can't. Old Doc Westfall like to got kilt tryin' to make Jezebel go over the bridge last year when Mrs. Conner had that stillborn baby."

It was broad daylight on a hot August morning, yet a chill cooled my arms. "That's tragic, Floyd."

"She was a pretty lady. Like you."

"Thanks." I didn't know if he was talking about Mrs. Conner or the departed Klancy, and I didn't want to ask.

"You look like a girl. JoHanna said you were cheated out of your childhood."

I tried not to show my surprise. Did JoHanna really say that, or was it more of Floyd's embellishments?

"She said you had po-tential."

The way he pronounced the word, I knew he didn't understand what it meant, and I also knew that JoHanna had really said those things.

"She and Duncan are coming home today. And Pecos. That's an ornery rooster."

The entire time we'd been talking, Floyd didn't move at all. It was as if his jaw were the only thing lubricated in his body. But suddenly he moved, swinging around to stalk Clyde Odom as he came out of the café and started to come our way.

Sure enough, I saw his hands hovering an inch or two above the handles of wooden guns he wore in too-small holsters on his hips. I hadn't noticed them before, but now he was in the gunslinger's crouch, watching warily as Clyde approached. I almost felt as if I should take cover, and then I blushed at the foolishness of my thoughts. Floyd might be an idiot, but he'd managed to snooker me twice in the space of ten minutes, once with a story and now with his gunfighting.

"Easy, Floyd," Clyde said as he came forward. "I'm in a peaceable mood today."

"On the count of three," Floyd insisted.

"Not this morning."

Clyde looked at me, embarrassment plain on his face. So he'd been encouraging Floyd in this farce so he could laugh at him, but he didn't want to do it in front of me.

"Go ahead, Mr. Odom. I always enjoy a good, fair fight." The words flew out of my mouth and struck him full in the heart, dripping as they were with the poison of sarcasm.

"One," Floyd said, his gaze locked on Clyde.

Clyde dropped his bundle of mail to the dirt and dropped into the stance of a fighter.

"Two."

I stepped back against the wooden wall of the telephone exchange building and let the air out of my lungs.

"Three!"

Floyd's hands were a blur of action as both guns came up and he made the explosive sounds of gunfire.

Clyde clutched his chest, spun around two times, and then staggered over to the building where I stood and fell against the boards not two inches from me. His hand brushed fully across my breasts.

"It's a game, Mrs. Mills," he said in a whisper. "Just a game with an idiot boy."

Aloud he said, "You got me, Floyd. I'm a goner."

Floyd lifted up first one gun, then the other and blew into the barrels as if he were clearing smoke. Eyes still squinted in concentration, he put them back in the holster and came over to me, ignoring Clyde Odom as if he truly were dead.

"I have to go to work. Mr. Axim has some new leather for me to tool. It's beautiful. I'm going to make the finest pair of boots in the world."

"I'm sure you will." I moved away from both of them. I wasn't certain who was crazier, but Clyde Odom was certainly more dangerous.

"Give Elikah my regards," Clyde said, standing away from the wall and dropping a bow at me. "He has fine taste in women."

I turned and fled, not caring that I wasn't supposed to run in town. But I wasn't quick enough to avoid hearing Floyd's gentle reprimand.

"You made her scared, Clyde. You shouldna done that."

I ran the two blocks to Mara's and fled into the warm, womanly smell of fresh bread baking.

⨍ Eight ⨍

THE car trip to Mobile was hot, hard, and boring. Only the ferry across Bad Creek roused me out of a lethargy that was part heat and part the fast growing concern about my condition. The morning nausea had gone away until the Friday we were to leave for Mobile. It returned with a fury that had left me spent and terrified.

In the hotel I washed my face in cool water and ate some of the icy watermelon that Elikah had gone to fetch me from the docks. The cool, sweet melon and the kindness from Elikah were the perfect cure. By early afternoon I was eager to see the city that had grown up beside the big Mobile River.

At first we wandered around docks and watched the men called stevedores unloading enormous boxes of cargo. Elikah was drawn to the bustle, to the undercurrent of men involved in men's work and the big ships groaning against the moorings. It was finally the sun that drove us back from the waterfront. Elikah let me pick a direction, and we wandered past the business district inland toward the residences.

Much older than Jexville, Mobile was sheltered by huge oaks dangling with moss. The branches laced together over the downtown streets giving some protection from the August sun. Walking along the shaded streets I peeked into the beautiful homes with their wide, beveled glass doors. It was like opening a book to see the polished wood floors, curio cabinets filled with painted plates and cups and saucers, and banisters that led to the second floor of a home where people lived in wealth and graciousness. Surely these people never committed an act of cruelty or meanness. They had everything. There was no need to hurt others. I thought of JoHanna. And Duncan. Their home was not this big, but it had the same air about it. People surrounded by color and comfort. And love.

Elikah waited for me as I sneaked up on the wide front porches to look in. My curiosity amused him, but at last he could stand it no longer and he pulled me down the street saying the people who lived in the houses would think we were beggars or thieves if I didn't quit staring.

I didn't care. I wanted to drink in the colors, the reds and blues and yellows that made such exotic pictures on something so common as a plate.

Janelle and Vernell had gone their separate ways, and we didn't see them again that day. Elikah said they'd gone to visit one of Janelle's cousins, but there was something in his tone that made me wonder if he was lying. I didn't care where they'd gone. Janelle made me feel young and stupid and I was glad to be rid of her even if it meant that I was alone with Elikah. Beneath the shelter of the oaks, among the bustle of the busy streets that ran between two-story homes or the brick business buildings all crowded together, tall and indestructible, Elikah was different. On the downtown streets I noticed how the women looked at him, eyes cast down but moving up quickly for another taste of him. For the first time in my marriage, I valued my place at his side. He held my hand as if I truly belonged to him.

That night, in a strange bed in a hotel so fancy it had an elevator, I thought I'd never rest. But as soon as I pulled the crisp clean sheet over me, I was asleep. I didn't wake up until Elikah touched my hip, murmuring that it was morning.

The nausea was gone again, and I was starving. Elikah said they would bring food up to the room for us, but I wanted to eat in the dining room with the patterned carpet of frosty white leaf designs on dark green and the two chandeliers that looked as if the lights were alive.

Electricity. I'd never stayed in a place where lights burned day and night just because they were pretty. I'd heard the lines were going to be run to Jexville. Janelle had said so, in fact, but I'd never bothered to consider that Elikah might have it come to the house. To flip a switch and have light in my home. Elikah's look said it was possible. As soon as breakfast was done, we left the dirty dishes on the table, got our things, and went to the station.

All thoughts of Mobile were left behind as we boarded the train. Almost as soon as we were seated, it began to rock and lurch us to New Orleans with a speed that was too fast through the stretches of Mississippi beach towns and too slow through the monotony of the pine forests.

Janelle sat across from me, a secret trapped in her blue eyes. To avoid her, I feigned sleep. I watched her through slitted lids with a growing despair. She waited for me to awaken. When Elikah and Vernell got up together and walked out of the car, she could wait no longer.

"We're going to the Quarter," she said, her lips so close to mine I could feel her shape the air.

"The Quarter?" Curiosity won out over dislike.

"The old part of town where they gamble and drink."

"They do that in Jexville." It was forbidden for the women to say a word about such things, and I was pleased to feel Janelle draw back in her seat and give me a prissy look. We weren't supposed to acknowledge those things, not even among ourselves.

"They do it in public. There are street women and music and dancing." She leaned down again. "Vernell said he would take me dancing if I swore not to tell anyone!"

I sat up. "Dancing?" The image of Duncan came to me, shiny shoes flying in the dust, dark eyes blazing with mischief and delight. "You think he really will?"

"I'm sure. Elikah is a wonderful dancer."

I leaned back against the seat. "Elikah won't even listen to a gramophone."

"This is New Orleans! We're not in Jexville. No one will know *what* we do."

I looked up to find Elikah standing behind Janelle's seat staring into my eyes. A half-smile quirked his lips up on the right, making him more handsome than ever.

"Ready for the city, girl?" he asked.

I couldn't answer. The way he was looking at me was both terrifying and exciting, as if the light of Louisiana pouring through the train window had given me some new worth.

"Of course she is, Elikah. Don't be silly. We're so ready we're about to pop." Janelle laughed, a feminine sound that seemed to cling to a man and wind around him.

"We'll be there in less than ten minutes. That big water we went over was Lake Ponchartrain. It won't be long now." He went back to find Vernell.

It had never occurred to me that Elikah had been to New Orleans before. He'd made it sound almost as if this were his first trip, too. But then he hadn't said that either. It was just a curiosity I pondered while I gathered our picnic basket and things and concentrated on not meeting Janelle's looks.

Dancing. I'd never even considered such a thing where Elikah was involved. I hated the idea that Janelle knew more about my husband than I did, but I also had to keep in mind that Janelle said things she didn't know for a fact. If Elikah wanted to dance, he would certainly let me know.

The train stopped and we got off, caught in a swirl of movement and bustle that swept us along the boarded platform of the station and out into the cobbled street. It was like walking into the page of a book. Men in suits, and women in the dark clothes of the office, swept by on urgent errands while cars honked and the harnesses of horses and mules mingled with a hundred other sounds. The buildings themselves were brick or plaster painted in muted colors ripened by age. Before I could catch my breath, Elikah took my arm and swept me toward a large wagonlike car with a lot of seats.

"It's a streetcar, Mattie. You'll love it," he whispered, giving my arm a little reassuring squeeze. And I did. I knelt on the seat and looked out the window as we lumbered and clanged our way on tracks in the middle of the street all through the heart of the towering city.

Janelle had not lied. Elikah and Vernell had booked us rooms in one of the oldest hotels in New Orleans, on Dumaine Street, a place filled with golden light and furniture that seemed to hold the glow of the afternoon sun half an inch deep in the wood. Even the bedspread shimmered with its own internal light. I had never been in such a beautiful place. Outside the open window, the sounds of the city beckoned, strange exotic languages, the cries of vendors and music that was happy and free.

The four of us walked the streets, watching artists ply their wares while music and laughter came out of places where men drank. I was numbed by the sights and sounds. We ate bowls of spicy food with shrimp and crab and turtle, a mixture that sounded awful but tasted better than anything I'd ever put in my mouth. We went in shops where jewelry as old as England and France could be bought, or merely picked up and examined. At Elikah's insistence, we went into a dress shop and I bought a new dress. He sat in a chair while I went into a dressing room, this one complete with a stool to sit on and a mirror, and tried on the red dress Elikah had selected. It was stylish, with short, filmy sleeves and a waist that dropped to my hip bones. Struck dumb by his selection, I put it on and went out. Elikah nodded. The dress was mine.

And finally it was night.

Janelle and Vernell had once again disappeared, leaving Elikah and me alone in the damp heat of August. Our room had a balcony where we could sit and look over the street. It was as if the people of the Quarter had all gone home and slipped into new skins. They moved with a different rhythm, more of a glide. On several street corners women dressed in flashy clothes stood, waiting for a cab while live music drifted around them from the open doors of what Elikah called "joints." Janelle said they were clubs, like the one Tommy Ladnier ran in Biloxi.

"Why don't you put on that red dress?" Elikah said. He was sitting on one of the little ornate iron chairs that matched the balcony railing where his feet were propped. He was smoking a cigarette from a pack he'd bought at a corner store that was filled with the strong smells of cheeses and the ripe green olives that I'd never seen before.

"Okay." I was shy. The dress made me look older, like a woman. Sexy. It would look wonderful on the dance floor, the skirt floating around my thighs, shorter than anything I owned. Frisky. As if I had suddenly become part of the strange, exotic night.

The material slid over my arms and head and torso, and I remembered the night after the Fourth of July barbecue when I'd poured the cold water over my head and felt as if I'd left behind more than the heat and dirt of the day. The red dress was the same. I put on the stockings he'd bought with the dress, and the strange red shoes that were so dainty and a little hard to walk in. I twisted up my long hair. I'd gotten better by examining the way JoHanna did hers. The woman who looked back at me in the lighted bathroom mirror was not Mattie Mills. This was another creature, one who looked almost pretty. If only I'd had the nerve to ask for a tube of lipstick. But Elikah had once seemed so disapproving of such things. I bit my lips to make them redder and then opened the bathroom door and walked out.

Elikah hung over the iron railing around the balcony and stared down at the street, his body tensed with desire to be down there, to be part of the night in a place where no one from Jexville could see. He turned slowly, tossing the butt of his cigarette into the street below.

"Well, Mattie," he said, his eyes moving over me as if he assessed each point. "My little bride has been hiding some kind of woman."

"Is it okay?" I wanted to rush toward him, to get so close he couldn't stare at me in that way that made me feel naked and vulnerable. The way he looked at me was so much more intimate than a touch.

"Red is your color." He motioned me out to the balcony and then handed me the glass of whiskey he was drinking. "Now take a sip. If you're going to look like a full-grown city woman, you'd better taste the pleasures of such a life."

The whiskey smelled terrible and tasted worse, and it burned. But I swallowed it and nodded, handing the glass back to Elikah. Maybe things would be different now that he could see me as more than a child. Maybe if I acted grown-up, he'd treat me like a woman, like a wife.

"That's some of the best whiskey money can buy. Tommy Ladnier delivers over here in New Orleans. I hear he's making a handsome profit, if some of the New Orleans gangsters don't have him killed off." Elikah laughed and handed me the glass.

I swallowed again, barely able to stop the urge to spit the stuff out.

Elikah motioned to the other chair. "Sit down, Mattie. I was thinking maybe we'd go to one of the clubs and hear some music. Maybe dance. How does that sound?"

I sat on the edge of the chair. The whiskey had sent a rush of heat to my face, and I wasn't certain I could manage an answer and maintain my grown-up dignity. "That would be . . . lovely."

He laughed out loud, but there was the ring of pleasure instead of mockery in it. "Lovely. Well, you've budded all of a sudden into a young lady. And it's a good thing." He chuckled again as he handed me the glass. "I told everyone in town you'd make a good wife, and here I get a lady in the bargain."

"I want to make you a good wife, Elikah." A wave of earnestness swept over me, and I blurted out the words. He'd shamed me and hurt me, but that could all be put in the past. It was the future I wanted.

Something of my own worth having, a handsome husband, a home; maybe, if we were really happy, I wouldn't mind thinking about a child.

"That's good, Mattie. You try hard, I'll give you that." He was suddenly serious, motioning for me to drink more whiskey.

I did, almost coughing, but managing to swallow it all. The warmth burned down my throat and then back up until it settled at the base of my skull, where fuzzy tentacles of warmth reached around and up my cheeks to the top of my head.

"Let's go see about some music." He offered me a hand and I took it, almost stumbling.

"Elikah, I don't know how to dance." I wanted to tell him before we got there and I embarrassed him.

"I think we can remedy that, Mattie." And he opened the door into the hallway and the waiting night. We stepped out into the street, moving from pool of light to pool of light just as the people I'd watched from the balcony. The whiskey had made me light-headed, free, and the night and the city were like a disguise.

The music crept out the doors of the bars and moved along the old sidewalk in a thick fog that we walked into. Suddenly, it was as if the sounds were all around me, inside me, speaking to my bones.

Elikah steered me into a club through a shuttered door. We didn't even go to a table. Elikah led me straight to the dance floor and pulled me into his arms. The music was slow, languid, and seemed to drift with the deep sounds of a giant fiddle, the night vibrating like the thick strings. Elikah's hand on my back was firm, and he pressed and released while he guided with the other until I felt my own body slide into the easy rhythm.

In the darkened room others were dancing, and there was the sound of laughter and talk and the smell of cigarette smoke and perfume and the feel of Elikah's hand drawing me closer until I was pressed against him and moving in a way that somehow wasn't decent but was too good to stop.

"You're a natural, Mattie," Elikah whispered in my ear, his breath a shiver of pleasure.

I couldn't answer. The music had pulled me deep inside where I shut my eyes and let his body tell mine what to do.

We went to a dark table where a woman brought us drinks in tall glasses filled with ice. The liquid was sweet, cold, easy to swallow. And we danced again, the skirt of the dress brushing the backs of my legs like a whisper while Elikah's warm hands touched and guided. I gave myself to him, to the music and the night and the strange dark city that had somehow become a deep blue note spiraling from the mouth of a horn.

I don't know how long we danced, but it seemed that my bones had softened in my flesh. At last, Elikah put his arm around me and walked me outside into the night.

"I think you're drunk," he said, laughing as he held me. "Can you walk?"

"Maybe." I lifted my leg and removed first one shoe, then the other. On my bare feet I had better balance. "I can walk."

Elikah's laughter was like a kiss. In response, I put my arm around his neck and stood on tiptoe to kiss him. "I'm having a wonderful time."

"And it's only going to get better," he promised as he led me back to the room.

Inside the bedroom he closed the door and helped me out of the beautiful red dress and into my gown. Then he walked me to the bed where I tumbled into it, laughing at the feeling of floating and the pleasure of the night.

Elikah pulled the sheet up over me and walked out to the balcony. Lying on my side I could see him, hands braced on the rail, staring down at the city. It was only ten o'clock. Late by Jexville standards, but early by the clock that ticked in the City that Care Forgot. JoHanna had told me that name. I knew exactly what it meant now.

"Elikah?"

"Yeah."

"Aren't you tired?" I wanted him in bed beside me, had grown used to the feel of him there.

"No, I'm not tired."

"Go on out," I told him. "It's been a wonderful day."

He turned to me, and I thought he might be mad. He didn't need me to say what he could do. He came to me and caught the placket of my nightgown in his fingers, holding the material gently, as if he were afraid he would bruise it.

"Okay," he whispered, then dropped his hand and left the room without his hat.

I got out of bed and went to the balcony and watched him cross the street, his boots sharp and clear on the cobbled brick streets. One of the ladies standing by a building stepped up to speak to him. He laughed and walked on, disappearing around the corner where the music seemed to come from.

Even as I stood there, after ten o'clock, the city seemed to grow more and more alive. Gas lamps on posts cast small pools of light, and I could watch the anonymous people move from pool to pool, like minnows in a vat, shifting without making progress.

The music teased me, reminding me of Duncan and her promise to teach me to dance. My feet were still throbbing from the beautiful new shoes and the dancing. It was all like a dream, and I closed my eyes and let the city invade my head.

When I found my head sinking to my chest while I sat in an iron chair on the balcony, I got up and went to bed. The sheets were heavy cotton, cool and smelling of sunshine. Crawling under the covers, I fell instantly asleep.

When the door to the room opened, I mumbled something to Elikah. The room was dark, unfamiliar, and my sleep as thick and heavy as a quilt spread over me.

There was the sound of his footsteps, a slight hesitation in the pattern that brought me fully awake. He came in with a host of smells, among them liquor and a heavy, sweet odor. Perfume. Perfectly still, I listened and watched the darkness.

Step, shuffle, step, step. Smaller, quicker steps that sounded as if he were being blown into the room. A confusion of noises, not like at home. But even in the strange darkness of the hotel room, I knew he was drunk.

The fear was like the prick of a needle. A warning. Elikah had been like a different man. In one day, I'd fallen a little bit in love with my husband, but I was afraid of him when he was drunk. We were alone in a city where no one knew us, no one cared.

Except we weren't alone.

I heard her then, the breathless giggle of her laughter. "Shush, Eli." She giggled as she made the sound. "She's asleep."

"And we're going to wake her up," he answered, laughing also.

❧ Nine ❧

THE rocking of the train was soothing, a sound and movement beyond my control. Without lifting my forty-pound hand, I was
hurtling through time and space. I sat with my face turned to the
morning sun, remembering how it was when Daddy worked the night
shift and he would come home in the mornings. Mama would be up
cooking bacon and biscuits, then making the red-eye gravy he loved,
and I would hear them talking, the low current of their voices much
like the movement of the train, the feel of the morning sun coming
through the window on the clean sheets of my bed where Callie and
Jane still slept beside me. I loved to listen to the kitchen sounds, the
knowing that the day had begun and would continue, with Daddy
going to sleep and us kids going out to pick the vegetables and help
Mama with the younger children. We'd draw lines in the dirt, setting out the rooms of our make-believe house around the old oak tree
in the backyard. The roots were gnarled, big and sturdy, making sofas
and chairs and nooks where we could nestle Josh, the baby, in his own
little room.

If I closed my eyes tight enough and gave in to the train, I could go
back there and draw my own room around me, the walls invisible but
respected by Callie and Jane, and even Daddy when he came out to see
what we were doing. He always used the space where the door had been
drawn, careful not to step on the furniture we'd outlined in the dirt. I
squeezed my eyes to hold back the tears.

Janelle took the seat beside me as soon as Elikah left. "That rich food didn't agree with you." She spoke as if it was a fact. "Elikah said you ate too much."

I gripped the edge of the seat and hung on to the motion of the train.

"I had the hotel make me up some tea. It's warm now, but it might help." She settled back against the seat.

"No, thanks."

"Did you dance last night?"

I remembered the room with the covered lights and the band that seemed to blow smoke from the shining horns. "Yes. We danced."

"I told you." She touched my arm. "Had a little too much to drink, didn't you? It wasn't the food at all. You drank."

I didn't dispute her. What purpose would it serve?

"Vernell did, too, but I didn't touch any of it. I don't feel sick today either."

We were pulling into the Bay St. Louis station, the first stop in Mississippi. We'd passed over Lake Pontchartrain, a mirrored sheet that stretched from horizon to horizon. Now the Sound waited out my window, glittering into the distance. The beaches were the color of muslin, not the pure white that I'd always imagined. It was a detail I'd failed to notice on the way over.

"Vernell told me to leave you alone, but I've been waiting for a chance to talk to you."

I tensed, feeling the involuntary pain curl through me. "I don't feel well," I told her.

"It's JoHanna McVay," she continued, ignoring me. "I know you're tenderhearted, Mattie, and a tad naive, but you can't go around with that woman. Everyone in town knows you were at that baptism with her when Mary Lincoln drowned. And that Duncan all but cursed her with it. Look, Elikah has suffered a lot of shame because of you. Don't you see, honey, you have to watch yourself? Everything you do reflects back on him."

My fingers dug into the seat, holding on, holding me back. I couldn't look at her or I would smash her pert little nose between her blue eyes. In my hot brain I could feel the flesh give beneath my palm, the point of her nose both hard and soft.

"Mattie, I'm not trying to lecture you, but there are some things you need to know about that woman. She's got a reputation. A bad one. Everyone in town knows she's had lovers. At least two."

I ignored her, keeping my gaze out the window where the pine trees passed in a blur. Off in the distance there was an occasional house, and along the beach there would be some of the bigger homes. Mansions.

"JoHanna flaunts herself all over town. Why even the way she walks is designed to bring attention to herself. And she's raised that child to be an outcast. The only friend that young-un has is that nasty old rooster."

"Pecos loves Duncan." I wasn't saying it to defend the rooster. He wasn't my favorite creature on earth, but he did love Duncan. "He'd kill anyone who tried to hurt her."

"That's ridiculous, Mattie. Roosters don't have sense enough to act like a watchdog. You're being silly. And even if the rooster was as smart as Thomas Edison, it still doesn't make what's happening at that house right. Two lovers! And I could name names."

"Does Will know?" I didn't believe such a thing. What woman would choose another man over Will McVay? It was just more of Janelle's gossip.

"Who knows what Will knows or why? Everyone in town says she has a cooter-lock on him anyway. And it's common knowledge that she got rid of a baby before Duncan was born. That's why she's so obsessed with that child."

The things she was saying were wicked, evil. Lovers were one thing, but getting rid of a baby was something else again. JoHanna would never do something like that. Never. Decent people didn't even think about such things. Not even when they were desperate and so afraid they thought they might die. Killing an unborn baby would be the biggest sin, the worst thing a woman could do.

"JoHanna can act like she doesn't give a damn, but she knows in her heart that God is going to punish her, and He has."

"Punish her? What do you mean?" Janelle had finally frightened me. I knew all about a punishing god. JoHanna didn't believe in such a thing, but Janelle did, and I wasn't certain exactly what I believed. It seemed to me the world was mostly made of punishment, whether a person deserved it or not.

"Look at what happened to Duncan, and that was just a warning. But JoHanna hasn't mended her ways at all. She's unnatural. She doesn't behave in a respectable way. I mean she dresses like a slut. She may think it's fashion and all that, but she's forty-eight years old and she dresses like she's a model from some Paris whorehouse. Those hats and those dresses, they're just indecent." She fluttered her hands in her lap. "God don't hold with such behavior in a decent town. She ought to go on over to Paris or Europe or wherever she thinks is so grand and fine."

"She's beautiful." I spoke so softly I wasn't sure she heard.

"Beautiful? If you like that all the men in town watch the way you move. Why, you can see her butt jiggle under those flimsy dresses. And no sleeves, and that little hellion of hers dancing like she's been possessed by Satan."

"Duncan can't dance anymore. She can't even walk."

"In that wagon with that rooster. It's ridiculous. She makes a fool of herself and a fool of you—and Elikah—when you're seen with her."

I let go of the seat and turned to her. "Why are you so afraid of her?"

She opened her mouth to speak, but nothing came out. "How dare you speak to me like that when I'm only trying to do you a service by warning you? How dare you?" She got up, holding to the back of my seat as the train lurched. "Well, I can tell you one thing. I won't waste my breath any further here, but just you mark my words; the day will come when you regret you ever spoke to that woman. And if you keep it up, you'll be ruined in town. No decent person will invite you into their home." She whirled around and fled.

"No decent person should invite me in," I answered her when she was gone.

❦ *Ten* ❦

BY the time I returned from New Orleans, JoHanna and Duncan had come and gone. They were back in Fitler with JoHanna's Aunt Sadie, according to Floyd. I suppose it was because Floyd was their friend, the closest thing left in Jexville to them, that drew me down to the boot shop on that Wednesday. I'd told no one about New Orleans, or about my nausea. I had begun to think of ways to do away with myself. Perhaps it was my own thoughts that drove me to seek out someone who could hold my desperation at bay with words and stories, and even the vaguest link to JoHanna. At any rate, I went to the shop under the pretense of having a pair of shoes made.

Floyd was in the back of the dark shop that smelled like leather and polish. Moses's Bootery was a long, narrow, wooden building that shot straight back from a few racks of display boots. The front display section was divided from the larger workshop in the back by the office where Axim Moses sat stooped over his desk. The office was solid wood on the bottom but with bars going to the ceiling, more like a horse's stall than anything else. A narrow passage bypassed the office and gave onto the room where Floyd was intently working by the natural light of a single window.

He straddled a rough wooden bench with a wooden foot situated so that he could work on the boots and shoes without having to hold them. With great care and no small degree of skill, he was piecing the leather vamp on a pair of fine boots. Mr. Moses was busy in the small office with some paperwork, so I went all the way to the back.

Floyd's smile made me want to cry. He was genuinely pleased to see me.

"Hi, Miss Mills."

"Don't stop," I told him, not wanting to interrupt his work for my make-believe mission.

"You want some shoes?" He looked down at the pair I was wearing. They were new, but they didn't fit exactly right. My long skinny foot seemed to bunch down at the toes after I'd walked for any length of time. "Those don't fit too good."

"I just came to look. Maybe later I can get some shoes."

He got up and came over to me, kneeling down at my feet, his gaze intent on my shoes, his fingers pressing at the toes. I had to catch my breath to keep from shifting away from him. Elikah pursued his handsomeness; Will took his for granted. Floyd was simply oblivious.

"These don't fit at all. Your toes are all cramped up in there." He pressed hard, drawing an exclamation of discomfort from me. "Sorry," he said, looking up. "You're gonna get the arthritis if you wear these shoes. Cripple your feet."

Somehow he managed to lift my foot and take off the shoe. It was a relief to stand barefoot, at least on one side.

Before I knew it, he'd inserted a piece of paper beneath my foot and extracted a pencil from behind his ear. Using great care he drew the outline of my foot.

"Now the other," he said.

"The other?"

"No two feet are alike. No point in making shoes that fit one foot but not the other."

I let him take off my shoe, standing barefoot like a fool. And I had said that Floyd was a loon. If Elikah walked into this shop and saw me standing barefoot with a man on his knees in front of me, I'd be more than sorry.

"Floyd, I—"

He grabbed my hand and put it on his shoulder so I could balance. "Just a minute more."

The pencil moved around my foot, tickling my instep.

"See here, it's that heel, and right at the big toe. You're narrow." He'd slid the drawing out from under me and was pointing with the pencil.

I looked up to be sure Mr. Moses was still busy in his office. His back was to me and his head was bent over the papers he had out on his desk.

"Sit down." Floyd waved me to a chair. He stayed on his knees, but edged toward me. "I have to measure more."

"Floyd, I can't afford shoes now." I had to tell him. He was so completely sincere that he made me ashamed. And nervous. "I just wanted to say hi. To see if you'd heard anything from JoHanna."

"They'll be home tomorrow. We're going on a picnic. JoHanna sent a note by Bruner this morning." He reached for my foot, a tape measure in his hand. "Stand up," he said, bending over my foot.

Moving from the length of my toes to the arch to the heel to the ankle, he took the measurements, making a note of each on the paper that contained the drawing of my foot.

"I can't have shoes," I told him again.

He motioned me back to my seat and lifted my left foot, examining as he turned it first one way and then another. He was so intent on his work that even I became interested. It was almost as if it weren't my foot at all, but someone else's. A strange, pale thing that had sprouted at the end of my leg without pain or warning. His fingers began to work over the soul of my foot, probing gently, and I was more than aware that it was my foot again.

I'd gotten a little more at ease with him hovering over me. It was just something he did with everyone who came to buy a pair of shoes or boots. It was pleasant, actually, the feel of his warm hands on my feet. His fingers probed the callouses on my heel and the ball of my foot.

"That's because your shoes don't fit," he said, nodding. "You're rubbin' there. Sure sign of trouble."

My feet were long and slender, but they were almost petite against his large hand.

"I've got some really fine leather. I'm making Sheriff Grissham these boots." He got up in a quick, fluid movement and went to his work bench to retrieve the half-made shoe. "See. Duncan helped me with the pattern."

I took the leather which still seemed warm from his hands. It was the vamp of a boot, highly ornate, with stitching that seemed to draw pictures, only it wasn't a picture of anything I'd ever seen before.

"That's timber rattler," he said, pointing out the strange design. "I made it just like Duncan told me. She drew the picture and told me how it was, and I knew how to make it."

"It's beautiful." I held it up, letting the broad shaft of light strike it. The snakeskin seemed to come to life in the sun, almost to move with the sinuous grace of its original owner. "It's really beautiful, Floyd." I'd never imagined he was such a craftsman. Fine leather boots, yes, he was known for his work. But the intricacy of this design was like a painting.

I looked up at him and saw that he was frowning. "What's wrong?" My bare foot on the floor felt suddenly indecent.

"It's from one of Duncan's dreams. She was upset."

I didn't completely follow him. "What dream? What came from a dream?"

"The picture on the boot. Duncan dreams about a man in the water. It's not like a whole dream, but only bits and pieces." He looked up at me, his fingers unconsciously massaging my foot. "He scares her."

More than likely it was Mary Lincoln's drowning that had Duncan upset. I figured that was why JoHanna was spending so much time in Fitler. After that baptism scene, it was better for them that they made themselves scarce. At least until Will got back from Washington. People in Jexville were acting like it was Duncan's fault that Mary drowned.

Floyd's hand on my shoulder startled me. "Duncan says the dream is like being trapped underwater. She hasn't told JoHanna. Only me." Pride was mixed with concern. "You won't tell, will you? Duncan would be mad."

"No, Floyd. I won't tell." His secret was perfectly safe with me. I had enough of my own, and no one to share them with. "You said JoHanna will be back today?"

"Maybe right now. Miss Nell is bringing them back. She went over to Fitler to see her mama's people and she's gonna give JoHanna and Duncan a ride home. I'm gonna get some rolls from Mara. To surprise Jo-Hanna and Duncan. I can get one for you, too."

I reached out and touched his arm, startled by the hardness of the muscle on his forearm beneath his shirt sleeve. "Thank you, Floyd, but I'd better stay home and make supper for Elikah." I couldn't go on a picnic, but I had to see JoHanna. Alone.

He nodded. "I'm gonna tell Duncan the story of the pirates on the Pascagoula River. It's a true story."

"Maybe I could hear it another time."

"The head pirate's name was Jean Picard." He grinned up at me, delighted with himself. "JoHanna taught me how to say his name. She said it was French. He was hanged in New Augusta. They built the gallows right by the courthouse. It was the same place they hung old James Copeland."

I'd heard of the outlaw James Copeland, but Jean Picard was a new one on me. Very likely something JoHanna had made up, passed to Duncan, and it had finally become another item in Floyd's treasure chest of tales. With repetition, he'd come to believe it was true. That was Floyd's weakness. He wasn't a loon, like I'd first thought, but he was an innocent. He believed everything people told him, even to the point that his real father had been a gunslinger. That was one of the crueler fabrications of the townsfolks, but Floyd had accepted it so completely that now not even JoHanna could dissuade him.

"I'd love to hear about James Copeland and Jean Picard, but I can't." I didn't point out that JoHanna had not extended an invitation to me.

"Okay." He leaned over toward me, his long arm sweeping up the drawings of my feet. "When you want shoes, I'm ready now. You just have to tell me what you want."

"As soon as I have some spare money, I'll be back." I got up, sliding my feet into my shoes. Floyd went back to his bench and picked up a small mallet he was using to pound the leather. I stood for a moment, watching him. What illness had left him with the trust and wonder of a child? Was it a gift or a punishment?

Watching him work the leather, I had to admit that Floyd was far happier than I was.

Eleven

"How about some bacon and eggs, Mattie?" JoHanna held the spatula in her hand as she turned to me. On the stove the cast iron skillet was spitting and popping with the strips of bacon that sizzled in it.

"No, thanks." I swallowed, running my finger around the edge of the cup of coffee I had not touched. Sitting in JoHanna's kitchen, I was terrified. I'd come to her because of Janelle's gossip, and watching her stand at the stove, her arms pale but muscular in the short-sleeved blouse, her head covered in a fine fuzz of chestnut, I couldn't bring myself to ask what it was I wanted.

"You haven't been sleeping lately, have you?"

She wasn't even looking at me. She was turning the bacon.

"No."

"Is it Elikah?"

"No." I swallowed again, letting the coffee warm my hands. "Well, yes and no."

"Are you pregnant?" She turned around and held me with that blue, blue gaze.

"I think I may be." I started to cry. "I don't want to die."

Her smile was immediate. "Most people don't die in childbirth, Mattie. You know that. It's frightening, but completely natural." She put the spatula down and came around the table to put her hands on my shoulders, lifting the heavy braid of hair that hung down my back.

I wanted to lay my head on the table and squall. As it was, though, I fought back my tears and straightened my back. I couldn't look at her, but I could tell her. "I don't want this baby. If I have to have it, I'll kill myself so it won't be born."

Her hands continued to pull at my hair, the slight tugs of a mother ordering a mess. At last she dropped the braid and went back to the stove and turned the bacon. She took it out, draining it on some brown paper, and moved the pan off the stove. "Let me fix Duncan's eggs," she said. "Then we can go for a walk."

I'd dried up my tears, and I was determined not to cry again. She wouldn't believe me if I cried. She'd think I was being a baby and was just upset over my circumstances.

With the skill of a practiced cook, she broke the eggs in the hot grease and flipped them. In less than a minute she had the plate ready. "Duncan gets breakfast in bed, but then she has to get up and try to walk. I think she might be getting a little stronger."

She talked as if she'd forgotten what I'd said earlier. It made me steadier, gave me a chance to compose myself.

She put the plate on a tray with some milk and toast. Pushing open the kitchen door with her butt, she stopped and looked at me. "Mattie, would you throw Pecos those crusts of bread?" Then she vanished through the door.

I took the crusts and went outside. Pecos was still not my best friend, but we'd gotten to the point where he didn't try to spur me anymore. I'd just finished crumbling the bread when JoHanna came out the door, her apron in her hand. She dropped it on the top step and signaled for me to follow her as she started across the backyard and into the woods.

We walked about fifteen minutes before we came to a small creek completely canopied by trees. We walked downstream to a place where the creek was nearly four times as wide, and deeper, the current a good bit slower. JoHanna began to take off her clothes. "I need a swim," she said.

I looked down at the ground, suddenly self-conscious. I'd never taken my clothes off in front of a woman except my mother and sisters, and that had been before I was married. JoHanna had said before that she swam naked, but I hadn't really believed her. She'd brought no bathing suit.

"In deference to your sensibilities, I shall swim in my underwear." Jo-

Hanna was teasing me with her tone and her words. I looked up to find her standing in her bra and drawers, hardly more than scraps of lace. "I think you should give this a try. I find that I think more clearly after a swim. And we don't have long. Duncan will need me to help her get dressed."

She walked into the water, giving a little shriek at the coldness of it. When she was knee deep, she dove in, surfacing on the other side of the black water. "It's cold at first, but the water's deep enough here." She pointed downstream. "Will gave some beavers a little assistance to dam it up so we could swim."

The thought of Will made me blush. It was not hard to believe that he and JoHanna had frolicked down here plenty of times, naked as Adam and Eve.

"Come on, Mattie. Your underwear will dry out before you get home. I swear, it'll make you feel better."

I stood up and unbuttoned my green dress. It fell around my feet, and I stepped out of it, leaving my shoes behind as well. The dirt was black, hidden from the sun by the thick growth of trees. I walked down to the water and waded in, stopping at my ankles. It was bitterly cold.

"Get in a little deeper, then dive. It's too hard to inch in." JoHanna was doing a breaststroke, the flow of water holding her stationary.

I could swim a ragged, unrhythmic stroke that kept me afloat and inched me along in the water, but nothing like her movements. Instead of diving, I sort of squatted in the water, the cold so abrupt that it made me feel as if my heart would burst.

"I love my hair short." JoHanna brushed her hand across the fuzz that she had managed to level out a little. Perhaps her aunt had helped her cut it. "Now, when I get hot, I just put my head under the pump. It's so cool. So easy." She laughed. "I always wondered why men wore their hair short. Now I know."

I was moving my arms and legs frantically to keep from freezing. But JoHanna was right. I was beginning to adjust. "Are you . . . ever . . . going to let . . . your hair grow back?"

She laughed at my question. "I suppose I'll have to. Duncan's life is hard enough without me making it worse. She'll have to go back to school this fall."

I hadn't even given school a thought. Poor Duncan. What was she going to do with all of the kids thinking she'd cursed Mary? And she would have to have a rolling chair.

"Come here, Mattie."

JoHanna's voice was soft. I looked up. She was standing with the water just above her breasts, which were clearly visible through the lace of her bra. She was motioning for me to come on out to deeper water beside her.

The bottom was sandy, except in places I could feel with my toes that it was hard clay. Not as slick as I thought it would be. I inched out toward her, aware, too, of the pull of the current. It was faster than it looked, even in the deep pool. If Will hadn't built the dam just below us, the water would have been a flash. Fighting the current, I made it out to JoHanna without being swept off my feet. As I got into the deeper water, there was less pull.

"Relax." JoHanna put her arm behind my neck and eased me backward. I had a terrible moment remembering how Mary Lincoln had struggled, but JoHanna's voice was calming.

"Relax. I've got you. Just lie back, and you'll float. I'll support you."

I could feel her hands beneath my shoulders. My legs had floated up of their own accord, and she had one hand under my knees.

"Close your eyes." JoHanna was smiling down at me, amused by my rigid posture. "I won't let you go, Mattie. I swear. I won't let you go under."

I closed my eyes and let my head relax back into the water until my ears were covered. I could feel the weight of my hair begin to stream out behind me. My head was pointed downstream and the water seemed to rush by me. The play of sunlight in the tree branches flickered on my eyelids. It was hypnotizing, and I felt my body relax a little more.

"Now that's it," JoHanna said.

She kept herself perfectly still, an act of will. She was my mooring, my anchor. As long as she held me, the current could not pull me away. I looked up into her face.

"Tell me what's wrong," she said.

I watched her lips move, shape the words. They were distorted, but I could hear her. All the hard edges were removed, softened by the water.

"If I'm pregnant, I don't want the baby. I would rather die than have his baby." My own voice was loud in my ears. I watched her face but saw no reaction.

"Does Elikah know?"

Her lips made the words again, and they came to me from a long way away, floating down to my ears.

"No."

She nodded. "Relax." She closed her eyes and began to move very slowly in a circle. My body followed her movements, buoyed by her hands, and I closed my eyes, letting the sun and shade play like the quick burst of fire poppers inside my eyelids. I had spoken my worst desires aloud to her, and she had not found me repulsive. She had not abandoned me. She did not think I was a monster.

I felt her hand beneath my knees drop, and my legs lowered very slowly, until my feet were in the sand. Pulling my head out of the water was hard. My hair was wet, saturated, heavy, and it wanted to hold me down. I stood and opened my eyes.

"There's a doctor in Mobile. When Will brings the car back, I'll take you. But you can't ever tell anyone, Mattie. And you should know that you might never be able to have a child."

I felt as if the water had hold of me, as if I had no control over what I said or did. "I never want children."

She reached out and touched my cheek. "Are you sure?"

"I'm sure." I knew by the look on her face what I was giving away. But she had no way to understand why I did such a thing. No words could explain it. I couldn't even really understand it myself. But I knew it was right.

"I'm going to swim for a few minutes. Why don't you get out and start to dry. Your hair is a lot longer than mine, and it'll take more time."

She knew I couldn't go home with my hair wet, but even though it was thick and fine, it would be dry long before I made the walk back to Jexville. It was going to be at least a hundred degrees by midday. A really hot one for Duncan and her picnic with Floyd.

JoHanna was talking of the scuppernong jelly that her Aunt Sadie had made. They had gone into the swamps beside the Pascagoula River and picked the wild grapes themselves. She was chatting away, trying to move the day past my terrible confession. We had just gained the edge of the yard when we heard the crash of dishes.

"Duncan!" JoHanna tore off across the yard leaving me to follow right behind her.

Pecos was in the window crowing and squawking to raise the dead as we ran to the back door and into the house.

"Duncan!" JoHanna didn't stop in the kitchen but ran to the bedroom.

"Mama!" Duncan's voice was upset. "It's the man again. He was under the bridge. He was reaching out for me. Mama, he was calling my name and reaching out for me!"

I stopped outside the room, terrified by what she was saying. Her voice was soaked in anguish, drenched in fear. I could almost hear her heart beating in her words.

"Oh, Duncan." JoHanna's words were both calming and afraid. "It's only a dream, honey. He can't get you. You know I'd get the shovel from the yard and beat him to death before I let him take you."

I could see her on the bed, Duncan pulled into her arms. Pecos was still in the window squawking, but he'd calmed some. I wasn't prepared for Duncan's response.

"You can't kill him, Mama. He's already dead."

I put a hand against the wall to brace myself. Then I walked to the doorway and surveyed the broken dishes on the floor and JoHanna in the bed with her daughter, holding her tight. Without saying anything I began to pick up the dishes.

"No matter that he's dead, I wouldn't let him have you."

I cast a glance at JoHanna to find that she was as white as Duncan. All of the healthy glow of our swim was gone.

She felt me looking at her. "Duncan has been having this recurring nightmare."

"I fell asleep after I ate breakfast." Duncan looked down at the floor. "I'm sorry, Mattie. I didn't mean to break the dishes. But I was trying to get away from him and I was running, but I was in the water and my legs wouldn't work right."

I put a hand on her leg and patted. "Hey, it's okay. Your mama has lots of plates." Beneath my fingers I felt her leg jump suddenly, as if she'd been pinched. "Duncan?"

"What?"

I stood up slowly. Perhaps it had been my imagination. "Your leg. It moved."

JoHanna sat up and put her hands on Duncan's legs. "Can you move them?"

Duncan's brow furrowed, her dark eyes narrowing with concentration. Her lips pinched together and she braced against her pillows with her arms.

"That's it!" JoHanna jumped from the bed and threw her hands in the air. "They moved! Both of them, Duncan! They moved!" She threw herself across the bed, hugged Duncan, then got up and ran around the bed to hug me. "They moved!"

Pecos fluttered into the room and landed on Duncan's bed. He gave me a look, cocked his head and looked again, then lifted his wings slightly, a warning to me not to get too close when the room was in a state of wild emotion.

"Pecos!" Duncan grabbed him by a leg and dragged him over to her. "Don't be mean to Mattie."

JoHanna swooped down and kissed Duncan's forehead. "It was all that swimming we did up at Fitler. I told you the river was magic, that it would bring the muscles back." She was almost jumping up and down with delight.

Duncan grinned up at her. "Nope, it was the dream. I dreamed I was running, and I tried. That's how I threw the tray off me in my sleep."

JoHanna grabbed her hands, bringing them up to her lips for a kiss. "Then thank god for the dream, Duncan. If it takes getting chased by a drowned man to make you run, then let's get him to come after us again."

"Drowned man?" My question fell into the joyous celebrations of the room unheard.

"Drowned man?" I asked again.

"The man in the dream. He's at the part of a bridge that goes in the water."

"The support," JoHanna supplied.

"He's sort of sitting up against it and he's calling me to come to him."

As Duncan spoke, JoHanna stilled. She was watching her daughter, listening to the dream with more care.

"He calls your name."

The child nodded. "He says 'Dun—can!' And he reaches out to me. There are chains around him, but they've fallen down to his lap because he's . . ." Her voice stilled. "He's sort of a skeleton, but not really. Except the fish swim out of his ribs." She closed her eyes. "He wants me to come and sit beside him under the water." The last she finished in a whisper.

"You didn't say that before," JoHanna said, stroking Duncan's head.

"Each time I dream it, I know more." Duncan looked up at her mother. "I don't want to dream anymore, Mama."

"Maybe once you start walking," she leaned down, "and dancing, the dreams will stop. Your body is used to being up and about. Usually, you fall asleep before your head touches the pillow." She kissed Duncan's head, rubbing her hand over the fine dark hair that had grown out about a quarter of an inch. The two of them, had they been blond and standing in the sun, would have looked a great deal like dandelions. "Your body and mind have been confused, but things are getting back to normal again. You'll see."

"Good." Duncan smiled at JoHanna and then at me. "Stay for the picnic, Mattie. Please! We're going to have such fun. Floyd likes you a lot."

"And how do you know that?" I entered her teasing spirit, eager to put the nightmare behind us all.

"I just know." Duncan's grin was wicked, but pleased.

"It's true," JoHanna said, joining in. "He does like you a lot. He says you're kind."

"I've hardly spoken to him." They were making me feel self-conscious.

"No matter. Floyd can read goodness in people." A crow's wing of dismay touched her eyebrows. "If only he could see meanness as accurately." She looked at me and smiled. "Anyway, he thinks you're good to the bone." JoHanna lifted the tray where I'd stacked the pieces of broken dishes. "Now I have to make some sandwiches for the picnic. Will you go with us, Mattie? Floyd is bringing some special sweet cakes from Mara's, and he said he was getting one for you, just in case you changed your mind."

What would Elikah say when he came home from lunch and I was not there and no food was cooked? What would he do when I came home? I didn't have to voice my questions. JoHanna read them on my face.

"I'll take care of him." She kissed Duncan again, then stood. "In just a minute Mattie is going to come help you with your legs. Do every exercise, Duncan. Don't cheat, okay?"

Duncan rolled her eyes. "Maybe I'd rather wait for a dream."

"Maybe I'd rather pinch you." JoHanna threatened to do just that until Duncan squealed and gave her promise.

JoHanna motioned me out of the room and into the kitchen, where she stopped in front of the phone. "Elikah has a phone at the barbershop, doesn't he?"

I nodded. He'd recently had one put in, claiming he needed it for business, but I knew it was more for gossip and the convenience of Tommy Ladnier and his buddies.

JoHanna cranked up the phone and asked the operator for the barbershop. She looked at me, her blue eyes suddenly merry. She put her hand over the mouthpiece. "You know this will be all over town, so prepare yourself."

I nodded, wondering what in the world she was going to say and what price I'd pay at a later date.

"Elikah? This is JoHanna McVay." She lifted her eyebrows. "I'm calling about Mattie, I'm sorry to say."

I could hear his voice but couldn't understand his words.

"I was headed into town early this morning and found her on the side of the road. It looks like she's . . . having some female difficulties. I brought her up to the house and have her in bed. I don't think she should be moved."

There was a space where he talked again, his voice more excited.

"Well, it's a difficult thing for a woman. I believe it would be best to leave her here. Since I've got Duncan, I'm housebound and I can look after her. She doesn't have any people around. Why don't you come up and have supper with us?"

I shook my head, but JoHanna was almost laughing. Her voice was terribly serious, very warm and cordial, but her eyes told a completely different story.

"I'm going to give Doc Westfall a call, too, but I think I know what to do for her. If the bleeding gets worse, I'll call you back."

He said something else.

"Well, I can't really talk right now. She's already upset and I don't want to make it any worse."

He talked again.

"Since you won't come for supper, I'll call you at the shop in the morning and let you know how she is." She hung up.

"What did he say?"

JoHanna looked at me. "He was awfully agreeable. Too agreeable." She waited for me to respond.

I wanted to tell her about New Orleans, but I couldn't. I simply could not say anything about it. I looked down at the floor. I felt her hand on my shoulder. "Mattie, what are you going to do?"

I shook my head. "I don't know."

"We'll write your mama."

I shook my head again. "I can't go back there. Jojo is just as bad. Just as mean." A tear dripped off my nose.

"Too bad he wouldn't come to supper. We could have poisoned him."

I looked up quickly, but I couldn't tell if she was joking to make me feel better or if she was serious.

∽ *Twelve* ∽

"TELL us about the disappearance of Mr. Senseney." Duncan held a half-eaten sandwich in her hand, waving it at Floyd as if it were her royal scepter.

"Okay." Floyd was leaning up against a tree, his thick hair a damp blond sheaf that was cut straight across at his jawline. It was a young boy's haircut and contrasted sharply with his bronzed, bare shoulders. JoHanna had said he was twenty-three. His tanned chest was hairless, but definitely not childlike. I looked down at the ground and listened to the easy bantering.

Instead of going for a long picnic, we'd decided to go back to the seclusion of the creek behind the house, where JoHanna and I had swum. We didn't want to run the risk that someone would see us on the road and mention it to Elikah. Or Doc Westfall. JoHanna had called him, giving him more graphic details of what sounded to me like a miscarriage. Doc had agreed to call Elikah and convince him that it was for the best for me to spend a few days with a woman friend, someone who could tend to me without causing shame or disgrace. She made me sound terribly pitiful.

Despite my worries and fears, I felt happy and carefree as we sat on the bank of the creek, stuffed to the point where I flopped over onto my back in the cool dirt as Floyd prepared to tell his story.

JoHanna was leaning against the same big, smooth trunk of a wild bay tree and she pulled Duncan up into her arms, so I was the most convenient audience for Floyd to look at. He sat with legs apart, hands balanced on his knees as he leaned forward to eagerly begin the story. As a gunslinger or storyteller, Floyd had his moments to shine.

"Have you ever been to Fitler, Mattie?" he asked.

"No. I want to go. JoHanna's told me some about it."

"It was the biggest town in this area, a boomtown." He leaned forward even more and looked around at JoHanna, proud at the use of her expression. "That was back around 1880 and up until Mr. Kretzler built the railroad here in Jexville. That sort of sucked the life out of Fitler."

"The railroad runs on time and the river has its own schedule," Jo-Hanna said. "Folks were more decent when they had to rely on the river. They couldn't get away with being as mean because they had to depend on each other more."

Floyd nodded, as if he'd seen such sights with his own eyes. "That's true. But the story is that if the bridge over the Pascagoula River at Fitler had been finished, then Jexville would have been the town to die. That's why it's such a mystery what happened to Jacob Senseney, the man who had the money to get the bridge built."

Duncan leaned forward in her mother's arms. She was exhausted from the nightmare and the exercises we'd done, without further leg improvement, but she was unwilling to give up the day and nap. "Old Mr. Senseney disappeared and was never heard from again. Some say—"

"Duncan!" JoHanna clapped a hand over her mouth and pulled her back into her chest, laughing as Duncan pretended to struggle. "You wanted Floyd to tell the story, so don't spoil it for Mattie."

Duncan squealed, then nodded yes that she would behave, and Jo-Hanna removed her hand.

"Anyway, Fitler was a hoppin' place." Floyd shook back his hair and smiled at me. "The main street was nearly a mile long, and there were five saloons and three of those had whorehouses on the top. Right beside the finest of the whorehouses was the jail, then a land office, and on down were three cafés and a restaurant with a French chef from New Orleans." He looked at JoHanna, who nodded. "JoHanna ate at the French restaurant. She said she had crepes!" He smiled big that he had used the word. "And other things that I don't want to think about."

JoHanna laughed. "My parents had come down to Fitler to invest in the timber business and the town. They were going to build a big sawmill there, to compete with the one in Pascagoula. But the hitch was, there had to be a way to get the lumber inland. At Pascagoula, they load it onto ships and sail it to market. Fitler needed an inland system. A railroad. And to get the railroad a bridge was needed. The ferry was very risky because of the river currents." She brushed her hand over Duncan's head and stopped talking.

I'd heard from Janelle how JoHanna's folks had drowned on that very same ferry. Yet she still took Duncan swimming in the Pascagoula as often as she could. Almost as if she defied the river. Or maybe joined with it.

Floyd picked up a small twig and twirled it in his big hands. "Mr. Senseney was a Yankee from up in Minnesota. From all the old tales, he was the black sheep of the family and had come south to avoid the law."

"What had he done?" I interrupted without thinking. "Sorry, Floyd."

"It's okay. There are a lot of different stories about that." He gave Jo-Hanna a look as if he expected her to jump in. When she didn't, he continued on with only a slight hesitation in his voice. "The best I could tell was that he was the second brother in a family and his daddy left everything to the oldest son. Lots of folks around here think like that, that the oldest boy inherits and the others have to fend for themselves. So the land won't be divided."

"For those families who have something to divide." I hadn't intended my comment to sound so bitter, but it fell into the middle of the story like a stone. For a few seconds there was silence, then the screech of a red-tail hawk, which broke the tension, and Floyd continued.

"Jacob Senseney was said to have stolen all the money from the family business and headed south to make his own fortune." Floyd grinned. "There's a tale that says he left a note saying he was taking only a portion of what should have been his fair share. That may be true or not. As far as I ever heard, no lawman ever came looking for him, and he made a fortune down in Mississippi in land and timber. He owned two of the saloons in Fitler and two of the really bad ones that were set up like houseboats and floated up and down the river. But his pride and joy was an old paddleboat called the *Mon Ami*. That's another French word for 'my love.' He did love that old boat, 'cause he stayed on it a lot, going up and down the river having card games and such."

I started to tell them about the card game that Elikah held on Sundays, but I held my tongue. It wasn't my business to tell, and I didn't want to even say his name on such a nice day.

"Mr. Senseney got in with JoHanna's daddy, and that was when the bridge became more than just a dream. It was going to cost a hundred and twenty-five thousand dollars to build, and the state wouldn't give a penny. The state engineers said the current was too strong right there at the fork of the Leaf and Chickasawhay, but Mr. Dunagan, that's Jo-Hanna's daddy, and Mr. Senseney hired their own engineer who said it could be done."

Floyd's voice had picked up a fast rhythm so that it seemed as if he'd told the story many times after learning it from someone else. Or perhaps he did have a flair for the telling. His face was alive, his blue eyes holding mine with a trust that finally revealed itself as his deficiency. He trusted me to listen, to believe as he believed. He trusted me to give as much as he gave, and for that he was the object of ridicule and sport on the streets of Jexville. In his complete innocence, he believed that Clyde Odom and others of his ilk were playing with him.

"Is something wrong, Mattie?" He was staring at me with concern.

"No, Floyd." I patted his knee and felt the rock-hard muscle of a young man. "I was listening too hard. Please go on."

He nodded, picking up the story. "So it was agreed that if Dunagan and Senseney built the bridge, then the state would improve the road north of Fitler to Meridian and south of Fitler to Mobile. The road was part of the old federal roadway, and a well-traveled route." He cast a glance at JoHanna. "The drawback being the ferry."

"Why didn't they build two smaller bridges over the Leaf and Chick-asawhay?" I'd never seen any of the rivers, but I loved the word Chicka-sawhay. It was like music in my mouth.

Floyd looked at JoHanna, who now supported Duncan's head on her chest. Duncan was fighting sleep, but her sharp eyes were becoming slow and lazy. Pecos had even settled onto a roost in an old huckleberry bush beside her.

JoHanna's voice was soft, low. "The swamps at the fork of the rivers are very dense, especially where the bridge would have gone. To go up-river would have meant abandoning all the benefits that the wider, deeper Pascagoula gave the town as far as river traffic. In Daddy's mind, and Mr. Senseney's, it was Fitler or nowhere. Especially since that was where Mr. Senseney owned so much land and where growth would have meant even more money for him."

I nodded.

"Well, there was the terrible ferry accident where Mr. and Mrs.

Dunagan drowned." Tenderhearted to a fault, Floyd said those words all in a rush and didn't dwell on them. "But Mr. Senseney was determined to go ahead with the project. It took him a year or two, but he got the supplies together and began to pour the cement supports that would hold up the bridge in the swift current. It was a wonder, and people came from all around to watch the work, which was slow as molasses. But finally the supports were in, and standing. That spring there was the worse flooding ever. One of the supports was hit by a barge that had come loose. The supports held! It was time to build the platform of the bridge!"

Floyd leaned toward me, his eyes bright. God, he was a handsome man. And not the least aware of it. I wanted to reach out and touch his face but knew that it would be wrong. No matter what my intentions, it would be wrong. It would not matter that what I wanted to touch was his tenderness, his sense of wonder. I held my own hand in my lap.

"That night Mr. Senseney was in his biggest saloon, The Watering Hole, and he was saying that he was headed out early in the morning to New Augusta to buy supplies there. Then he was going straight down to Pascagoula to buy more supplies there. It was his plan to start building the bridge from both sides! He said it would be done in six months, and then he had an appointment with the head of South Central railroad. See, if a wagon bridge could be made across the river, then he was certain a railroad bridge could be put a little farther downstream. At the bar he was so excited he bought drinks for everyone, and drank a little too much himself. Then he went home."

Duncan had fallen asleep with the familiar story, but I was spellbound. "What happened?"

"Since Mr. Senseney said he was leaving before daybreak, no one missed him for several weeks. It would have taken him some time to go to New Augusta, get back and he'd said he was going straight down the river to Pascagoula, and the *Mon Ami* was gone. Everyone thought he was on board her. But after five weeks and there was no sign of him or his supplies, folks began to wonder. He didn't come to collect his rents or take care of his business, and the *Mon Ami* returned and the captain said he hadn't seen hide nor hair of Jacob Senseney. They telegraphed a family by his name in Foley, Minnesota, but he wasn't up home with his folks. He'd just vanished."

Floyd lifted his eyebrows over his kind blue eyes. "And he was never found."

"What happened to the bridge?" I asked.

"It was never finished," Johanna said. "The supports are still in the water, holding as firm as he and Daddy said they would. But no one ever had the money to buy the materials, and when the railroad decided to go through Jexville, it was the end of Fitler and the dream of the bridge."

"That's a sad story." It had left me with a hollow sensation. "All of that work, all of those dreams. Where do you think Mr. Senseney went?"

"Folks thought he was murdered, but there was never a body. Some said he got scared and took the money and left. Part of it was Daddy's money and I was supposed to get some of it." JoHanna acted as if she was talking about marbles or jacks, something unimportant.

"Part of a hundred and twenty-five thousand dollars was yours?"

JoHanna's smile was tired, as if she'd spent all the energy she ever would on this subject. "Half of it. Daddy put up half the money for the bridge, and Mr. Senseney said he would finish Daddy's dream and then give me my money back plus a portion of the profits he made on his land."

"And what happened?"

"There was no written agreement. His property was sold or stolen, and I guess they sent the money to his family in Minnesota."

"JoHanna, that's awful."

"I haven't done without much." She shrugged, careful not to awaken Duncan. "Don't feel bad for me, Mattie, I've had a good life. Very good. Except for a few misfortunes, I've been very lucky. I never knew the money before it was gone, so I didn't regret it that much. Just at times." Her smile was even tireder. "Just at times when I think it could do some good. But . . ." She shook her head, dismissing the rest of whatever she was going to say. "I think someone killed Mr. Senseney. Folks said he was a crook and that he ran off with the money, but I never believed it."

"The law didn't hunt for him?"

JoHanna's smile was hardly a smile at all. "The law is only as good as the community it serves."

"And Fitler was an evil place?" To hear JoHanna talk about it, Fitler was wild, but she'd never led me to believe it was corrupt.

"Jexville became the county seat. The sheriff was here. There wasn't a lot of interest in what had happened to Mr. Senseney."

"Because it was to the benefit of Jexville." It didn't take a blood-hound to track down that trail.

Floyd picked up the last of the sandwiches and bit into it. He chewed and swallowed. "They say Mr. Senseney's ghost walks the old main street of Fitler. JoHanna and Duncan are gonna take me one night to see. I'll bet I can talk to him."

"I wouldn't doubt it, Floyd. You're an innocent, and spirits know to trust you." JoHanna reached around the tree and patted his arm. "Now Mr. Moses is going to expect you to get back to the shop and work this evening to make up for being gone today. Remember, you can't tell anyone about Mattie being here. It's our secret."

"Mattie's gonna stay out here with you and Will?" Floyd grinned at me. "Maybe I can stay, too."

"I have to go home to Elikah," I told him. "Tomorrow."

"I have to go to work." He stood up and began to pick up the picnic things. "Let me take Duncan," he said as JoHanna tried to rise holding her. He lifted the child up into his arms as if she were made of fluff. Her little legs dangled, pale and fragile-looking with a few blotched scars, but she slept like a rock. The fact that she had made no progress during her exercises this morning had disappointed her greatly.

JoHanna caught one lifeless foot in her hand and held it, as if she were examining it for the first time. "Duncan had the dream again."

Floyd looked down at her. "No one will hurt her, JoHanna. I'd never let them hurt Duncan."

JoHanna rose. "I know, Floyd. You and Pecos are her guardian angels."

"Duncan helps me with my work." Floyd tilted Duncan into his arms so he could look at her face. "She tells me things."

"I'm sure she does." JoHanna sounded slightly skeptical.

"She gave Floyd a design." I felt some strange need to take his side, to be sure that JoHanna knew he was telling the truth, not just making it up. "It's beautiful. For one of the boots he's making."

JoHanna brushed Duncan's head, the fine, dark hair rippling like sleek cat's fur. "Maybe Duncan will be a painter."

"Or a dancer," I said. "When her legs are well."

"Or a storyteller," Floyd added.

Johanna lightly kissed Duncan's head. "We don't care, do we, as long as she's happy."

"She can be anything she wants, as long as she's happy," Floyd said.

JoHanna picked up the picnic basket, nudged Pecos with her knee, and motioned for me to take the lead with her as Floyd carried Duncan home in his arms.

∞ *Thirteen* ∞

JOHANNA turned on the path, laughing at something Floyd had said about Pecos as we came out of the woods. I was the first one to see Will's car. It was parked beneath the chinaberry tree, a gleaming red monster of a car.

Two thoughts struck me almost at once. Will was home, and Jo-Hanna would be able to take me to the doctor in Mobile. I felt as if all the air had disappeared out of my lungs and all the sounds of the earth had stopped. There was only the pounding silence, the heat and sun-light, white-hot light, that danced on the hood of that red car.

"Mattie!" JoHanna's hand caught my elbow, shoring me up as Floyd came up behind me and put a hand between my shoulder blades.

The sounds came back and the light dimmed and I could breathe again. "I'm okay."

"I didn't expect Will until much later." JoHanna sounded worried and excited.

"You want me to put Duncan in the hammock or take her to bed?" Floyd asked. He looked toward the road. "I'd better head back. Mr. Moses will be thinking I left for good."

"The hammock will be fine." JoHanna looked again at the back door, as if she expected Will to appear.

"Thanks for the picnic," Floyd said as he eased Duncan into the hand-knotted sling that was tied between the chinaberry tree and a much smaller grancy graybeard. Both trees cast thick shade, lowering the temperature by a good ten degrees. A mockingbird squalled an insult at us for interrupting her privacy.

"Thanks for the story, Floyd." I answered because JoHanna was looking at the back door again. "Go on. I'll stay here and watch Duncan."

Floyd waved and took off, his long legs moving with pantherlike grace, completely unaware that his body rippled with a signal his mind did not comprehend.

"I'll be back in a moment." JoHanna walked to the clothesline, where she rested her left hand. Her eyes were trained on the kitchen window. "Would you mind keeping an eye on Duncan?"

JoHanna acted nervous, almost afraid. Had she and Will had a fight? "Go on and see about Will." I went over to the hammock and took a seat on the ground, bracing against the smooth bark of the chinaberry to the further fury of the bird. I ignored the squawking and focused on Duncan. Whatever nightmare had tormented her this morning, there was no trace of it on her face now. Her eyes were softly closed, her mouth pursed in the rosebud of innocence.

JoHanna watched me and Duncan for a minute, then let go of the line. She hesitated a moment like a doe at a branch when she smells a human approaching, then started forward to the door. Once she was in motion, there was no doubt, no weighing of alternative actions.

"Will?" she spoke his name as she went up the steps and opened the screen door. He stepped out of the shadows, caught her against him and picked her up with a growl.

They seemed to struggle, and I half rose from my position on the ground. My hand closed around a piece of lighter that someone had put in the yard with the intention of splitting. The screen door slammed with terrific force, and they disappeared into the kitchen. There was the sound of the oven slamming shut. I stood up slowly, the wood in my grip, and made sure that Duncan was still asleep. I heard them again.

"You bastard! You've been in my pot roast. No wonder you were so quiet coming home! You didn't even come looking for us!"

"A good wife would have been here to feed me."

"Good wife, is it? Is that what you want, a good wife?" JoHanna's voice escalated with the question. I looked over at Duncan again. She was still sound asleep, and I still held the wood in my hand.

Will's laughter was sudden, loud. "If I'd wanted a good wife, I would never have married you."

"Do you want roast, or do you want this?"

JoHanna's voice held a challenge, an edge of something that was wild and daring. I knew without looking what she was offering him, and I sat back down under the tree, my legs weak with relief.

"You're a shameless hussy," Will said, laughing again. "I hope you haven't been corrupting Mattie with such behavior."

"Ah, Mattie." JoHanna's laughter died, and her voice dropped to a level that I could not hear.

I leaned back against the tree, my fingers releasing the wood. A small splinter had lodged itself under the skin of my thumb, and I set about trying to pick it out.

There was the sound of the oven slamming again, the murmur of voices, but I no longer needed to hear what they said. What JoHanna told Will about me, I didn't want to know. My gaze fell on Duncan's sleeping face. JoHanna had been thirty-nine when Duncan was born. Her first child. Her only child, as far as I knew.

Duncan had JoHanna's nose and eyebrows, and Will's jaw and eyes. She had his thick, black eyelashes, too. And JoHanna's spirit. She was a perfect blend of the two McVays, a creature unique. I reached out and touched the soft fuzz of her hair where it was growing back. In her sleep she smiled at me.

My hand was trembling, and I withdrew it before she woke up. The sunlight filtered through the lacy chinaberry leaves and warmed her skin to a pale cream. She was a beautiful child, engaging and alive. I looked down at her legs, a paler shade and marbled with blue, as if there was no circulation. The burns had healed, and the scars were slowly fading. Perhaps they would eventually fade completely. Even as I looked, her foot twitched.

I felt her staring at me, and I looked back into her brown eyes.

"My legs are getting well," she said. "I want to go to Fitler and swim in the river. Mama says the water is magic."

"I'm sure JoHanna will take you back up to visit your aunt. She seems to like staying in Fitler more than staying in Jexville."

"Where's Mama and Daddy?"

"Inside."

Duncan smiled. "They fighting?"

"I thought they were at first, but I don't think so."

Duncan's smile widened. "It's hard to tell, isn't it? Sometimes they act like they're going to tear each other apart." She saw my expression. "No, really. I'm not making it up. One time Daddy tore her blouse right off her. She was standing at the kitchen sink and he came in and—"

"Duncan, I don't think—"

"But it's just them. Mama told me that a man and woman should have passion for each other. Of course, Daddy thought I was spending the night with Aunt Sadie." She rolled her eyes. "He was very funny. All apologetic."

I couldn't help myself. "He tore her blouse off? What did she do? Hit him?"

Duncan laughed. "She tore his shirt off him. Then they started kissing real hard and he was leaning her down on the kitchen table when I came in the back door." She grinned at me. "They broke a bunch of plates and glasses. Shocking, isn't it?"

Her grin was infectious. "Yeah, it is."

"Tell me a story, Mattie."

I listened to the silence of the house for a few seconds, determining if it was best for me and Duncan to stay. The image of Will, torn white blouse in his hands, wouldn't get out of my head. My skin felt overheated and I didn't want to leave the shade of the trees. The laughter had stilled inside the house. There was only the breeze rattling the leaves above us and the irregular anger of the mockingbird. We were okay where we were. "I don't know any good stories like Floyd does. Where I grew up, there weren't any stories that I knew about the town and such. Mama used to tell us a little about living up in West Virginia, where her daddy was killed when a coal mine caved in." Mama had loved her daddy, and it seemed to comfort her some to talk about him, to describe how he'd walk the road up to the mine every morning, his lunch pail in his hand. But it wasn't something Duncan needed to hear, a story about thirty-seven men being buried alive beneath a mountain of dirt.

To me, whenever I imagined it, I just thought of Grandpa walking up a road into a grave. The opening of the cave was shaped just like a coffin standing on end. And I could see him walking, walking, slowly walking, up to the opening and disappearing in the dark and never coming out. I'd never known him, of course, but I could see him clearly.

"Her daddy was buried alive?" Duncan had caught hold of the morbid and was giving it a good gnaw.

"Uh-huh. Why don't I tell you a story that I read in a book?" I'd forgotten about the library books I could check out for free. There had been one red one, leather bound and filled with stories from all over the world. I loved that book. I checked it out so many times the librarian said I couldn't have it again for six months. When I went back, someone had stolen it.

"I have a lot of books." Duncan's brown eyes were considering. "Maybe you'd like to borrow some of them."

"That would be great." I didn't care that they were books for a nine-year-old. My reading was good, but I loved any kind of story.

"Tell me one you read."

So I told her "Walissa the Beautiful," a story about a hut on legs and a little girl who got trapped in it. She liked that so much I told her about three men who traveled the country with magical abilities. Their names were Longshanks, Girth, and Keen. The names tickled her, and she listened closely.

"You don't tell stories like Floyd, but I like yours, too. In a different way."

"Why don't you tell me one?" I suggested. The afternoon was passing, but there had not been a sound or a movement in the house. I cast a quick look at Duncan, but she had no interest in her parents.

"Mattie, will you stay in Jexville forever now that you're married to Mr. Mills?"

Her question caught me by surprise. I didn't like to think about the future. Particularly not about forever. I couldn't really even think about going home. With a lie or two, JoHanna had bought me an afternoon and evening in her home. After that? The answer to that question brought on a feeling of blankness that was scarier than pain.

"You don't like Jexville, do you?" Duncan asked.

"I haven't really been here long enough to say." I didn't want to talk about this. "How long have you had Pecos?"

"I guess you don't want to talk about yourself." She nodded. "I got Pecos when I was eight. Daddy got him at the feed store."

"From the Leatherwoods?" I was surprised. I suppose I'd given Pecos a more exotic heritage than Jexville Feed and Seed.

"He had a broken leg and Daddy took him. Mr. Leatherwood was going to kill him."

"Will set his leg?"

"Mama. She knows things about how to make animals heal. And people, too." Duncan reached down and touched her legs. "I'm going to get better. She told me so. Each time we go to Fitler, I can feel my legs getting stronger." She rubbed the top of her foot. "I can feel more."

The house remained silent, and for the first time since I could remember, I didn't have a long list of chores to finish. Since I wasn't going home, there wasn't anything I had to do. Just me and Duncan and Pecos in the yard.

"Look." Duncan pointed to her left foot. "See. I can make it point and flex."

"Point and flex?"

"It's ballet. Or it's something a ballerina does. An exercise. Mama was showing me before I got struck."

"Ballet?" JoHanna was an endless surprise.

"Well, Mama said it was her version. It was just for fun."

"Maybe when you're well, she'll show both of us." That would truly send Elikah over the edge. The idea that I was dancing ballet. It would make him hate me in that dark way that frightened me and also gave me a sense of power. The power was worth the fear.

"Mattie, will you take me inside?"

I hesitated. "Maybe we should wait out here until JoHanna gives us the word."

"Don't be silly. Whatever they're doing, we won't bother them. They go in their room and shut the door, and I leave them alone. We have a deal. Sometimes I can hear them laughing, but I've never knocked on the door."

"Why don't we get the wagon and go for a ride? I'll pull you." I didn't want to hear Will's laughter or imagine him without a shirt.

Duncan considered the idea. "Okay. When we get back, we'll get Mama to make us some lemonade. I haven't had any in a long time, and I know Daddy brought me back some lemons." She looked up at me. "He never forgets."

ᴄᴏ *Fourteen* ᴄᴏ

WHEN Duncan and I got back from our wagon ride, JoHanna had a big pitcher of lemonade made for us. Will was taking a nap. I couldn't be certain, but there seemed an extra spark in JoHanna's eyes, and her step was light as she finished putting together the peas and okra and the cornbread that would comprise our dinner. It was only when Duncan was in the bathtub that she pulled me down into a chair in the quiet kitchen.

"Will is leaving me the car for tomorrow. Are you sure, Mattie?"

No matter how sure I was three seconds before, whenever I tried to speak of it, I felt as if I were suddenly cocooned in a womb of bright light and heavy silence. The husk of my body sat at the table, but I was somewhere distant, wrapped in light and the pounding sound of silence, unable to reach out.

JoHanna touched my shoulder. "You don't have to do this. Having a child isn't the end of the world. A baby could bring you joy and love and happiness you've never known."

I found a voice, something strained and awful that felt as if it were tearing my throat. "With a baby I'll never escape."

JoHanna stood up and came to me, cradling my head against her bosom. She hushed me, stroking my hair like she did Duncan's. "Hush, Mattie, hush. No one is going to make you do anything. But this is dangerous. You could die. You could become sterile."

I let her stroke me, hungry for the comfort of her touch. My mother had always had a child on her hip and one at her feet. She had not had caresses and tender words for us older children. It never crossed her mind.

"I just want you to be sure, Mattie. You don't have to stay with Elikah. If you want to go home, I'll take you to Meridian. I'm sure we can arrange things. If that isn't good, then there are homes where you could go. Decent places that would find a loving home for your baby."

I didn't want to go to a home where there were other girls pregnant, girls who would give birth and then pack their clothes and leave, shedding their baby like an old skin. A child wasn't something I could walk away from. How could I explain that in my life there had been a series of Jojos and Elikahs, and women like my mother, who were too beaten down, too weak to defend their children. There was only one way I could guarantee that my baby would not go to a home like that.

"Don't make a decision now." JoHanna talked to the top of my head, her breath a puff of tenderness on my part. "Don't think about it. Tomorrow we'll see what the doctor has to say. Then you can decide what you really want to do." She grasped my shoulders and knelt down so we were eye to eye. "I have to tell you, though. Mattie, an abortion is dangerous. There are so many risks. To your body and to your mind. If that's what you decide, you have to promise me that you'll never look back. Regretting the past is an indulgence few people can afford."

"Coming to Jexville like I did, I don't have a past, and if I'm pregnant, I certainly don't have a future."

"Oh, Mattie." JoHanna's eyes filled. "You have a future, but you have to take it. Some people get one handed to them, an open path with no hurdles in front of them. You were born in a crevice, but you can squeeze and push yourself out of it. You can. You're strong."

Her blue eyes willed me to believe her, to share her strength. "I don't know," I answered.

She nodded. "Tomorrow." She stood up and went to the stove to check the cornbread. The day was still hot. Too hot for baking, but Will was home.

"Let me get Duncan out of the tub and heat some more water. I think a good hot bath would make you feel better," she said.

"No." I stood up. "I think I'm gonna walk back to the creek. It's so hot."

She put her hands on her hips and leaned back against the kitchen sink. "You want a suit? I have an extra."

I shook my head. "No, thanks."

"Have fun." She smiled. "There are towels on the clothesline. Help yourself."

"Duncan said I could borrow some of her books."

"They're in the bookcase in her bedroom."

I selected a thick one. I could hear Duncan in the bathtub, singing away. It sounded as if Pecos was adding some kind of rooster song. With the book in my hand I went out the back door, careful not to let the screen slam. I took a bright green towel and a yellow one from the line. The afternoon stretched before me, a block of time completely cut away from my life. I felt as if a dark box had opened and sunlight had been allowed to filter down to me. I had the beautiful solitude of the woods and the magic of a book for an hour or two.

When I came out of the woods, my hair wet and dripping down my back, I stopped beneath the last of the pines to watch Will and Duncan. She was in a swing and he was pushing her. I could see the vast improvement in her legs. She was able to hold them out in front of her, pointing her toes as she flew squealing through the air.

Will pushed her with force, sending her flying up into the branches of the magnolia tree, where the pods were thick with red seeds. My brothers and sisters and I had often thrown the heavy pods at one another, sometimes in jest and sometimes in earnest. They could draw a welt. Still, they were interesting to look at and touch. JoHanna would gladly give me as many as I wanted. I wondered if I could germinate one, make it grow in my barren yard. In Elikah's yard. At that thought, I knew I had not escaped him.

"Mattie?"

I turned to find JoHanna in the hammock. I'd completely overlooked her. "Will ate half the roast, but there's plenty left for supper." She was smiling as she watched her husband and daughter. "Duncan's legs are getting well."

"I know." I took my seat against the chinaberry trunk. From that vantage point I could study JoHanna as I had earlier studied Duncan. In the afternoon light the tiny wrinkles around her eyes were more noticeable. The short haircut made her look older, more worn. Nothing could dim her blue eyes, though. They were ageless, like some hard substance forged in the heat of the earth, then glazed by the sky.

"Will is going to New York tomorrow. We'll give him a ride to the train station in Mobile."

"And Duncan?" I couldn't believe JoHanna would take Will with us. Not when we were going to the doctor. And certainly not Duncan. Not a child to witness what I would not even try to imagine because I knew it was going to be gruesome.

"I didn't tell Will anything except that we were going shopping. Duncan can spend the day in the boot shop with Floyd. I've already called Mr. Moses and asked."

"Thanks." I could have wept with relief. "You didn't tell Will?"

She shook her head. "I love him more than anything, except Duncan. But men are men. Some things they don't need to know. Some they don't want to know. This is between us, Mattie. For the rest of our lives. Only us."

"Why are you doing this?" I had wondered. Abortion was illegal. JoHanna could go to prison. The doctor, too. And me? I would be as guilty of murder as they were.

JoHanna reached down and plucked a tall strand of bahia grass. She crushed the juicy stem with her teeth. "I think maybe the worst thing in the world is not to be wanted. The second worst is being the weapon used against someone you love."

That wasn't exactly an answer to my question. "You're risking so much. Why? Why for me?"

She chewed more of the stem, drawing it into her mouth with her lips. "In a perfect world, Mattie, only people who wanted a child would get pregnant. I don't know the truth about you, and I'm not asking for details, but I feel like maybe you didn't have a choice." She looked away from me, dropping her gaze to the ground. "I want you to have a say in this. Of all the people in the world, the mother should want her child."

The night in New Orleans rolled over me, a furnace of shame and horror and revulsion. "You don't know what he did to me." I dug my fingers into the ground. The grass roots held tenaciously to the soil, clumping in my hand, giving me something to cling to until the worst of it passed.

"Tell me if you must," she said so softly I had to calm myself to hear her. "I'll listen. And I promise that I won't tell anyone. But I can't promise you that I won't hate him, and some very strange things grow out of hatred."

I looked up at her.

"Love and hate. Both nourish some powerful actions, good and bad."

The compulsion to tell her was stilled in me. To hear such a thing would change us forever. She could never know the way it was. I could not tell her truthfully, because it changed with each hour, each day. There were times it didn't seem so bad. I could shrug and honestly feel that it was past and gone, one night in a million, a nightmare that I had endured and survived, banished by the day. Other times I felt as if the core of me had been touched by rot, that I was dying by degrees.

If I told her, what truth would it be? If I told her, it would change me even more.

"When we get back from Mobile, will you take me to Fitler with you and Duncan?"

JoHanna reached from the hammock and picked up my wet hair, lifting the mass of it so that the cool suddenly touched my damp back. "You'll love Fitler, Mattie."

I felt the need for action, for some task that would define me, at least for a few moments. "You stay here and rest. I'll go put supper on the table. Shall we drink the lemonade?"

"For Duncan, yes. Will brought us a bottle of wine from one of the senators. A good merlot. It'll be perfect with the roast. The glasses are in the dining room, the smaller bowl-shaped ones."

I'd studied the different shapes of her glasses but I didn't know Jo-Hanna had seen me doing it. Somehow, it made me feel like a child, like a loved child, and I smiled at her before I turned and ran across the yard and up the steps. At the top step I caught a whiff of the roast, and it made saliva spring into my mouth. I'd never felt so hungry, so ready for food.

The day was still hot when we sat down to eat, but Will had to be at the train station early, not to mention that we also had to be in Mobile as early as we could. To my surprise, I ate and laughed as if I hadn't a care in the world. Will McVay could do that to a woman.

He teased me outrageously, making Duncan and JoHanna laugh at the blushes that added to the warmth of the evening. He told us about his meetings in Washington with powerful men who worried about the wax on the cars they drove or whether their coats were cut in an elegant enough fashion. He made us laugh at those faraway figures I'd never even thought to consider as human beings. With that laughter, he pried open the door to the world a tiny bit wider for me. When he told us that next summer, when Duncan was completely well, that he would take all of us to New York on the train with him, I felt as if I could do it. New York. With Will to show the way, it was within my grasp.

JoHanna had been there, more than once, but Duncan had not. We would share that adventure together.

"You'll certainly have to teach me to dance before we go," I told her across the table. "I've read about the hotels where there are orchestras that play all night and clubs where people go to dance and listen to bands." A sudden image of a negro band in a blue-lit room made me stop. A giddy, sweet taste of bootleg rum choked me. My fork slipped from my fingers.

"Mattie?" Will was sitting beside me and grasped my arm. "Are you okay?"

My eyes connected with JoHanna's. A piece of cornbread was in her hand, halfway to her mouth, and she didn't move. Whatever was on my face made her eyes fill with tears. Even Duncan paled and looked down at her plate.

Will stood up, my arm still in his hand. "Let's go out to the swing and get a breath of fresh air." He assisted me from the table, casting a look back at JoHanna that asked her what the hell was happening.

He put me in the swing and sat beside me. Not close and not far away. The distance of a friend. He pushed the swing enough to get us going and to set up the steady, comforting song of the creaking chains.

When I didn't speak, he sighed. "Mattie, if he's hurt you in any way, tell me and I'll take care of it."

I don't think anything in the world had ever frightened me as much as those words. Once, when Jojo kicked me in the stomach, and I saw his foot draw back to kick again, I thought I was going to die. But this was different. This was even more terrifying. I could not look at Will for fear he would see something that would make him act. I did not doubt that he would get in his shiny red car, drive to my small house, and drag Elikah out into the street and beat him to death. There was about Will a sense of definite action. He was like JoHanna's stride, a force of nature that could not be stopped once it was started.

We rocked on, the silence growing.

"Mattie, if that man has hurt you in any way, you have to tell me."

I had to speak. "It's okay, Will."

"He's hurt your feelings then?" There was relief in his voice.

"Yes. My feelings." It sounded so silly, as if he'd said my fried chicken was too dry or my biscuits flat and heavy. But dear God, I did not want Will to know what had really happened.

His hand on my arm made me jump, and when I looked at him in the dying light of evening, I knew he didn't believe me.

"Mattie, if he ever hurts you, I'll take care of it."

I could not look away from his brown eyes. The amber center was gone. They were all dark and hard, angry, but a cool anger.

"No man has a right to hurt a woman. Not for any reason. Not under any circumstances. A man who hits a woman is a coward."

I thought for a moment that he might have somehow known what Elikah had done, but he thought he was beating me. The relief gave me the strength to nod. "I'm okay." I nodded again.

"Are you sure?"

Outside the screened porch the frogs and crickets had set up their evening song. Even the heat had gentled, lying on my skin like a soft, warm touch. "In a lot of ways, I've never been so lucky." I lifted my chin. "I've never had friends who could stand up for me. Now I have you and JoHanna. I'm not so alone."

He reached across the swing and brushed my cheek with his fingers, testing, I think, to see if I'd flinch. "You're a lovely child, Mattie. And you'll grow up to be a beautiful woman. I don't intend to let Elikah or anyone else disturb that process."

"I'll be fine."

For that instant, I believed it.

∽ *Fifteen* ∽

JOHANNA wore her hat with rooster tail feathers to Mobile. She loaned me a loosely cut navy dress, dark but sleeveless and cool in the baggy cut of it. She also gave me a hat, navy with a veil. I held it on the carseat beside me as Will drove the back roads out of Jexville toward the old federal road that led to Mobile.

Will had gotten up at dawn and taken Duncan to have breakfast in Reba's Café, one of their favorite places. JoHanna told me I could not eat or drink water, that it would make me sick. I could not have eaten anyway. The appetite of the night before was long gone, as was my small, budding hope that things would be okay. I rode in the back seat, silent and afraid. Though JoHanna cast me reassuring looks, they did no good.

At the train station we waved Will off. He gave JoHanna a big, dramatic kiss right in front of everyone. A kiss that drew smiles from many, frowns from a few. They didn't care. JoHanna waved until the train had disappeared in a hiss of steam and a cloud of grit.

She didn't talk as we went back to the car. JoHanna drove with the same determination that she walked. Both hands on the wheel, eyes straight ahead, she aimed for her destination. I didn't want to talk. If she asked me again what I wanted, I might be too afraid to do this thing.

The building we stopped at was dark brick, three stories high. Beautiful curlicues of wrought iron formed small balconies at double doors on each level. It looked somber, serious, but not dirty. It did not look like what I had imagined. We parked in the shade of a live oak that seemed to bend over the entire street, a gesture of good will.

"Wait here," JoHanna said. "I have to talk to him."

Real terror struck me. "He may not do it?"

She didn't say anything for a moment. "Mattie, you may not be pregnant. It could be something else wrong. And yes, if you are, he may not do it."

"But he's done this before?" I was desperate. I gripped her arm.

"He's a doctor." She shook her head. "Whether he wants to or not . . . The less you know, the better. For me, for him, and for you."

The possibility that he would not help me settled over me like the dirt of a grave. I was suffocated by my own helplessness. I nodded, indicating I would wait in the car.

She got out, crossed the street in that long, long stride, and went inside the building.

I don't know how long she was gone. A while. The leather car seat grew hot, even in the shade of the tree. My mind seemed to stop working. I sat and watched the people come and go along the street. It was mostly men; some wore suits, some the pants and shirts of common laborers. Some stared at me; some passed as if I did not exist. I put the hat on, drew down the veil, and waited.

JoHanna came back, her face set in an expression that told me nothing. She came around to my door, opened it, and motioned for me to get out. Together, we walked to the back of the building. Inside there was a staircase. At each landing there were double doors that led inside, but we went straight to the third floor and into a long hallway darkened by heavy paneling.

JoHanna led me to a room centered by a narrow cot with a light at the end. The veil cut the room into tiny diamond bites, little fragments of horror. Sun slatted into the large windows through wooden blinds that were semiclosed. Several shafts fell across a neat arrangement of silver instruments on a clean white cloth. On a counter was a bottle beside a silver strainer, a cotton cloth. There was nothing of familiarity in the room, except JoHanna, and I edged closer to her.

"He'll have to examine you." JoHanna looked down at her feet. "I have to wait outside."

"Stay with me." I grabbed at her hand. "JoHanna, I'm afraid."

She met my gaze, her own emotionless. "He won't let me. I have to wait outside. Mattie, he's risking a lot to do this. It's his way or not at all."

"Will it hurt?"

"Yes." She never flinched. "He can't give you any ether. He said it re-laxes the uterine muscles and can make you bleed too much." She swal-lowed and her throat worked. "He'll give you morphine, but you won't be completely asleep. I can come and sit with you when it's over. Then we'll go home. We have to leave before it gets dark."

I looked around the room. The instruments were hideous. I reached out to touch one, and JoHanna's voice stopped me.

"Don't touch anything."

"Are there others?"

She didn't answer.

"Are there other women having this done? Where are they?"

Still she hesitated. "No. This is special."

"Then why is he doing this for me?"

She took a breath, gauging how much truth to tell me. "Because he doesn't have a choice."

I didn't want to know what she knew that was forcing a doctor to risk his career, his freedom, his future. She saw the paralyzing fear on my face and spoke again.

"No one in this room wants to be here. Not you, not me, and not him. None of us are sure we're doing the right thing. But that doesn't matter now. What matters is that you come through this safely."

JoHanna was the strongest person I'd ever known, but she couldn't give me what I needed. "You'll wait outside?"

"Right outside the door." She reached out to me. "Mattie, it's not too late to change your mind."

"How much does this cost?" I hadn't even thought of money. Why hadn't I thought of the cost? I would never be able to pay JoHanna and Will back.

"Money isn't an issue here. It's the last thing to worry about." She waved her hand in the air, brushing it aside.

She looked back through the open door of the room. A shadow moved on the opposite wall. The doctor was out there, waiting. By the way he shifted, I knew he was impatient.

"I have to go," she said. "Mattie . . . ?"

"Go." The word was barely a whisper.

"Take off your underwear and get up on the end of the table. Just lie back and close your eyes. Don't open them for any reason. Don't look, and that way you won't have anything to remember."

She was talking fast, desperate. She was scared, and that made me afraid. What if I died? What would she do with my body? She couldn't leave me in this barren room. How would she get me back to Jexville?

"Oh, Mattie." She turned and fled the room.

I took off my undergarments and didn't know what to do with them. Lying on the floor they looked obscene. I balled them up in my fist and held them and got up on the hard, narrow cot. I closed my eyes and waited for the door to shut.

The doctor did not talk to me. I held my eyes as tightly closed as possible. I tried to remember summer days when Callie and Lena Rae and I played in the field behind the house. Days before Jojo, when the red clay dirt and Mama were all we needed.

When he hurt me, I didn't cry out, but concentrated on staying perfectly still. He never said I was pregnant, but he didn't say I was not. He did not talk at all.

He lifted my arm, turned it so that the bend was exposed. There was a sharp bite. I tried to draw away from him, but he held me, his grip much stronger than I'd anticipated.

"It's morphine," he said. He put my arm down and stepped away from me. I could sense that he had withdrawn. I heard him at the tray, the rattle of those metal instruments. I wanted to cry, but I was afraid he would leave in disgust if I did. He cleared his throat, but the noise was strange, something deformed trying to make a sound.

In the darkness beneath my eyes there was a strange swirl of noise and color all blended together. There was the sound of a large bird calling my name and the pulse of water against land. I opened my eyes a tiny slit and saw him, a man of middle age with glasses and a worried expression. He was standing beside me and he lifted my arm. There was the feel of some restraint and I tried to struggle, but my arms were mine no longer. My body did not respond to my command to flee.

"You have to be very still," he said. There was no emotion in his voice. No sympathy. No anger that he'd been forced into this situation. "The morphine will help, but it may hurt. Please try not to scream."

I tried to talk but my mouth was dry, my lips thick and gummed together. He positioned my legs and the pain began.

How long it lasted, I can't say. At one point, JoHanna hovered over me, crying herself as she held a towel to my mouth to muffle the sounds I was making. There was trouble. I heard it in the panic in her voice and the doctor's response, now electric with concern. My heavy body wanted to get up, to leave, but I could not move. Whether it was the straps or the morphine, I couldn't say. I gave in completely to my terror and guilt and shame.

I awoke in a dark tunnel. In the distance there was the sound of children singing. I knew if I moved to the sound, I would be saved. Their voices would lead me to safety. JoHanna was calling to me, but I wanted to go with the children. The tunnel was black, and I ran. At the very last minute I stopped. There was a steep ledge. Below were the children, all looking up and waiting. They held sharp instruments and their eyes were blank, hungry. Fire burned all around them, and there was the smell of sulfur. I felt my throat ripen and explode with the scream.

"Mattie." There was the whisper of a cool damp cloth over my face. "It's over, Mattie. You're coming around."

My eyes felt glued shut, but after the dream I wanted to open them and see where I was. I knew it had been a dream. A nightmare. But my heart was still pounding and I felt as if something had been ripped out of my body. "Am I going to die?" My voice was raspy, raw, and it hurt to talk.

"No." JoHanna put the cloth on my eyes, letting the cool water seep beneath my lids.

"The doctor?"

"He's gone."

"Can we leave?"

"In a bit. If you don't start bleeding again."

I tried to reach down my body, but JoHanna caught my hand.

"Don't, Mattie. Just be still."

She gave me a tiny piece of ice. The nausea was almost instant, and she held me while I heaved into a pan.

"Try not to do that," she said as she wiped my mouth. "It can start the bleeding again."

I nodded, unwilling to risk speech. What was going to happen to me? I opened my eyes. I was still in the same room, still lying on the narrow cot. The only difference was the slant of light in the window. It was late afternoon.

"We need to leave here, if you can," JoHanna said. She looked around nervously. "I'll go and get the car and bring it to the back of the stairs. You wait right here. Don't try to move."

I wouldn't have moved for a million dollars. My body was on fire. It throbbed with a burning pain that made me sick. I had not asked what they would do to get rid of the baby. I hadn't wanted to know. Now I would never forget.

Time meant nothing as I waited for her to return. I would drift away for small fragments of time, coming back to a reality that was too awful to be real. But I knew it was, and I waited. I heard her step and heard the door open. I felt her hand on my arm. With her help I sat up and forced my eyes open again. The room was the same. For some reason that amazed me.

"If you can make it down the stairs, we'll head home." She picked up my hat from the floor and put it on my head, adjusting the veil.

I had no faith I could make the stairs, but I had no choice. We needed to go. I heard the desperation in JoHanna's voice. It was a long ride home. It was getting dark.

"Duncan?" I asked.

"Floyd will take care of her." She grasped my elbow. "Duncan is fine, Mattie. It's you I'm worried about right this minute. Once we get home, everything will be better."

I slid from the table and felt my feet on the floor. I was amazingly steady, and with JoHanna's support, I walked across the room and down the stairs. The cramps started again when I was in the car seat, but I didn't say anything. JoHanna was already worried. Once we got back to Jexville and I could lie down, I'd be fine.

"Go," I told her as she got behind the wheel.

And she did. Faster than Will drove and with less regard for anyone else on the road. We drove into the setting sun, and I closed my eyes and entered a red-hot place where blood ran down the walls and babies screamed in a distant room.

Sixteen

WE stopped in Jexville only long enough to retrieve Duncan. She and Floyd were at Nell Anderson's. I cowered in the car seat, webbed in nightmare images, while JoHanna went in and rounded up Duncan, Floyd, and the rooster. In a matter of moments, we were, all five, on the way to Fitler and JoHanna's Aunt Sadie.

As soon as Duncan and Floyd caught sight of me, they fell silent. JoHanna asked about their day, apologizing for being so late. "Mattie is sick," she said. "Aunt Sadie will know how to help her."

"Where's Mr. Mills?" Duncan asked.

"He has to work. He couldn't come." JoHanna pressed the gas harder, pushing the car to a reckless speed on the rutted road. In the three hour drive back from Mobile, my body had come fully awake. The pain was so large, so intense, I couldn't begin to say where it came from. I wanted to curl into a ball and hide. Not even the mention of Elikah's name bothered me. He could not hurt me worse than I was already hurting.

"What's wrong with Mattie?" Duncan asked. She reached over the seat and touched me. "She's sweating, and she's cold."

"She's, ah, had a chill." JoHanna's lie rang false in my ears. Duncan didn't believe her. I could tell that. But she pushed back in the seat and turned her questions to Floyd.

Above us the night sky was starlit velvet. It was early September. Soon the nights would begin to cool and the sky would get blacker, harsher. October was normally dry, but November could be either. I went through the months and the seasons, finding patterns, predictions, a future that had not changed in the last twelve hours.

If there was a town of Fitler, I missed it completely. There were trees and stars and the bald patch of road that the car headlights illuminated. And suddenly there was a front porch, and the car slowed to a stop.

"Floyd, could you carry Duncan in for me?" JoHanna asked. "Duncan, hang on to Pecos until I can get him in your room. Sadie will have a fit if that rooster starts running all over her house. Floyd, please tell Aunt Sadie that I'm out here and need her help. Tell her to bring a lamp."

I tried to move, but my legs ignored me. "I can't seem to make my body obey," I said, laughing a little at the foolishness of it.

"Be still." JoHanna's voice was firm, in control.

A figure appeared at the door, a small woman, erect. She held a lighted lantern and she came out to the car, to the passenger side. She held the lantern so she could see my face. "What's wrong?"

"Bleeding." JoHanna said it on a sigh. "We have to get it to stop."

"Floyd can bring her in." Aunt Sadie stepped back with the lamp and returned inside. She came back out with Floyd and held the lamp while he picked me up.

I tried not to cry out, but I did. I sounded like a wounded animal, but I couldn't help it. Floyd carried me into the house and to the room where Aunt Sadie directed him. The bed was narrow, a single bed with crisp white sheets. Floyd put me down and then stepped back. I could see my blood on his left arm, saturating the sleeve. "Am I dying?"

"Maybe. Maybe not." Aunt Sadie motioned Floyd out of the room. "Take care of Duncan," she directed him with a bluntness that sounded callous. "JoHanna, go put some water on to boil." She spoke to her niece with the same crispness.

When the room was clear, she turned to me. "Did you miscarry or did you abort?"

"A doctor . . ."

She didn't give me time to finish. "Were you bleeding when you left Mobile?"

"I'd stopped."

"Good. Now stay as still as you can. That ride more than likely opened up a bleeder. It may stop on its own. If it doesn't . . . well, it will probably stop by itself. I'm going to make you some tea, and you have to drink every drop."

The idea of swallowing anything made me sick, but this small woman wasn't to be denied. She left the room, and I allowed my body to sink into the soft mattress.

JoHanna brought the tea, and I drank the nasty stuff. I fell asleep, and in my dream I heard Duncan and Floyd. They were dancing. Duncan was a young woman, her hair all grown, her body complete and whole. And Floyd had somehow found his wits. They were to marry and leave Fitler, together, happy.

When I awoke, a small elderly woman was standing at the foot of my bed staring at me. Her eyes were clear, hard blue. The wrinkles around them were not from laughing. She looked as if she'd stared too hard at life and found it sad.

"The bleeding stopped of its own accord," she said. "If you don't start again, you'll be fine. JoHanna's making some eggs for you. Eat everything. You look like a heifer that's been left in a bare lot. If you'd lost any more blood, I couldn't have saved you."

She left the room on that bright note, and I eased up in bed.

The room was small, but there was an open window that allowed the fresh September morning in. Outside was a green tunnel where the road wound between oak trees as big as those in Mobile, and just as laden with the gray mass of growth that hung in lacy gobs. Spanish moss. Elikah had told me that in Mobile.

Looking harder I saw the outline of what appeared to be buildings. Blackened timber against the sky. From the bed I couldn't determine if buildings were going up, or if they were the decaying scaffolding of the boomtown that I'd heard so much about.

JoHanna brought a tray in to me. "It's Fitler. Or what once was the town," she said, putting the tray across my lap. "Aunt Sadie says you can't walk today, but in a day or two we'll go down there. I'll tell you about it."

Day or two. I had a surge of worry. I had been gone all day yesterday and all night. Without telling Elikah a word. And now I was in another town and he had no idea where I had gone.

"If you're worried about that husband of yours, don't. It'll do him some good to wonder where you are, and I'll have Floyd deliver him a note tomorrow or the next day." She motioned to the tray. "Now eat.

Duncan had another dream last night." She shook her head. "That child has an imagination, but she's insisting that I take her to speak with Mr. Lassiter."

"Mr. Lassiter?" I'd never heard the name.

"He runs a logging company. Really nice man. Duncan insists that he's going to drown." She smiled, but it wasn't exactly sincere. She was worried and didn't want to show it. "I'll send Duncan in to tell you her dream. You can decide for yourself."

Sadie brought in more tea and shooed JoHanna out of the room. This had a slightly different flavor, and it had been sweetened with honey to hide the taste of what had to be moonshine. The bite was quick, clean, and hot. It seemed I had hardly finished the cup before my eyes closed and I was adrift on a warm wave of air, floating over trees that swayed in a delicious breeze while the Spanish moss danced and cast strange patterns of shadow on the Fitler sand.

I awoke with the sound of voices. At first I had no idea where I was or who was talking, but I soon heard JoHanna's voice. Nervous. Then Duncan's and Aunt Sadie's. A fourth voice was added, male. But it wasn't Floyd's kind and gentle voice. This man spoke in deep, rich tones crackling with intelligence and with an authority that expected to be obeyed. I was certain it was the sheriff, come to get me and JoHanna.

Through the weight of fear, I forced myself to listen, to catch the words and comprehend the meaning.

"She insists on telling you in person, Red." JoHanna's voice was apologetic. "I was going to take her down to the river to talk to you, but she sent Floyd without my knowing."

"He has to hear." Duncan had no such apology in her voice. There was anger. "You don't believe me, Mama, but he has to hear this. If he doesn't stay off the water, he's going to drown."

"Duncan." JoHanna's tone was a reproach.

"I told Mary Lincoln and she didn't listen. I told her plain as day. I wasn't certain then that it would come true. But I know it will. I saw it clear this time."

"Duncan . . ." JoHanna sounded hot enough to sizzle spit.

"Jo, it's okay. Let her tell me. The child is trying to help me out." Beneath the sincerity there was amused tolerance. I could well imagine how that condescending tone would sit with Duncan. If she could walk she'd probably kick him in the shins. But the explosion didn't come. Instead, Duncan started to talk.

"It was a crisp day, sort of one of those cool ones thrown in at the end of summer when it doesn't look as if fall is ever going to come." Duncan paused. "The weather was good. That's what I remember, because Mama and I were going along in the sand. I was in the wagon, so I hadn't got the use of my legs back yet. We were going to get Floyd down at the river where he was fishing."

If nothing else, the wealth of her detail had silenced them. They were listening, and so was I, distracted from my own nightmare by the images Duncan cast out to us.

"You had your men down at the river with a big raft of logs. I asked Mama to take me closer. I like to watch the men herd them up and tie them. Daddy has said one day he'll take me down the river on a raft."

There was another pause and I knew she was daring JoHanna to object.

"Tell the dream," JoHanna said, her voice neutral.

I knew the camping trip on a raft would come up for later discussion, when the man had gone on about his business.

"You were out on a raft the men were pulling together. You had one of those hooks and were pulling in a big log. Everyone was laughing. The weather was so fine and the river was shallow, but deep enough to float the logs on down to Pascagoula." Duncan took a breath.

"I don't know what happened, but the log twisted under you. It seemed for a minute that you were going to get your balance back. The men were laughing. Then you stumbled. Your right leg went down between the logs, and they came together real hard."

There was a dead silence. I felt my skin chill and prickle.

"Tell the rest, Duncan." The man's voice was not condescending now.

"I heard the bones crush, and you cried out. You tried to pull out, but the logs were crushing your ankle and leg. The men ran toward you, jumping on logs and running across the river faster than I'd ever seen anyone do that before. But the logs that had hold of you opened, and suddenly you were gone, down under the raft. And you drowned."

"Well, that was some dream." The man's voice had a false note of joviality in it. "And you know it was me for a fact?"

"Yes, sir. So I knew I had to tell you. Just stay off the rafts while the weather is good. Then it won't come true. You won't have a chance to get caught like that."

"Good advice."

"Listen, Red," JoHanna broke in, "she insisted on telling you. And I agree with Duncan, it's better that you know."

"Well, sure. A man can avoid a train if he sees it coming."

I could tell he didn't completely believe what Duncan had said. But she had rattled him some, and maybe enough to keep him off the logs for a while.

"When I woke up, I could still feel the hot sand on my bare feet where I had been running," Duncan said.

"Red . . ." JoHanna didn't know what else to say.

In my bedroom, separated from the voices by a heart of pine wall and open doors, I pulled the sheet up to my chin. The day was hot outside. I could see the heat devils wavering in the sand beyond the tunnel of oaks outside my window. Duncan's words chilled me. The child had the gift of words, if not prophecy. I had no doubt that everyone sitting around that kitchen table felt the same touch of death that I had.

"Do yourself a favor, Red. Stay off the rafts. What could it hurt? If the child has a gift, you can save yourself. If she doesn't, you've got men who can do the work as good as you. You won't lose anything." Aunt Sadie's voice was as hammer-hit hard as always.

The woman was to the point. Direct. But there was a comforting lack of judgment in her. She knew I'd had an abortion, but it was only another fact to tote up so she could figure out how to help me.

There was the sound of chairs scraping back on hardwood floors. "Thank you, Miss Sadie, for that delicious pound cake and the coffee. I know you let my men come over here once a week for cake and coffee." He laughed. "I appreciate it. They work hard and lots of them don't have their families with them for long stretches at a time."

"A little sweet cake and hot coffee is a simple gift. Through the years you've been good to me, Red. You and your men. If you see JoHanna and Duncan down around the water, get your boys to watch them. Jo-Hanna thinks she's part fish and Duncan, well, I don't know what Duncan has decided to be."

"A dancer," Duncan said.

There was a split second of awkward silence as her words called to everyone's mind the fact that she couldn't use her legs. Not yet. They were getting stronger. But dancing was a long, long way away. It was then I remembered her final image, the hot sand as she was running in her dream. Duncan wasn't a prophet. She was a little girl with a vivid imagination.

"JoHanna's brought that sweet boy Floyd up here with her. He's down at the river fishing now." China rattled and I knew Aunt Sadie or JoHanna was picking up the dishes from the table. "He's a handsome boy, but innocent. Keep an eye on him, too. He doesn't know the currents of that river, has no idea how it can snatch a man and pull him down and hold him."

"Floyd will listen to whatever you tell him," JoHanna added. "He's no trouble, but if you do see him in a dangerous spot, just tell him. He listens."

"Will do. Now those men are thinking I'm stealing all of Miss Sadie's cake and coffee. They won't work a lick out of jealousy."

Footsteps traveled to the back door.

"Come back, Red," Aunt Sadie said.

"Take care," JoHanna added.

"Don't drown," Duncan sang out from the kitchen table where she still sat. "Take me in to see Mattie, please," she requested as soon as the man was gone.

JoHanna was silent, but I heard the chair scraping. She was picking Duncan up. In a few seconds they appeared at my doorway.

"You're awake." Duncan was delighted. "You look much better. Last night you looked horrible. Put me on her bed, Mama."

I nodded at JoHanna's questioning look. I was feeling much better. The cramps were gone. I was starving again. I was delighted to see Duncan.

"Want to play cards?" Duncan asked. "Mama always plays cards with me when I'm sick."

JoHanna stood in the door waiting to see if I wanted Duncan to stay or not. That simple gesture made me tear up.

"Mattie?" JoHanna stepped forward.

I laughed, letting the tears run down my cheeks. "You're waiting for me to decide what I want. It just touched me." I laughed, and Duncan and JoHanna joined in. "I'd love to play cards with Duncan." I looked up, brushing the wetness from my cheeks with the back of my hand. "And I'd love a piece of that cake and some coffee."

"Well I think we can handle that order," JoHanna said. "I'll get the cards first."

She disappeared from the doorway, and Duncan gave me a serious look. "I really like Mr. Lassiter," she said. "I got Floyd to bring me by your room before he went fishing, but you were asleep. I was going to tell you my dream."

"I heard."

She looked down at the cream-colored chenille bedspread, her fingers picking tufts of the pattern. "I think he listened." She looked up, her brown eyes dazed and lost looking. "Sometimes, since the lightning, I can feel colors."

I put my hand on hers as it had fallen motionless on the spread. "What do you mean, Duncan?" I wasn't certain I wanted to know, but she'd decided to tell me.

"I feel them. Like hot and cold, only more."

"More how?"

"Like Floyd took me out in the woods and we found this wildflower. It was so blue that it made me ache. I felt as if my heart were breaking in two."

She was completely sincere. A little girl slightly afraid of the power of her senses.

"Has that ever happened to you?" she asked.

"No." I tried to remember, but I couldn't pinpoint anything like that.

"I saw a cardinal out the window day before yesterday. He was going from the clothesline to the chinaberry tree and then down into the yard to mess with Pecos." She grinned. "Sometimes other birds mess with him because he's not certain he's a rooster."

"Where is Pecos?"

"Aunt Sadie doesn't like him in the house. He's out under the porch, but I'll get him inside by tonight."

"What about the cardinal?" I was strangely compelled to hear this. Outside there came a burst of laughter, men working on the river. The echo had that wavery sound of being cast back from water.

"That's Mr. Lassiter's men. He has six or seven camps in the woods cutting the trees and getting them together. Then he has men who float them down to Pascagoula." Her smile slowly faded. "Anyway, the cardinal was out there, and I was watching him. Suddenly it was like the rest of the world lost color. There was the bird, and the red was so red that I could feel the bird's heart beating. He was too red to live long. His heart beat so fast. And I started to cry because he was so beautiful and born to die so soon." Her eyes had filled even as she talked.

"And this color thing has happened to you before?"

"Since the lightning. I have to be alone, and . . ."

"And what?"

"It's like it feels wonderful, but it hurts so much, too." There was a question on her face. "At first, the color feels like . . . like all the joy in the world is inside my chest. It's that way for just a few seconds, and then the pain comes." She looked at me as if she expected an answer.

"I don't know, Duncan. Can you stop it?"

"I don't know. I don't know if I want to."

I heard JoHanna moving in the kitchen, the rattle of dishes. She was fixing my cake for me. "What does JoHanna say?"

Duncan looked down at the spread and picked once again at the tufts of creamy fabric. "She says that in life pleasure and pain are twins. One comes, but the other is never far behind." She looked up at me. "She said to experience feeling intensely is a gift, but that I have to learn when to feel, that I have to learn to guard myself." She took a deep breath. "Because, she said that if I don't protect myself I'll become afraid to feel, and that I'll die by degrees."

I could hardly believe that JoHanna had told Duncan such a thing, but I saw it plain on Duncan's face. She was frightened, and it scared me. "It's always good to guard yourself." I tried to pick a path through emotions and fears I didn't understand. What was JoHanna trying to warn her daughter of?

"Mattie, have you ever been afraid of your feelings?"

Yes, oh, yes. I caught a shimmer of the night in New Orleans. My shame had almost killed me. I was afraid. Of Elikah and what he had done to me, but also of myself. Of what I had become capable of. Duncan was watching me with such intensity that I knew I didn't have to answer. She saw it on my face. "Duncan, I think maybe it's other people's actions you have to guard against." I faltered. "The colors you feel are pure. That's you. If you feel that . . . completely about others, you put yourself at risk." I wasn't certain I was helping. Either of us. I heard JoHanna's footsteps and felt an immense relief. I didn't want to talk about this. I didn't want to think of Elikah. I shifted in the bed to a better sitting position and I felt his mark all over me. I could not escape him, but I would not bring him into this day, this morning, this moment with the sun shining out the window and slanting across the bed. "Here's your mother."

"It's pound cake," Duncan said, her mood already shifted. "If Floyd can find another wagon, Mama said we could go to the river later today."

JoHanna appeared in the doorway with a tray laden with a quarter of a cake, steaming coffee, and a rose in a tiny vase. I didn't see the October-sky pink as intensely as anything Duncan had described, but the sight of that beautiful flower stung my eyes.

"I said Mattie could go to the river *if* she felt like it and *if* Aunt Sadie said so. But give her a chance to eat her cake and see." She gave me a look.

"Maybe walking would do me some good. I'm kinda sore." There were places where the sore was bad, but there were other places that felt like if I could move around, they'd limber up.

"We'll see." She put the tray down on my lap and lifted the deck of cards from it to hand to Duncan. "A couple of games. Then you and I are going to the store."

"When's Floyd coming back?"

"Lunch. Then we'll see about the river." She walked over to the window and looked out. "If you stand up you can see her," she said.

"The river," Duncan interpreted. "Mama says water is a female." She saw she had my attention. "She said calling the Mississippi the 'father of waters' was the only mistake the Indians ever made, except not killing the first white men who came here."

"I don't think the Indians meant father of waters." JoHanna spoke to the window. She turned toward us, and I saw the light of mischief in her eyes. "Father is the interpretation that the Spaniards put on the Indian term. Spain was, at that time, and still is, I should add, a very patriarchal society. Any figure of reverence or authority would naturally be male." She lifted her eyebrows. "According to the men who heard it."

I was surprised by my own laughter. "Where do you think of these things?" I asked her.

She grinned, a real complete grin. "Will asks me the same question. But he doesn't wait around for the answer. I don't think he really wants to know. Do you?"

I was suddenly aware of the risk. What she offered was not a simple answer to a question—it was revolution. I felt my smile slipping, and I tried to hold on to the lighthearted moment.

JoHanna left the window and came up to the bed. She put her hand on my forehead. "Cool," she said. "You've weathered the worst, Mattie. Aunt Sadie promises. I do believe you can get up after lunch, if you want."

"I want."

"Good, then we'll go to the river." Duncan's eyes were bright, an imp of mischief dancing there with the same abandon that Duncan had once danced the Charleston. "*She* wants to meet you, Mattie. *She's* heard lots about you this summer from me and Mama."

Seventeen

THE Pascagoula was not what I'd expected. In my mind's eye it was a deep blue river with willows bending over the banks, a picture-book river winding placidly past small towns. I was correct in visualizing it as low on one side with high bluffs on the other, but that was as far as my imagination took me into fact.

We had come to the end of the road where the bridge was to have been built some thirty-odd years before. It was the easier route for us, because of our disabilities. Before us, the water was a mesmerizing element.

The river itself was yellow-red, sluggish looking. Looks were deceiving. Rains north of us had clouded the river and bloated it, giving it that lazy look, JoHanna said. But it wasn't slow, she warned us. Far from it. The current wasn't a steady flow, as I had imagined, but a confusion of small eddies. In places, it was smooth as glass. Suddenly a churning motion would break the water and a swirl of suction would be revealed. Whatever luckless object happened by would be suddenly sucked deep into the river. It could be a floating branch or a bottle, or a man. The river took whatever it could, JoHanna said. Sometimes the object would disappear, the vortex closing as fast as it had come. Later, it might be released far downstream, or it might not ever be seen again. JoHanna said there was a treasure of riches and broken dreams on the bottom of the Pascagoula.

JoHanna said the water would clear by tomorrow and that then we could swim, if Aunt Sadie gave her permission for me to get in the river water. A hot bath was definitely in order, JoHanna said, but Aunt Sadie didn't believe in the healing properties of the Pascagoula, and she feared some infection would get me.

Since I tended to agree with Aunt Sadie, I was relieved. But I was glad to sit on the bank and watch Duncan and JoHanna and Floyd, and even that crazy Pecos, as they ventured closer to the murky depths.

Since JoHanna had insisted that I be hauled in a wagon by Floyd while she pulled Duncan, we didn't go as far upstream as Duncan wanted. There was a place with a sandbar that Duncan loved. JoHanna said we would go there tomorrow if we could walk and swim. For today, though, we were to look only.

The enormous brick and mortar pilings that reared out of the current were a melancholy reminder of the bridge that was never built. More than fifty feet in height and wide as half a locomotive, they rose above the river, still resisting the constant tug of the current. Set in twos, there were fifteen pair. I couldn't begin to imagine how the men got them down to the bottom of the river without being swept away.

"Daddy drew the way the bridge would look," JoHanna said. "He wasn't an architect, but he had a flair for being able to conceptualize things. He had it all, down to the little decorative iron touches." She smiled. "I'm glad he never lived to see these barren supports here. That would have broken his heart."

"Do you think Mr. Senseney is alive somewhere, building other things?" I was still wondering about the hundred and twenty-five thousand dollars that had disappeared along with him. JoHanna's sixty-two thousand, five hundred dollars included in it. I'd done the arithmetic.

"I don't think so." JoHanna held the handle of Duncan's wagon. "I don't think he's alive at all. I think he was killed up in New Augusta, when he went to buy the supplies. That whole neck of the woods is fraught with outlaws and their kin. I think Mr. Senseney had too much money on him, and he was the kind of man who liked to show off a little."

JoHanna's eyes had a rare distance in them, so I thought of something else to talk about. "When we go back, can we stop in the town?" We'd passed through it as fast as they could pull the wagons in the sandy road. JoHanna had said very little about the gaunt wooden frames that were left, skeletons of the past. I couldn't tell if JoHanna wanted to race through the town because she didn't want to talk about it, or because she was so eager to get to the river. Duncan had told me how much she hungered for the water, just to see it.

"I'll give you a tour," JoHanna said.

"Then I want to come back and fish." Floyd looked at the water. "There's a big one in there. I've heard the stories about that big tabby." He looked at us all, one by one. "He weighs over a hundred pounds. If I could catch him, I'd be somebody."

The handle of Duncan's wagon hit the dirt with a soft thud. JoHanna was at Floyd's side in one swift step. Her hand was on his cheek, directing his gaze deep into her eyes. "You are somebody, Floyd. You're very special. You don't need to catch a fish or do anything to prove it."

Floyd's grin was lopsided, and a flush warmed his cheeks. "You say that all the time, Miss JoHanna. *You* think I'm somebody, but the people in Jexville don't. They think I'm a fool."

I looked down in shame. Floyd wasn't as simple as I'd thought. He was aware of the way people spoke of him. How could he not be? They did it to his face, as if he couldn't understand.

"You can't be responsible for the shortcomings of others, Floyd. You're who you are. That's plenty. You give some folks honesty, and they don't realize the value. Give them a pretty dress, and they think they have something worthwhile." She brushed her fingers across his jaw. "You're very special. Catch the fish if it makes you happy, but do it for you."

"Maybe I'll get my picture in the paper." Floyd turned away from her and looked into the water. "Now that would be something. Maybe my mama would read about me and know that I'd grown up to be someone she shouldn't have left behind."

Down river there was the sound of men rafting the logs, someone whistling a ragged tune. I looked at my hands, so pale in the bright sun.

"Let's head back to town," JoHanna said. "We'll see what the river has to tell us tomorrow."

"I'll be back today." Floyd made the promise to the river before he turned the wagon I rode in and started back toward the ghost town of Fitler.

The town proper of Fitler, or where it had been, was only half a mile from the river. Unlike Jexville, where all trees had been chopped down to make Redemption Road a straight line, Fitler's main street snaked around the huge oak trees. The buildings had once been set back from the street where unruly shrubs now dominated. We were in no hurry as we meandered along the road, stopping to look at wild flowers or the prickly pear that could pierce thin shoe leather. I had the nagging sense that someone followed us, just beyond the shelter of the trees that grew on both sides of the road. In my perch in the wagon, I looked up often but saw nothing. My own guilt was playing games with me, as if Elikah had left his barbershop to come to Fitler and spy on me. As if he knew what I had done. I tried to ignore the sense of being watched.

At the middle of town, JoHanna stopped the wagon Duncan rode in and looked around. "When I was a little girl, there was a piano in that bar. Mr. Senseney's bar. All evening long it would be going with the lively songs the men liked to hear. But sometimes, early in the morning, one of the whores would come down and play it. I always wanted to ask her the melody, it was so strange and haunting. I would sneak out of Aunt Sadie's and come over and hide in those old bushes in my nightgown and listen to her play. I could see her through the curtains, and she didn't look much older than me. She was killed, though, before I ever got to talk to her."

"Killed?" I asked.

"Some man cut her with a knife, and she bled to death before the doctor could get there." JoHanna stared at the two-story frame. "Corpses would float up, down in Pascagoula, sometimes two a week. The high-stakes card games brought a lot of violent men here. A lot of the killing went on at the floating saloons. There were houseboats that would dock, pick up a load of gamblers, and then move back out into the river, where they could tie up at some out-of-the-way place. No law ruled those hellholes."

"There's pirates' treasure, too," Duncan said.

"That tale drew plenty of fortune hunters up to Fitler," JoHanna agreed. "Floyd knows some stories about that."

"Where did everyone go?" I looked at the rambling structures, what looked like the town had been thirty or more businesses. The only thing left was a small grocery that also served as a postal and telegram office with a bait shop on the side. The wooden frames of buildings past were like a mirage. They gave the idea of a town, but when I looked closely, it wasn't there. I wasn't certain it ever had been. The contrast to what I'd come to know in Jexville was too extreme.

"Most of the folks went to other river towns. The coast." JoHanna pulled the brim of her ever-present hat lower to shade her eyes from the afternoon sun. "I heard Lonnie and Frank, the bartenders at the Last Chance, are working for Tommy Ladnier. His private home. I remember them as handsome young men. I'm sure they add a note of elegance to Tommy's little soirees."

"Mr. Ladnier has nice clothes," Floyd said. "I'm making him a pair of boots. Very special."

I looked up and down the abandoned street. "What would have happened to Fitler with Prohibition?"

JoHanna shrugged. "Nothing. Like the coast. Like Jexville. There's liquor in every cabinet, folks just hide it and pretend not to drink. This country is in love with hypocrisy."

The skin on my neck prickled just as Pecos shrilled with alarm and flew off the back of Duncan's wagon. All of us were startled, and we all swung around at once to find a tall, dark-haired man standing not five feet behind us. He'd come up so silently that we hadn't heard a thing.

"You're right," he said, as if he'd been part of our conversation. "The people in this country want to live the life of what they see in the film-strips, but they don't want others to know what they do."

JoHanna should have responded. She should have said something to the man for frightening us, for sneaking up on us and eavesdropping on our conversation. Instead, she looked at him and caught her breath as if she had a sudden pain. His dark gaze was proud, direct. Effective. He spoke to her, communicating something that made my skin prickle. Her lips parted to speak, but whatever she'd meant to say did not come out.

"Who are you?" she asked instead.

Before he could respond, Floyd swung around on him. Dropping into his gunslinger's crouch, Floyd inched his hands up until they hovered over the wooden pistols he wore wherever he went.

The stranger's face shuttered, his eyes narrowing as his legs bent slightly and he lifted his hands to his sides. "Can we talk?" he asked, his voice a threat and a request.

"Be careful, Floyd," Duncan warned.

Floyd hesitated, shifting just enough so that his body protected Jo-Hanna if the lead began to fly. "Put your hands in the air." He drew his right pistol and pointed it at the stranger's chest.

The stranger complied, large hands moving slowly into a position of surrender, though surely he could see that Floyd's guns were wooden. The stranger wore no weapon that I could see. His face registered no trace that this was a fool's game. He treated Floyd as if he had a cannon. Floyd's face was flushed with success, and pride.

"Easy, Floyd." JoHanna placed a steadying hand on Floyd's arm, as if she too believed he carried a loaded weapon.

I wondered if they had all gone insane.

"Now maybe he'll tell us his name," JoHanna prompted, "before you have to do away with him."

The stranger stepped forward, left hand still in the air while he extended his right to her. "John Doggett. And you are JoHanna McVay." He looked at Duncan. "You're the daughter, Duncan. And?" He looked at me and Floyd. I found that I, too, was holding my breath. He was a highwayman, a figure of dark fantasy. Surely if I blinked he would be gone.

"Mattie and Floyd, my friends." JoHanna finally stepped forward as if to shield all of us from his too obvious interest.

He gave Floyd a nod. "You did an excellent job of protecting Mrs. McVay." He looked at me, assessing my place. "And her family." He returned his attention to her. "I've heard many things about you." He spoke to her as if they were alone. Then he instantly dispelled that notion by giving Duncan a smile. "And your beautiful daughter."

"I'm sure you have. Gossip, like hypocrisy, is a delicious little sin, isn't it?" JoHanna's voice held a strange note of haughtiness.

Instead of getting angry, he laughed at her. For one crazy instant I thought of Will.

"Part of the gossip I find so delicious is your understanding of the river." By the end of the sentence he was no longer teasing. "You know the power that it has."

JoHanna was caught in a draft of erratic wind. She seemed to be blown back from him, then toward him, yet her body never moved a fraction of an inch. "I have respect for the river. For all of nature."

The strange man nodded, his dark gaze sculpting her face. He was without age. Or I should say indeterminate. He could have been twenty-five, or he could have been forty-five. His skin, an autumn bronze, seemed more natural than sun-kissed, and his dark hair, I finally noticed, was pulled into a thong at the nape of his neck. There was no gray, but a shift in his facial features would age him, then the hint of a smile would hurtle him back to a younger age. Somehow, I had the craziest notion that he was actually from the past.

"My people once lived beside the river."

The words he said weren't strange, but the effect on JoHanna was profound. She was unable to stop looking at him.

"Are you from around these parts?" Floyd had moved beside Duncan, where he'd put his big, gentle hand on Pecos's head, stroking the bird's ruffled feathers.

"Yes."

It wasn't really an answer, and it wasn't designed to be one.

"Do you live here in Fitler?" I asked. He made me uneasy. Not that I was afraid of him. Not in the least. But he commanded all of our attention in a way that concerned me. He was a presence, and I knew then that I could not blink him away.

"Sometimes." He smiled at me and I felt safer, and more annoyed.

"You're Chickasaw, aren't you?" JoHanna stepped toward him, examining his features as if he were a statue, something that could be walked around and studied without giving offense. She lifted her hand, as if to touch him, then dropped it back to her side.

"Pascagoula, Chickasaw, Mingo, Scot, Irish, Welsh," he compressed his lips and raised his eyebrows, "barbarian."

JoHanna laughed out loud, and Floyd and Duncan joined her. I sat in the wagon, the sun beating down on my head, and wondered if this was a sun-induced fantasy. I took in John Doggett's clothes. He wore a collarless shirt, unbuttoned at the neck, gray pants that were well worn along the contours of a body fit and lean. Scuffed boots that had once been expensive. There was nothing unusual in his dress, except that his clothes seemed an afterthought. Barbarian. It fit him well, except I could find no hunger for blood in his eyes. There was something there, but not cruelty.

"What are you doing in Fitler, Mr. Doggett?" JoHanna picked up the handle of the wagon.

"I've come to learn from a harsh mistress."

JoHanna laughed at his teasing. "The river, I presume."

"The river is part of her domain." The teasing was gone. He was serious, even though he spoke in riddles. "It's nature. I've come to try and figure out where I fit in with her."

JoHanna cast him a sideways glance, but she didn't say anything.

"And where is this wagon train headed? Since we've determined that I'm barbarian, mostly Indian, and you have a worthy cowboy to protect you, perhaps we could stage a battle."

JoHanna shook her head. "No more gunfights today. We're headed home. Duncan and Mattie both have had enough sun." She started walking, and Floyd followed suit, pulling me behind.

John Doggett dropped in alongside us, walking a step or two behind JoHanna and to her left. He didn't offer to pull the wagon for her, as if he knew intuitively that she would not allow him any control of her daughter. He didn't seem to notice that Floyd and Duncan and I were right there with them; he talked only to JoHanna.

"The old town interests me. I like the area. I was thinking of buying some property and building a home."

"Hard to make a living in a ghost town." JoHanna's voice wasn't critical, just stating fact.

"I write. It's hard to make a living at that anywhere."

JoHanna looked back at him. "What kind of writer are you?"

"I write about the truth."

The man was chockful of answers that didn't say a thing, but if Jo-Hanna noticed, she didn't seem bothered. Her attention was drawn to the river, where a group of six men were standing in a cluster while three others were out on the logs, organizing them into a raft that could be floated. The upstate rains had raised the river to an unexpected high for September, and the men were eager to move the logs while the high water held.

"Do you write books, Mr. Doggett?" I asked.

"I write about the past. About the way life once was."

"A historian," JoHanna pronounced.

"Amateur. And to be truthful, I take whatever work I can find to see me through. I've traveled a great deal."

"A drifter." It was a harsh assessment, and I don't know why I said it. He'd done nothing to harm me.

He turned back and gave me a half-smile. "Some would call me a drifter, but I've been called worse." His smile widened. "Some have called me a lot nicer things, too."

JoHanna's laughter made me flush.

"Why are the two young ladies riding in wagons?" he asked.

Duncan had been left out of the conversation too long, and she answered promptly. "I was struck by lightning and my legs don't work. Yet. And Mattie was bleeding last night."

Crimson washed over my closed eyelids, a red tide of burning shame. When I opened my eyes, no one was looking at me.

"Struck by lightning?" John Doggett was staring at Duncan with renewed interest.

"A direct hit." Duncan took off the straw hat JoHanna had spruced up for her with red ribbons. "My hair was burned to a crisp. And Mama cuts hers off, too. I think she lost her mind, but we both like our hair this short. We might not let it grow back until Christmas." She rumpled the downy fuzz, showing the white of her scalp as the hair slipped beneath her palm.

"What about your legs?" John Doggett dropped back so he could stare into the wagon at Duncan's pale white legs.

"Mama says the river is going to make me well." Duncan had taken a shine to the stranger.

"May I?" he asked as he leaned over and made as if to pick one up.

JoHanna had been watching over her shoulder, and she stopped the wagon. We'd left main street Fitler behind, and Aunt Sadie's house was just around the next two bends. We were almost home, and I was tempted to tell Floyd to take me on. But I didn't. I sat silent as a stone as John Doggett knelt down beside the wagon and picked up Duncan's left leg. He placed one hand under the knee and held her ankle with the other, working the leg as if it belonged to a puppet. I looked the other way at the men on the water. They were laughing and joshing the men on the logs, daring them to roll the big timbers. The day was warm and the water not unpleasant. Two of the men were setting up to compete. They were both standing on a single enormous pine trunk. While one would start it spinning in one direction, the other would try to balance and turn the spin. It was a contest I'd seen before on the Pearl up near Meridian. I focused my attention on the river, trying as hard as I could to tune out John Doggett and whatever foolishness he was going to start with Duncan. It made me angry that JoHanna would allow this. The man would get Duncan's hopes up with some silly predictions, and then she'd be upset for weeks if her recovery wasn't as fast as he'd promised.

"The muscles are there, just weak," he said, his fingers probing along her calf and thigh. "Can you stand?"

"No." Duncan sounded uncertain at last.

John Doggett lifted her from the wagon. I opened my mouth to protest, then turned back to the river. JoHanna was standing right there. I couldn't understand why she stood, planted like a pine, with the wagon handle in her hand and nothing coming out of her mouth.

With great care, John Doggett lowered Duncan to the ground. He braced her as he encouraged her to take a step. With such effort that it strained her face, Duncan managed to lift one leg and move it forward several inches. John Doggett's hands balanced her, his voice encouraged her, "Do it, Duncan. You can. I've got you. Take a step."

JoHanna breathed her daughter's name on a sigh of hope, "Duncan."

The men on the log had stopped. They both stood motionless, a feat in itself on a floating log. But something in their stance made me look slightly to the north. It was a man I hadn't seen before, a man with ropes and pegs and a hammer. He rose to stand fully erect, and I saw him falter.

From the distance of three hundred yards, where we stood in the road, it seemed as if he had merely lost his balance. There was the snick of trees colliding in the cushion of water, a crash muted by the river that washed them apart and then pushed them back together again.

I looked to the river but heard Duncan's sharp intake of breath. I swung back to her, saw the knowing on her face as she lifted her hands in front of her and began to scream.

"Red! Red! Red!" She ran a step with each cry.

As she fell, I heard the scream of a man in agony. I looked up to see the tall man with the hammer sink down on the raft. He went down slowly, as if he'd been brought to his knees to pray for forgiveness for some terrible sin. The log rollers began to run toward him, as if they intended to spring across the top of the river without falling in. But they were too slow; the river too fast. The logs pushed apart, and Red Lassiter disappeared beneath the raft.

Eighteen

THERE was no Doc Westfall to call for Duncan, and no need to call one for Red Lassiter. He was gone, taken by the river. They found Red's boot caught in the logs, but he had slipped from it. Vanished.

John Doggett carried Duncan in his arms to Aunt Sadie's house, Jo-Hanna running at his heels while Floyd was left to wallow through the sand with me and the wagon. I would have gladly walked, but JoHanna made me promise, and to be truthful, I didn't know if I could support my own weight. Since the abortion, I had been beset by strange sensations and thoughts. At times my mind was filled with tortured images, and I wasn't certain this moment was real. I could have dreamed it. I wanted to believe that I would awaken to find no one had drowned before my eyes. Though I'd never met Red Lassiter, I had liked his voice, his manner of speaking.

At the front porch I insisted on walking in and found JoHanna and Aunt Sadie ministering to Duncan. The child had been laid on Sadie's brocade sofa. Against the colorful cloth, she was too white, her eyes shut as if in death, one hand dangling as if never more to lift. Only her too rapid breathing proved she was alive. I could see she had slipped back into the place where she neither walked nor talked, a safe place guarded by the thin skin of her eyelids and the deep recesses of her mind.

"She walked," JoHanna whispered as she hovered. "She actually walked, Sadie."

"She ran," Floyd corrected as he stepped to stand beside JoHanna. "She wanted to save that drowning man."

I lingered in the door, wondering what to do. John Doggett was nowhere in sight, and I was not surprised. I'd half expected him to disappear before my eyes on the road. Now I was glad for his absence. He disturbed me in a way I couldn't define.

"Duncan?" JoHanna touched her daughter's cheek. "Duncan?"

There was fear in her voice.

"Do you suppose Red told anyone about Duncan's prediction?" Sadie's question was as blunt as ever, her implications crystal clear to me.

"I don't know." JoHanna wasn't thinking. "Why?"

"If word gets around that she's predicted another drowning, it's going to be harder than ever." Sadie went to the window and lowered the shade to block the sun from Duncan's face. "Let her sleep. I want you all to come in the kitchen with me." She took JoHanna's arm with an iron grip and led her to the kitchen table where she pushed her gently into a chair.

Since I was doing nothing but standing in the doorway, I was glad of some direction. I followed Sadie immediately, and at her signal began to put coffee on. With my hands busy, I found it easier to breathe. I had been holding my breath until my ribs ached.

"Is Duncan going to wake up?" Floyd clearly didn't want to leave her alone even though she was in the next room on the sofa. He touched JoHanna's elbow. "What if she wakes up and no one is there? Maybe I should go sit beside her."

JoHanna stilled herself long enough to look at Floyd. She brushed his thick honey-blond hair back from his forehead with a gesture of kindness. "Will you sit beside her, Floyd? Maybe you could tell her one of her favorite stories. I know she's asleep, but I think she can hear you. The story will be like one of our marked trails in the woods. She can listen to it and follow it back to us, here." Her voice clouded with emotion, but she smiled, blinking back her tears. "Could you do that, Floyd?"

He stood up, a man in stature but a child at heart. "I'll lead her back," he said, brushing JoHanna's tears from her cheeks. He turned and went into the other room.

In the silence of the kitchen, before the kettle boiled for coffee, his voice came to us clearly.

"I think your favorite story is the one about the ghost of Miss Kretzler at Courtin' Bridge. That's the one I told you the most, so I'm gonna start with that. But you have to remember it was a long time ago, during the Great War . . ."

"God bless him," Sadie said. It was one of the softest things I ever heard her say. "Sit right there, JoHanna, before you drop. That's all we need is another bed filled with tragedy."

She must have caught the sudden shame that flared in my cheeks because she turned squarely to me. "That wasn't meant to hurt you, Mattie. I just don't want JoHanna to keel over. I've got to go down to the river and find out what Red Lassiter told those men. Red was a good man, but he liked to talk as much as the next one." She shook her head. "The sooner we know what the talk is, the better we can prepare." She reached behind her and untied the apron she wore. She handed it to me. "Make JoHanna drink a cup of good, strong coffee. Make her sit still while she drinks it. You drink one, too, but put plenty of cream and sugar in yours. Just sit at the table, the two of you, until I get back. Draw a good breath, because when I come back we're going to have to start preparing."

She turned and walked out the back door, letting the screen slam hard behind her. I walked to the kitchen window and watched her going down the road, her small feet leaving shallow prints in the sand as she went toward the place where Red Lassiter had drowned.

"This is too much." JoHanna sat with her elbows on the table and her face in her hands. "Duncan said it was a fall day. She said the day was cool. This is September. It's practically summer."

The kettle began to boil and I poured the hot water down in the well of the dripolater and busied myself getting out the cups and saucers, the spoons and cream and sugar. The day was really too hot for coffee, but I needed it.

Floyd's voice continued on from the living room, rising and falling as he told the story that Duncan loved. Suddenly I was blinking back tears, and just as quickly irritated by my own maudlin weakness. JoHanna had been strong for me. She'd held a towel to my mouth to muffle my screams while terrible things were done to me. Floyd was reaching out to Duncan, a lifeline of words that she loved. And I couldn't make coffee without falling to pieces.

I poured two cups and pushed one to JoHanna. "Drink it," I said.

JoHanna looked up at me, then lifted the cup to her lips.

"When does Will come home?" I was wondering if the ancient telegraph office could possibly get word all the way to New York.

"Two weeks. I won't call him unless Duncan gets much worse."

"JoHanna." The word was total disbelief.

Her bosom lifted with a deep breath. "This trip is important, Mattie. It's our livelihood. If I call Will home, he'll come. If I don't have to have him, it's wrong to worry him. He's a thousand miles away by now. Think how he'd feel if he knew what had happened. He'd be sick with worry, and even if he was here, there's nothing he can do now. Nothing."

What she said was true. I walked to the door of the living room and looked in at Floyd. He'd pulled a chair right beside the sofa and sat, holding Duncan's limp hand and talking as if she were wide awake and hanging on each word. Instead, Duncan had chosen to return to a deep sleep. To wake her suddenly might do more damage than to let her surface on her own. Will could only stand and watch her, as I was doing. I turned back to the kitchen and walked to the table.

JoHanna was putting herself back together. I could see it happening, like ants rebuilding after a storm.

"What if there's trouble in Jexville? Will you send for Will?" *If* word of Duncan's prediction got back to Jexville, there would be trouble.

"They won't burn her as a witch." JoHanna's smile was wan, but it was there.

"You should stay here, in Fitler." I put the heavy cream in my coffee with a liberal hand, then added three spoons of sugar. I normally drank it black, but I craved the richness of the cream, the jolt of the sugar. "Floyd and I should go back. We can try to stop what's happening."

JoHanna lifted her coffee, but she didn't drink. "And Elikah?"

His name was a shadow in Sadie's bright kitchen. What of Elikah? "I don't know."

"You aren't afraid?"

With the focus on me, JoHanna was almost completely repaired. Her back had straightened, her head lifted, the blue returned to her eyes.

"Maybe I'm afraid, but I have to go back. Or I have to leave." I drank the coffee, licking the sweetness from my lips. "I'm not ready to leave yet. I don't know where to go," I added. "I'm not ready to think about where to go." That was closer to the truth.

The screen door creaked open and Sadie came along the porch and into the kitchen. She went straight to the stove and poured herself a cup of coffee before coming to sit at the table. She looked at me, then at JoHanna. "He told the men."

JoHanna didn't move a muscle. I knew then that she'd expected this. She'd known.

"What are they saying?"

"That Duncan is a prophet. That she can see the future." Sadie unbuttoned the top two buttons of her dress, and I realized then that she was perspiring heavily. She'd walked too fast in the heat of the sun. I went to the pitcher of water she'd drawn and got her a glass. She took it with a nod of thanks.

"How bad is it?" JoHanna asked.

"Hard to tell. They don't really believe it, but they believe it enough to be curious."

"Curiosity isn't so bad." JoHanna spoke the words tentatively, as if she didn't believe them either.

"The folks here won't amount to much. It's Jexville. They're not going to take it lightly that Duncan has the ability to foretell death." Sadie's gaze connected with JoHanna. "They're already afraid of you, Jo-Hanna. They may decide to take it out on Duncan."

JoHanna nodded, but she kept her head up. "They already take it out on Duncan." A spark lit her eyes. "Fear may be our biggest ally."

Sadie shook her head. "Don't do anything to egg this on. I know you, Jo. I know you to the bone. You can flaunt your ideas and fancies at them and manage to skin by. Not this time. This is the hand of God they're seeing. Or the work of the devil is more likely the way they'll interpret it. For Duncan's sake, don't provoke them. Let this die down and pass off."

Her words chilled me. JoHanna lived with Will and Duncan and Pecos in a sunny house outside the narrow boundaries of the town. She read her books and listened to her music and waited for Will to come home and tease and love her. She didn't hear the whispers of the men downtown or watch the other women tilting toward each other behind their hymnals, their whispers like angry wasps. JoHanna wasn't naive.

She knew the women talked about her. But she couldn't know how hard the feelings were against her. It was still a puzzle to me how Will was so well liked and JoHanna so despised. And Duncan would inherit her mother's mantle. Had she been a boy, she would have been pitied as the child of JoHanna McVay. As a female, though, she was a miniature JoHanna. This prophetic ability would bring only sorrow.

"What do you suggest that I do?" JoHanna's voice was cool, and I knew she'd been badly wounded by Aunt Sadie's words.

"Stay here with me. At least until Will comes home. Maybe longer if that's what it takes."

"What about school?"

Sadie snorted. "As if that ever mattered a whit to you. Duncan doesn't go half the time. What she knows she learned from you. The child can read and write and do her numbers. You think that pinheaded teacher can tell Duncan more about the world than you? I wouldn't doubt Cornelia still believes the earth is flat."

I got up and refilled all of our cups to hide my smile. The situation wasn't amusing. Not in the least. But Aunt Sadie's assessment of Cornelia Tucker was perfect. Heavy bosomed and heavy hipped, Cornelia Tucker directed the Methodist choir and the public school in Jexville. She taught, wrote policy, chose curriculum, and said the morning prayer. To make sure no one challenged her right to do all of the above, she even provided the school building.

"Duncan should have a right to go to school." JoHanna was angry. "Will pays taxes. Duncan should be able to attend without being ridiculed and punished."

"If you want Duncan in the school, then you should let your hair grow out, buy some foundation garments and bake some cookies." Aunt Sadie slammed her coffee cup into the saucer, cracking both. "Dog in the manger. That's how you're behaving, JoHanna. Talk about rights. Talk about wanting Duncan to go to school. Well, powder my ass with talcum, 'cause all this pretending is chappin' me raw."

JoHanna stopped, coffee cup in midair. I froze, just getting ready to take my seat. Sadie's coffee spilled through the broken dishes and moved across the table in a wet brown march. I watched it, fascinated, but I was too afraid to make a move for the dishcloth.

"Well." JoHanna spoke the one word as she broke her locked gaze with Sadie and looked at me. "Well, I'll be damned." She started laughing. "I'd like to powder your ass, you old warhorse." She laughed again until she had to lean back in her chair.

Sadie started laughing, too. It was a high-pitched laugh, in complete contrast to her normal brisk tone. More like a rusty hinge that had been broken loose. Then I got started laughing and didn't have time to listen to Sadie or JoHanna. It was as if a dam had broken and our laughter rushed over us, freeing up the pain and fear that had nearly walled us up. Each time we looked at each other we laughed afresh, until I was half lying on the table too weak to sit up and JoHanna had gotten up to get a cloth to blot the spilled coffee.

Sadie stood and put the broken dishes in the garbage. "So it's settled," she said, still chuckling. "You and Duncan will stay with me."

I didn't want that. I wanted JoHanna to come back to Jexville with me. To be there. But it was better for her and Duncan to stay. Floyd and I would go back, each to our private lives.

"It's settled," JoHanna said. She stood up. "But you don't have to go back right away, Mattie. Stay another day or two."

Sadie caught the sudden tension between us. "Excuse me, I'm going to check and see if the wash is dry." She was out the back door with another healthy slam.

I met JoHanna's gaze. "Elikah." The word was like an illness. Something I couldn't cure and couldn't escape.

"I'll send him a note by Floyd."

I wanted to believe that JoHanna could write something magic that would make it okay for me to stay longer. But I was afraid. Elikah wanted things to be just so in his home. His breakfast with the eggs fried so that the whites were done but the yellows runny, his bacon crisp but not dry, his toast the color of hay baking in the field. There were so many things to be done his way, and if I was gone, no one was doing them.

"Mattie, if you go home and have relations with him, the bleeding could start again. It might not stop. You could die."

JoHanna spoke matter-of-factly, but my face flushed with blood. "I won't do that." I swallowed the bile that threatened to rise in my throat.

"I get the impression that Elikah doesn't listen to you when you say no. If that's the case, it could cost you your life."

I looked down at the floor and heard Sadie scuffling at the back door. No doubt her arms were filled with clean sheets and our laundry that she had thoughtfully washed out. She had a kind streak even though she hid it well. "I need to go home." I sounded stubborn.

"Do you want to go home?"

She was pressing me hard, and I looked up at her. Her blue eyes were not unkind, but they were unyielding. "No."

"Good. Then you're staying for another day or two." She went to a drawer and pulled out a tablet and a pen. "I'll write him a note and Floyd can take it to him, all sealed up. I promise, it will do the trick."

"He's going to be furious."

JoHanna sat down at the table and put the pen to the page. "He might be, but he won't dare touch you," she said as she began to write. "He won't dare."

She composed the note in a few moments, without hesitation or blotch. Then she read it to me. "Dear Elikah, I've brought Mattie to my Aunt Sadie for help. She has a high fever and has been talking out of her head. She is afraid someone is going to hurt her, and then she calls out for you. It would do her a world of good if you came up to see her, but I know you have a business to run. Therefore I will take care of her until she gets better. She is really raving, not knowing what she is saying and talking about all sorts of outlandish things. Wherever could she have learned such things? Don't worry, we'll take good care of her. Jo-Hanna McVay."

I looked up to see her expectant gaze. I wasn't so sure this was a good idea. "He's going to think I'm saying that he's been hurting me."

"Yes, but the best part is, I'm writing as if I don't believe it. So he'll just hope you come to your senses before I believe what you're saying. And he won't want you back in Jexville for fear Doc Westfall will have to be called and will hear your wild ranting and raving."

Playing on Elikah's fear was both exhilarating and frightening. He was a man who could shave off half his toe just to make a point.

"How will Floyd get home?" I hadn't agreed to the plan, yet.

"Nell will be up here this evening, or one of the folks around here will go into Jexville for supplies." She gave me a grin. "And to spread the latest gossip."

"Does Floyd want to go back?" I just realized that his story had ended about the time JoHanna and Sadie started yelling at each other.

"He does." JoHanna shook her head slowly. "Floyd loves his job,

Mattie. Making boots is something he does better than anyone else. It gives him pride. He needs to go back."

"They laugh at him."

"Yes, but they hire him to make their fancy boots." She rose from the table. "For Floyd, that's enough." She went to the doorway and looked in at Floyd, who sat silently holding Duncan's hand. When she turned back, her eyes had filled with tears.

"What am I going to do?" she asked. "What if we're back at the beginning, where she can't speak or walk?"

"Don't be silly, JoHanna." I lifted one shoulder in a gesture I didn't know I knew. "The shock of what happened has made her want to sleep. When she wakes up, she'll be just like she was. And each day she'll continue to get better." I went to her and gave her a hug, knowing for the first time in my life what it meant to lie to another for the haven of a moment. I gave her a chit of what she so gallantly gave all around her. Hugging her tight, I knew she needed me to stay, and that gave me strength to stand against Elikah.

Nineteen

I HEARD my name called as if from a distance, then there was the rapid slither of something crawling down my cheek. Bursting up out of sleep, I forced myself awake even as I fought against whatever crept across my face. I was met by Duncan's smile, framed by her fingers which dangled, spider-like, over my nose.

"Get up, sleepyhead," she said. "Sadie has breakfast cooked and she says to tell you to come in your gown."

Holding Duncan in his arms, Floyd was grinning, not at all discomfited by the fact that I was a grown woman in my bed. I saw clearly that he viewed me as nothing more than Duncan and JoHanna's friend. Instead of pulling up the sheet, I reached out and grabbed Duncan's hand. "So, you're awake and speaking to us." I tugged her as if I intended to pull her from Floyd's arms, and she shrieked with delight.

"She woke up hungry." Floyd jiggled her in his arms. "And me, too. Come on, Mattie. Aunt Sadie made biscuits and ham gravy."

I threw back the sheet and padded into the kitchen on bare feet, my hair a nimbus around my head. As I slipped into my place at the table, JoHanna laughed at me.

"Why it's a fairy child, come to dine with us, Duncan."

The relief and joy were palpable in her voice. She pulsed with happiness, sending waves of it around the room. Looking at the table, I saw that Sadie had responded to Duncan's recovery in typical Southern fashion. A platter of ham was centered in the table. Around it were biscuits high as cakes, a bowl of eggs scrambled with rat cheese, a jar of

Sadie's wonderful Mayhaw jelly, butter, and she put a steaming bowl of yellow grits on the table as I watched. I actually had to swallow, my mouth was watering so hard.

"Dig in," she said in her brusque way.

Floyd needed no second invitation, nor Duncan. They fell upon the food with great competition while JoHanna and I shared a glance.

The night before we had finally gone to our separate beds, with Duncan still in a deep sleep. Her color had returned, and her legs twitched, like a dog in a dream chasing a rabbit, and it was that simple reaction that gave JoHanna the strength to hang on and wait. Floyd had moved her from the sofa to JoHanna's bed, where we had all stood around for half an hour, watching. Pecos had taken up his position in the open window, flapping his wings whenever anyone moved too suddenly. Aunt Sadie ignored him, unwilling to argue about the bird in the house when Duncan, in between twitching a little, was lying as still as a corpse. Worried but unable to determine an action that would help, none of us had bothered with supper.

Wherever Duncan had gone, she had come back to us during the night. Sleep had healed her, or at least given her the strength to fight. The skin beneath her eyes held a faintly bruised sheen, and her smile was a bit forced, but her appetite was a delight to behold. She and Floyd were forking slabs of ham and reaching across each other for the biscuits and butter.

Once the two predators had filled their plates, JoHanna, Sadie, and I began to serve ourselves. Words were not necessary. The clatter of knives and forks said it all. The giggles that slipped between Floyd and Duncan were plenty of conversation.

I ate until I could not swallow another bite. I would have been ashamed of myself for my gluttony, but it was a sin shared by all at the table. JoHanna actually groaned as she leaned back and rubbed her stomach. "I'll pay for this meal," she said, laughing.

"What we need is a good swim. To use up the food." Duncan's eyes were determined. "You said we could go to the river today, Mama. And Floyd has to leave soon. And Mattie will have to go in a day or two. We don't have a lot of time to waste."

I couldn't believe that Duncan wanted to go back to the river not twenty-four hours after she'd watched a man drown. The Pascagoula was a beautiful sight, I wouldn't deny that. But she was a force to be reckoned with. One I didn't feel I could match in any way. And certainly Duncan could not, without even the use of her legs. If the current caught her, she'd be a goner.

Hesitation crossed JoHanna's face. "It might be better for us to stay close to home, Duncan."

I knew her love of the river, and her tone of voice surprised me. Maybe it was the talk she was worried about, not the river. Out of sight, out of mind might be what she was thinking.

"You think because Mr. Lassiter died that I'll be afraid of the river." She put her knife and fork across the top of her plate. "It's not like the river is bad. I know that."

Silence fell over the table, an awkward lull that no one but JoHanna could fill. "We'll go to the river, but I can't promise a swim." She placed her hands on the table and stood. "It all depends on the current and how clear the water is. Yesterday it was too muddy. We'll see."

"It'll be clear," Duncan predicted with such certainty that once again all noise in the room ceased.

"If we can't swim, we can fish," Floyd said, amenable to either prospect. Whatever JoHanna ruled was law with him.

I helped with the dishes and then excused myself. The events of the day before had started a small amount of bleeding, something I hadn't told JoHanna. She didn't need additional worries on top of Duncan, and I had gotten Sadie to brew me a cup of her herb tea before I went to bed. But the journey to the river concerned me. Whether Duncan was afraid or not, I was. The yellow waters of the river looked thick as dirt. Able to weight a body down and hold them beneath the surface.

While I dawdled with my toilet, Aunt Sadie packed up a picnic lunch and Floyd dug worms for his fishing. JoHanna bathed and dressed Duncan, and before the sun was too terribly hot, we were on the way.

I insisted on walking, and Duncan convinced Floyd to ride her piggyback. Without the wagon, Pecos would have to make his own rooster way along the sand. He entertained us by running ahead, pecking maniacally around the ground as if he might find diamonds and emeralds, and then running ahead again. JoHanna carried the picnic basket, and I held Duncan's hat for her.

"I'm afraid to let her swim," JoHanna said as we dropped a little behind Duncan and Floyd. "For the first time in my life I'm afraid of the river."

"Yesterday was enough to make anyone afraid."

JoHanna shook her head. "It wasn't Red's drowning. It's Duncan's dreams." In the shade of her hat her eyebrows were still drawn together in a frown. "It's the dream where the man under the water keeps calling her." She shifted the basket to her other hand.

"You think there's going to be another drowning?"

JoHanna's teeth snagged her bottom lip. I was close enough to see the tissue pale beneath the pressure of her bite. "I think it may be Duncan," she whispered.

Her words rocked me as if she'd punched me as hard as she could. "But it's a man, she said." My whisper was so urgent that Floyd hesitated and Duncan's head twisted to look back at us.

"What's wrong?" she asked, her brown gaze riveted to JoHanna. When JoHanna didn't answer instantly, Duncan wiggled around until Floyd shifted her from his back into his arms so that she could see over his shoulder more easily. "What's wrong, Mama?"

JoHanna's teeth released her lip and she smiled, the pale place slowly filling with red color. "Mattie said she didn't want to get in the water today. And I was telling her that we'd sit out with her."

I looked over at Pecos, aware that it was the first lie I'd ever heard Jo-Hanna tell Duncan. It was also one I didn't want to dispute. I was afraid. So it was sort of the truth. The rooster felt my gaze upon him. He turned, darting his head in that bullying way, and hissed at me.

Duncan's laughter made me look at her. She was undisturbed by Jo-Hanna's decision, generous enough to allow me my fear and not make a scene about it. "Pecos is after you, Mattie."

"Pecos is always keeping me in line," I said, smiling at last.

"We can picnic and Floyd will tell us a story." Duncan struggled up over his broad shoulder and then leaned down his back and pinched his behind. He jumped forward and then began to spin in the road, holding her by her legs and swirling her around in a long, slow arc that made her scream with delight.

We were completely alone on the road, free of all the restraints I felt in Jexville. I unbuttoned the top of my dress and let the morning air cool my neck and chest. It occurred to me then that JoHanna had not brought suits. She'd never intended to allow Duncan to swim.

We walked along, Floyd teasing Duncan in his gentle way. JoHanna said no more about her fears for Duncan's safety, but I could see the worry still in her eyes. It seemed to give the blue of her eyes a slightly purple cast, a little bruised.

Instead of going to the supports where we'd gone the day before, Duncan directed us farther north, where the narrow road became more and more crowded with elderberries and huckleberry shrubs. Dogwoods clustered in the woods, their leaves beginning to turn a bright green that signaled their deaths. Fall would be upon us in a few weeks, my favorite of all the seasons.

Most of the wild trees and shrubs were familiar to me, as was the tangle of scuppernong vines that also showed the first hint of fall. Not ten feet from the road, the land became a jungle of smaller trees and shrubs woven and knotted with the thick vines.

Following Duncan's directions, Floyd led us to an opening in the wall of vegetation. It was almost a small tunnel, so low that we had to stoop over to make it through the dense green, especially Floyd. I was so busy watching my feet that when I burst out into the sunshine on the other side, I was dazzled for a moment by the brightness of the sun and the white sand.

I had dreamed of azure water and sugary sand beaches. I had never expected to find half of that dream in Fitler, Mississippi. There was no turquoise water or pounding surf, but the sand was as pure as mountains of sugar or ice. It extended in a long line, disappearing around the curve of the river, a sharp contrast to the yellow-brown water.

"It's beautiful." I reached and picked up a handful of it, letting the pure whiteness of it drift between my fingers.

"Take off my shoes," Duncan cried, jouncing about in Floyd's arms. He slipped her shoes from her feet, dropping them into the sand, then pulled off her socks. With great care he stood her on her feet and held her.

"It feels wonderful." She curled her toes in the sand, digging out a little hollow.

"Wonderful." JoHanna agreed, but she was watching Duncan's feet. Duncan had gained more use and control, even from the day before.

"Go ahead, Mattie. Take off your shoes. You, too, Mama," Duncan ordered. "Then we're going to walk to the edge of the water." She looked up. "All of us."

JoHanna sat down in the sand and eagerly pulled off her shoes, and I followed suit.

"Floyd?"

Duncan looked up at him while he still balanced her on her feet.

"Are we gonna swim?" He looked at JoHanna.

"Let's see Duncan walk first," JoHanna hedged. She stood up and un-fastened her skirt. She must have felt my gaze on her because she looked down at me and laughed as she stepped out of the skirt and left it billowing in the sand. "My slip is perfectly presentable. I advise you to do the same," she said, unbuttoning her blouse.

I didn't move at all as she shook it down her arms and let it fall beside her skirt. The camisole she wore was fringed with white lace and tiny pink embroidered roses, the same lace and roses that edged her slip. Cotton. They fluttered in the breeze from the river.

"Don't be a dunderhead, Mattie. Get comfortable. It's the river!" Duncan's voice teased me, and I looked up to see that she was in her underpants, her own dress left at Floyd's feet. The thought that he might drop his pants sent a flush of heat to my face, and I quickly looked away.

"When it's just me and Mama, we get naked." Duncan was teasing me, but I knew it was true. Floyd was completely unaffected by the idea.

It struck me that perhaps they were all truly innocent and I was the one tainted by sin. Maybe I'd heard too many times how indulging in some harmless pleasure, like feeling the sun and water on my skin, would lead to something else. Beneath my lowered brow, I studied Jo-Hanna as she left me to go to Duncan and scoop her up into the air, twirling her around and around until they both sank into the hot, white sand, laughing. There was no harm in what they did. No harm in the way Floyd smiled down at them, happy at their pleasure. The wrong was in my own sense of shame, that I could not enjoy an innocent action.

My fingers moved to the buttons on my blouse, but there they stopped. I could go no further. A terrible reality struck me so that my hand faltered and fell to my lap like a blasted dove. Duncan, Floyd, even JoHanna, were innocent. I was not. First at the hands of Elikah, and then with my own decision, I had stepped beyond innocence. I knew things that I had never wanted to learn, and I was forever changed. I could not risk dropping my dark skirt. I could not be certain that I had not bled. I was not a carefree mother frolicking with my daughter. My child would never stand in the hot sand beside a river.

JoHanna started toward me, then stopped. I saw my pain was reflected in her eyes as she looked at me. Unable to help me, she spared me and turned to Duncan, holding out her arms. "Can you walk to me?" she asked her.

Duncan's smile turned into a frown of concentration. As Floyd held her steady by her shoulders, she clenched her jaw and stared down at her right foot. "Move," she commanded.

Her leg trembled, but it did not inch forward as it had the day before.

"Move!" Duncan's voice cut into the sounds of the woods, and for an instant the small thrush's moving about in the underbrush ceased. Pecos, pecking away at the edge of the water, lifted his head and froze.

Duncan lifted her face to her mother, and I saw that her eyes held dread. "Mama . . ."

JoHanna smiled. "It's okay, Duncan. You walked yesterday. You'll walk again."

"Mama!" Duncan's eyes darkened, and without any warning she lifted her fist and crashed it into her right thigh. "Damn you!" She lifted her hand again but Floyd was quicker and caught it before she could strike herself. She struggled to free her hand as JoHanna ran across the sand toward her.

"Duncan." JoHanna scooped her into her arms. "Oh, Duncan."

"I thought I could do it. I knew I could." Duncan was heaving with sorrow, but she was not crying. "I hate my legs! I hate them. They won't work anymore, and I'm sick of being carried around like a baby. I want to run! I want to dance!"

I sat in the sand, not knowing what to do. Floyd stood over them, as helpless as I. It was Pecos that sounded the alarm. Feathers bristling, he half ran and half flew from the water's edge back toward the green tunnel where the path to the road lay. I looked up to see a tall, darkly handsome man standing just hidden by the woods.

John Doggett walked across the sand toward JoHanna and Duncan. Ignoring Pecos as if he didn't exist, he gave me a nod and Floyd a smile, but JoHanna was his destination, and he never slowed a step in reaching her. Kneeling down beside her in the sand he looked at Duncan.

"There are some things you can do in the water that will strengthen your legs. The muscles are there. They've been asleep, and yesterday you woke them up rather abruptly."

His voice was strong and clear and soothing. Duncan lifted her angry face to him. Her mouth opened to speak, something angry, I could tell. But nothing came out, and the pain faded from her features.

JoHanna did not turn to face him. She reached down and placed her palm on Duncan's face.

"May I take her into the water and show her some exercises?"

"JoHanna has already done that. We're not getting in the water today." I spoke as I stood. My intent was to go and get JoHanna's clothes and hand them to her, but at the last minute I couldn't bring myself to do that. Jo-Hanna finally looked at me, and surely she saw the consternation in my face, because she shook her head. A gentle gesture, but one I saw clearly.

"What exercises?" Duncan's fury was spent. Her frustration had faded with the hope of help.

"Kicking, lifting. The current can help you do the movement, and at the same time the weight of the water forces the muscles to work." He spoke to Duncan as if she were an adult. "I'm sure Floyd will help me so that your mother feels you're safe enough."

"JoHanna has already said we're not going in the water today." I closed the distance between us, circling around so that I went up on Floyd's side where I could face JoHanna and John Doggett.

"Mattie . . ." JoHanna looked confused. "What's wrong with you?"

I looked at JoHanna, ignoring Doggett as he stared at me, as if he were putting the pieces of me together and I wasn't a very difficult puzzle. He wasn't upset at my harsh tone. It was more as if he were curious about why I was reacting so strongly to a simple offer of help. I spoke to JoHanna. "You said you didn't want to get in the river, remember?" I felt my courage slipping. I wanted to remind her of the dream again, but Duncan was listening.

"We'll hold her tight," Floyd assured me. "I'll never let her slip." He smiled down at Duncan. "Want to do it?"

"Sure." Duncan held out her arms to him.

Floyd lifted her up, slipping out of his shoes as he started walking toward the river. John Doggett stood up and joined them, hopping on first one foot and then the other as he drew his boots off with two long, smooth pulls that tightened the shirt across his back.

"JoHanna!" I spoke her name in an urgent whisper. "You don't know a thing about that man. You've let him take Duncan." I still couldn't believe what was happening. I looked around for the rooster. Even Pecos wasn't doing his job. He'd given his flap of warning and made a run at Doggett, but he'd turned back to pecking at the drying mussel shells in a patch of dark clay.

"No," JoHanna said, her gaze on the three at the lip of yellow water. "I let Floyd take her. John Doggett is just a bit of lagniappe."

"He could be a killer."

JoHanna's smile was bemused, but she didn't look at me. "No, he's just a man with excellent timing and a bit of kindness toward a little girl."

"What makes you think he knows anything about helping her legs?"

JoHanna finally looked at me. "It doesn't matter what he knows or doesn't know, Mattie. What matters is that Duncan believes he can help her. She was about to give up. If she quits trying, she'll never walk again. What he gave her was a new hope. Some bit of magic to keep her going."

I snorted. "Duncan wasn't going to give up. She's just frustrated."

I half expected my persistence would make JoHanna angry, but it didn't. She gave me a look filled with what seemed to be pride. "Little Mattie, the briar." She stood up and started toward the river.

"I'm not thorny." Her words stung me.

She turned back toward me, the sun directly overhead, and I realized for the first time that though I'd seen her shorn head and had grown used to it, John Doggett had not, yet he had not even glanced at her. "A briar has more than thorns, Mattie, but you have a few of those, too. It's a quality of survival." She laughed as she turned back to the river and took those long, long strides until she had joined the group in the waist-deep current.

∽ *Twenty* ∽

I SAT in the sand for half an hour, until the dark folds of my skirt had turned into an oven. Not even pulling the material up enough to reveal my calves was any real measure of relief. For the first twenty minutes I'd watched Doggett like a hawk, but his attention was on Duncan. He held her in the water on his hands and urged her to kick. A time or two he lowered her enough in the water so that she floated on her own. As far as I could tell, he paid no attention to JoHanna, though her slip was now wet and melded to her body.

It gave me a chance to ponder her, though. She was forty-eight, well into middle age. She had not gone to fat as many women had. The mark of her years was in the slight droop of her breasts, the bit of extra flesh at her thighs. If her waist had thickened, it was still small enough, and firm. Her arms, where most women age first, were long and slender. Graceful. She reached and lifted and held and motioned with the fluidness of a young girl. *Vital.* I smiled at the word. JoHanna McVay was vital. Perhaps that was the secret of her youth.

She gave no more attention to Doggett than she did to Floyd, but she laughed with both men while Duncan fought against the weight of the water with a grim determination that I recognized as fear. JoHanna knew her daughter well. Duncan was afraid she'd never walk. That confidence she spouted had been for JoHanna's benefit. And mine. And Will's. And Floyd's. For herself, Duncan feared the worst.

The thought of Will gave me a feeling of uneasiness. What would he say to the spectacle of his wife in the river in her underclothes with two handsome men, one of them definitely virile? But JoHanna was so natural, so completely at ease, surely she was not doing anything that Will would object to. She loved her husband.

In contrast to Doggett, Floyd's childlike nature had never been more obvious. He'd instantly assumed the role of servant to the master, doing whatever Doggett told him to do. And Doggett gave his orders guised in a silky tone, a voice that told Floyd how much he was helping even as it set out the task—to lift Duncan's leg, to support her head. Doggett was a man who'd learned to get his way, from whoever crossed his path.

I felt a ticklish presence at my elbow and looked over to find Pecos standing beside me, his feathers just grazing my arm. His beady gaze was fastened on the scene at the river, and I felt an unexpected kinship with the bird. He didn't like Doggett either.

The hot and glaring sun had given me a headache, and my heavy breakfast had consolidated to lead. I knew that I had to get up, to move, to find some relief from the hot sun and my worries over the scene before me. As I put my hands behind me to push up, JoHanna swung around suddenly in the water and stared at me.

"It's time for lunch," she said, wading out of the water, her slip clinging to her stomach and hips and thighs. Laughing, she ran across the sand to me and lifted her slip. She twisted it in her hands and the cool water cascaded down on top of my head. I wanted to be angry, but the water felt good, and JoHanna's face was alive with joy. She leaned down to me.

"She moved her legs strongly. They're coming back to life." She placed her palm on my forehead, concern darkening her eyes. "You're too hot, Mattie. I shouldn't have left you in the sun." She stood up. "Floyd!"

"I can get up." I shook my head at Floyd as he came out of the water, Duncan in his arms. At least she hadn't called Doggett to assist me.

JoHanna's hand on my arm steadied me, and Pecos served as my guard as I walked across the hot sand back to the beckoning green of the woods. It was amazing. As we stepped beneath the boughs of a huge water oak laced with the sinuous coils of a wild wisteria, the temperature dropped at least ten degrees. The thick foliage blocked the white hot glare of the sun, and I forced my forehead to relax. The relief was instant. My headache began to clear, my stomach to settle.

"Mattie, you could have had a heat stroke sitting out there in that dark skirt, and with no hat." JoHanna's voice was half rebuke at me and half criticism of herself. "I thought we both had more sense."

Why hadn't I gotten up and moved to the shade? I wasn't an idiot. I'd spent my entire life in Mississippi and knew the dangers of the sun. I touched the top of my head and felt the heat. My part would be sunburned, as would my face. The fact was annoying, but not a tragedy. I'd been sunburned before and had the freckles to prove it.

Floyd ran back to the river and retrieved the jug of tea he'd anchored in the deep, cool water, and we sat down to eat again. My breakfast was still with me, but I knew if I didn't make a small effort to eat, JoHanna would get even more upset. I took the sandwich wrapped in a beautiful cloth napkin and the glass of tea Floyd poured and settled back against the trunk of a magnolia grandiflora. When I'd first arrived in Jexville I'd seen the last blooms of the season on such a tree in Jeb Fairley's yard. They were at least a foot wide with a scent of lemony heaven. Jeb had seen my interest and told me that one touch on the vanilla white petals would turn them brown. Delicate. A symbol of Southern womanhood, he'd said. But then Jeb was an old-style gentleman and not one given to beating his wife.

Elikah rose up before me, a specter of fear and longing. I sipped the sweet tea and tasted the bitterness of my marriage, of what I had become because of it. What had gone wrong? As everyone remarked, he was a handsome man. Not like Will. Elikah suffered from a streak of vainness that Will didn't possess, and a big helping of cruelty. I had wanted so much to love him. In the first days of my marriage, I had thought it was possible. I looked down at the sandwich in my hand and slowly began to unwrap it, watching JoHanna through the safety of my eyelashes. I wanted what she and Will had together. I wanted to laugh with my husband, to play and love and talk. To start a child that would be wanted and loved.

"Mattie, are you going to eat?"

Duncan's question snapped my head up, and I found that everyone was staring at me. I unwrapped the sandwich and took a bite, forcing myself to chew and swallow, aided with a swig of tea.

"Why don't you tell us a story, Floyd?" JoHanna said, drawing the attention off me. She'd settled against a sweet gum and was chewing one of the twigs, her own sandwich half eaten in her lap. In truth, we'd all overindulged at breakfast. Only Floyd and Duncan, who was too young to ever completely fill, were hungry. Doggett was eating a ham sandwich at a leisurely pace.

"Maybe John would know a story." Duncan's bright eyes dared him to rise to the challenge. "Floyd's the best storyteller in Chickasaw County. Mattie's pretty good, too."

Doggett's smile was slow. "I know a few stories. But I don't claim to be any storyteller."

How cunning he was. He'd said he was a writer. Of course he could tell a tale. Why was he pretending to such modesty? I shifted my sandwich into my lap and tore off some bread for Pecos. The bird and I were developing a stronger and stronger link. He didn't threaten Doggett, but he wasn't having anything to do with the man.

Like me, he watched.

Doggett turned into my stare, his smile holding but his brow furrowing for a brief few seconds. "I do know a story about the river," he said. "It's been handed down from my people."

"The Indians, the Irish, or the barbarians?" I snapped out the question.

JoHanna stopped chewing and stared at me, but she left Doggett to handle the situation on his own.

"The Indians," he said in that soft, composed voice of his. "The Pascagoulas. They left little behind but their legends and burial mounds. The white man drove them west on the Trail of Tears, those he didn't murder outright."

Even though I was girded against him, his sad anger touched my heart. The story of the Indians wasn't written in any history book. For the Seminoles and Choctaws and Creeks, their entire history was condensed to a paragraph or two on "first settlers of the area," or a single phrase, "filthy Indians." The campaigns to eradicate them were not taught to young children. But I'd seen them first hand in Meridian, which wasn't far from Philadelphia, where the remnants of a tribe had been herded up on a reservation. They were a people without a past or a future. What they'd once been, the white man had eradicated. What they might have been was forbidden by law. Indians did not have a tenth the rights or power of the Negroes.

"It's a story about this river?" Duncan had scooted forward in JoHanna's arms until she sat on her own, only a few feet from the tips of John Doggett's booted feet. I noticed again how handsome the boots were, if only they were brushed and polished. The design sewn into the vamps looked to be some type of leather I'd never seen. It was the only scrap of vanity I could find about the man, and after paying for rare boots, he didn't care for them properly. Perhaps they'd been stolen off a dead body. The satisfaction of that thought made me smile.

"Well, I think Mattie is ready now." Doggett lifted an eyebrow at me, and I felt a chill travel down my arms. I wasn't afraid of him. But he was like a snake. Beautiful, mesmerizing, and very likely deadly. Still, I couldn't deny his charm. He didn't have to touch me for me to feel him.

"Back many years ago when the moon shone only on the red skins of my people, there was a beautiful Indian princess by the name of Anola. Her father was the mighty ruler of the fierce Biloxi tribe."

Doggett was no storyteller. He was a poet. His voice was an instrument that set the melody, his words the lyrics. He pulled and tugged at me, drawing me close to his warmth. I forced myself to look around and saw that he was having the same effect on everyone there. Even Pecos seemed lulled into a stupor.

"It happened that Anola was promised in marriage to a young warrior of her tribe, a man she did not love, but as the daughter of the chief, she knew her duties. So it was that she was sent to the easternmost portion of the Biloxis' territory to learn the ways of a wife and begin the beading of her wedding skins."

"Did she have to soften the skins by gnawing on them?" Duncan's question was spoken with the utmost sincerity and total lack of judgment.

"Anola was a princess. Such duties did not befall her." Doggett smiled as he answered, amused.

"Where did she get the beads?" Duncan asked.

"Of course there weren't beads like you have today." Doggett picked up a stick and began to draw in the dirt. "They used shells of a beautiful color, or they were painted with natural dyes. And precious and semi-precious stones, feathers, carved and painted wood. The Indians were quite resourceful."

"The artwork I've seen, bits of jewelry and pottery, is primitive but very beautiful," JoHanna joined in. "Some of the natural dyes are remarkably intense."

Doggett's gaze lingered on her a fraction of a second too long. Then he started again. "For the bride, the wedding skins were bleached by natural herbs again and again until they were a light buff color and the beadwork would be more noticeable. But Anola didn't get far into her wedding costume before fate offered her another path. She had gone out into the woods to hunt for special items to add to her dress. It was a warm fall day, and she decided to venture down to the edge of the Pascagoula River. She'd been warned not to go close to the water. The current was treacherous, and also there were parties of Pascagoulas wandering along the banks. The river marked the boundaries between the two tribes, and there were hostile feelings between the two."

He paused as he looked at JoHanna. "As a woman, Anola was not able to understand how one tribe could hate another when they didn't even know each other. She did not believe that another Indian, no matter what tribe he belonged to, would hurt a harmless maiden as she searched for the bounty of the earth to adorn her wedding dress."

"They killed her!" Duncan was wide-eyed with horror, as was Floyd, who'd edged up to sit close beside her.

"No, they didn't kill her." Doggett dispelled that idea immediately. "Anola was digging up a mussel shell from the thick dark clay with a stick when she heard laughter carried down the water. Sound travels easily on water, especially a river with a good current. She knew the man laughing was not near, but she could not resist seeing who was making such bold sounds in the woods without fear of being heard. Abandoning the many items she'd gathered on the banks of the river, she crept back into the woods and started upstream.

"What she saw would change her life forever. A Pascagoula warrior was bathing in the river, splashing and laughing at his own pleasure. Even as Anola hid in the bushes, the young warrior stood up, water sliding down his gleaming body, and came toward her.

"Legend has it that Anola rose from her hiding place at the sight of him. He saw her, and they stood staring at each other for a long time, while all the creatures of the forest stilled at the thing that was happening before them. Anola and Altama fell instantly in love. The beautiful young maiden never went back to reclaim her treasures on the banks of the river or her wedding gown or her intended groom. She walked straight into the river and swam across with Altama, the prince of the Pascagoula tribe."

Doggett's voice lowered, and he looked down at the tips of his boots pointed into the air. Almost self-consciously, he reached and brushed at the top of them as if he'd suddenly noticed they were dusty.

"I didn't expect a love story." JoHanna's comment was wry, but her lips were slightly parted and moist. She'd been as affected by the tale as the rest of us.

"Did they live happily ever after?" Floyd asked.

"No, they didn't." Doggett's answer took us all by surprise. "I wish I could say they did. I hadn't really thought of it before, but not even in legend do the Indians have happy endings. The love between the beautiful Anola and her warrior prince Altama ended in a war." He looked down at the meaningless designs he'd drawn in the dirt.

"Did Altama and the Pascagoulas win?" Duncan asked, prodding him for more detail.

Doggett sighed, as if the events he recounted had just happened in the past week. "It was the night of the full moon when the Biloxis attacked the Pascagoula, intending to kill them or take them as slaves."

"The Indians had slaves?" Duncan was impressed.

"Slavery is an ancient practice," JoHanna answered her and then lifted a finger to her lips so that Doggett could finish the story.

"Anola climbed to the highest bluff of the river. She'd selected the spot so that the moon silhouetted her, so that the Biloxis would know her shape. She called out to her father, begging him to stop the bloodshed. She told him that she had gone with Altama of her own free will and that she loved him more than life. She pleaded with him, as the daughter of his heart, to call a truce and for both tribes to live in peace. But her father paid her no heed. As the bride of Altama, she was no longer a Biloxi."

"How could he be so cruel?" Duncan was crying.

"The Pascagoulas were a gentler tribe, and they had been decimated by high fevers and sickness. Worse than death, though, they feared slavery. It was Anola who found the solution to their dilemma. Calling the tribe around her, she led them to the edge of the water where the moon silvered a path to the land of the spirits. Her sweet voice, thickened by tears, directed them as they all joined hands, forming one straight line down a sand bar much like the one in front of us. Fearing death less than slavery, they walked into the water of the river, singing their death chant as they drowned. On still nights, when the moon is full and the color of blood, you can hear their voices beneath the water."

Wind rattled through the wild wisteria above me, sending down a sudden scattering of leaves. A young female cardinal, her reddish gray feathers less obvious than her mate, perched on a limb beside Doggett and eyed Pecos. She gave two long trills that ended on high notes, as if she questioned the rooster about the company he kept.

"Is that a true story?" Duncan's voice held hope that it was and hope that it wasn't.

"It's a legend of my people. It happened long before I was born, but I can tell you that it's true about the singing. That's why the river is called the Singing River."

"You've heard it?" Floyd asked.

"Yes, on two occasions. Both in the light of the Hunter's Moon."

Duncan reached over and touched his shin. "Will you take us to hear it, this October, on the next full moon?"

Doggett looked beyond her at JoHanna, waiting to see her response to the request. JoHanna's nod was slight, but it was there.

"Of course. I'd be delighted, but you have to promise me that by then you'll be walking. I want us to wade into the water a bit, so we can feel the vibration of the voices against our skin."

I opened my mouth to protest, but stopped. I had no right to object, but I could not believe JoHanna was going along with such foolishness. Duncan walking into the river in October at night. It was insane. What if she wasn't walking by then? It was wrong to put such pressure on the child.

"I'll be walking by then, don't you think?" Duncan's faith was shining in her eyes. "You'll help me, won't you, John?"

"As much as you need me," he answered.

"Can we work on my legs some more in the river?"

Once again Doggett waited for JoHanna's nod. "Certainly, but not too much longer. It has to go a bit at a time. Waking up a muscle is like waking up a person. You don't want to do it fast and startle her."

Duncan laughed, and Floyd stood without being told to carry her back to the water. JoHanna rose and I did, too.

"I think I'm going to go back and help Aunt Sadie with some herbs. She said she'd show me some of the things she uses to stop bleeding. I'd really like to learn."

JoHanna wasn't fooled by my earnest little speech, but she didn't press me.

"It's not much fun to sit in the hot sand." Her glance traveled down to my skirt. "Are you bleeding?"

"I don't think so." I shook my head. "I just can't be certain. I'm perfectly fine, but I've had enough of the sun. And I do want to learn what Sadie is willing to teach me."

"She's virtually a witch." JoHanna handed me her hat. "Wear that home. The top of your head is already glowing, even here in the shade."

"What about . . ."

"Believe it or not, the way my hair is cut it deflects the sun."

It was the craziest thing I'd ever heard, and it made me laugh.

"Go on, now. Just take your time and be careful. You want me to walk you back?"

"And leave Duncan in the hands of John Doggett and Floyd? Not on your life."

She laughed again and waved me toward the tunnel of green even as she turned back to the river and the two men standing waist-deep, their boots and shoes scattered like Hansel and Gretel's bread crumbs as a trail back the way they'd come. Duncan's squall of mock horror was the final straw. JoHanna was moving away from me toward her child even before she knew it. She turned back, still walking away. "Be careful, Mattie. And don't worry. Everything is fine here. Duncan is getting better."

I waved, saying nothing, and turned toward the road.

I took my time, examining strange leaves and bushes, plucking several things I wanted Aunt Sadie to name. Maybe I'd even bring her something she needed. I took only the unusual, sometimes pulling up leaf, flower, root and all. As I grew more absorbed in my collecting, I felt the anxiety slip away from me. Perhaps John Doggett was exactly what he said, a writer who was part Indian and loved the area and had simply come to write about it. Maybe it was my own attraction to him that I felt, and not JoHanna's. Although he frightened me for reasons I couldn't fathom, I was still honest enough with myself to admit that he fascinated me. And excited me.

In truth, he tempted me, offering me some indefinable something that seemed both delicious and dangerous all at once. Forbidden. And again I thought of the snake, and of Adam and Eve.

As it was, my thoughts were already a bit sinister when he stepped out of the woods not five feet in front of me.

I didn't scream, but I bit the inside of my mouth in my efforts not to do so. "What do you want?" The question was rudely put.

"I didn't mean to frighten you, Mattie. I took a shortcut through the woods to catch you before you got too far along."

"Where's JoHanna and Duncan?"

"In the river with Floyd. Waiting for me."

"Then why are you here?"

"A point of curiosity. Why don't you like me? Or should I say why do you dislike me so strongly? I've done nothing to harm you."

I thought perhaps he knew already and was merely taunting me, but his dark eyes were troubled.

"I'd like to be your friend."

His directness forced me to look down. I could not meet him with openness.

"You think I'll do something to harm JoHanna, don't you?"

That brought my head up, and my gaze locked with his. "Yes."

"I'd lie if I said I wasn't drawn to her."

There it was, between us. "She's married to Will, and she loves him." I felt as if I couldn't get enough air to make my sentences complete. "They love each other. Don't mess with them, Doggett. Leave them in peace."

He didn't mock me, as I expected. "I mean her no harm."

"And Will? Can you say the same of him?"

His smile was not mocking, but sad. "He has a champion in you, so he must be a good man. I can see that you're a little bit in love with him yourself."

"I'd never—"

He shook his head slowly, stopping my denial before it could be spoken. "You're a noble young woman, Mattie. I don't question that at all. And far too young to be married to Elikah Mills."

His use of Elikah's name was like a sharp slap. "What do you know of Elikah?"

"Enough." He didn't look away from me.

I remembered then that he'd said he heard the singing of the drowned Indians twice, both on the night of the Hunter's Moon. So he'd been in Fitler, or somewhere along the river, for at least two years. Had he been in Jexville? Had Elikah sent him to find me? I opened my mouth to find air, I was suffocating.

His hands grabbed my arms. "Steady," he said, watching me. "Elikah is some kind of man that the mention of his name terrifies his new bride."

There was scorn in his voice, and I knew he hadn't been sent to spy on me or bring me home.

"How do you know my husband?"

His dark gaze was shadowed by what looked like pity. "Do you want the truth?"

I shook off his hands. "Of course I want the truth."

"I know Elikah Mills by reputation. He has one in some of the bigger towns."

A wave of shame smashed over me, but I stood my ground, refusing to look away from him. I knew what reputation Elikah must have been building.

"I only meant to say that I see goodness in you. And innocence. I regret that you married Elikah, because I see little goodness in him."

As much as I wanted to defend my husband, I could not. I swallowed. "I didn't choose my husband, but I have chosen my friends. Whatever you're thinking, don't do anything that makes trouble for JoHanna or Duncan." I swung away from him and started down the sandy road back to Fitler. Just above the tops of the big oaks in the distance I could see the blackened scaffolding of some of the taller buildings.

I felt his gaze on my back as I hurried along, but he didn't call out to me and I didn't turn around until I had rounded a curve. Sneaking back, I peeked around a big live oak and found the roadway empty.

He'd undoubtedly stepped back into the woods, taking some shortcut that I didn't know. But I had the most disturbing sensation that he'd completely disappeared.

Twenty-one

FROM the flowers, roots, and leaves that I'd gathered, Aunt Sadie put five out to dry. One small plant, less than a foot tall with dull yellow trumpet flowers that opened on deep purple throats, she continued to examine. I'd picked it more for its flower than anything, but Aunt Sadie held it in her palm as if it weighed at least five pounds.

"What is it?" I reached to touch it, but she lowered her hand.

"Folks call it several things. Where'd you find it?"

Intrigued by what once had been a white picket fence, I had wandered off the road toward an old homesite. "In a small cemetery. Eckhart was the name on the tombstones." I felt like I was confessing to trespassing. "The place had been abandoned a long time. Nothing left but a chimney and some old boards."

"I know the place." Aunt Sadie went to the stove and turned on the kettle, the plant still in her hand. "Was it growing by the road?"

"I was picking those spider lilies around a crepe myrtle and I saw the old headstones. When I went over to look, the flowers caught my eye. They're unusual."

"Were there more?"

"Just around one grave. Lillith Eckhart. She died in 1885. She wasn't all that old either. She was born during the war."

Sadie lifted her hand and stared at the plant. "The War Between the States. Lillith was close to my age, we both came to Fitler about the same time. She was a beautiful young woman when I knew her." She pinched a leaf and sniffed it, backing off it quickly. "Smells like tobacco."

I waited for her to continue, but she didn't. "What kind of plant is it?"

"Folks call it Jupiter bean, or devil's eye."

"Is it a good plant?"

"Yes. It can be very soothing to a person in an agitated state."

"Like chamomile tea." Aunt Sadie had given me more than one cup of that, and it did make me relax.

"Yes." She went out to the porch and put the plant down in a shady corner.

"Is it the root or the leaves?" I asked her. She'd been telling me how different plants had different parts that were useful.

"Both of those, and in a few weeks it'll go to seed. Those are good to use, too. But there isn't a great need for devil's eye when there's chamomile tea." She put her hand on the kettle just as it started to whistle. "How about some tea and a nap for you? That sun has blistered your skin and drained your energy. You look done in, young-un."

I was exhausted. The sun, the anxiety of John Doggett's presence, then the coolness of the house, the safety that I felt in Aunt Sadie's presence, all had combined to sap my energy. I had to admit that I wasn't as strong as I normally was. "I think I'd like a nap if you don't want me to help you with the plants."

"Take your rest while Duncan and that rooster are out of the house. Land's sake, why I ever let that fowl in my home I'll never know. Filthy creature."

I smiled at the emotion in her voice. I was the only one she could speak to about Pecos. Duncan, Floyd, and JoHanna defended the bird's right to be indoors. Even I had kindlier feelings toward him since he'd not taken to Doggett.

The thought of Doggett made me frown, something that Aunt Sadie didn't miss.

"Anything wrong?"

"That man, John Doggett, he says he's a writer. Is it true?"

"I'd heard he was living somewhere up on the Chickasawhay and working on some kind of history story. Up until yesterday I thought he'd left the area, though."

"Then he's been here a good while?"

"He comes and goes. Just when folks get used to him being around, he's gone. I've heard he's part Indian."

"He is, or so he claims."

Aunt Sadie's interest was piqued. "Up until he stood in the yard yesterday, I was beginning to think he was a ghost. There's been talk, but hardly anyone actually claimed to have laid eyes on him. He's a handsome devil."

He was handsome, but I didn't want to admit it. "He's different." I shrugged one shoulder and accepted the cup of chamomile tea she'd steeped for me. The honey jar was sticky as I moved it beside my cup. "He's down at the river with Duncan and JoHanna and Floyd." I glanced up to see what reaction that drew. None, to my disappointment. I might have said Nell Anderson was there.

Aunt Sadie wrang out a dishcloth to wipe down the stove top. "I hope JoHanna finds out about him. Satisfy my curiosity. He comes and goes, but he mostly keeps to himself." She chuckled softly. "I like that in a person. Shows they can get along with themselves. Lots of people can't do that."

"Or else they have something to hide."

Aunt Sadie's smile faded. "What is it, Mattie?"

I held the hot tea, glad for the feel of the thick cup in my hand. "I think he likes JoHanna."

She didn't register any reaction, but she pulled out a chair and sat down on the edge of it. "Are they up on the sandbar?"

I nodded. "They're working on Duncan's legs. Mr. Doggett said she'd be able to walk by the full moon in October. I hope she isn't disappointed."

Sadie dried her hands on her apron, stood, then reached around behind her to untie it. She picked up JoHanna's hat that I'd put on the chair beside me.

"I think I'd better take this up to her. She's getting a little too old to have the sun beating down on her face."

"Want me to go with you?"

She shook her head. "No, you just take a nap. I need to look for some sassafras root, and there's a patch not far from the sandbar. I can kill two birds with one stone." She plopped the hat on her head and started toward the front door, turning back with a sly smile and a little lift of her chin. "When I was a young woman I loved my hats. I suppose JoHanna takes after me in that regard. Even now, I put on a hat and I think I can still strut." She closed the door behind her, softly, as she left the house.

I was still smiling as I finished my tea and unbuttoned my blouse and skirt. The heavy white sheets of my bed looked awfully inviting.

I awoke to the wonderful smell of something baking and the buzz of conversation in the kitchen. Duncan's laughter swung, bell-like, as if the wind blew it to me in soft waves. Stretching, I lay in bed and listened, a shameless eavesdropper on the McVay clan. Their lively talk soothed me, reminding me of the rare mornings when I overslept and Mama and Callie and Lena Rae got in the kitchen to get all the other children up and fed. My stomach grumbled loudly at the aroma of peanut butter cookies.

"I'll be walking in two weeks," Duncan promised. "John said the muscles were ready to wake up."

"You'll walk when you're ready, but you'll walk," JoHanna answered her.

"It's a shame John wouldn't come home with us for supper," Aunt Sadie answered.

"It's a shame Floyd had to go back," Duncan responded, a note of wistfulness in her voice.

I got up then, the pleasure of lingering sleep slapped from me by Sadie's comment. She had invited John Doggett to eat with us. The man had worked his charm on her as surely as he had everyone else. Except me and Pecos.

My hair was a jumble, but the top of my head was too sore to allow a brushing, so I smoothed down the wild hairs as best I could and went into the kitchen.

"Mattie." JoHanna came to me and took my hands. There was a smudge of cookie dough on her left cheek. "How are you?"

"Fine." I hid my concerns. "The sleep did me a world of good. Something smells wonderful."

"I was able to walk in the river." Duncan claimed my attention as she sat at the table, a half-empty saucer of cookies in front of her. Pecos sat beneath the table, accepting the cookie crumbs she offered him out of her hand.

"How long have you been back?" I felt as if weeks had elapsed.

"About an hour. Long enough to bake cookies, most of which Dun-

can has consumed. Or at least the part she hasn't given that evil bird."
Aunt Sadie looked over her glasses at Duncan to let her know she wasn't
getting away with feeding Pecos under the table.

"I walked in the river." Duncan demanded a response.

"You walked?"

"John said the water held me up, but that with practice and *hard
work*, I'd be able to walk on the land. He said I was amphibious!" She
slapped the table lightly with her palms and laughed. "Like a frog.
They're better in the water than on land."

The shock must have shown clearly on my face, because JoHanna put
her arm around my shoulders and took me onto the small screen porch
off the kitchen where Sadie had hung my plants to dry.

"Mattie—"

"What if she doesn't walk!" I turned on her. "You're letting that man
set her up for bitter disappointment."

"Mattie—"

"How can you do this, JoHanna? You don't know a thing about
him."

"Mattie—"

"What would Will say?"

"Mattie!" Her voice cracked out, pulling me up short. I looked at her
and found that I was panting.

"Duncan's legs are much better. She walked yesterday; today she
made even more progress. John isn't leading her on. She'll walk in two
weeks. I'm positive."

"Just because he says it, how can you be so sure?" My voice was soft.

"She'll walk in two weeks." She reached up and brushed a tendril of
my unruly hair from the corner of my mouth. "I'm the one who said two
weeks. John only repeated it. He didn't make it up."

That took the wind out of my sails, and I shifted my weight so that I
was standing a little further away from her. "I'm sorry. I shouldn't have
said those things."

"You don't care for John, and you don't want to see Duncan hurt. It's
okay, Mattie."

"Floyd has gone home?"

"He caught a ride with Nell."

"I think maybe I should have gone with them." I hated myself as I
said those words, but somehow John Doggett had squeezed me out of

Fitler. His presence had changed everything. The only place for me to go was back to Jexville. The longer I put it off, the harder it was going to be to go back.

"You don't ever have to go there."

She could say that, but it wasn't true. I had to go back. Either to finish what I'd started or to continue on. "If I were you, I wouldn't have to go back. But I'm not you." I couldn't look at her. "I don't feel I have another choice."

She put her arms around me and hugged me, holding me against her body warmed by the oven. "Oh, Mattie. You have to do what *you* feel is right. If it's going back, then that's what you have to do. Just promise me if that man tries to harm you in any way, you'll call me."

I wanted to say that I'd call Will, but I crushed the impulse I had to hurt her, not understanding it even as I knew it was wrong. "If he acts mean, I'll leave again," I promised her.

"Jeb is coming up here tomorrow to help search for Red Lassiter's body. I'm sure he won't mind giving you a ride back." JoHanna sighed. "I wish we could all stay up here forever."

"Why don't you move up here?" Will was gone a lot, but he could drive from Fitler as well as Jexville. "Or y'all could move to Natchez or New Orleans or New York, for that matter." A lot of Will's business was big city clients. It actually made more sense for them to live in a city, and JoHanna would be far happier in a place with theater and dance and libraries and other free-thinking women.

She watched my thought processes in my eyes, her smile widening. "I live in Jexville, contrary to Aunt Sadie's caustic statements, because of the schools, for Duncan. In case you haven't noticed, there aren't any other children in Fitler. And Will's brother has a place over on Kali Oka, there's that family tie." She shook her head. "And it's part Dunagan stubbornness. My parents came here to make their fortunes. I guess I don't want to leave this area because some narrow, righteous people make me uncomfortable. And last but not least, there's Aunt Sadie. She's getting on up there and I don't want to leave her alone. Now she doesn't want me underfoot all the time, but I need to be close enough if she needs me."

What could I say to all of that? At least she didn't stay out of fear.

"Whatever you decide today, there's always tomorrow. If you go back to Jexville, you can leave in a week, or a month. Or a year."

I felt the pressure of my unexpected tears, hot and scalding behind my eyes. "Unless I have a child." I swallowed. "How can it be that the one thing I could love with all of my heart is the thing that might destroy me?"

JoHanna caught my shoulders in her hands and held me tight. "A child is always that for a woman, Mattie. Always the risk of potential destruction, if you love them enough. When you're older and stronger, you might not feel it's such a risk. Or you might not care."

Looking at her kind face, I knew then that I would never have a child. It was as sure as knowing that I would grow no taller or that my hair would never be blond like Callie's. It was a physical fact. One that no amount of grieving or remorse could change. My hands crossed instinctively over my stomach. JoHanna saw the reflex, but she didn't understand what it meant to me.

"Are you hurting?"

"No." I dropped my hands to my sides. "No, I'm fine." But I knew that something inside me had died. Perhaps not an organ or tissue, but something necessary to bring forth new life. Whether the doctor's instruments or my own fear had killed it didn't matter.

"Mattie, are you sure?" JoHanna's gaze scanned my face, then dropped down to my body. "You're not bleeding?"

"No, really." I lifted my shoulders. "I'll just have to make certain that I don't get pregnant again."

"And how will you do that?"

There was a hint of teasing in her question. If I went home, I was not foolish enough to think that Elikah would not expect me to fulfill my duties as a wife. I focused on a worn place in the floor, feeling the heat of my sunburn more intensely than before.

"There are ways to prevent pregnancy." JoHanna had taken pity on me and stopped teasing.

"Elikah wouldn't wear one of those." He'd expounded too many times on the pleasures of the "natural" feel of a woman. Besides, he wouldn't do anything that marred the picture of perfect manhood he felt he presented.

"There's something else. You put it up inside you and take it out when you're finished."

"Inside me?" I looked at her at last, half repulsed by what she said and half expecting to see the glint of the devil in her blue eyes. But she wasn't teasing.

"Contrary to popular belief, Mattie, your fingers won't fall off and you won't grow horns if you touch yourself."

I couldn't imagine. "What is it?"

"It's like a sponge. It stops the sperm from getting up inside you. A blockade, if you will."

Now she was grinning again, and the image she'd created did have some amusement value.

"How do you get it out once you've put it in?"

"You take it out yourself. It'll take some practice, but you can learn to do it. And the best thing is that Elikah won't even know what you're doing."

"It'll work?"

JoHanna wiped the cookie dough from her face. "Nothing is perfect, but it works pretty well."

I was still having trouble imagining that I could do this, but when I thought of the doctor in Mobile and what I had done there, I knew I could manage a bit of sponge.

"Where can I get this?"

"Doc Westfall."

My head snapped up. "I can't ask him for this. It would humiliate Elikah. No one can know!" The safety she'd offered me was suddenly snatched away, and panic flooded me.

"Doc won't tell Elikah. Besides, he suspects you've had a miscarriage. He'll think you want time to heal before you try again. You can even tell him that."

I hardly dared to believe her. "He won't talk to Elikah about this? Those men all talk."

JoHanna's smile reassured me. "Doc won't talk. Especially not to Elikah."

I nodded. "I can do this." I took a deep breath. "I can."

"You can." She walked over to the line where Aunt Sadie had hung my plants to dry. "Comfrey," she said. "I'm sure Sadie was pleased to get this."

There was no sign of the strange flower I'd found. I suspected she'd thrown it away but didn't want to hurt my feelings. For all her gruffness, Sadie had a tender heart.

"Mama!" Duncan's happy cry pulled JoHanna back toward the kitchen. "Pecos pecked Aunt Sadie on the butt!" She laughed, and there was the sound of Sadie's angry tirade at the bird.

"I'll get you, you filthy creature!"

"Mama!" Duncan's voice held alarm.

We ran into the kitchen to find Sadie chasing the bird around and around the kitchen table with a broom.

"Save Pecos!" Duncan was laughing, but there was worry on her face.

"You'd better get out of my house, you claw-footed Satan!" Sadie gave a mighty swing that toppled a chair over.

"Sadie!" JoHanna jumped into the brawl, going for her aunt rather than the chicken.

"Run, Pecos! Run!" Duncan pounded the table and shouted encouragement at the rooster.

Pecos made a dead run for me, and since he'd sided with me against John Doggett, I ran to the back door and held it open. Pecos made a clean getaway, flapping into the backyard, where he stopped, cocked his head at Aunt Sadie, who was panting in the doorway, broom held at the ready.

"I'm going to cook that bird," Sadie vowed. "With tender dumplings."

Pecos lifted his wings and shook them at her, lowering his head and giving a mean chicken squawk.

"You devil!" Sadie shook the broom at him. "Your days are numbered."

JoHanna was trying not to laugh, and even I couldn't help grinning.

"More like Pecos is going to give you a stroke," JoHanna said, putting a gentle hand on the broom handle. "Come on back in the kitchen and I'll pour us all a little of that scuppernong wine you keep hidden under the sink."

Sadie swiveled on JoHanna. "He's pushed me too hard, JoHanna. I bent over the oven to get the cookies out, and that brown bastard pecked me."

JoHanna's laughter spilled out. "Tough as your old butt is, I doubt he did any damage. Now let's go have a drink."

ᘒ *Twenty-two* ᘒ

JOHANNA poured me a cup of coffee and gave me a promise that it would help the headache that pounded behind my eyes. I had discovered, belatedly, that Aunt Sadie's scuppernong wine carried a healthy afterkick. We had all three gotten a little tipsy, laughing and cranking up the gramophone in the living room. Aunt Sadie had taught me to waltz, while JoHanna gave me instruction in the livelier steps of the Charleston. Duncan, happy in the belief that she would soon be dancing herself, shouted instructions and encouragement from the sidelines. Exhausted from the pleasure of it all, I had tumbled into bed, tingling with silliness and joy, unaware that misery hovered over my pillow and waited for the dawn.

"It's only a hangover," JoHanna said. "It'll pass."

I glared at her, wondering how she could not be suffering. She'd had as much to drink as I had. Maybe more.

"Practice," she answered, reading the look on my face. "I'm also twenty pounds heavier than you. Once you get some meat on your bones, you'll be able to drink more and suffer less." She chuckled.

Aunt Sadie came into the room perkier than I'd ever seen her. She was wearing a beautiful lavender dress that shimmered in the soft white morning light. Behind her glasses her eyes had been touched with something to darken the lashes, and there was a tint of subtle pink on her lips. Instead of laying her low, the wine seemed to have given her new life, new blood.

"Where's Duncan?" she asked.

"Asleep." JoHanna smiled. "She wore herself out in the river, and then watching us dance last night. She'll sleep another hour or two."

Sadie nodded, bringing her cup of coffee to the table with us. "That's a good thing. They'll be dragging the river today for Red's body. When I went to check the mail yesterday, Karl said they were bringing men over from Jexville and Leakesville. It would be just as well if Duncan didn't see that."

"I agree, but . . ." JoHanna's eyes were troubled. "We're going to have to make an appearance at the river, though. To stop the gossip. If we hole up here in the house, it's only going to make it worse when we do go out."

Aunt Sadie drummed her fingers on the table. "Wouldn't that be better done some place other than the river, especially when they're dragging for a body? No telling what they might pull up, or how it's going to look."

"The river's the place to take a stand. We won't stay long enough for Duncan to see anything. We just have to put in an appearance and let folks know we're not hiding. If they've got something to say, I want them to know I'm not afraid to face them. And Duncan's not afraid either. We'll get down there early, just as they're getting started, and then come right on home." JoHanna looked down into her coffee cup as she finished.

She wasn't afraid. Not for herself. But she was afraid for Duncan, and she couldn't hide it from me. I could only hope she was a good enough actress to hide it from the men she was going to confront. If they sensed any weakness in her . . . I could imagine the pleasure Elikah would take in recounting even the smallest sign of JoHanna's fear. Elikah was not alone in his desire to see her brought low—no matter what the occasion.

"Jeb will be down there." Sadie got up to put another stick of wood in the stove. "French toast," she said, letting us know the menu. "Duncan asked for it last night."

My stomach roiled at the thought of food, but I was also hungry. The conflicting needs made my head pound worse.

"Starches will help soak up the alcohol. If you can eat it'll make you feel better." JoHanna still had a smile for my condition, as worried as she was about Duncan.

Sadie got up and began to crack eggs in a bowl. "I'm going to get started in here. I've got things to do this morning."

Standing, JoHanna took the bowl from her aunt. "I'm quite capable of making French toast for Duncan, when she wakes up. And you should go tend to your business." She arched an eyebrow. "Even if it is monkey business."

Sadie slapped JoHanna lightly on the arm. "I'm too old to be teased."

"You're never too old, Sadie. Never." She leaned over and kissed her aunt's cheek, then shooed her out of the kitchen. "Stay out of here, now, or I'm going to have to sic Pecos on you."

Sadie's voice came back to us from her bedroom. "If that damn bird puts one gnarly little claw in my house, he's going to find himself swimming in a pot of dumplings."

Duncan's voice joined the fray. "Aunt Sadie, maybe if you kiss Pecos he'll turn into Prince Charming." After the laughter, she continued. "Mama, I'm starving. Will you come get me?"

I signaled JoHanna that I could manage Duncan. I couldn't carry her with the effortless strength of Floyd nor with the sureness of practice that JoHanna showed, but I could get her fifteen yards from the bed to the kitchen table, even if I had to stop and rest. I rose too suddenly and found that the slightest effort set my head to pounding like Abe Woodcock was in there standing at his anvil and pounding on a hot horseshoe. I swear, my ears were ringing with the blows, but I went to Duncan's room.

"You look sick." Duncan greeted me with a grin.

"Headache."

"Hangover," she said knowingly. "You overindulged." She laughed at my condition.

"It isn't exactly funny."

"No, it isn't." Her voice had lost its teasing edge. "I had the strangest dream." She held out her arms to put around my neck, clasping me close to her. I froze bending over the bed.

"What kind of dream?"

"It was awful." Her voice was a rich contrast to her words. She sounded completely at ease, unafraid.

I lifted her and started toward the kitchen.

"I'll tell you and Mama at the same time. It gets tiring having to repeat something two or three times."

"Right." I jiggled her. "You love the attention."

I put her in her seat just as JoHanna placed two batter-soaked pieces of bread in the sizzling bacon grease on the stove.

"I dreamed there was a terrible storm. The wind blew so hard it tumbled houses down and flung trees everywhere."

Duncan's words seemed to stop time. There was only the bread frying in the grease, the occasional pop and sputter. JoHanna didn't move, and I was caught up in Duncan's words.

JoHanna recovered first, flipping the bread expertly. "At least no one drowned."

"Oh, but they did. Dozens of people." Duncan leaned forward. "It was a horrid tragedy. Bodies everywhere, some even up in trees."

"Duncan!" JoHanna turned to her, her voice sharp.

Duncan's face, so lively and eager, fell into hurt. Tears welled in her eyes, and she blinked against them.

JoHanna dropped the spatula into the pan and went to her daughter. "I'm sorry. It's just that you sounded so . . . excited, about death."

Still fighting tears, Duncan looked up at her mother. "It was exciting." She swallowed. "Am I evil?"

JoHanna pulled her child to her breast and held her. I got up and rescued the toast from the pan, stacking it on a plate before battering two more pieces and putting them into the pan. Now the sizzle of the grease was comforting, blending as it did with the sound of Duncan's soft tears.

"Oh, baby, you're not evil."

"You acted like I was." Duncan's voice was muffled by her hurt and JoHanna's chest.

"I didn't mean to. It's just that I'm a little on edge about your dreams."

"I don't ask for them to come."

"I know." JoHanna rocked her gently. "I know." She drew back, wiping Duncan's eyes with the front of her blouse. "Now tell us the dream while we have breakfast. Thank goodness for Mattie or the toast would be burned."

I put a plate before each of them and put more bread in the pan for me. I was hungry, yet I didn't want to eat. But I wanted to get over the hangover more than I wanted to mollycoddle my stomach. And I wanted to hear Duncan's dream.

"It wasn't as clear as the one about Red Lassiter." Duncan took the pitcher of syrup JoHanna handed her and poured it over her stack of toast. "It was more confused. Like parts of it had been jumbled up and I couldn't tell what came first. And I didn't know a single dead person."

"That's comforting." JoHanna's voice was crisp, but her hand shook as she took the syrup. "Then perhaps it wasn't Jexville or Fitler where the dream took place."

A wad of toast in her jaw, Duncan stopped chewing. "That may be it," she said, licking a dribble of syrup from her lips. "I didn't recognize anything. And it was sort of like . . . flying. I could see things but they moved by so fast I couldn't really remember them. If I ever knew where they were to begin with."

"Things?" JoHanna waited, her plate untouched.

"Trees blown over. Buildings knocked down." Duncan put her fork down and hesitated. "The bodies in trees, it was as if they'd been picked up and hurled there. Like in the stories when old Zeus gets mad at the mortals and pitches a fit." She lifted her chin in a gesture that was pure JoHanna. She met her mother's worried gaze. "It was terrible to look at, but it didn't make me feel bad."

"Then," JoHanna hesitated, "it wasn't like the dreams about Mary Lincoln or Red? I mean the bodies were all on land, not drowning?"

"There were people on the boats out in the ocean. They were having a terrible time, like waves fifty feet high, crashing down on them. The wind was blowing so hard. But I don't really know what happened to the boats or the people in the houses. I sort of moved on. But all around me there was the sound of wailing and crying. Like an entire town was carrying on."

JoHanna pointed toward the glass of milk beside Duncan's plate. "Drink it," she said. There was relief in her voice, in her manner. "It sounds as if you dreamed of a big storm. Perhaps Floyd has told you about the hurricane that hit these parts twenty years ago. It did terrible damage, even as far inland as Fitler."

Duncan's eyebrows lifted. "Floyd did tell me." She nodded, and I could see that she was as relieved as JoHanna no matter how blasé she'd been when recounting her dream. "I've dreamed before about some of his stories. Especially Miss Kretzler, down under the Courting Bridge, all drowned and lonely." She shivered.

JoHanna's balance was perfectly restored. She got up and refilled our coffee cups. "Drink your milk, Duncan. For your bones. I think your dream is just something Floyd told you and it came back to you while you were asleep." She rubbed Duncan's head. "And you said it didn't frighten you."

Duncan's mouth was too full to answer. She shook her head, swallowed a big gulp, and took a breath. "No, it was like I was up above looking down." She spoke carefully, choosing her words. "I couldn't help anyone, even the ones crying and begging for help. I could only see what had happened."

"Well, since it hasn't upset you, I think we should forget it. You need a bath. Jeb Fairley is coming today, and we need to go down to the river with him."

"They're looking for Mr. Lassiter, aren't they?"

My coffee cup clattered into the saucer. Duncan was too astute for her own good.

"Yes." JoHanna pushed her half-eaten breakfast back. "And we're going to take some food down there. I don't want people to think we're afraid or that we're hiding."

"Because I told him the dream and then he told other people. And then he drowned."

JoHanna nodded as she got up. "That about sums it up."

"Are people going to say that I'm evil?"

JoHanna had picked up her plate and was shifting toward the sink. She stopped and gave her daughter a long look. "They might. We don't want to encourage such talk by acting afraid, but we aren't going to let it bother us if they do say such things."

Duncan didn't say anything, but she pushed her plate away, her French toast only halfway eaten. "I guess I wasn't as hungry as I thought I was."

"I'll take care of these dishes while you give Duncan a bath," I said, sliding between JoHanna and the sink before she could take her place there.

"Jeb should be here in an hour or so. He'll want a cup of coffee, and Sadie got up this morning and baked a pound cake." JoHanna's face softened into a smile. "Now let's get cleaned up and we'll take ourselves down to the river and see what they're saying for ourselves."

Duncan rode in the wagon, Pecos perched beside her with all the pride of a vain rooster. Aunt Sadie had disappeared out the back door half an hour before we were ready to leave. She'd been in a big hurry and was wearing a straw hat with wild lupine and asters around the crown. It was too modest to be one of JoHanna's creations.

We walked at our leisure, drifting from the shade of one big oak to the next. If JoHanna wanted to halt the gossip, she made no effort to do so by trying to appear less odd. She did wear her big hat, which was in and of itself a statement, but one less provocative than her close-cropped hair. Duncan's head, now a silky fringe of black hair, was bare, and she bumped her heels in the bottom of the wagon in time to Jo-Hanna's walk. Had I been JoHanna, I would have taken the car, and I would have locked Pecos in the house.

There were thirty or so men gathered where the bank sloped gently into the river. They spoke softly among themselves, pointing out different areas of the river. Several men had waded into the water, their hands on the wooden sides of the fleet of small boats that were clustered there. As we approached most of the boats began to pull away, each with two or three men aboard.

The day was unnaturally still. No laughter rang out on the water, no jokes or teasing calls. As we drew closer we could hear the sound of the water lapping against the remaining three boats.

"Aunt Sadie asked me to tell you that she'll be bringing over some chicken and dumplings at noon." JoHanna spoke to a tall, angular man who had just waded into the water in preparation of boarding a boat. He was bronzed from the sun and carried a coil of stout rope over his shoulder. He turned her way, his gaze going past her to Duncan.

"The men will appreciate that." He looked nervously back to the river.

"Come on, Diego." The man in the boat signaled him impatiently. "It's going to get hot as hell out on the water."

Diego lifted the rope, swinging it high over the water. The sun glinted off the four prongs of a sharpened hook as it arced through the air and landed with a thud in the wooden bottom. He cast another look at Duncan, then turned his back. Hands moving quickly he made the sign of the cross before he got into the boat, shoving off with his foot.

"They won't find him this morning." Duncan's clear voice carried easily on the water to the men. The one called Diego gave her a frightened look before he lifted his paddle and put his muscular arms to work.

JoHanna held the handle of the wagon in her hand and watched as the men fanned out along the river, beginning at the point where Red had disappeared beneath the raft and moving downstream.

"He could be halfway to Pascagoula by now," Duncan said to no one in particular. "Once that river gets hold of something . . ." She didn't finish the thought.

"Let's go make those dumplings." JoHanna started back toward the house.

"What about a swim? I want to exercise my legs." Duncan had a hint of petulance in her voice.

"Not today." JoHanna stopped and gave her daughter a long look. "I'll come back down here with the food, and I'll wait until the men come and eat it. And Duncan, you and Mattie will stay at Sadie's, and you will say nothing that even sounds vaguely like you're making a prediction."

"They won't find him this morning." Duncan's jaw had squared. Her brown eyes were filled with anger and a flash of hurt.

"They may never find him, Duncan, but I don't want you to say that."

Twenty-three

THEY found Red at three o'clock. When the sharp metal hook snagged him on the bottom of the river, it brought up something else, too. A cap, once white, carefully crocheted for a newborn baby. A girl. The tiny knotted brim was laced with the remnants of a pale pink ribbon. The treacherous current of the river had wrapped the long ties of the cap around Red's hand, and as they dragged the body to shore, the white material floated beside him.

I'd gone down to the river to retrieve Sadie's dumpling pot while Jo-Hanna and Duncan took a nap. I had hardly loaded the big pot in the wagon when a wild cry echoed off the river. It was Diego's hook that found Red's body not two hundred yards from where he'd been caught between the rafts.

The boat came toward shore towing the body. I saw a hand lift from the water, almost as if Red were waving, or trying to swim. But he wasn't. His arms were frozen in a position that looked as if he'd tried to shield himself from some terrible sight.

Diego cast me a nervous look before he leaped into the shallows and towed the body up to the narrow strip of sand. I couldn't look away, not even when he bent to remove the hook. I heard a muttered curse and a string of Spanish as he pulled the body to the shore. The little cap clung to Red's arm.

Diego's cry brought the other searchers in, the small boats moving toward the shore with the somberness of a ritual. Red Lassiter was drowned. The river had yielded up the proof.

* * *

Jeb Fairley was waiting for me back at Aunt Sadie's when I returned with the dumpling pot and the news that Red Lassiter had been found. Jeb abandoned his seat on the porch and went down to the river, returning less than an hour later, ready to head home. He paced the yard impatiently while I said my good-byes. Aunt Sadie gave me a brisk hug and attempted to catch Pecos to put in the car with me. Duncan waved from the porch while JoHanna came out to tell Jeb to keep an eye on me. They would wait for Will, she said, unless something unexpected happened.

We drove east. At our backs, the setting sun dusted the moss-draped oak trees with pink flames. Wrapped in sheets, the body of Red Lassiter had been placed in the backseat. There was no time to waste. The warm water of the Pascagoula and the September heat had already begun to do its work. Red was wrapped tight from head to toe. I didn't ask how they got his arms down at his sides. Jeb had removed the baby's cap from his arm and left it to dry on Sadie's porch. Sadie couldn't remember a baby drowning at Fitler, but there had been several ferry wrecks where trunks of clothes had gone to the bottom. And there was no telling what tragedies had occurred upstream. It was something I tried not to ponder as the light shifted and changed and the car moved steadily toward Jexville.

Dark had fallen before Jeb spoke, his voice soft, as if he didn't want to disturb Red in the backseat.

"Jexville is in a stir about Duncan." He looked at me. "And you haven't been spared."

"How's Elikah?" I laced my fingers in my lap. My husband would not be happy that I had called attention to myself.

"He's been quiet."

The road was rutted and the going slow, and Jeb wasn't pressing the old car too hard. He cleared his throat, a warning to me, and I fought hard not to cringe. What had Elikah said?

"I should have married Sadie."

I thought at first that I hadn't heard him, but when I looked, I saw that I had. He was staring straight ahead at the small vanguard of light the headlights threw on the red dirt road. His hands were gripped on the wheel, looking relaxed, but not. For the first time I noticed that he was older than I'd thought. I also remembered that Aunt Sadie, hat perched atop her head, had been gone all day.

"Why didn't you?" As far as I knew, neither of them had ever married.

"I've given that a lot of thought. I came up with a hundred good reasons, all to hide the fact that I was a coward."

My hand started across the distance of the seat, to touch him, to give him comfort, but the set of his jaw stopped me. He did not want comfort from me. He wanted something else. Something far more difficult to understand.

"I came to Fitler in 1883, back when this area was still recovering from the ravages of the war. It was an accident that I happened onto the place, but the first thing I saw when I got off the riverboat was Sadie. She was standing in the shade of a big oak with another young woman, laughing over something one or the other had said. I've been told that Lillith was the true beauty, but I swear to you, I never saw her. There was only Sadie."

The cooler air of the September night blew in the open car window as we motored along. The drone of the car's engine, at first loud, had receded in my mind. There was the distant sound of frogs as we passed a small pond where beavers had dammed a stream. There was not another living soul for miles around, and I was riding in the car with a man lost in the past and a body wrapped in sheets. I wondered then if it was Red that Jeb Fairley was talking to as much as me.

"I fell in love with Sadie that moment. And I've loved her ever since."

"Why don't you marry her?" I still had not learned the art of governing my tongue. My question might have been ill-phrased, but it was sincere. They were both free to marry. There weren't even any children—that I knew of—to object.

He glanced at me. "You haven't heard the whole story."

We rode along in silence for a bit, and I wondered if I should prod him on or let it go. Just as I was giving up hope that he'd speak another word to me, he started again.

"Lillith D'Olive was a strange girl. Her father was a tung oil farmer, and they owned lots of property north of Fitler. He'd brought his daughter to Fitler to stay with his sick sister and to meet some men. She was twenty and more than old enough for marriage. There was no dearth of proposals; it was just that Lillith couldn't make up her mind. She had an idea of what it was going to be like to fall in love and get married. Lillith couldn't pass down the street without drawing every man in town out of the stores and saloons to walk along with her. She could have had her pick of any man in the territory, and God only knows why she decided it would be Edgar Eckhart."

Lillith Eckhart. I could almost feel the cool marble of her headstone beneath my hand. She'd died in 1885, only two years after Jeb had come to Fitler.

"She was very young. How did she die?" Sadie hadn't told me that part.

"She was hanged." He kept looking at the headlights dancing on the road. "The only woman ever executed in this part of the country."

I felt as if my breath had been punched out of me. "Hanged?"

"They built a gallows in the main street of town."

"In Fitler?" I sounded dumber than dirt, but I couldn't help myself. In all of the stories JoHanna and Duncan had told me, in watching Sadie and her love of the town, I'd never thought of a hanging. Especially not a woman just twenty-two years old. "What did she do?"

"She was tried and convicted of murdering her husband."

The pain in my abdomen almost made me cry out, but I gripped the door handle of the car and gritted my teeth. Sweat popped out on my forehead, and I moaned slightly, but the wind from the open window whipped it away from Jeb, taking it back to the ears of a man who no longer heard. It was not a real pain I felt, only the memory. It passed as quickly as it came.

"Edgar Eckhart was a son-of-a-bitch. He was a violent man, though he could be quite charming when he chose to be. Lillith loved him beyond reason."

"She was a fool." I made my pronouncement with no sympathy for this long-dead woman. How was it that a woman could love a man who hurt her? This wasn't something I could understand. I did not love Elikah, though I wanted to. At first. I learned quickly, though, that while I could not protect my body from his belt, I could safeguard my heart. "She was a stupid fool."

"No bigger fool than I." He slowed the car, pulling off the road beneath the straight limbs of a red oak.

The big leaves blocked out the clear night sky, and I felt a twinge of apprehension. I didn't want to stop. We would already be arriving late, after dark. If we tarried long, I might lose my nerve and never return to Elikah.

He sensed my apprehension because he turned to me. "Do you mind if we stop for a few minutes? Red doesn't care." He chuckled softly. "He was a patient man with his friends, but he told me almost forty years ago that I was a fool. He named me correctly."

Jeb Fairley had been a kind neighbor, an older man who minded his own business but who always had a nod and a smile for me. His voice was raw. Whatever grief he was suffering needed attention now. "Did you love Lillith?"

"No, not Lillith. It was always Sadie that I loved. Even now."

I remembered the perky hat, the hint of lipstick. Sadie loved him, too. They had obviously spent the day together. The feelings were mutual. What kept them apart? "You're confusing the dickens out of me." I couldn't help the irritation in my voice.

"Everyone in Fitler soon knew the circumstances of Lillith's marriage to Edgar. He would drink in the saloons and go home and hit her. At first she tried to hide it by staying home. But Sadie kept going down there and dragging her into town. She and Lillith would walk up and down the main street with both of Lillith's eyes punched black and her hair pulled out in hunks."

My heart was beating too fast now. Jeb Fairley had stumbled on dangerous ground. He lived too close to us. How much had he heard? How much did he know of my marriage?

"Sadie thought for sure that someone would intervene. But once Lillith had married Edgar, she was his wife. Folks didn't interfere with a man punishing his wife and children. It was private business."

I could feel him looking at me as he spoke softly again. He knew—I just didn't know how much. I swallowed and said nothing.

"Even when it shouldn't be, it's still private business. And that's how it came to be that Lillith poisoned Edgar. When no one else would help her, she killed him."

I didn't want to hear any more of this story. "And they hanged her for it."

"Indeed they did. In front of the entire town. And not a man amongst us tried to stop it, even though we knew that she was only defending herself."

"So Sadie wouldn't marry you."

"I wish that had been the case." He drew a ragged breath. "You might as well hear it all. I never made the offer. You see, Sadie climbed the scaffold with Lillith. Sadie looked down on the men of the town and called us the cowards we were. Sadie stood by her friend and tried to defend her, and for her troubles she was ostracized and shunned. Sadie didn't marry me because I didn't ask her. And neither would any other man."

In the darkness I didn't see him move, but I heard his car door open as he got out to crank the old car. It lurched several times, then smoothed out as he climbed back behind the wheel.

We rode the rest of the way to Jexville in silence. Jeb had revealed his past to me, but he had also given me a fistful of terrible truths.

Instead of going to the undertaker, Jeb looped around by my house. He braked the car in front and let the engine run. "Want me to go in with you?"

There was a lamp burning in the kitchen, but other than that the house was dark. Elikah was probably at a card game. "No." My voice quivered, and I couldn't help it. I was afraid.

"Mattie," his hand brushed my cheek, turning me to face him. "I hope it doesn't ever come to this, but you have my word. I won't be a coward twice. You come to me if Elikah hurts you again."

"I'll be fine." I opened the door and inched out, wanting nothing more than to climb back in the car. In the backseat Red Lassiter had slumped against the opposite door, a drunken mummy. It struck me suddenly that not a single member of his family had been at the river to hunt for him.

"Does Red have a wife?"

Jeb cleared his throat. "No, and I don't know this for a fact, but I think he fell in love with JoHanna. When she married Will, he just sort of determined that he was happier by himself."

I stepped back away from the car. "If they need me to help with him, I'll come."

He eased away from my yard. "Take care, Mattie." He drove away, leaving me standing in front of my darkened house.

Twenty-four

"MATTIE."

My heart stopped beating as the blood rushed into my ears with the roar of a train. Elikah's voice had come from the front porch. Dear God, he was sitting on the swing in the dark. I'd never known the man to frequent the porch for any reason.

"Are you going to stand in the yard or come up?"

I couldn't answer him so I started up the steps with the intention of going in the front door.

"Come over here and sit in the swing with me," he said. "I've been sitting out here in the cool night air thinking when you were going to come home. I was beginning to wonder if you might never come back."

No matter how hard I searched for the warning edge of anger in his voice, I couldn't detect it. He sounded sad, a little beaten. An Elikah I didn't know—or trust. The true test would be his breath. If I got close enough to smell it.

"I'm tired, Elikah. Mr. Fairley and I brought Red Lassiter back with us. They found him in the river today."

"Terrible tragedy." The swing creaked as he shifted his weight. "Everybody liked Red. He was a little strange, living up there in Fitler by himself when five dozen women chased him for the past thirty years. But nobody ever said he wasn't as honest as the day is long."

I put my hand on the screen. What he said didn't require an answer, and he made me nervous. This new Elikah, so quiet and introspective, sitting out on the swing alone. I didn't trust this at all. The last time

Elikah had decided to show me another of his faces, well, my body still flooded with shame at the thought.

"Come sit out here with me a spell." He patted the swing. "I'll push us both. What did you think of Fitler?"

Where was his antagonism toward JoHanna? Why wasn't he mad at me for leaving the way I'd done? Had he really believed the note that JoHanna had sent him? Maybe he just wanted to get hold of me, save himself the trouble of having to chase me so he could hit me. My fingers holding the handle of the door had grown stiff and old. I could not let the handle go; it was my lifeline, yet I could not pull the screen open.

In the darkness he fumbled on the seat beside him. "I've got something here," he said, his voice shimmering with a soft darkness. "I was sitting out here smelling your hairbrush. Your hair always smells like rain, Mattie. At night, when I wake up, I like to smell it on the pillow beside me."

I looked out to the street. Had I come to the wrong house? Was Elikah so drunk that he had forgotten the way of our marriage?

"Come over here and let me brush your hair."

Dear Jesus, I was too afraid to move. This was worse than his anger, worse than his cruelty and bullying. Worse than his strap.

"I'm tired." I managed to croak out the words, hating myself for my cowardice.

"You lost the baby, didn't you?"

Was there a hint of accusation in his tone? I wanted to run, to dart down the steps and run screaming onto Redemption Road. I wasn't quick enough. He'd catch me and drag me home. There was no one to help me. Jeb Fairley was still down at the funeral home.

"Come on over here, Mattie. I'm your husband." He patted the swing again.

There was no help for it. I had to go. My fingers released the door handle and my feet began to move across the gray boards. When I was at the swing I turned and sat down, giving him my profile.

"You lost the baby?" he asked again.

"Yes." I looked across the porch toward the blackness of the night.

"That's too bad." He didn't bother to hide his relief.

I had thought he would be angry, but it was his relief that made it even worse. He didn't want his child. He was as unnatural as I was.

"Turn around." His hands grasped my shoulders and shifted me so that my back was almost to him. "Now just be still."

I felt the brush grasp and tug at my hair. My scalp was still a little sunburned, but I didn't flinch. Elikah was the kind of man who found excitement in a little bit of pain. I did not want him excited. "I can't be a wife to you. Not for a while." I spoke to the darkness and found that my fingernails were digging into my palms.

"Says who?" He plied the brush with a slow, steady motion.

"JoHanna talked with Doc Westfall."

"JoHanna likes to poke around in our business, doesn't she?"

There it was, that whisper of anger. "I was so sick I scared her. The bleeding wouldn't stop. She called him because she was afraid I was getting worse."

"But the bleeding's stopped now." It was a statement, not a question.

"Mostly." I wanted to bolt from the swing, to run and run until I burned away into speed. The brush moved through my hair slowly.

"Your hair is so soft."

He leaned forward. I could feel his breath on my neck as he lifted my hair. My skin prickled. His breath was warm in the cool of the night. His lips were heated, barely brushing my skin. I felt the tears smarting in my eyes, but I willed them away.

He retreated, bringing the brush back up again, moving it through my hair that had been tangled by the car ride. He worked the knots gently, the silence between us growing bigger and bigger so that it drank all the air on the porch.

The brush came up again, the bristles whispering beside my ear.

"I thought you might be running back home." He never slowed the stroke of the brush, drawing it all the way to the end of my hair, then moving it up to start again.

"No, I'm not going home." Going home would solve nothing. At least in Jexville I had JoHanna. And Duncan and Floyd and Will. In Meridian my own mama couldn't help me if I got in trouble. "No, I'm not going home." I repeated the words without intending to.

"When did Doc say you can 'be a wife to me'?" He mocked me lightly with his tone.

"Two weeks."

"That's a long time for a man like me. I thought I married a good, healthy girl. You reckon your step-pa sold me a bill of goods?"

"I suppose that's something you'll have to take up with Jojo." I stood up suddenly.

In the darkness his hand was quick. He grasped my wrist in a tight hold and drew me toward him with a steady tug.

"Elikah, if the bleeding starts . . ." I didn't resist him. I knew better.

He pulled me into his lap, his hands now on my shoulders. "Simmer down, Mattie." He spoke softly. "I just wanted to tell you that I missed you."

I sat on his lap, making certain not to move at all.

"Didn't you miss me, even just a little?"

This was a new side of his torment. Never before had he tried to make me say things. Elikah was a man of action.

"I was too sick to miss anyone."

"And as soon as you felt better, you came home to me."

I didn't deny it. There was no point in provoking him.

"You've grown up a lot since you came here." His thumb stroked my cheek, the softest of touches. I'd seen Elikah shave a man before. He could be deft with his hands when the mood suited him.

"You're growing into a fine-looking woman, Mattie." His thumb traced the edge of my bottom lip. "So soft." He parted my lips with his thumb, barely touching my teeth. "Don't you even have a kiss for me? Just a welcome home kiss."

The image of JoHanna and Will came back to me, the way he'd grabbed her and kissed her when he'd come home from his trip. I felt the sob welling up in my throat. Leaning toward him, I kissed him lightly on the lips. To my surprise there was not the smell of alcohol on his breath.

"That's a good girl, Mattie." He shifted, letting me know that I could stand up. "I'll bet you'd like a nice, hot bath, wouldn't you?" He stood alongside of me.

I didn't know how to answer him.

"Mattie, would you like a bath? I'll draw the water for you."

He was completely insane. This was all some evil trick, but I couldn't fathom it. "I'd like that." I stepped toward the door.

"At last, you've finally said what you'd like." He opened the door, ushering me into the house. All the way to the kitchen, he walked behind me. The house was surprisingly neat. Even the dishes in the kitchen were washed and put away. I turned to him, my amazement showing.

"I'm glad you're home, Mattie." He picked up the big kettle for the water. "Now I'm going to see about fixing that bath for you."

"Who cleaned the kitchen?" I couldn't believe he'd done it. Maybe he'd eaten every meal at one of the cafés.

He stopped in the doorway with the kettle in his hand. "Oh, I guess I forgot to mention my cousin."

Elikah had no relatives. Or none that he'd told me about. "What cousin?"

"Lola. She's been dropping by to, uh, see to my needs. Since you're not up to being wifely, maybe she'll stay on a few more days. To help with your chores." He came to stand beside me, the empty kettle swinging in his strong fingers. "Of course, if you've got any objections to this arrangement, Lola won't mind making room for you in the bed."

He must have read my thoughts in my eyes because he laughed and ran his finger gently down my collar bone to my breast. "I always suspected you enjoyed that night in New Orleans. Once the shock wore off, you liked it a lot, didn't you?" His hand molded around my breast, tightening slightly. "That was something to see, the two of you."

"Elikah . . ." I could barely say his name. There was nothing I could say if his mind was made up. I'd learned that in New Orleans. Begging would only excite him more. "I can't . . . do anything. The doctor . . ."

His fingers squeezed hard, once, then released me as he went to the bucket and filled the kettle before lighting the stove. When he turned back to me the laughter had gone from his face. The light from the lamp made his eyes hollow, unreadable. But his voice was clear, and I understood that he enjoyed the waiting, the torment. "Maybe not tonight, Mattie. Or tomorrow night. But it won't be long before you can do anything I tell you to do. Now get ready for your bath."

Twenty-five

IT was not the fact that Lola came and went from Elikah's bed that bothered me most. My feelings on that issue were strangely confused. My unexpressed anger came from the fact that he allowed her to come and go from my kitchen as if she were a guest. Elikah made it clear to both of us that this arrangement was only for the length of my recuperation. Once I was able to be "wifely" again, Lola's role would change. And so would mine.

The possibility brought only a bored shrug from her as her flat brown gaze roved over the cabinets, lingering on canisters and bins.

She ate like a starved hound dog. And with about the same finesse. In the morning, when Elikah went to work, she vanished from the house.

Where Elikah had gotten her and where she went when she wasn't with him, I had no idea. She wasn't local. Her destination, once she left our home, didn't seem to trouble her. She was where she was for two purposes. To service Elikah and to eat as much as she could swallow without exploding. Looking into her vacant eyes, I couldn't begrudge her the food she ate, but it stung me that I was left to cook the food, to wash the dishes. The terms of this arrangement were clear. If I could not perform my conjugal duties, I could maintain the house.

Two days passed, with me cooking and spending as much time as possible in town. I went to the dry goods store and explored every dusty bin, every bolt of cloth, every box of lacy underwear. Olivia showed me the stockings that felt like air, drawing them slowly up her round, white arm to demonstrate their sheerness. Watching the other side of the store to be certain old Mrs. Tisdale was busy, she showed me how to roll the stockings just above the knee for the most fashionable look. I caught her watching me with a look of curiosity, but it was only kindness and an offering of friendship that she demonstrated.

I spent an hour or two in the bakery, watching Mara's strong fingers work the dough. She taught me to knead the dough, to feel the life in it, and then to braid the elastic strands to make the sweet loaves that sold for a penny each. Glad for the extra pair of hands, even if they were inexperienced, she didn't ask why I wasn't at home waiting for my husband. In fact, no one I passed seemed surprised that I was not the loving wife I should have been.

Part of the day I spent with Floyd at the boot shop. He was making great progress on the beautiful boots for Sheriff Grissham. Even more wonderful were the boots for Tommy Ladnier, the bootlegger. Mr. Ladnier had taken his occupation to heart when he'd drawn out the type of boots he wanted. They were tall and black, beautiful in their simplicity of line. From the few glimpses I'd caught of him, I knew he'd look like a pirate with his white silk shirts and those knee boots. He struck me as a man who wouldn't hesitate to run his sword through anyone who resisted him. But Floyd said he was very easy to work with on the boots. Floyd said his voice was like the Pascagoula River washing against the shore, and that he never sounded angry or impatient, not even when Floyd measured and measured again because the boots were cut to fit his calves so closely and went all the way to the knee.

Mr. Moses didn't mind that I sat on a three-legged stool in the back and kept Floyd company. Once he even asked me to manage the cash drawer if anyone came in. I took it as a sign of trust, and it made me feel welcome in the shop, until it occurred to me that Axim Moses knew about the woman in my house and that his gesture had been motivated by pity. Elikah was the kind of man who would brag about such a thing, I felt sure. I could sometimes go to the window of the boot shop and look across the street to the barbershop. Elikah kept a steady clientele, and the men came out rubbing their freshly shaven cheeks and grinning. Elikah would walk by the window, snapping the barber's cloth before he placed it around his next customer, and the sound of laughter would tumble out into the road. The sound of that laughter scalded me, sending me to the back, where Floyd labored in the light of a window.

It was Floyd who told me about Red Lassiter's funeral. We decided to go together, a united front should anyone try to question us about Duncan. We would go for the McVays.

The funeral was set for ten the next morning, and I awakened from my bed on the sofa to discover that fall had slipped through the town. The trees had been hinting for days, whispering with the rustle of leaves still green, but the sun had burned as hotly as ever. Now there was a touch of chill in the air as I found my clothes and slipped into them. It was time to make Elikah's coffee and breakfast. Time to feed the hound. If the thumping and groaning of the night before was any indication, she'd be starved.

I put on the coffee, started the bacon and grits, and began cracking eggs in a bowl for Elikah and Lola. In a peculiar way I'd come to welcome her. She hadn't spoken a word to me since her arrival, and I didn't want to talk to her. I resented feeding her less, though. Strangely enough, I had to admit to myself that I didn't resent *her* at all. Elikah came to the table and ignored both of us. We were women, there to serve. I cooked, she serviced. All in all, it wasn't a bad arrangement.

"What's the secret, Mattie?"

Elikah's question almost made me drop the bowl of eggs. I couldn't tell him how much I liked the punishment he'd constructed for me. I slid three eggs into the hot bacon grease before I answered. "Red's funeral is today."

"And that made you smile?" He tapped the table with his fork, impatient with me.

I flipped the eggs. "They've waited three days for some of his family members to show up, but they can't find anyone. I'm just glad they're getting on with it. Red deserves a decent funeral. Are you going?"

"No. I'm closing the shop, but I've got some accounts to go over. I can use the time to do that."

I nodded as I scooped up the eggs, put four slices of bacon on his plate, dished up some grits, and put it all on the table. In a few seconds I had four pieces of perfectly browned toast from the oven.

"Lola!" Elikah yelled at her though she sat only three feet away.

"What?"

"Tell Mattie what you want."

She shrugged, but she eyed his plate hungrily. Her hair was a pale brown, almost blond, and it hung in her eyes, as straight as a board. She shrugged. "Whatever she cooks is fine."

I fixed her the same thing I'd given Elikah, then took a cup of coffee for myself.

"Eat some food, Mattie. You're never going to get better if you don't eat more."

"I'm getting better, Elikah." I went to the doorway. "I've got to get ready for the funeral. I have some errands to do beforehand."

Floyd sat beside me on the cushioned pew, the blue of his flannel shirt the perfect color of his eyes. The church had white walls, but the timbers above the high ceiling were dark, unfinished wood. It gave the sanctuary a sense of gloom. A center aisle split the dark rows of pews and led to the altar, where the coffin rested on sawhorses. Black-eyed Susans and wild asters had been woven into a blanket to cover the new pine of the coffin. They gave the room the only color, the only sense of beauty.

We'd arrived early and taken a seat in the back. Folks took notice of us, but not unduly. We were there, showing our respects to the man whose death Duncan had predicted. We were there for JoHanna, and for Duncan.

Janelle Baxley slipped into the seat beside me. "I didn't think Jo-Hanna would have the nerve to show." She looked straight ahead. "I tried to warn you about her. Everyone in town is talking, and not just about those McVays. They're talking about you, too."

The entire time she spoke she stared at the front of the church, where Red Lassiter's corpse resided in a varnished pine box. Janelle spoke out of the side of her mouth, never glancing at me or acknowledging Floyd in any way, as if she could not be seen associating with the likes of us. In contrast, Reverend Bates kept casting long, hostile glances at me and Floyd from the small vestibule off to the side of the altar. I had heard a minister from Waynesboro would preach the funeral. If I'd known Bates, who'd sprawled on the bank of the creek while Mary Lincoln drowned, was going to preach, I might not have come. He was not a man of God by any definition I knew. Janelle's voice buzzed in my ear like a big green blowfly.

"It would curl your hair to hear some of the things JoHanna McVay is capable of doing." She clutched a handkerchief in her hand, her fingers working it into a sweaty knot. "That woman needs to be run out of town. She and that little prophet of death. Red would be alive today—"

"I was there to see what happened, Janelle. Duncan didn't have a thing to do with what happened, and Red would tell you that himself, but I don't think he's up to gossiping."

"Mattie!" She turned her blue eyes on me, shock blanking out the tiny wrinkles that had crept around their corners. "He's dead!"

"Thank goodness for that if we're going to bury him." I waited a heartbeat before I went on. She wanted details, gossip, something shocking to gnaw and worry. "I was there when they found the body." I couldn't stop myself. "That Spaniard, Diego, hooked him not very far from where he went under the raft. JoHanna said it was unusual for the river to pull someone right down and keep them there. She said it was almost like the river was holding him close, like a lost child to a mother's bosom."

Janelle started to rise, but Agnes Leatherwood and her husband, Chas, slid into the pew, a perfectly groomed Annabelle Lee between them. There were a dozen other children in attendance. Agnes leaned forward to look me over, to see if the taint of JoHanna had rubbed off on me like a manure stain. She didn't speak to Floyd. He sat on the other side of me, unaware of the slight. He didn't expect to be acknowledged by these women. I understood then that they would have been kinder to an ugly idiot. It was his handsomeness, his per-fection of body, that earned such harsh treatment. These women didn't want to seem to take notice of him because they were so painfully aware.

"Did Duncan really tell Red he was going to drown?" Agnes leaned over Janelle to get her question to me. She tried to speak softly, but her whisper carried up the pews, causing heads to turn and stare at us with disbelief, disapproval, and curiosity.

I had rehearsed and rehearsed my answer for this, but it suddenly seemed inadequate. In the end, what answer would best serve Duncan? I felt Floyd's fingers grasp mine on the pew between us. He would not talk to these women. Somehow, he'd been warned not even to look at them. But he heard.

I turned to face Agnes and Janelle. They didn't have the intelligence of Pecos. "Duncan had a dream and she told Mr. Lassiter that the rafts were dangerous. That's it."

"But we heard she told him just hours before he drowned." The pleasure of gossip had pushed Janelle over her shock at me.

"Red stopped by for some coffee and cake, and Duncan chatted with him. Then he went out to the river and began working on one of the rafts. He drowned. But everyone with good sense knows those rafts are treacherous. It just so happened Red—"

"That child is dangerous. First Mary, now Red. Who's going to be next?" Agnes Leatherwood put her arm around the plump Annabelle Lee and pulled her against her bosom. "If she says one word about my baby I'm going to . . . to . . ."

"To what, Agnes?" I stared into her, daring her to make a threat. "Duncan did not hold Mary Lincoln underwater. She didn't push Red under the raft. She's a little girl and she can't even walk. Why are you so afraid of her?"

Stung, Agnes had finally straightened her shoulders a bit. "Who do you think you are?" she asked. "You were *sold* to your husband. Everyone in town knows it, and you act like you're the queen of England."

I had turned the ire from Duncan onto myself, but it wasn't exactly what I'd intended to do.

Janelle looked around the church and found that more than half the people were watching us as we argued in terse whispers. Reverend Bates took three steps toward us, then hesitated as a tall, white-headed man in a black coat stepped toward the pulpit. Janelle put one hand on me and one on Agnes. "That must be Reverend Ellzey. Now calm down, Agnes. Mattie, I told you if you took up with that woman you'd end up in a mess. Now everyone is talking about you. You've shamed your husband, Mattie."

The complete unfairness of that remark was almost my undoing. Floyd's hand held me down in my seat, but I managed to turn to Janelle. "You don't know a damn thing about shame. Nothing! If you had any idea . . ."

"Mattie." Floyd reached over with his free hand and grasped my shoulder closest to Janelle, turning me forcefully, holding me as I struggled to swing back around to them. "Mattie, be quiet." He spoke softly, but his hands held me so that I faced the front of the church.

"My God, look at that!" Agnes stood up at the sight of Floyd's hand on me. "He touched her. He actually had the nerve to touch her, telling her what to do like she was his . . . Not only is JoHanna raising up a child that has the talents of Satan, they're letting the town idiot touch them." Agnes cowered back from me as if I had leprosy. "We've tolerated Floyd in this town because we were sorry for him. But now, we'll call a town meeting and see what's to be done about him. He can't be left on the loose."

Everyone in the church turned to look at us. In my ignorance, I had made a bad situation worse. For myself. For JoHanna and Duncan. But mostly for Floyd. He would suffer for this. They would always turn on the weakest.

I carefully removed Floyd's hand and rose to my feet facing Agnes in the pew. "Floyd is an innocent." I wanted to tear her stringy hair from her head and make her swallow it. "He isn't capable of the evil you're filled with. He touched me, yes, he did. And that fact saved you from the beating of your life. Whatever dirty things you see in Floyd come from your own filthy mind."

From the pew in front of me Rachel Carpenter stood, her wide hips almost brushing her husband into the aisle as she turned. Her stout face was white with fury. "How dare you come into our town and threaten us. Everyone tried to help you, to ignore the fact that you were poor white trash. But we won't be threatened. Not by you or that spawn of Satan or that idiot."

Floyd rose slowly, his fists clenched at his side. He towered over me, daring any one of them with a look to take this further.

Rachel Carpenter stepped back out of his reach. "I can see plainly how you've driven your husband into the arms of a whore." She pushed her husband's shoulder. "Let's find another seat." She stared at Agnes. Chas had risen also, his hand on his wife's rounded shoulder. The look he gave me was half pity and half contempt as he dragged Agnes backward with him as he moved, Annabelle Lee crushed between them.

Janelle, her big chest moving in and out in rapid, shallow breaths, scooted away from me. She cast one fearful glance at me and Floyd before she stood up and ran to the other side of the church. I turned to find the out-of-town minister who had come to preach Red Lassiter a farewell sermon standing in the pulpit, doubt and concern tightening his mouth. Even as I looked his expression changed, and I followed his gaze to the front door where JoHanna stood, Duncan in her arms.

"JoHanna!" Floyd's cry was filled with relief. He brushed past me and rushed toward her, scooping Duncan into his arms.

Freed of the weight of her child, JoHanna stepped forward. Her blue gaze was white-hot as it swept the room. Agnes Leatherwood actually cringed back into her husband's chest. Rachel Carpenter looked down at the floor. Janelle gave a small cry, as if she'd been stung by a wasp.

"This is a time to show our respects to Red Lassiter," the minister said softly. "Please, let us take our seats and begin."

Reverend Bates swept up to the pulpit, his long arm pointing at Jo-Hanna. "That woman doesn't belong in a house of God." He pointed at me and Floyd. "Get out of here."

The visiting minister refused to move aside. "Stand back, Reverend Bates. God's house is open to all."

Reverend Bates looked around at his congregation, taking strength from them. "This will not be allowed. . . ."

"You sicken me." JoHanna's words echoed eerily in the sanctuary of the church. "You turn on a child of sixteen and a young man who hasn't the ability or desire to defend himself, and you do it in a place you claim to be sacred to your religious beliefs." She swept her hand around the wooden sanctuary. "If there were truly an all-powerful God, he would send a blight down on you and take what you hold dear. He would destroy everything you possess." She nodded at me and I hurried to join them at the doorway. "I'll pay my respects to Red at the cemetery." She turned, leading our small procession out of the darkness of the church and into the brisk fall morning. Pecos awaited us, perched on the back of the rocking chair that was once again strapped in the wagon.

The rumbling of the congregation within could be heard out on the street. It was a swarm of hornets, a nest of snakes. The two ministers were shouting at each other, and that was the only thing that delayed the congregation from boiling out of the doors after us.

"I'm sorry, JoHanna." I had started to cry. "I'm so sorry."

"For what?" She was furious. Grasping my shoulders, she shook me until I looked at her. "For what? Because you're not cowardly or cruel. I heard enough to know that you were defending Duncan and Floyd. Those people are narrowminded, bigoted fools. They see evil because they are evil."

Floyd had placed a very quiet Duncan in the wagon. He picked up the handle, turned it around, and started toward Peterson Lane. He sensed the need to get away.

"We're not running away." JoHanna suddenly realized what he was about and ran after him, grabbing his shoulder. "I came to the service to show them I'm not afraid of them. If they think I'm afraid, they'll only get worse."

"We're taking Duncan home." Floyd didn't stop and he looked only at the ground as he moved forward, one long step at a time.

"We are not running." She grabbed his arm and dug her heels into the ground.

Floyd pulled her along as if she were a reluctant puppy.

"Floyd, stop it! We can't run now."

He finally stopped and turned to look at her. His blue eyes were troubled. "They don't like me or Mattie." He shook his head in disbelief. "They don't like you or Duncan. They wanted to hurt us. Why, Jo-Hanna?"

That finally stopped her. The hand she placed on his arm was gentle. "Because they're ignorant, Floyd. It's only ignorance that makes them the way they are." She sighed. "You're right. Let's go home. Now isn't the time to confront them."

I hung back, hoping they would leave and get home fast. I could not run to the safety of Peterson Lane with them. What I had done in the church would be at the barbershop in a matter of minutes. Left to brood about it, Elikah would be truly angry by suppertime. It was best to confront him head-on and get it over with.

They had gone two dozen yards before Pecos gave a loud squawk and jumped off the wagon and ran toward me.

Duncan swiveled and found me standing, the bird running around me in a circle, pecking at the backs of my heels, as if he intended to herd me along.

"Mattie isn't coming." Duncan's face was still pale.

Floyd stopped the wagon, and JoHanna started walking back to me.

"I have to stay. I have to face Elikah now."

JoHanna stopped. Worry etched the fine wrinkles of her face into more permanent lines. The sun had done its damage to her, and in the coming years, it would show. "You don't have to stay here."

I nodded. "I do."

"Is it true what Rachel said? About Elikah?"

"He's moved a whore into the house." I felt my lips twist into a bitter smile. "Until I can be wifely again."

JoHanna pressed her lips together. "Why go back there?"

I didn't have an answer to that, except that I had to. I was also afraid. JoHanna and Duncan had only Floyd to protect them. If I remained in town, maybe the anger would be drawn to me. At least until Will returned, and I intended to make that happen as soon as possible.

"I'll send Floyd to check on you." JoHanna was clearly worried.

"No!" That would be the worst thing she could do.

She understood, and she bit her lip in frustration. "Please, Mattie. Come with us."

"I have to face them. I'd rather get it over with before it has time to fester in Elikah."

Duncan lifted her chin and stared directly at me. As if at some unspoken signal, Pecos abandoned his attempt to herd me along and ran crowing to the wagon. With one awkward leap and a flap of his wings, he was beside Duncan. "Don't worry about them in town, Mattie." There was the ghost of a smile. "It won't be long before they'll be too busy to hurt you." She looked down at Pecos and began to stroke his feathers.

Twenty-six

THE cool cloth on my face, the soft voices strained by worry, awakened me. I kept my eyes closed, wondering where I was and what had happened to me. I didn't recognize the woman's voice, but her touch on my throat was gentle as she felt for a pulse.

"You likta kilt her." There was no accusation in the voice, only stated fact.

"A wife doesn't shame her husband the way she did me, letting that half-wit touch her. Talking to Mrs. Leatherwood and the other ladies." Elikah had lost some of his bravado, though his words were still bold.

"If you'd hit her one more time, she'd likely be dead. And you'd be going to prison."

I knew it was Lola who spoke. It was Lola who had put the cold cloth on my face. I tried to open my eyes, but they wouldn't. I lifted one hand, and there was a raspy breath of recognition from Lola that I was truly alive.

My fingers crept along my face and discovered that where my eyes should have been were puffy slits. I remembered Elikah slapping me, hard enough to bust my lip. Apparently, he'd also used his fists on me. I took a deep breath and cried out with the pain.

"Her ribs are broken." Lola spoke with authority. "That was when you kicked her." She was talking to Elikah. "You'd best get the doctor."

"No!"

There was fear in his voice. Real fear, and not for my condition. He was terrified of having to pay for what he'd done. JoHanna had read him correctly. He did not want anyone to know of his treatment of me.

"You don't get the doctor, I'm not gonna stay here. If she dies, I don't want nobody saying I had a hand in this."

Lola was far smarter than I'd ever thought. I wanted to smile at her, to give her some encouragement, but I could only moan. My tongue was swollen to the point that I could not make a comprehensible sound.

I felt the trickle of cold water at the corner of my mouth, and I opened it enough for Lola to dribble some in. Swallowing made me gasp with pain.

"Go get the doctor. I'll say she tripped in the road and a horse stepped on her." Lola spoke as if she were an old hand at making up excuses for wounds and injuries.

"What horse?" Elikah was grasping at the story she'd concocted.

"Any fuckin' horse you want me to say." She splashed the cloth in the water and replaced it on my face, her touch not as gentle now. "Your horse, in the yard. You can't say anybody else's."

"You're right." Elikah was calculating the odds. It gave me a sense of satisfaction to know that I was causing him at least a little discomfort. "You go and get Doc. I'll stay here. You tell him about the horse and how I dragged her in and tried to help her."

Lola stood up. "Funny," she said with bitterness in her voice, "I didn't take you for no hero."

"Shut up or I'll give you—"

"You get any ideas about what you'll give me and I'll go straight to the sheriff."

Lola's blank brown eyes apparently hid a sharp mind. And a nerve I'd never suspected. I didn't want her to leave me. Elikah might decide to kill me while she was gone, and I could hardly lift a hand.

"Get out!" Elikah gritted out the order. "Just as soon as Doc examines her, you're gone. You understand?"

Lola's laugh was sharp, almost a bark. "I understand plenty. I'll be more than glad to get away from a mean bastard like you, but I ain't goin' without plenty of money. You'll make it worth my while to go. You'd better keep it in mind that I ain't your wife. You can't treat me the way you treat her and get away with it."

"Get!" He picked up something from the dresser and threw it. Lola screamed among the sound of breaking glass. He'd broken the scent bottle JoHanna had given me. A small loss compared to what he'd done to my body. I wondered what else, along with my ribs, might be broken. I didn't have the heart to try to find out.

There was the sound of Lola's footsteps going through the kitchen and then out the front of the house. How did she know where Doc Westfall's office might be? I forgot about Lola as I felt Elikah's fingers grasp my hand.

"You're going to be okay, Mattie."

I tried not to breathe. If I could have held my breath and died I would have gladly done so. There wasn't an inch on my body that didn't hurt.

"What possessed you to let that idiot touch you?" He didn't pause long enough for me to answer even if I could. "He's not so harmless as folks make out. He may be slow, but he's smart enough to recognize a willing woman."

I shook my head slightly, and the pain shot red flares in my skull. Two of the teeth on the left side of my jaw were loose. Unable to help myself, I felt hot tears leaking out of my eyes. What if I was blind? What if he'd damaged my eyes?

"Don't cry," he said, his touch light on my face. "If you cry, your head will stop up and it'll be worse."

He spoke so reasonably, so kindly, that the fury inside me burned away all my tears. The bastard had backhanded me in the barbershop in front of three men and then dragged me down the street by my hair. Not a single person had tried to help me, and once he got me home, he really set in. Whatever else she was, Lola had tried to hold him back.

His grip on my hand tightened. I tried to pull free, but even the slightest movement sent a sharp pain in my side and set off echoey pains all over.

"You keep your mouth shut to Doc, you hear?"

I nodded. I couldn't talk, and I didn't want him to kill me before Doc had a chance to get there.

"You had this coming, Mattie. You know you did. You got off with JoHanna McVay and forgot who you were. Her husband may let her run the country flaunting herself and doing how she pleases, but I'm not Will McVay. I won't be humiliated by you." He increased his pressure on my hand until I thought the bones would snap. "Don't ever forget that again. You hear?"

I nodded and gasped when he released my hand. I heard him stand up and move away from the bed. His footsteps retreated to the kitchen, where there was the sound of wood going in the stove.

"I'm going to heat some water for you. A good hot bath will help the soreness."

The idea made me want to cry. I didn't think I could move, much less get in a tub.

"I'll help you, and then you can sleep. No telling how long before Doc gets here. I heard he had to go over to Greene County to see about birthing a baby. We'll have plenty of time to clean you up before he gets here."

Halfway through the bath I fainted, sliding down into the blood-tinted water until Lola pulled me up. Elikah and Lola managed to get me out of the tub and into a nightgown and bed before Doc Westfall got there.

I came to when I heard Doc's voice and opened one eye enough to see his worried face, framed by the cloud of fine white hair that was backlit in the bedroom window. The sight of him did me more good than any medicine.

He took a look at me and shooed Lola out of the room. Elikah tried to remain, but Doc said his examination was private. Elikah could leave or Doc said he would get some men and a stretcher to take me to his office where he could do a proper exam. Showing all kinds of husbandly concern, Elikah retreated to the kitchen, but he left the door open so he could hear what I said, if anything.

"What kind of horse would do this?" Doc asked as he pried open my eyes and squinted at me.

Maybe, at long last, I'd learned to keep my mouth shut. I had no intention of saying anything that would make Elikah hurt me more.

"The woman who came to get me said you fell under a horse. How'd that happen, Mattie?"

I concentrated on breathing. When he touched my ribs I cried out in pain.

He moved down my body, taking his time, inspecting the bruises and the swollen places. Of great concern was my abdomen, which he poked and prodded until I moaned. Then he checked lower, removing the cloths that Lola had put there to catch the bleeding.

"Sweet Jesus," he whispered as he poked around more.

"How is she, Doc?" Elikah called out.

Doc didn't answer him. He started in with the bandages, helping me to sit up while he wrapped long strips of cotton around my ribs, binding me tight.

"My eyes?" My words sounded like they were spoken through layers of cotton.

"I think your vision will be fine, but you're going to have a couple of black eyes. Lucky the cheekbones weren't broken."

"Is she talking?" Elikah came to the door.

"She was asking about her eyes. I've never seen a horse give a person two black eyes." He didn't stop with the bandages. He didn't expect an answer from Elikah.

"It was the damndest thing I've ever seen. She just went right under old Mable. That horse is steady as a rock, but she just went crazy. Mattie kept trying to roll out from under the hooves and she just kept right under the mare. If I hadn't heard her screaming and gone out there to pull her out, she might have been trampled to death."

"I'm sure." Doc put his finger on my lips. "Open up there, Mattie." He peered into the small slit I was able to manage. "Get me some cold water."

When Elikah didn't obey, Doc looked up at him. "Get some cold water. I don't care if you have to sell your miserable soul to Satan to secure it. Just get it and bring it to me now."

Elikah slammed his fist into the doorway. "This is none of your affair, Doc."

Doc Westfall took his fingers out of my mouth. "Her ribs are broken, her eyes are swollen shut, you've knocked her teeth loose," his voice rose with each item, "and that's the minor stuff. She's hemorrhaging, Mills. Her uterus is bleeding. I don't know if there's something busted up inside her or if you've managed to beat her into a miscarriage. But if she doesn't stop bleeding, or if anything else happens to her, I'll see you hang for murder."

"This is my home. She's my wife—"

"Heed my words, Elikah. You've damaged this child enough. Whatever she did, she didn't deserve to be beaten nearly to death."

"A man has a right to punish his wife when she shames and humiliates him."

"This is punishment?" Doc Westfall sat down heavily. "Get that cold water and then get out of here. Maybe you'd better send for JoHanna McVay."

"Damned if I'll send for her. She's the cause of all of this."

Doc sighed. "Then get that other woman in here. She'll have to take care of Mattie."

Elikah stalked back into the kitchen. "Lola!" He yelled her name. "Lola!"

But there was no answer. Lola had gone, whether for good or not I couldn't say. If she had any sense she'd never look behind her. When he returned from his search, he brought cool water, which Doc trickled into my mouth, ordering me to swallow.

"She has to drink water, and I'm going to give her something for pain." He leaned down to his bag and drew out a bottle and a syringe. "It's just a little morphine, but it'll help her over the worst."

"No." I managed to get the word out. I remembered the morphine from the doctor in Mobile. "No."

Doc hesitated. "It'll cut the pain some."

"No." I didn't want to be dreaming and at the mercy of Elikah. I needed my wits about me or else he might kill me in my sleep.

"Mattie, those ribs are going to be painful, and I can't tell how bad the other will be."

"I'll be okay," I whispered. I wanted only to get well enough to crawl out the door and start toward JoHanna's. If I could get word to Floyd, he'd get JoHanna to come and get me. And Will.

"She doesn't want anything. She's not hurt as bad as you think." Elikah stepped more fully into the room. "Now if you're done, maybe you should get out of here. Just because you're a doctor doesn't give you the right to pry into a man's personal affairs."

Doc rose. "I'll be back tomorrow, Mattie."

"Doc, this isn't anybody's business. You understand."

Doc Westfall snapped his bag. I opened my eyes a slit and managed to bring him into focus as he stared at Elikah. "It doesn't take much of a man to beat a young girl half to death. I knew you were hard, Elikah. There's been rumors about you. But I never thought you'd stoop to such violence against a young woman." He brushed past Elikah and walked out of the house, his footsteps slow as he left.

Elikah came over to the bed. He touched my foot beneath the covers. "Well, Mattie, it's just you and me. You'll be back to yourself in a day or two. You'll see. I didn't do you any permanent harm."

He walked out of the room and left me to my tears.

* * *

Lola was gone for good. With her she managed to take Elikah's money clip and over twenty dollars. Suspecting that Elikah had no intention of buying her silence, she took what she could get and escaped. I was sick with envy of her.

Elikah spread the word in town that I had gone home to visit my sick mother for a week or two. He made it a special point of stopping by the boot shop to tell Floyd so that the word would get back to JoHanna. He wanted to make certain that she didn't come looking for me. If Janelle or Rachel or Agnes knew better, they told no one. I was alone in the house with Elikah, dependent on him to bring me food and water, to empty the chamber pot beneath the bed. He did these chores as if I were his most beloved wife, someone he cared about and cherished. After feeding me my soup, he would bring his plate to my bedside and fill me in with all the gossip of the day as he ate his supper. I could not understand his motivations. He behaved as if I were someone he cared about. As if my helplessness gave him pleasure.

My humiliation, and isolation, were complete. Only Doc Westfall came to see about me, and Elikah made certain that my room was tidy and that I was well groomed and clean.

By the fourth day, I could get around the room. While Elikah was at work I went into the kitchen, making sure that no one could see me through the white eyelet curtains I'd hung during the first days of my marriage. The curtains had been a gift from Callie. She'd given them to me with a hug, saying that all of the young brides in the stories she knew had eyelet curtains on their kitchen windows to make it homey. I touched the fabric and wished myself back in Meridian, back to a time when I was safe. It had all been so long ago, before Daddy was killed, but it was still there in my mind, and I found that I could go there and linger for longer and longer periods of time. Only Elikah's return brought me back to the present, back to the torment of my life.

Standing at the kitchen window, or looking out the one in the bedroom, I watched as fall settled in for a lengthy visit. It was mid-September, and the cold snap that had come in the day of Red's funeral had remained. Massive banks of clouds had begun building on the southern horizon, but they didn't move toward Jexville. They kept their distance, teasing me with the promise of a fierce storm. The days were perfect, but there was a need for rain. I could see it in the drooping leaves of the bushes and the parched brown of the grass.

Sitting at the open windows, making certain that the curtains hid me from view, I heard the call of Bruner, the vegetable man. Sometimes I would catch a glimpse of Jeb Fairley as he walked to and from his home. I wanted badly to signal him, to have him come over to help me. But I was afraid. Elikah had come very close to killing me, and his most recent days of consideration had me scared and terribly confused. It was not possible that the same man who'd grinned as he kicked me in the ribs was now the one who spooned soup into my mouth. No matter how hard I tried, I could not make the pieces of it all fit together. Some part was missing, and I couldn't remember what it was.

I knew when Floyd touched me in the church that Elikah would be furious. I had thought he would let me explain. In my wildest imagination, I'd never thought he would nearly kill me. I'd expected a spanking. A hard one. But not a savage beating. But I couldn't deny that I had let Floyd touch me in a familiar way. In public. Janelle had warned me of the consequences, the fury that any husband would display.

The hours of the day passed as I worried the knot of my problems. Doc Westfall came every day, checking the stove to make sure that Elikah was feeding me properly. My teeth had miraculously stabilized, but he warned me to eat only soft foods. The bleeding had stopped once again, and though Doc was curious about my "initial incident," he didn't ask any questions that I couldn't avoid. He told me that after the scene at Red's funeral, JoHanna and Duncan had returned to Fitler. He said that word had come back to him that Duncan was finally walking a little. Even though the days were cooler, JoHanna was taking her to the river every day for her exercises.

There was no mention of John Doggett, and I came to believe that he had been part of a dream. His image haunted me in my sleep, a tall, silent man who required no words to make his presence felt. He stood behind JoHanna whenever she came into my nether world. Was he guarding her or threatening her; I couldn't determine. He grew more dreamlike with each encounter. John Doggett was the first warning that I was having difficulty discerning past from present, real from remembered.

I moved about the house, tracking the rising and setting of the sun. Looking out the front windows I watched the storm clouds gather while the sun burned golden among the changing colors of the single sycamore tree in the empty lot across the street. I fancied myself a little girl again, scuffing through the first crisping leaves that had fallen. Sitting at my window, I could feel the delicious crunch beneath my feet. The long walk on the way to school. The first cedar smell of unpacked sweaters. Thick socks. Fall. My favorite of all the seasons.

As the pains in my body lessened, I was able to reconstruct the small fragments of joy from long ago. More familiar than the present was my fancy, single moments of the past spun into days where all of my senses were amazingly acute, and there was no suffering, no cruelty. Elikah would come home to find me at the window, gazing out into some scene I'd taken from the past and embellished and carved until it was as real as the touch of the windowsill beneath my hand. With a queer kindness, he would lead me back to bed and feed me, talking of this and that, trying to draw my interest in a place and a people I had never known and completely wiped from my mind.

I had at last escaped Jexville.

I was not unhappy. Perhaps I was happier than I had ever been. I no longer had the ability to judge such things. There were the windows, Elikah, the food he brought me. I knew those things to be real, but real had no value any longer. As soon as my meal was finished or Elikah had finally fallen asleep, I would ease out of bed and return to a window. There I could feel.

The kitchen window had a view of the paddock where Mable grazed. I knew the mare, and some of my fantasies included sneaking out to saddle her and ride. There was no place I wanted to go, but I wanted the sensation of riding. I knew better than to leave the house, though. Elikah had made it clear that I was "away." No one in town, other than Doc Westfall, could know that I was in the house, crisscrossing the rooms in search of another view. The idea that Elikah thought he had me trapped amused me. I had learned how to travel far away to places he could never even imagine. He was the prisoner, not me.

I wasn't so far gone that I didn't appreciate the fact that he had also become the servant. I had not tried to light the stove or wash a dish. Those were skills of another Mattie. I had no need for food or dishes, except what he insisted that I take. I needed only my window, where I watched a childish Mattie following the sounds of a crying infant. The baby was in distress, and young Mattie, with her thick, curly hair in pigtails down her back, hunted through the narrow green tunnel of foliage that led to the sparkling white sand of a reddish river. There, in a shallow trench dug in the white sand, was a baby. Delighted, Mattie lifted the child high into the blue sky. The baby reached down to Mattie, holding out chubby fists, content at last.

"Mattie?"

Someone called me from the tunnel of green, someone hidden from view, but I knew the voice though I could not place it.

"Mattie?" There was fear in the voice, an emotion that made me jerk away from the window and whirl. A woman with hair clipped so close to her head that it looked like a bathing cap was standing in the doorway of the kitchen. Behind her were Doc Westfall and Elikah.

"Mattie, it's me, JoHanna."

I knew her voice, but the way she looked at me made me afraid. I put my hands up to cover my face.

"Mattie!" She took three long strides across the room and pulled me into her arms. She held me tight, so tight it made my ribs ache, but it was also good because I felt her warmth. Her tears struck the top of my head, hot little nails of emotion.

"You're a dead man, Elikah Mills." She spoke with such anger that I thought her words might slice across the room and cut Elikah in half. I imagined him, cut down the middle like the chickens I'd cooked long ago for a barbecue in a place I couldn't remember.

"I'll get a few of her things." Doc Westfall started toward the bedroom while Elikah stood in the doorway. His hands hung down at his sides like something dead. I'd admired his hands as he was feeding me, the way they scooped just the right amount of potato on the spoon, lifting it all so smoothly to my mouth. Never spilling. Never miscalculating. Now they were lifeless. He would not look at me.

When Doc came back with a small bag, a pair of my underwear hanging out, Elikah stepped out of the doorway, out of the way. Her arm still tight around me, the woman led me through the house and out into the grayness of an approaching storm. The sun had disappeared and the heavy mass of clouds had finally begun to move our way.

Twenty-seven

KNEELING before me in the bright yellow kitchen, the woman with the funny hair cried as her fingers traced the still-bruised tissue of my face. A young girl, her head also strangely clipped, stood in the doorway and cried, too. They both looked at me as if something terribly important was missing. I held out my hands and checked my feet to be sure all of me was there. Several days had passed since they brought me to this house, and each day they cried over me first thing every morning. They would make coffee, put a cup on the table for me, and begin to touch me and cry.

"Mattie, look at me." The woman put her palm against my cheek and drew my face down so that I gazed at her. She had the bluest eyes. Looking into them was like being touched by her. And she was crying again.

"What's wrong?" My voice sounded funny because I hardly talked any more. In the places that I liked best, there was no talk. Only movement through time. And sensation. I looked beyond her, out the window where a big rooster perched, cocking his head this way and that as if he watched us. At my look, he lifted his wings and made a menacing sound. He seemed to dance toward me, puffing out his chest and waving his wings. The rooster was constantly around, too.

"Pecos." The girl chided him. "If you can't behave go outside."

But I didn't mind him. He was interesting. I'd never seen a rooster in a house before.

The woman took me to a bedroom where she turned back the cool cotton sheets. The most beautiful peach-colored curtains lifted on the wind. I could smell the storm coming, and I turned from the bed to look out the window. The storm had been building for days, massing dark clouds on the horizon. Now, at last, it had begun to move over us.

"Mattie, I'm going to write your mother. And your sisters, Callie and Lena Rae. I'm going to tell them how Elikah beat you and ask them to come see you."

"Callie?" There was something I had to tell my sister. Something important. I remembered! "Tell her not to marry. No matter what Jojo says."

The woman pressed her palm lightly against my jaw. "Yes, Mattie. Callie and Lena Rae. They love you. We love you, Mattie. Me and Duncan. Try to remember." Her face brightened, and she hurried out of the room to return with an enormous straw hat with fancy rooster feathers on it. "JoHanna McVay and her daughter, Duncan. Remember us? Do us a little dance step, Duncan."

With a laugh, Duncan sang and hummed a ragtime tune and did a few awkward dance steps with her stiff leg. When she finished, the woman applauded, and I did, too, to be polite.

"JoHanna," the woman said. "Say it, Mattie. Say my name."

"Jo-Hanna." Warmth tingled deep inside me. "JoHanna McVay."

Her face shifted into surprise, then joy. "Yes, Mattie, yes. I'm Jo-Hanna." She motioned the girl to her side and pulled her close with one arm. "And Duncan."

"Gramophone." I remembered her with a gramophone.

"Oh, Mattie." The woman hugged me on one side and the girl on the other. Then she kissed both of our heads. "You're coming back to us, slowly but surely. And now I want you to sleep. Doc Westfall said sleep was the best medicine." She knelt down beside me and began unlacing my shoes. The girl joined her, taking my other foot. I could have done it myself, but it was easier to let them than to fight about it. When they were done they lifted my legs and put them in the bed, drawing the soft spread up to my chin.

"You can still see out the window." JoHanna pointed to where the curtains billowed on a hot, fast breeze. "I have to go and cook us some supper. Give a holler if you need anything." She kissed my forehead. "Anything at all."

Something in my head buzzed a warning. She was too close, too real. I would be hurt. I looked past her out the window, where it was safer. Clothes on the line were snapping in the sudden gusts of wind. My younger sister stepped from behind a sheet. She and my next sister were playing among the clothes. I couldn't remember their names, but I knew them, knew they were eleven and ten, respectively. They darted among the wash, laughing and trying to tag each other. I smiled and waved at them, but they couldn't hear me because of the storm.

"Mama, there's no one out there," the girl in the doorway whispered. "Who's she waving to?"

The woman shook her head to silence the girl. "When Doc came up to Fitler to get us, he said Mattie was having trouble telling what was real from what she imagines. *She* sees someone out there, Duncan. She sees *them* better than she sees us. So we're just going to have to make her focus on us again."

"How?" The girl tottered into the room on unsteady legs. The right one dragged a bit behind her as she walked.

She was distracting me from my sisters out in the yard. I got up and went to the window where I could see outside better. The sky was getting grayer and more overcast, the wind blowing hard. It was going to be a bad storm.

The woman came and led me back to the bed. "Rest for a while, Mattie." Her words were gentle, but they were also a command. I'd learned from Elikah about commands. I lay down on the bed, my hands resting on my stomach.

"Geez, she looks like a corpse!"

"Duncan!" The woman shook her head. "She can hear you, even though she acts like she can't."

"He beat the dickens out of her." Duncan's voice broke. "Is she going to get better, Mama? Is she?"

Her anguish hurt me, but there was nothing I could do. I would have soothed her if I could, but I had nothing to give her to make it better. I glanced at the window, wondering when they would leave me so I could go and look outside.

The woman took the young girl by the shoulder and they left the room, taking care to see the door was left ajar. I lay on the bed and listened to their voices. A man had joined them. He had a deep, pleasant voice, and he spoke softly. When I was certain they were deep in conversation, I got out of bed and went to the window. There was an Auburn Touring car beneath a chinaberry tree, and I stared at the automobile. It was beautiful, and I remembered a handsome man, dark hair neatly groomed, chocolate eyes laughing and teasing. But the buzzing started in my head again, and I saw that the car was a fire truck. My sisters were hiding behind the other side, laughing at me as they peeked around the big silver front bumper. They were older than when they'd played in the clothes on the line. Older and prettier. They wore dresses, and they laughed at the handsome firemen on the truck. But it was me the firemen pointed out. They held out their hands and urged me to come out the window and climb on board the big red truck. They were going to take me for a ride.

"Mattie."

I ignored the man's voice as he spoke from behind me. The firemen didn't talk. They only smiled and touched and nodded, saying without words that they liked me, that they wanted me to come with them on the big red fire truck.

Strong hands grasped my shoulders. Too real, they went through my dress and skin right to my bone. I struggled to free myself, thrashing and twisting against those big hands that seemed to want to hold me in a place I didn't want to be.

"Mattie." He spoke calmly, though he was fighting to keep his grip.

"Mattie." He shifted me toward the bed, and when he managed to get me down on it he held me with one hand while brushing his long, black hair out of his face.

"Easy, Mattie, it's me, John Doggett."

The name echoed around my head and then left.

"Easy." He held me with one hand and pulled a chair up beside the bed with his free one. "Easy." He moved his hand away from me inch by inch, always watching to make sure I didn't try to bolt and escape. I knew better than to move. He could still hit me.

"JoHanna and Duncan have gone to get Floyd. I told them I'd stay here with you until they returned. I said I'd tell you a story."

He smiled, and I thought how handsome he was. If only he wouldn't talk aloud. If only he'd shut up and talk with his eyes. I reached up to put my fingers on his lips, and he closed his mouth. He caught my fingers in his hand and held them tightly before putting my hand beside me on the bed. Very gently he held it there. Then he nodded and stared at me.

His eyes were intensely black with straight eyebrows that were now drawn together in concentration. He shifted closer, so that I could see the texture of his lashes, thick and long, the bristle of his beard beneath his skin. Though my gaze strayed, it always returned to his eyes. And then I saw myself in the black depths. The swelling was gone from my face, but the bruises were still dark, fringed in green. They were healing. I reached up to touch my own face and saw my hand in the reflection of his eyes.

Mattie.

He did not speak the word, but I heard it.

Mattie, come back to us.

He called to me with his gaze. He did not speak. His lips did not move.

Please, Mattie.

I heard his voice, but his lips did not move. I touched his lips again and felt them curve only slightly in a smile.

"JoHanna asked me to tell you a story, Mattie." He spoke against my hand, his life puffing lightly against my fingers. "I've picked out one I think you'll like. If it isn't right, Floyd will be here soon to take over as the master storyteller. For the moment, my story is about a young girl who decided to have an adventure on a river."

I closed my eyes and felt his words against my fingers, and I began to listen.

I awoke to unnatural blackness and the sound of panic. In the darkness people were scurrying around and there was the sound of breaking glass as a woman cursed with great ability. I had no idea how long I'd been asleep or where I was. But I had slept. After nights and nights of sitting at my windows watching, I'd finally slept. Inside my head the memories were quiet.

"Where's Pecos?" The young girl who had trouble walking demanded. I recognized her voice easily.

"Duncan, that bird has sense enough to get someplace safe. That's why he's been missing for the last hour. He's smart enough to realize we're in for a bad storm and he's found himself a safe place to be. Now we're going to do the same."

"I'm going to hunt for him."

"Over my dead body. I've got enough to worry about without you going out into a bad storm."

"I'm not afraid of storms." There was defiance in the words.

"I'm not either, but you're not going out there. This isn't just a thunderstorm, Duncan. Can't you feel it? This is a grandfather of a storm."

A man's soft voice spoke. "Imagine it, Duncan. Zeus up there in the clouds getting ready to pour some serious tragedy down on us mortals. A little entertainment for the gods."

"Right." She spoke with sarcasm. "It's just an old storm. Ever since I got struck by lightning, Mama acts like a little rain is going to kill me."

"Duncan, you're staying inside this house. If Pecos wants to come home, he will."

"I'll go look for Pecos, Duncan."

This was a different voice. Younger than the other man. Golden and light. I liked the sound of it. I knew this man and he made me feel safe.

A door closed and footsteps went down the wooden steps.

Someone had come into my room and closed my window, so I got up and went and opened it. The peach curtains, slinky as silk, fluttered in the wind and draped around my body, teasing my skin with cool caresses. It was as dark in my room as it was outside, so I had no concerns about being seen. Beyond the window I heard the golden man calling for the rooster named Pecos. The storm had blocked out all signs of moon or stars, and the clouds seemed thick and dense, moving close to the ground like the march of a midnight army.

I saw the man in the light from the kitchen window. His hair was longish and golden. Floyd. I knew him. I knew that I liked him. He was tender, gentle. He had been kind to me sometime in the past, though I couldn't remember when or why. The wind pressed his shirt into his brawny chest, and he lifted his chin and called for the rooster. "Pe-cos! Pe-cos!" He called strong and hard, but the wind whipped the words from his mouth and tore them apart. "Pe-cos!" He moved toward the outside shed. He tried to force the door open, but the wind blew against him. I could see he was strong, but the wind was strong, too, and it came in gusts that made it hard to fight. The door gave suddenly, swinging out toward him. A squawking, flapping blast of feathers shot from the shed. The bird half ran, half flew across the yard directly to the window where I stood.

Before I could move, he flew up, talons extended, and came at me. I felt his claws dig into my arm, and I heard my scream, though it sounded as if it came from a great distance away.

Behind me there was the sound of running feet, and then the man and woman and the young girl were all around me. The woman held my arm while the man put pressure on it to stop the flow of blood. In the light of a lantern I watched the dark red blood drip off my fingers and dance against the waxed wood of the floor.

It didn't hurt, not yet, but I knew it would. Reaching up to push the hair out of my face with my other hand, I saw the other scar, the curved hook in the center of my palm. That, too, had been made by the rooster. I remembered. Pecos. The red-brown flurry of feathers and claws as I stood in the hot yard pulling a wagon and a gramophone. Pecos! I remembered!

Around me JoHanna and Duncan and John Doggett were chattering and getting bandages and turpentine. In a corner of the room the rooster waited, his beady little eyes following each and every movement that I made. We looked at each other, and he lifted his wings out from his body and shook them at me, a warning.

"Damn you, Pecos," I said. "That's the second time you've spurred me. I ought to cook your scrawny ass. I think Aunt Sadie was on the right track when she wanted to make dumplings with you."

Everyone around me went completely silent, and I looked at them.

"What time is it?" I asked.

"Nearly ten o'clock. You slept for twelve hours straight." JoHanna's voice was rigidly controlled, a calm, steady voice.

I nodded. JoHanna was giving me the strangest look, and Duncan had finally stopped crying. Floyd stood in the doorway, and John Doggett sat beside me on the bed, his large hand holding the cloth against the six-inch slash that Pecos had opened up between wrist and elbow. I had the clearest memory of John's eyebrows and the way his lips moved when he talked about some girl who went to live with the Indians on the Pascagoula River.

"Welcome home, Mattie," JoHanna said. She brushed her hand over my face and lifted my chin up to the kerosene lantern she held in her other hand. She studied my face intently. "Do you know me?"

"I know you aren't Mary Pickford."

My response brought laughter that started rather feebly but continued to grow as they each looked at one another. Finally, they were all laughing until tears came from their eyes.

"Who would have thought Pecos would bring her out of it?" Floyd asked. He went and got the rooster and put him on his shoulder. "As soon as John finishes with Mattie, I think we should put the boards across the windows. The wind is getting mighty high. This is going to be one bad, bad storm."

Twenty-eight

ONCE the wound given to me by Pecos had been cleaned and dressed, I ate a bowl of potato soup and went back to sleep. I awoke, infrequently, to the sound of Pecos's claws clacking on the hardwood floor beside the bed. Either he was serving as sentinel to my sleep, or he was angry because I'd taken Duncan's bed. I didn't waste more than a few seconds on the question but immediately returned to the soft darkness of a dreamless sleep. When I finally surfaced, it was to an eerie gray light and the howl of wind. The rain, driven by the wind, hammered the windows that were crisscrossed with boards in long gusts that sounded like rocks being shaken in a jar. My first impulse was to pull the sheets and pillows over my head. The house groaned as if it were coming apart at the seams, while outside the trees fought their own battle against the gales. They moaned and strained, a subtext of noise to the challenge of the wind.

I knew instantly where I was, and my arm, and Pecos's presence in the room, perched on the back of the rocking chair JoHanna had sat in to watch me, were testimony that I had not dreamed the events before I went to sleep. I lay in Duncan's bed and decided I was glad to be back in the present. My retreat had been into the past, but a past that had never existed. I knew that. It had been a choice—to avoid a present I could not tolerate. JoHanna's rescue of me, the strange power of John Doggett's voice, and Pecos's unintentional attack. Somehow the combination had given me the link to the present, a path back.

Stretching against the clean cotton of the sheets, I felt the most peculiar sensation seep into me. During brief lulls in the wind I could hear voices in the kitchen. The storm was blasting the house, and because of where I was, I felt safe. I was also a little afraid, but mostly safe. I got up and slipped into the robe JoHanna had placed at the foot of the bed and went to find her.

I found them all in the kitchen, huddled around the table. Duncan sat in JoHanna's lap, and Floyd and John sat on either side of her. Pecos followed me into the kitchen, and I took the fourth seat at the table.

"It's a hurricane," JoHanna said. "A lot of people are going to suffer." A single lamp on the kitchen table cast a golden globe of light on our hands and faces. It was strange illumination. The outside light was pearlized, a glowing gray, as if the sun had forsaken us and sent a weaker cousin in her place.

"Is it going to blow the house down?" Living in Meridian, I'd heard about hurricanes, but they only affected the coastal area, or so I thought. Jexville was a good forty miles from Mobile Bay, and then another goodly piece from the open water of the Gulf of Mexico. But the big storms obviously had a long reach.

"This house is well made." JoHanna looked around the kitchen just as a big limb slammed into the side of the house. "If one of the trees falls on it . . ." She didn't have to finish. The big oaks out front had deep root systems, but they also presented a big target for the wind to catch. I wanted to look outside, but I was unwilling. The noise of the wind was enough to convince me that the storm's raw power was more than I wanted to witness. I would linger in the safety of the lamplight with my friends.

"What about Will?" I asked.

"He's still in New York. I'll get word to him that we're safe as soon as I can." She wrapped her arms tighter around Duncan.

Duncan shifted, loosening JoHanna's hold. She cocked her head, a gesture that Pecos, standing beside her, immediately imitated. "I like the storm," she said softly. "Listen to the wind. It's terrible, so angry." She took her mother's hand. "But none of us were in the dream. It was only strangers."

There was an undercurrent of emotion around the table. Fear? Apprehension? I couldn't be certain.

"You like it because you think it won't affect us." JoHanna was frowning. "A lot of people are going to be hurt by this. The last storm that came through in 1906 leveled the pine timber from the coast up to Fitler. The destruction was complete. Some folks haven't recovered yet, and here it comes again."

Duncan twisted so that she could look behind her, reading her mother's expression more than her words. "You always say that nature is supreme, that people forget her power. You say that nature is the only force to bend humans to her will, and that it's good for us to know we aren't all-powerful."

When no one spoke, Duncan continued, her voice more determined. "You said that when man is able to control the weather that he'll destroy the earth." She turned in JoHanna's arms to look at John Doggett. "You said it, too. I've heard you talking with Mama."

Doggett's smile was sad. "It's true, Duncan. But some lessons are painful, and hard to watch. Nature tends to punish the good and the bad without discrimination."

His words struck me at the base of the spine, a tingle of apprehension. I had so fully accepted his presence in the house. I had climbed out of myself using his words as footholds. But why was he here? I lowered my chin and watched him through my eyelashes. He was at ease, but sad.

"Some people need to hurt." Duncan's gaze turned inward, her mouth taking on a hard line that looked older. "This is what I saw in my dream, and it's going to happen to everyone in Jexville. They're all going to be touched." She put her cards, face down, on the table. "I keep remembering the dream, and I know some of it's here, in Chickasaw County. People drowned. Water running in creeks and ditches." Her forehead furrowed and she rubbed it with one tired fist. "But it doesn't make sense. It's land like a farm where the bodies are. Not all on the coast."

JoHanna gathered her daughter to her chest, hugging her tightly. "Hush, Duncan." JoHanna looked over the top of Duncan's head and into Floyd's worried eyes.

"What is it?" I felt the tension, but I didn't fully understand. The storm was going to do awful things, but we couldn't stop it, and we were safe. Will was safe in New York. What was going on that I didn't understand?

They exchanged a glance, as if trying to decide whether to tell me or not.

"We should all leave for Fitler as soon as we can." JoHanna's gaze dropped to Duncan's hands on the table. "It would be best."

They were all afraid, or if not afraid, at least apprehensive. "Why?"

"Mattie, do you remember Red's funeral?"

The scene came back to me with blistering shame. I hadn't forgotten it. I'd simply buried it away. I felt the flush rise up my cheeks as Floyd turned to gaze at me. He'd touched me. Not in any suggestive way, but a simple restraint. That was why Elikah had beaten me. Oh, I remembered.

"I see you do remember." JoHanna hesitated. "I made reference to a natural disaster, a plight brought down by God. Well, here it is." She held her palm out, fingers pointed toward the window. "This is going to be the final straw. They'll think Duncan and I called this down on their heads. They won't call it witchcraft, but that's what they'll believe. In their hearts."

"They don't have hearts." I spoke with great bitterness. "And who cares what they think?"

"I do. I've lived here most of my adult life not caring what they thought. I've always irritated the people here, but I've never been afraid of them. But this storm . . . the helplessness against it. They could turn on us. On Duncan."

And they would. She didn't have to say it. They would. The fury of the storm was nothing compared to what they would do. They were frightened, and threatened. A helpless child was the perfect target.

"I left Tommy Ladnier's boots out on the counter." Floyd got up and paced the room. "I should go put them away."

"They'll be fine," JoHanna and John said in unison. As an afterthought, JoHanna went to the phone on the kitchen wall. "Maybe we can ring through." She tried, but the phone was dead.

"Trees on the line," John said. "It would have been a miracle if it worked."

"Mr. Ladnier will be very upset if something happens to them." Floyd turned at the stove and came back toward the table.

"You can't help a hurricane, Floyd." John pushed back his chair. "I'm going to light the stove and make some coffee. It's chilly now, but once the storm passes it'll get hotter than blue blazes."

"Summer's over." I ventured the assessment.

"Not by a long shot. Watch and see. After the storm it'll get as hot as August. Sticky hot. I'll have my coffee now and be hot later." He went to the stove and readied everything as if he'd spent the better part of his life in JoHanna's kitchen.

I started to comment, but it was pointless. And coffee sounded good. Coffee and maybe some toast. I was starving again.

Worried about Tommy Ladnier's boots, Floyd suffered more than anyone else through the long hours of the storm. We drank coffee and talked. John had lived all along the coastal rim, and he knew about storms from Key West to Galveston. With amusing stories he kept our spirits up. He believed that we'd caught the western side of the storm, the weaker side. It was the eastern edge, and whether the tides were low or high, that determined the power of destruction, he told us.

Through the long hours of wind and rain, the crack of tree limbs, and the sudden assault of some windblown object against the house, we passed the time as best we could. JoHanna and Duncan taught us to play gin, a game that Floyd did not care much about. To John's delight, I discovered that I had a talent for cards. When JoHanna and Duncan tired of gin, he taught me to play poker. It occurred to me that Elikah would be scandalized, and it gave me a stab of pleasure. I spent what few moments I spared Elikah visualizing him beneath the weight of the biggest tree in existence.

We made more coffee and ate more toast when the clock indicated it was past noon. I thought there was a slackening in the force of the wind when I went to the kitchen window to look out.

John Doggett came up beside me, his hand lightly touching my back. "We were lucky. The worst is over for now."

"Do you think it did much damage?" I saw a big tree, the tip of Elikah's boot showing from beneath it, and I hoped.

"Not the hurricane. Some trees, a few barns and houses. The real danger for us, this far inland, is the tornadoes that come with a hurricane. There are sure to be some, and those are the real forces of destruction."

Perhaps Elikah had been picked up by a twister and carried off, never to be found again. I liked that even better than the idea of the tree. I wouldn't have to pretend to mourn his death. I could simply say that he was gone. Just gone.

It was after two o'clock before the winds died and the rain stopped. Just as John predicted, the sun returned with a vengeance. John and Floyd got hammers and crowbars and began pulling the boards from the windows. No glass had broken, and as the boards came down we were better able to see the yard.

Small limbs and leaves were scattered about in the side yards. The chinaberry tree was undamaged, and John had moved Will's Auburn out into the more open field where green and brown leaves had been plastered to the bright red paint, but otherwise it was undamaged. We slipped out the back door and made our way, JoHanna holding Duncan in her arms, to the front.

The big oaks that bordered the road had survived with the loss of only a few big limbs. With some cleaning up, they would not show the ravages of the storm by next spring. But the cedar had not been so lucky.

The trunk had snapped about fifteen feet from the ground, and the entire tree had fallen over, the green boughs taking up half the side yard.

"Oh." JoHanna set Duncan on her feet and ran to the tree. She stopped at the trunk and put both hands on it, her palms sliding over the red bark much the same way she'd felt my body for broken bones.

"If we cut it below the break, it may live." John walked beside her and put his hand on her shoulder. "I'm sorry, Jo."

"I spent many an afternoon under these branches." JoHanna sighed. "Get the bow saw out of the shed. Maybe you and Floyd can take care of it before we go to town." She started walking back to us, stopping at Duncan to brush her head. "The fronds were too dense. The wind . . ." She shook her head.

Floyd got the saw from the shed, which had lost its door. JoHanna went in the house, but Duncan and I shook the leaves out of the hammock and sat in the shade to watch. I was acutely aware of John as he worked. He was slighter across the shoulders than Floyd, but when he took his shirt off, the bumps and ridges of his muscles were hard and lean. He was a man who worked for a living, and not just with a pen. He pulled a string from his pocket and tied back his long dark hair as he bent to the saw, working in complete rhythm with Floyd. They were perfect contrasts, one dark, one light. Although Floyd was as hot, he worked with his shirt on. He was eager to get to town to check on his boots.

Duncan grew weary of the heat and wanted to go back in the house. I held her arm as she made the walk with slow, deliberate steps, awed by the grim determination that forced one foot in front of the other again and again and again. She was stronger. Much stronger.

I helped stack the smaller pieces of wood, wondering if JoHanna would actually burn her tree in the fireplace this winter. Floyd assured me that she would. JoHanna loved the tree, but letting it rot in the yard would not bring it back. And JoHanna had her hope that the trunk would survive.

An hour and a half later we were done. Twelve feet of red trunk remained intact. The rest of the tree had been sawed and split into stacks. The sun burned down with a fury that had begun to condense the puddles of water, giving the air a soupy humidity that made me long for a cold swim.

Instead, Floyd, John, and I took turns pumping water over our heads, gasping at the cold. JoHanna and Duncan appeared at the back door with towels, a picnic basket, and the keys to the car. We were going to drive Floyd to the boot shop to rescue his work. Then we would take a tour of the countryside and finally go to Fitler to make sure Aunt Sadie was okay. John warned us as we got in the car, me and Duncan and Floyd and Pecos in the back, that the roads might not be passable. JoHanna's cedar would not be the only casualty of the wind, and chances were, plenty of trees had fallen across the road. The bow saw was packed in the trunk, along with gloves and jugs of water.

An hour and two trees later, JoHanna conceded that it would be faster for Floyd to walk into town. Peterson Lane dead-ended not far past the McVay house, and there was little traffic on it. The busier roads would be cleared, but for the next day or two, JoHanna would not be able to drive anywhere.

JoHanna put sandwiches in Floyd's pockets, and then looked up when John selected several for himself.

"I thought I'd go with Floyd, take a look at the town while he's gathering up his stuff. See how much damage there was." An undercurrent cut through his words.

"Yes, that's a good idea." JoHanna looked down the road as if she expected to see General Sherman headed our way, torches in hand. "Thank you, John. You're a good friend to us."

"I'll see about Mattie's husband, too." A muscle jumped in John's cheek, his eyes flattened with fury. In that instant he was transformed. Barbarian. The word suited him. I almost hoped he would meet up with Elikah. My husband found it easy to beat a woman. John Doggett would give far better than he got.

"Don't start anything, John. There are innocents . . ." Her gaze drifted to Floyd, who stood in the middle of the road, legs slightly parted, as he patiently waited for John.

John's muscle twitched again.

JoHanna's voice took on an urgency. "You can leave, John. I can, if it comes to that. And Mattie can come with us. But Floyd won't. Not even with me. This is his home. The only one he wants."

The dark head nodded once, swiftly. He shifted the sandwiches to his other hand and then brushed a kiss on JoHanna's cheek. The action startled me, though it was done without the passion of a lover. I looked away, at Duncan and Pecos, to give JoHanna and John the privacy they needed.

JoHanna spoke again, and her words pulled my head up to look at her as she gave her instructions to John.

"Would you stop by the telegraph office and have them send a message to Will at the Waldorf that we're fine here? I don't want him to worry."

John nodded, then stepped back and joined Floyd at the road. "We'll be back later. If they need help in town, we'll give them a hand. You girls will be okay, won't you?"

"I want to see." Duncan had climbed up to sit beside Pecos. "I want to see if it was like my dream. I'll know it if I see it."

JoHanna ignored her daughter. "Test the waters, John."

"Will do." He strode off, matched step for step by Floyd.

John came back alone, filthy and concerned. Floyd had decided to stay and help Axim Moses reorder the shop. Elikah's barber pole, although once securely anchored, had been pulled loose and hurled through the front window of the boot shop. Heavy rains had flooded the shop. Tommy Ladnier's high-dollar boots, sitting on top of the counter, were undamaged, but the rest of the shop was a mess. Relieved, Floyd had felt a desire to help Axim put things in working order.

Jexville had escaped with minor damage, a few broken windows, trees down on phone lines, sheds and outbuildings destroyed. With one exception.

Chas Leatherwood had been killed. The high winds had ripped the roof from the large hay barn beside the feed store, and a wall of hay, soaked with rain, had fallen on him as he was trying to set a new brace.

JoHanna heated water on the stove for John's bath as he sat at the kitchen table, hay stuck in his hair and clothes, dirt and mud grimed up to his ears, and gave her the temperament of the town. I took a seat across from him. Duncan, exhausted by her efforts at walking and her frustration at not getting to see the storm damage, napped in her bed with Pecos as guard.

John ran through the scene at the feed store where Chas was killed. Agnes Leatherwood had been hysterical. Annabelle Lee had been sent to Rachel Carpenter's while Doc Westfall had calmed Agnes with a dose of laudanum.

"Did Agnes mention me or Duncan?" JoHanna tried not to sound worried, but I could tell she was. Really worried.

John sipped the sweet tea she'd given him and looked at me. "She did."

JoHanna's hand dropped to his shoulder as she stood behind him. "How bad was it?"

"I think you and Duncan should leave. Maybe take Floyd with you." He pushed some strands of hair out of his face. "There was talk of retribution. Of coming here to confront you."

"And Mattie?"

"Seems to be the thought of the day that Elikah has brought Mattie under control."

His words were bitter, and his grip on the tea glass whitened his knuckles. "The prevailing attitude is that Mattie was led astray by your wild and dangerous ways, but that Elikah managed to beat some sense into her. I guess they aren't aware yet that you have her back in your clutches."

"Agnes is upset. Chas was her entire world." JoHanna fumbled over the words. "They'll get over—"

"It wasn't just Agnes. The others, the men, they were talking crazy, JoHanna. As soon as they got the body out, I came on back. I didn't want to leave you alone."

"And Floyd?" JoHanna looked toward the back door as if she expected to hear his step.

"He's okay. He's with Mr. Moses, and they're down at the other end of town. He said he was going to stay with them tonight."

JoHanna paced to the door. "I'd feel better if he was here with us."

"We're not exactly in the best position. We can't get away, remember."

JoHanna nodded, but she kept her gaze out the window. "And they can't get here. At least not by car or wagon."

"It's just talk, JoHanna." I tried to sound like I believed it. I'd heard angry talk about JoHanna before, talk of their dislike for her. What type of retribution did they have in mind? I wanted to ask, but I didn't really want to know.

"We need to get to Fitler." John started to get up, but he glanced at me and didn't. "I sent Will a telegram. The lines are down, but they'll be back up." John lifted his chin a degree. "I told him to come home as fast as he could."

JoHanna turned at the door. Her hand moved up between her breasts and rested there. "I suppose that was smart."

"No one in town knows anything about me." He rose slowly, standing at the table. "They asked a few questions, but I told them I was traveling through and got stranded by the storm. Some of the men had heard reports from other places. The storm hit hard. The devastation in Florida is bad. Thousands are dead. And in Mobile there's damage down along the waterfront. Looks like the storm hit Florida and then went back out in the Gulf to take another swing here. Even if Will gets the message tomorrow or the next day, he might not be able to get back here for four or five days. I thought it best that he got started."

JoHanna nodded. "Yes."

"You're right, JoHanna. I can leave here at any time. You need Will. The men in town respect him. Maybe they're even a little afraid of him."

JoHanna shifted so that her back was to us. "Mattie?" Her voice shook.

"Yes."

"Would you keep an eye on Duncan? I, uh, I need to see about some things outside."

She was crying.

"I'll listen for her when she wakes. I thought I might make some persimmon pudding. There's a tree just down the road. When Duncan wakes up, we can go down there and pick up the ones the wind blew down."

"Thank you." JoHanna's long stride moved her across the kitchen and out the back door. The screen slammed hard behind her, and out the window I caught a glimpse of her running toward the path to the creek.

John shifted his weight uneasily from one foot to the other. He started to speak, then stopped. Worry etched hard lines around his mouth.

"I'm afraid for her," he said carefully.

"From the men in town or from you?"

"From both." He strode out of the room, the screen door slamming behind him.

He caught up with her at the edge of the woods. One hand grasped her shoulder and pulled her around to face him. With a small cry that I barely heard, she stumbled into his arms and cried against his chest.

Twenty-nine

DUNCAN awakened in the afternoon and helped me gather the small, firm persimmons that grew in abundance in the wild. We had to be careful. If they were the faintest bit green, they'd draw our mouths together in a pucker that took a while to wear down. But once ripened, the wild fruit made a delicious bread-type pudding. The late afternoon drifted away as we sifted the ingredients for the pudding, pulped the persimmons, and then put it in the oven to bake. The aroma wafted through the kitchen, tantalizing Duncan. But even though JoHanna and John returned by dark, they were not hungry. I had no interest in food. After supper, Duncan and I went to bed, sharing the double bed in her room.

Heat and darkness settled over the house as if we were in the bottom of a large black cauldron and someone had put on the lid. Duncan had fallen into a sound sleep, but I could not relax. JoHanna and John had stayed up in the living room talking for several hours, but now the bedroom door was firmly closed. No sounds came from within the room.

The long, dark hours of the night passed, interrupted only by Duncan's occasional soft murmur, the sound of Pecos shifting about the room, and the hum of mosquitoes at the screened window. And the heat. The oppressive, suffocating heat, which had the sound of my own heartbeat.

Too warm in the bed, I got up and went to the window. The beautiful peach curtains hung limp. Not even a whisper of breeze fluttered them. I remembered John's prediction. He'd been too right. It was hotter than August. Nature was not finished with us yet.

On her side of the bed, Duncan stirred. Her arms pushed out from her body and she twisted.

"No." The word was small, strangled sounding.

She didn't move again, and I waited. She was dreaming, but perhaps the nightmare had moved on, leaving her in peace.

She twisted again, her hands coming up as if to ward off a blow. "No. No!" She spoke louder, more clearly.

I walked to her side of the bed and put a hand on her heated forehead. She didn't have a fever. She was just hot, like everyone and everything else left a-kilter in the path of the hurricane.

"Please." She switched her head from side to side. "Please don't."

"Duncan." I brushed my hand across her face, hoping to soothe her back into the deep emptiness of sleep. "It's okay. It's only a dream."

"No!" The word was a cry. She sat bolt upright in bed, her eyes wide open and catching the glow of the moon from the window. Her look was purely insane. "Mother!" She screamed the word. "Mother!"

I grabbed her by her shoulders and shook lightly, then harder when she didn't respond. "Duncan, wake up!"

"Mother!" Her eyes were wide, the whites showing. Foam had gathered in the corner of her mouth. "Mother! No!"

JoHanna's bedroom door was flung open with great strength. Wearing only Will's robe, JoHanna ran into the room. Behind her John Doggett wore only his white cotton drawers.

"Duncan." JoHanna pushed up to her daughter's side. "Duncan, I'm here. What's wrong?"

Duncan blinked, the madness leaving her eyes as she looked up at her mother and allowed the tears to fall. "He had me again. Down at the bottom of the river. He had me and he wouldn't let me go and I was drowning!" The last word was a wail. "There was dirt in the water, and I could feel it in my nose and throat and eyes, all grainy in my eyes! And I looked at him, and an eel came out of his eye socket. I could see his teeth in the white bones of his jaw!" Her face crumpled in upon itself, and she wailed blindly.

JoHanna crushed Duncan to her, stroking the child's back as she rocked her gently. "It was only a dream, Duncan. Only a dream. You're safe. You're here with me and Mattie and John. It was only a dream."

John and I stood at the foot of the bed, helpless to do anything. Duncan's terror had frightened me. Goosebumps defied the heat and humidity, and I felt a chill shake me like a teasing breeze.

John excused himself and went to find his pants while JoHanna rocked Duncan and I went to the kitchen to put on the kettle for some tea. There was no milk for cocoa. With the road blocked, there was no way to get into town. Unlike most of the people who lived in the country, JoHanna didn't keep a cow. Will was gone too much, and JoHanna liked to be able to go to Fitler when the mood struck. A cow was something that just couldn't be left behind to fend for itself. So I made the chamomile tea Aunt Sadie had taught me to use to calm and soothe.

JoHanna brought Duncan to the table, where she lit the lamp and we all gathered. After Duncan had sipped the tea and calmed enough to breathe without sobbing, JoHanna took her hand.

"Tell us the whole dream, Duncan. All of it."

Duncan shook her head. "It's awful. I don't want to say it."

JoHanna kept a firm grip on her hand. "But you must. You told us all the other dreams, about Mary and Red. About the storm. And you've told us about this one before. Tell it all to us."

Duncan looked into her mother's eyes. "No."

"Duncan, maybe if you talk about it we can try to understand it. We have to be able to figure out why this dream frightens you so much when the others didn't."

"If you had some man with hunks of loose skin hanging off his bones and an alligator gar staring at you from his rib cage, and he was trying to catch hold of you and keep you underwater with him, you'd be upset, too." The more she talked the angrier she got.

"That's a good start, Duncan. Tell us the rest. Do you know who this man is?"

Duncan's eyes were black. They snapped with anger. "I want Daddy."

JoHanna never faltered. "Will can't help you out of this, Duncan. This is something you have to confront on your own. We'll help you. Me and John and Mattie. And Floyd, when he comes back tomorrow. Right now, though, tell me, did you know the man?"

Duncan hesitated. The fire left her eyes, and they filled with tears again. "I knew him, but I couldn't figure out who he was." She took a ragged breath. "I didn't like him. He tried to hold me under with him."

"Was there anything about him that you recognized?" John asked softly.

Duncan nodded. "The boots." She whispered the answer.

JoHanna caught me with her look. "His boots? What about them?"

"They're like the pair Floyd is working on."

"The ones for Tommy Ladnier?" I asked.

She shook her head. "The others. With the pretty design. It's the same design from the boots. That's how I knew how to draw it, because the man under the water has the design on his boots." Duncan looked down into her cup of tea, and a small shudder touched her. "He was pointing down at the boots, and his jaw was working, but no words came out. But he was trying to tell me something. Something about the boots." Duncan looked up suddenly, her eyes wide and glazed with fear. "I'm worried about Floyd, Mama. I'm afraid something's going to happen to him."

Instead of denying the fear, JoHanna kissed Duncan's hand and pressed it against her cheek. Holding it there she reached with her other hand to stroke Duncan's face. "I'm worried about him, too. Maybe John will go tomorrow and bring him back here to us. We'll look out for him."

Duncan sighed. "Please, John?"

"Certainly." John's shoulders sagged in relief. I knew then that if Duncan had asked him to leave, he would. I wasn't certain if she understood what role he played in her mother's life. Or her father's. I wasn't certain of anything, not even my own reaction to it.

"Tell us the whole dream," JoHanna coaxed her.

John pulled his chair closer. "There may be a clue in it, Duncan. Something we need to know. To protect you or Floyd."

Duncan sipped her tea with a tiny slup of noise. "Okay," she finally agreed. "It's just so awful." She glanced up at me. "Did I frighten you, Mattie?"

"You did." I grinned at her. "But not as bad as you frightened yourself."

"I suppose not." She gave a half chuckle. "It all starts when I'm standing on the banks of the Pascagoula. It's springtime and the river is running high, just at flood stage. There are all sorts of things floating past me. Rocking chairs with old women in them, bathtubs with strange men taking a bath, chickens floating by on bales of hay." She shook her head. "It's all very strange because all of those things would have drowned, sunk to the bottom. But they go by real fast on the current because the river is in a hurry."

I watched JoHanna's face. She was extremely worried, and doing her best to hide it. I remembered her fear—that Duncan was predicting her own drowning, and I felt the finger of death in the room.

"I think I was a lot older, standing on the bank. Older than Mattie even. I was full grown. Anyway, the water kept rising and coming up until it covered my feet, and then my ankles, and then my knees, and when I tried to move back, the mud had me. I knew I was going under, but it didn't bother me because I wasn't afraid of the river."

We leaned in closer and closer to Duncan, transfixed by her words and by the lamplight casting strange shadows on her face, now shiny with perspiration. The night was not overcast, but the heat seemed to have thrown up a fog that blocked the starlight and stilled the breezes. Duncan was not afraid of the river in her dream, but I fought the horrible sensation of suffocation that her words generated.

"The water came up fast, and as soon as I slipped beneath it, the mud let me loose." Duncan's hands were clenched into fists, but she held them still on the table. JoHanna's hand was beside her, but not touching.

"I saw the man. He was down by the supports of the bridge, watching me. Waiting for me to come down to him. The current was moving very fast around me, but I was still, like a big fish that can hang in the water without seeming to move. I sort of pointed myself toward him and began to go against the current. I remember the feel of the water against my eyes, the pressure. It was murky and I couldn't see all that good, but I wasn't afraid. The man was sitting against the support, his back against the stones as if he were taking a break after some hard work. When I got closer, I saw that—" For the first time she faltered. "That he wasn't all there. Parts of his flesh were missing. Big hunks had fallen away in tatters."

John picked up one of Duncan's hands and he smoothed out her fist, straightening her fingers in the strength of his own.

"Tell us the rest, Duncan," he said softly.

Duncan lifted her gaze to meet his. Her dark eyes, so much like Will's, were frightened. "He lifted his hand and motioned to me to come closer. He said, 'Duncan, you know me. Tell the truth. You're as guilty as the rest.' " She took in a fractured breath. "Then he pointed to the boots. His leg bones were jammed down in them, but they looked new and beautiful, with that pretty vamp. And while I was looking at them, his bony fingers grabbed my wrist." She was looking at the table now, recounting the dream in a voice almost expressionless. "I looked over at him, and there was an alligator gar staring back at me from inside his rib cage. The fish grinned, then swam away. An eel came out of his eye socket, and his jaw dropped open to show his teeth, and there was the sound of him laughing, only it wasn't a laugh. It was bubbles of air. That's when I noticed the chain wrapped around him. It was big and heavy and rusty, and he said soon that the rust would free him and he'd rise up to make all of us pay." She took a breath that was ragged and weary. "That's all."

"Who do the boots belong to that Floyd is working on?" John asked.

"Sheriff Grissham," I answered. I remembered the day I talked to Floyd about them and he told me how Duncan had imagined the design of the vamp. "He's making them special order for the sheriff."

"Are they finished?"

I couldn't remember exactly, but he'd been almost done when I last went by the shop. Before my beating. "Probably."

John nodded slowly. "Well, I must say, Duncan, that's some dream." He still held the hand he'd forced open. He brought it to his lips and kissed it. "I think you're going to grow up to be an actress. Or maybe a writer. What do you think, JoHanna?"

JoHanna's smile was forced, but it was there. "I always thought Duncan would be a dancer. Like her namesake. Someone a little scandalous, but very beautiful."

"Like her mother," John said.

They were trying to put a better angle on Duncan's dream, and for Duncan they were succeeding. She was smiling a little, a hesitant smile. Telling the dream had been the right thing. It had cleansed her of it. I got up and took her cup to make her some more tea. Dawn was just beginning to break, and we had agreed to try to clear the road to town if we could. It was going to be a long, hard day, especially without Floyd to help John on the saw. But I wanted the road cleared as soon as possible, just in case Will got back sooner than anyone thought. I didn't know what Duncan's dream meant. I didn't believe she was going to drown. But I wanted Will to return. Sanity would return with him, I was certain.

⤿ *Thirty* ⤾

W E were up and through with breakfast by seven o'clock. Only Duncan looked as if she'd slept at all, an irony, to be sure. None the worse for her dream, she teased me and her mother about the dungarees we wore. JoHanna had insisted that if we were going to work like men, we should dress like men. Skirts were dangerous around saws and trees. It took little to convince me. Even though the pants she gave me were big, I snugged them at the waist with one of Will's cut down belts and felt a freedom I'd left behind in childhood. I was standing in front of the chevalier in JoHanna's bedroom, hands on my hips, admiring my masculine silhouette, when Duncan caught me.

"You're getting to be just like mama," she warned. She was standing in a shaft of white-yellow light that flooded into the room from three big windows that also washed the bed in sunlight. She, too, wore pants. A jaunty tam sat on the side of her head. "Pretty soon all the men in town will be afraid of you, too."

"I can only hope." The words came out with an anger I hadn't been aware of until I spoke.

She realized what she'd said, and she flushed. "I'm sorry, Mattie." She leaned against the doorway. Her legs were getting stronger, but she still found it tiring to stand for any length of time without support. "I'm sorry for everything that happened to you. But the bruises are going away. And your ribs must be much better."

Staring at myself in the mirror, I'd failed to notice the green bruises beneath my eyes and the scab on my cheekbone. I had looked at myself but had failed to see the remnants of the beating. The features of my face had not registered at all, but I was healing, and soon all exterior physical traces of Elikah's beating would be gone. I felt like working. In fact, I was eager to help clear the road. I needed hard labor. Something inside me was growing, and it was pushing against my skin, wanting out. But I was afraid to let it out, afraid of what it might become. If I could work until exhaustion, perhaps I could exorcise it that way.

"I'm going to be fine." I realized Duncan was watching me in the mirror, waiting for some answer.

"When Daddy gets home, he'll beat the hallelujah out of Elikah for you." Duncan's offer was made with quiet force.

I turned around to face her directly. "I don't want Will to do that."

"You don't?" Duncan's face fell. "Why not?"

Why not? The idea of Elikah's face, smashed and broken, pleased me greatly. Somewhere in the midst of the storm, an idea had stolen over me. The only way to get on with a bully was to bully him back. That was true. The only sign of fear I'd seen Elikah display was when he was on a collision course with JoHanna. He did not fear her physically, but he did fear what she *would* do to him in town. Doc Westfall was bound by his oath not to discuss his patients. JoHanna was not. She could, and would, tell everything he'd done. And he couldn't intimidate her the way he did me.

"Are you going to put him in prison?" Duncan asked.

"Where did you get that idea?" It hadn't even crossed my mind. He was my husband. No court of law would put him behind bars for hitting me.

"I heard Mama and John talking. John said maybe the best thing would be to get a good lawyer and bring charges against him. John said even if he wasn't convicted, the shame of it would likely make him behave. If he didn't kill you outright before you got a chance to testify."

Formal charges were a thought, but along with Elikah, I would be shamed, too. The night in New Orleans slammed into my mind, a seething twist of images that made me break eye contact with Duncan.

"What's wrong, Mattie?" She came into the room, her steps slow and careful. Reaching out, she put her hand on my shoulder. "What's wrong?"

"I don't know that the court is the place to fight this out." I forced a smile. "I sort of like the image of Will's knuckle prints in Elikah's face."

"Me, too." Duncan grinned. "Daddy is an excellent boxer. Did you know that?"

"Will?" He was so perfectly dressed, such a gentleman, I could hardly picture him, fists lifted, punching another man in the face for sport.

"He was on the boxing team at his university."

I had suspected Will had gone to school. "Where was that?"

"Oh, some place in Virginia." Duncan shrugged. "He said he liked it well enough but was glad to get out."

"And then he became a salesman?" I had spent many an hour wondering about Will. Where had he come from? How had he met Jo-Hanna? Was it like it had been for Jeb Fairley and Sadie, love at first sight? But while those perfect fantasies had entertained me, there was also a much darker edge to my fantasies about JoHanna and Will. John Doggett. I no longer hated him. We were linked by circumstance and our mutual love for JoHanna. But because I could even like him, it made me feel disloyal to Will. I could only wonder what Duncan felt. And why JoHanna put her in such a position. It was clear that Duncan loved her father better than anyone on earth. Maybe she didn't realize what JoHanna's relationship with John would do to Will. Maybe I didn't. Maybe I didn't understand anything at all about life.

"Are you girls ready?" JoHanna appeared in the doorway. The pants she wore emphasized her rounded butt and a waist still small. She wore one of Will's too-big shirts tucked in her pants, the collar unbuttoned down to her cleavage. She looked smart, and sexy. I glanced back at the mirror. I looked like a boy. My recent illness had robbed me of the curves I'd been developing.

"Come on, you two. John's got the car packed, and I want to get into Jexville, get Floyd, and get on the road to Fitler."

She didn't say it, but she'd begun to worry about Floyd. She'd halfway expected him to walk out for breakfast. It wasn't that far, and he often appeared at the back door just as she was putting the food on the table. It was a special treat for Duncan, to have Floyd at the beginning of the day.

We hurried out into the sunshine that was already too hot. October was only a week away, yet it felt like July. John waited behind the wheel of the car, a fact that made me stop in my tracks. It struck me as wrong. Dead wrong, but I got in the backseat with Duncan and the rooster and didn't say anything.

"When we get the road cleared, I need to go to the grocery store and get some supplies." JoHanna settled into the passenger seat.

"Not in those pants, you're not." John spoke matter-of-factly, but his tone made JoHanna's head whip around.

"I—"

"I don't want to have to bury you before the sun sets. JoHanna, the town is already buzzing. You want to pour salt on the wound? And I'm not going to ride in with you either. There's enough talk."

JoHanna looked straight ahead. In the backseat, Duncan punched me lightly on the knee. She made a face. "How are we going to get some food?" she asked. "We need some milk and bread, and some of Mara's sweet rolls with cinnamon. And cornmeal. And—"

John rolled his eyes at her in the backseat. "Poor starving child," he said. "I'll get out of the car before we get to town. I'll walk in and get whatever you want. I think it would be fine for you to drive around town, let folks know you aren't afraid. Just don't start new trouble by getting out in those pants. You can pick me up on the way home with the groceries."

"I see you've thought it all out." JoHanna's voice was impossible to read with her face looking out the front window of the car.

"I'm not trying to boss you, JoHanna. I'm afraid. That town is hotter than a hornet's nest. I don't think you realize. The men . . . they're afraid. And fear can bring down some powerful actions. Ones that people regret later, but it's too late by then."

JoHanna's shoulders relaxed, and so did mine. "You're right. We don't want to provoke them any more. It just makes me furious to think that I have to kowtow to their stupid rules and codes."

"I hardly think you kowtow," John said, his deep voice rich with amusement. "If it weren't for the storm and the damage, I'd say wear your pants. But folks are upset. They've been hit by a force they can't control, and it has them looking for someone to blame. As you well know, that's you. And Duncan. And me and Mattie if we get in the line of fire."

"You're right." JoHanna yielded with a degree of grace. "That's a good plan, John. Now let's get on to the first tree."

The severe wind damage to the trees shocked us, and then finally numbed us as we made our way slowly toward Jexville. In places the stands of timber had been twisted and torn, in others they had been snapped only feet from the base. John explained to Duncan how the pines worked off a deep tap root. In contrast, some of the water oaks and red oaks had been pushed over, their shallow, extended root system exposed to the hot sun. Lying on their sides, too big to be righted, they would die a slower death. JoHanna looked at the casualties, then turned away.

"What about the people?" Duncan asked.

"We'll find out in town," JoHanna told her in a tone that halted further questions.

We removed five trees from the road by lunch time, but only one of them was really big, a virgin loblolly that had somehow missed the logger's saw. When the pine was moved from the road, we drove on a little more, surprised to find that someone had already started clearing out Peterson Lane, working from the town side toward us. Since the road was clear, we pulled the big Auburn into a grove of mostly undamaged smaller trees and had our picnic. We weren't completely hidden from the road, but John took care to park in such a manner that we were partially concealed and so that we could get out in a hurry—headed for the open road toward town. As we unwrapped the sandwiches and poured the glasses of sweet tea I listened intently for the sound of approaching vehicles or wagons. There wasn't a sign of anyone coming our way.

"Do you suppose the rest of the main roads are cleared?" JoHanna asked, puzzled by the fact that a dead-end road had received such attention.

"Could be." John stared down the hot, red-dirt lane. His face had a closed look, as if whatever thoughts he had were too private to share.

JoHanna read him easily. "You think they were headed out to the house, don't you?" she asked.

"It did cross my mind." He stood and took his handkerchief from his pocket and wiped his brow. The egg salad sandwich JoHanna had made was half eaten on the pale yellow linen napkin beside him.

"Why did they stop?"

"Maybe the work of removing the trees burned out their anger." He shifted his position against a sycamore tree that had been stripped of every leaf. "Maybe all of the roads have been cleared and they were working on this one when dark fell." He drew one knee up to assume a posture of comfort, but his eyes belied his casual pose.

Staring at his face I felt a chill touch me. He had not told us every-thing about his adventures in town the day before. His caution had been deliberately understated so as not to antagonize JoHanna further. But he was worried. And as he leaned forward to pick up his sandwich, his pants shifted up above his boot. Tucked in the top was a pistol.

He must have felt my gaze upon it because he looked at me and waited until he caught my eye. He didn't have to speak to tell me to keep my mouth shut. In that strange way he had, he communicated clearly with me. The gun was to protect JoHanna and Duncan, and me, if it came to that. But it was not necessary to call attention to it. It would be better for JoHanna if she did not know.

I heard him clearly, and I got up and walked the short distance to the car to pour us all some more tea. Behind me I heard his soft tread in the green pine needles that had been stripped from the trees and scattered to carpet the ground.

"Can you use a gun, Mattie?" he asked softly.

I concentrated on filling my glass with tea. Once, when Jojo was drunk, he'd forced me to fire his gun. I could remember the feel of the gun in my hand, the cold metal and the kick when the trigger was pulled. Jojo had found it amusing because he put the gun in my hands, stood behind me, and held my hands on it as he pointed and aimed it at Callie as she ran around the yard. His finger had made my finger pull the trigger while Callie screamed and ran and I fought to stop Jojo from killing her. The smell of his rot-gut whiskeyed breath made me nau-seous, but I couldn't faint because I couldn't allow him to kill Callie. I had to wrench the gun down when I felt his finger beginning to squeeze the trigger. Jerking the gun, I watched the dirt kick up at my feet as Cal-lie screamed and ran to hide behind another tree or an old barrel.

John's hands caught me on the shoulders. "Mattie?"

I took a deep breath of the clean, sweet air. There was no smell of whiskey, no smell of gunpowder and fear. I looked up at him as he light-ened his grip on me. "I'm okay."

"Can you use a gun?" Urgency rippled through him.

"If I have to." Had I been able to wrench the gun from Jojo's hand, I could have shot him. To save Callie, I could have killed him. And I could do it again for JoHanna and Duncan.

John reached into his pocket and brought out a tiny silver derringer. "This is accurate only close up. There's two shots in it, so make them count. Go for the heart. The chest is a bigger target and easier to hit. Also less traumatic afterward. And Mattie," he said as he closed my fingers over the beautifully carved bone handle. "Use it if you have to. Don't let them get Duncan, if they try. They'll kill her. They may regret it later, but that wouldn't bring her back."

"Does JoHanna have a gun?"

He stared into my eyes. "No. I honestly think you're more capable than she is. I've put my faith in you."

He started to turn away, but my fingers closed on his white shirt and held him. He turned back to face me, his features settling into a calm mask.

"Why don't we go back to the farm? We don't have to go to town. Maybe if we wait a bit this will blow over. Why are we going in there to provoke them into hurting us?"

"Because I'm afraid if we don't go there, they'll come out to us. If they surround the farm, take us by surprise, Duncan and JoHanna won't have a chance. At least this way the main roads are cleared. She's got the car, and there's not another in Jexville that can come close to the speed of the Auburn. I can block off one end of town and hold them until she can drive away."

"And what will happen to you?"

His grin was daring, another of his masks, the Errol Flynn derring-do man. "I'm tired of trying to write my book anyway. Once they calm down, they won't take it out on a man." He shrugged free of my fingers and went back to the area in the woods where JoHanna was gathering up the picnic supplies with quick, determined movements.

As I watched the two of them I knew JoHanna was as aware of the dangers as John. She'd tried to hide them from me, and from Duncan. Now the pretenses were down. We were driving into a place where anything could happen. People I'd come to know, people she'd known most of her life, were capable of any betrayal. Even an attack on her child.

When we got back in the car, JoHanna got behind the wheel, John in the passenger seat. At JoHanna's instruction, Duncan held the rooster down beside her on the seat. In retribution, Pecos pecked me on the hip, causing me to scootch as far away as possible.

Just at the railroad tracks on the west side of town, John got out of the car and I climbed into the front seat. "Let them see you. Drive slowly, but not too slowly. Don't stop. No matter what they do."

JoHanna nodded, her hands gripping the wheel. "I'll head down to-ward Mobile and then turn around and come back and pick you up on the back road. Forty minutes."

John nodded. "Your list."

JoHanna pulled the piece of paper from the pocket of Will's shirt. I saw it had only three items on it as I handed it over to John. Milk, sweet rolls, and cornmeal. All requested by Duncan.

"There's nothing on it I really need." JoHanna reached after the list even as I handed it to John.

"If there's a problem, I won't waste my time trying to find sweet milk for you." He grinned, then stepped back from the car. "It's up to you, Mattie," he said softly.

We drove away and left him watching us on the side of the road.

Just on the west side of the tracks, JoHanna turned onto Redemption Road and headed toward town. We bumped over the tracks and slowed. The destruction at the feed store was awful. The store itself was mainly undamaged, but the big hay barn that had once stood behind it had completely collapsed. I couldn't tell for certain, but it seemed that maybe the storm had blown a section of roof away, which in turn had allowed the rain to soak the huge stack of hay. Once the hay was wet, it must have started sliding into the support timbers. That was when Chas Leatherwood had gone out to try to shore up the support and keep the entire roof from caving in. But the hay, sodden with rain, was already beginning to slide. As we drove slowly by, we could see the pile of hay, dark and heavy. There was the musty smell of mold even though the sun was bright. John had said they'd gotten Chas's body out from be-neath the hayslide. He had suffocated, the weight of the hay and the lack of oxygen beneath it, combining to kill him. It would have been a horrible, frightening death.

There were at least a dozen men working in the yard beside the barn, and as JoHanna drove slowly by, they eased their saws and ropes to a halt to stare at us. We didn't wave, and we didn't turn away. We drove on as if we were running an errand in town.

I saw JoHanna's gaze flash to the side mirror and remain several sec-onds. Trying not to draw Duncan's interest, I turned slowly to look be-hind us. The men remained clustered in the woodyard, pitchforks and saws hanging at their sides in grips that had gone loose and limp. They were knotted tighter, a smaller group, as if they huddled to speak. To plan. Even as I watched, a teenage boy broke from the group and started to run, his thin legs pumping hard. He was headed toward the center of town, cutting through the back lots and back yards. I felt the power of the men's gazes as they turned their attention from the boy back to us and watched as the Leatherwood house blocked us from their view. My hand slid into my pocket and felt the gun. It didn't make me feel safe, but it made me feel better.

The Leatherwood house was separated from the feed store by a three-acre field that was now the parking place for two older vehicles and three wagons, one belonging to Doc Westfall. The curtains were closed on all the windows in the house, and JoHanna took a left on Paradise and then another left on Canaan to stop at my front door. Even as the wheels ceased to move, my panic grew. There was safety in movement. Flight. But one glance at JoHanna's throat told me she knew the danger, and she had a plan of her own.

I looked at the house I had come to as a new bride. The front porch swing was still hanging but two shutters were missing. The barn in the back looked to be fine, and Mable was standing at the gate chewing a mouthful of grass as if she'd weathered the storm without trouble. We'd gone past Jeb Fairley's house, and I was relieved to see that his magnolia grandifola had made it through the hurricane. I was afraid the big tree had been knocked down.

JoHanna put her hand on the key but she didn't stop the engine. "Run on inside and get some more clothes," she said. "I'll wait here with Duncan. I'm counting on the fact that Elikah is too cheap to miss opening his shop today." She didn't say it, but I knew this was my last chance to claim whatever I wanted from Elikah's house. In JoHanna's mind I was not coming back here. Not for any reason.

"I don't want any of my clothes." Looking at that house gave me the creeps. Even the front porch, once my haven, had been despoiled by Elikah's touch. I didn't want anything to remind me of my life with Elikah Mills. What I wanted was a fresh start someplace else.

"Are you sure?"

Was there anything in that house I'd miss? Anything I considered mine? I nodded my head. "I'm sure. We can go."

JoHanna eased off the clutch and we turned around and headed down Canaan to Mercy. We took a right and slowed as we went by the grocery where John would buy our food.

Something had broken the store window and several men were busy inside mopping and cleaning. At the sight of the red touring car, all of them stopped work and stared out at us as we drove by. As if magically drawn, they dropped their mops and brooms and stepped through the broken glass window and out onto the street.

They followed us. They did not hurry, but they followed, and I felt the skin along my spine prickle and dance.

We took a right at Redemption, headed east again, and I braced myself. The stores along the main road were not badly damaged, some of them not at all. But we would go by the barbershop, and there was a chance I would see Elikah. And that he would see me. My fingers sought the carved handle of the derringer in my pocket. I wondered if JoHanna knew John had given it to me. Probably not, or she would have demanded it herself.

Elikah's shop was on one side of the street and the boot shop on the other. All three of us looked to the boot shop. The window was clearly broken, and the shop was dark inside. Perhaps Floyd and Mr. Moses were in the back, or maybe they'd gone to his house over on Liberty Street for more supplies. I studiously avoided looking to the left, to the barbershop. JoHanna slowed, but she didn't stop.

"Should I stop and look for Floyd?" she asked.

"I don't think so." I looked to the end of town. There were wagons and trucks parked along the street but it was clear that business was much slower than usual. The sun beat down on the red dirt road without mercy, and I wiped the sweat from my forehead before it could sting my eyes. "We ought to keep moving."

JoHanna reluctantly pressed the gas, her gaze lingering on the boot shop. "If there's anything up with Floyd, John will find out."

In the backseat, Duncan was unusually quiet. She cuddled Pecos to her side and stroked his head as she stared into the boot shop. "I wish we could talk to him," she said softly.

My attention was focused on Duncan when JoHanna slammed on the brakes, tossing me into the dash, and Duncan and the rooster against the backseat. Scrabbling to right myself, I looked out the front window to see five men blocking the road, Sheriff Grissham in the center. My first thought was of Floyd. He would slink into his gunfighter's crouch and draw down on these men, standing as if this were a shootout in the Wild West. Grissham's right hand even hovered in the air, and I wondered if he wore a six-shooter beneath his coat.

JoHanna stopped the car, but she had no intention of killing the motor. She put her arm out the driver's window, leaned over slightly and called out, "Afternoon, Sheriff."

For a long time no one moved. The men stood there, blocking the road but undecided what to do next. JoHanna leaned on the door, as casual as a cat in the sun. Behind us, the men from the grocery and the feed store were coming. Had Elikah joined them as they passed his barbershop? I could not stop the lurch of fear that came with that thought.

"Have you come to see your handiwork?" Grissham's voice was strained. His fingers flexed over his right hip and I knew he had a gun.

"I came to see how the town had fared. I noticed someone was trying to get out to check on us. The road was mostly cleared. That was a nice thought since Will is out of town." JoHanna's foot eased on the gas pedal, making sure the car would respond if she let off the clutch. "I was sorry to hear about Chas Leatherwood."

"I'll just bet you were," one of the men sneered at JoHanna. He took a step closer to my side of the car, and even from a distance I could smell the liquor on his breath.

"I am sorry." JoHanna saw the man's eyes dart back to Duncan, who sat very still in the middle of the backseat with Pecos in her lap. "I'm not so sorry that I wouldn't run over you like a bug, Boley Odom, if you make a move toward my daughter."

She spoke in the same soft voice she'd used before, conversational. It took a few seconds for the words to register on the man. When they did, he stepped back a few paces before he caught the sheriff's eye and stopped.

"Folks in town got some concerns about you, JoHanna. You and that girl. Folks believe you're in league with Satan." Grissham's eyes were colorless. I couldn't tell if he believed what he was saying or not.

"Folks can believe whatever they want. I don't think there are any laws in this country stopping folks from believing foolishness. It's an American right." She smiled. "Just as I have a right to drive down this road. Unless you have some legal accusations to make against me."

"Maybe you should be taken in. For your own protection." He matched her smile with a cold, hard grin.

"Sheriff, as long as you're willing to suffer the repercussions of such an act." JoHanna's voice was knifelike, cutting. All softness was gone. "You know that Will and I will take this as high as we have to. Will had some business with Senator Brady just last week. I'm certain the Senator will be glad to give you an interpretation of a sheriff's rights to detain a law-abiding citizen for her own protection. If you want to send a wire, I'll be glad to wait for a reply."

JoHanna had pushed him too far. I saw the man on the far left bring the gun out from behind his back. It was a casual movement, and all the more deadly for that. He wasn't afraid or excited. He was calculating. The man named Boley Odom also brought a pistol out of his belt.

I could see the pulse jumping in JoHanna's neck. Each tiny jump matched the harsh thud of my own heart. I reached over the backseat and took Duncan's hand, squeezing it hard to let her know to be still.

"Turn off the car, Mrs. McVay." Grissham's voice was deadly.

"I think not, Sheriff. I have some errands to tend to, and I want to take my daughter home. If you want to come and get me later, come on. I suggest you send that telegram before you do anything you'll regret."

The power JoHanna threatened was a thousand miles away, far removed from this moment in Jexville. Will's connections to Washington had been the one thing that had kept JoHanna safe. Now it wasn't enough.

The men from the feed store and grocery had come up behind us. In looking back to check on Duncan, I saw that two of them were armed. We were blocked in. JoHanna would have to drive over the men in front, or back over the ones behind to get away. I didn't think even the big Auburn was fast enough to do that without all of us getting shot first. My only consolation was that Elikah was not among them. I knew none of the men except Boley Odom, Clyde's brother, and the sheriff.

"Get out of the car." All disguise of civility was gone from the sheriff's voice. "There's some feeling in town that you and that crippled girl know more about Chas Leatherwood's murder than you let on."

"Hold it, Sheriff." The male voice came from up above, and I swiveled to the only two story building in Jexville to find Doc Westfall's window open and a shotgun pointed at the street. Doc's white hair was a nimbus behind the gun as he sighted down the barrel at the sheriff's chest.

"Doc," Grissham called the words out loud and strong, "better back out of this while you can. This isn't about doctoring."

"No, it's about stupidity and fear." Doc never lowered the shotgun. Behind him I saw a slight movement. John Doggett. He had gone to Doc when he saw JoHanna in trouble. Or had I imagined the passing of a shadow behind Doc's white hair?

Grissham spoke again. "You don't want to spend your last days in jail for murder, Doc."

"The way I figure it, Quincy, I can shoot you in the gut and if one of your gunslingers doesn't kill me, I can make it down the steps and patch you up before you die. It would hurt something fierce, but it wouldn't kill you. Worst I'd get is attempted manslaughter. And by the time I went to trial, I daresay the sentiments of the town would have changed a good bit. Folks would come to their senses and be ashamed of how they were afraid of a nine-year-old girl. Now back off and let Mrs. Mc-Vay and her daughter pass."

"You're gonna regret this." Grissham didn't move for a few seconds, but when he took the first step back, I knew we had won. I released my grip on the derringer and put my shaking hand in my lap.

JoHanna eased the clutch, taking care not to make the car jerk or shudder. We drove slowly through the men, clearing the end of town without further incident, and headed for open country. We had topped two hills before I saw JoHanna breathe.

"I don't think this worked out the way I had hoped," JoHanna said, her eyes on the road.

"I hate them." Duncan spoke with such vehemence that JoHanna touched her foot to the brake, slowing the speeding car. I kept my eyes on the road, looking for the trees that might wreck us because JoHanna wasn't paying attention.

She reached into the backseat and grabbed Duncan's knee. "Don't hate them, Duncan. I don't hate them. I'm even sorry for some of them. For Agnes. She'll be lost without Chas to tell her what to do." Her voice saddened. "They fear us, and we pity them."

Her words were like a slap. "It's gone beyond that now, JoHanna. Save your pity; they would have hurt you. Or Duncan. Or . . ." I stopped myself before I said Floyd's name. "This isn't some lesson you're going to teach them. You act as stupid as they do. They aren't going to suddenly understand. They don't want to understand. They want to lash out and hurt. It gives them pleasure to do that."

JoHanna's face colored, and her foot hit the gas pedal, sending the car forward with a spurt of gravel. "You're right, Mattie." She pressed harder on the gas. "We'll drive for a while, give Doc a chance to settle them down. Maybe now that we've had a confrontation, they'll let it go. John will be able to tell us." Her face cleared as the breeze struck her cheeks and cooled them. She pointed toward a stand of loblolly pines that were twisted and broken. "Looks like the wind did about the same amount of damage out this way. See how all of the trees fell in the same direction. That's a strong force of wind. Now a tornado will lay the trees in different directions because the wind currents are circular and tight." She pointed out other damage as we drove, allowing us all to calm before we had to turn around and head back toward Jexville.

"Mama, turn to the right up here." It was the first words Duncan had spoken since her angry outburst. The road she pointed to was narrow, a red slit between two tall water oaks. If Duncan hadn't seen it, we would have passed it by.

"Why?" JoHanna asked. "It's hardly a road."

"I want to see something," Duncan whispered. "I don't remember Jexville in my dream, but this road . . . I saw this road, and the family on it." A frown creased her brow.

"Duncan, it looks muddy. We can't afford to get stuck out here now. Especially not today." There was no traffic coming in either direction, and JoHanna slowed the car and stared at the red-dirt road. "It has a peculiar name, but I can't remember. I think it's a dead end, maybe a few farm families on it."

"Please, Mama." Duncan's plea held something else, a whisper of something sinister. "It's from the dream."

"We'd better not." JoHanna eased off the gas and put the car in motion at a fast clip. "We'll take the old Scott Dairy Loop Road."

"Mama!" Duncan grasped the back of the seat and shook it. "Please go back. Please. I have to see if it was . . ."

Duncan was spoiled, but I'd never seen her pitch a fit. I turned back to give her a warning look, but her face stopped me. "What is it, Duncan?"

She'd let Pecos go and he was perched on the top of her seat, the wind ruffling his feathers in what I thought must be as close to flight as an awkward old rooster would ever achieve.

"There's something on that road. Please. I have to look."

At the next opportunity, JoHanna turned around and we went back to the narrow red lane that cut between the oaks. We bumped along the ruts to Pecos's indignant squawking. On the main road he could dream that he was an eagle soaring down the roadway. Here he had to hang on for dear life or be thrown out of the car.

After a mile of bumping and jarring, JoHanna slowed the car to a stop and turned around in her seat. "Duncan, I've had about enough of you and this road. It's going to knock the car apart. The only good thing I can say is that there haven't been any trees in the way."

There were fields on both sides of the road, no trees to blow down, just flat, unkempt pastures fenced with rusted barbed wire.

"Just a little farther," Duncan urged. The darkness in her face had been replaced by confusion. "Please. Just a little more." She was pale, the green tam only serving to highlight the alabaster of her skin.

"What exactly is it you expect to find?" JoHanna turned completely in the seat. "We're not going on unless you tell me."

"Remember the dream of the storm? I said it wasn't anyone I knew. That there were bodies in the trees." She gripped the front seat with her small, strong fingers. "This is the place."

Whether it was true or not, Duncan's words were impossible to ignore. JoHanna eased the car forward. The road narrowed more, until the branches of small scrub trees reached out to grab at the side of the car. JoHanna's foot eased off the accelerator and she began to look for a place to turn around. "We have to meet John," she said. "I don't think this road goes anywhere, Duncan."

"Listen," Duncan ordered. "Listen."

JoHanna stopped the car, listening. In the distance there was the sound of an animal in distress.

"Cow," I finally determined. "Sounds like it might be hung in a fence or in some kind of trouble."

"It's not calving season," JoHanna noted.

I shrugged. A lot of dirt farmers didn't go by season. They just waited for a chance to get their cow to the closest bull, and they didn't care whether the calf was born in spring or winter.

JoHanna eased the car forward, clearly unhappy about doing so. "This is beginning to give me the creeps," she said, trying to make light of it. Duncan was anxious, and even though the sun was shining I felt a chill at the base of my spine. "You said no one around Jexville drowned. Folks around here would have to wade in a creek or lay out in their yards with their noses in the air to drown in the rain. It isn't like we live on the coast."

JoHanna talked and Duncan dug her fingers into the back of the front seat. I found myself fondling the gun in my pocket. Never in a million years would I have ever guessed that a gun could have given me such a sense of safety. Scanning the sides of the road for trouble, I knew I would use the gun without hesitation. I would have used it in town on men I had spoken to when passing them on the street. I would not be a victim again.

The desperate lowing of the cow grew louder and louder, until I spotted the animal in the pasture. She stood, legs straddling a big udder, crying her distress. At the size of her milkbag I knew the trouble. She hadn't been milked in a long time. She was in great pain, and though I was a fair hand at milking, I didn't know if I'd be able to bring the milk down and give her the relief she sought.

"Can you help her, Mattie?" JoHanna asked as I swung open the car door and got out.

"I'll see."

The cow was in too much pain to run from me, so it was easy enough to examine her, but touching her strutted udder brought on an entirely different reaction. She cried in pain, and I had to steel myself to pull on the teats to make the hot, discolored liquid zip into the sparse grass. JoHanna was standing at the cow's head, stroking her and talking. In the car, Duncan was crying at the cow's suffering.

I'd never been one to credit cows with much sense, but this one seemed to know we were trying to help her, and she stood still for the pulling and jerking that finally drained her bag. When I had finished, I was drenched in sweat and my back was throbbing.

"Mattie, is she better?" JoHanna asked.

The cow had stopped her bellowing as the tension on her bag eased.

"She's better for now, but we'd better find her owner. Must have been a couple of days she's gone without milking."

"Maybe she ran off in the storm." JoHanna rubbed her between the eyes and earned a lick from a big, sloppy cow tongue.

"She looks well fed. I don't think she'd run away and not go home unless the storm got her disoriented." The cow was on a slight rise in the pasture, which gave a better view. I looked toward where the road led. I couldn't be certain, but it looked like a cluster of oaks that might be a homestead. "Maybe she lives there." I patted her hip. "Let's go see."

"Then we have to go back for John. I don't like the idea of him standing on the road alone, waiting for us." She didn't have to say more. If Doc hadn't been able to calm the town, they might take their anger out on a stranger. Especially if they had any idea he was linked to us.

"We can turn around at those trees. If she isn't theirs, maybe they'll take care of her."

JoHanna took her long strides to the car and had it cranked before I could get in the passenger seat.

Duncan had sat back in the seat, but she wasn't any more relaxed as we turned beneath a canopy of oaks to find a small farmhouse. Several chickens clucked up to us, but they backed away when Pecos leaped out of the backseat and ran at them.

"Pecos!" Duncan shouted, going after the bird for all she was worth. Her legs were slow, but she was determined to capture the rooster before someone came out the door and shot him.

JoHanna and Duncan were busy with that damned rooster, but I had time to look at the house. It stood square and solid, gingham curtains in the front windows. No one came to a window or door. No one was coming out. There was a stillness about the place that made me swallow. JoHanna, too, finally sensed something. She glanced at me.

There was a general air of neatness about the place, but the storm had blown down limbs that were untouched. One of the front windows had blown out, and there was no sign of anyone trying to clean up the mess. JoHanna got out of the car and started toward the front door. In contrast to her normal stride, she walked slowly, cautiously, and I hurried to catch up with her.

At the door she knocked, but the sound echoed hollowly. There was no one home. The house had that silence of emptiness, as if it had been abandoned for a long, long time. As if the occupants had fallen under some spell of enchantment.

"Maybe they went out of town and couldn't get back because of the storm. Maybe we should leave them a note saying we milked their cow but they need to see to her." I spoke into the vacuum that cloaked the house. My words seemed to disappear into the old boards, swallowed whole.

"Mama?" Duncan's voice was peculiar.

"What?" JoHanna went to the window that had been destroyed and peered inside.

"Mama?" Duncan's voice was more demanding.

"What?" JoHanna's answer was short, and she turned to face her child with a frown on her face. The expression on Duncan's face froze her, and she followed the way that Duncan's finger pointed until she saw them.

We saw them.

Almost at the same instant.

Hanging from the limbs of the oak tree at the back of the house were five bodies. Three children, one a very young girl, and a man and a woman.

JoHanna reeled on the porch, stumbling into me. We managed to catch each other as we backed down the steps and to the car. Pecos chose that moment to make a run at the chickens, and they scattered beneath the hanging corpses.

"Sweet Jesus," I said, my breath sounding like the rattle of cornhusks on the wind. "Sweet merciful Jesus." I couldn't take my eyes off the little girl. She wasn't more than three, her nightgown hanging past her feet.

JoHanna breathed through her mouth. "What happened?"

Standing by the passenger door of the car, Duncan stared at the bodies. "He killed the wife and then the children. He held them in the ditch in front of the house and drowned them in the middle of the storm. And then he killed himself."

"Duncan!" JoHanna broke the horror of the scene by running around the car to her daughter and gathering her up in her arms. But Duncan pushed her mother away. "The dream was so confusing. I saw the bodies in the trees, but I couldn't see the ropes. I knew they'd drowned, but it wasn't clear why they were in the trees. I thought it was the dreams of people afraid of drowning. Now I know. Now I see what happened." She looked up at her mother, fear tracing diamonds in her eyes. "It was exactly as I dreamed it."

Thirty-one

IN our rush to leave, we almost forgot Pecos, but Duncan realized our mistake and JoHanna backed up so that I could leap out of the car and catch the rooster. To my horror, Pecos refused to come to me. He feinted and wove, determined not to be captured when there were hens to impress. When I cornered him by the fence, he ran under the oak tree where the corpses hung. He took his stand beneath those dangling legs and dared me to come after him.

"Pecos!" I hissed at him. At that moment I would have gladly wrung his neck. He made a foray out toward a hen, and at last I caught him by his tail feathers and stalled him long enough to get my fingers around his scrawny throat. He pecked me once on the cheek, ripping an angle of skin free so that it flapped, but I held him tight and handed him off to Duncan in the backseat. JoHanna set the car in motion before I could sit down and close the door. Without slowing her pace, JoHanna gave me a clean handkerchief to staunch the flow of blood from my cheek, and Duncan gave me an apology for the rooster, who showed no remorse.

Tree limbs tore at the side of the car as we raced over the rutted road, but JoHanna did not slow. Her eyes were wild and her knuckles white as she gripped the wheel and pushed the car to dangerous speeds. When we came to the main road, JoHanna burst onto it without letting up. The car slued in the gravel and then righted itself as we sped toward Jexville. In the horror of what we'd seen, Jexville seemed a lesser evil.

"Mama, we can't just run off and leave them hanging in the trees like that."

Duncan's calm voice made JoHanna slam on the brakes so hard that Pecos was thrown into the back of the front seat.

"Mama! Dammit!" Duncan kicked the seat and then gathered Pecos in her arms. She refused to say another word until she'd examined the rooster and had him perched beside her again.

"Duncan McVay!" JoHanna's voice cracked with fear and command. "What we saw back there is forgotten. Your dream is forgotten. None of this will ever be spoken of again."

Duncan busied herself stroking Pecos's feathers, her face averted. I saw the big tears splash on her pants, the moisture immediately soaked up by the brown material.

"Duncan, do you hear me?"

She nodded, creating another cascade of tears.

I knelt in the front seat and reached back to her, lifting her face so that JoHanna could see her tears.

"Oh, Duncan." JoHanna turned off the car and climbed into the backseat herself. She caught Duncan to her and held her, lifting her face to kiss her. "I'm sorry, Duncan. I didn't mean to yell at you like that. It's just that those people are dead, and I don't want us to be blamed for any part of that. We've got enough trouble in town without five dead people."

JoHanna was right about that. Just sitting in the middle of the road made me nervous. The sheriff or anyone else could be waiting for us off in the trees. I scooted over behind the wheel and set the car in motion. John Doggett would be waiting for us. He'd know best what to do about the dead folks on that narrow, rutted road. I couldn't shake the image of them, hanging like so many deer and hogs, strung up for butcher. What in the world had happened at that neat little farm? Had the man really murdered his family, as Duncan said? Or had some other person, some passerby, stopped to take advantage of a family isolated by a raging hurricane?

The day was hotter than six degrees of hell, but cold sweat trickled down my ribs and in the bends of my knees. I eased the car along, praying that I could remember how Jojo had showed me to shift gears. He'd taught me to drive so I could get his liquor for him when he didn't want to get out of the house.

Jojo wasn't the kind of teacher who had a lot of patience with scraping gears and faulty starts, so I drove fairly smoothly, but it had been a long time since I'd tried. The car lurched forward twice, then leveled out. As we drew close to town, I turned left onto the back road. Through the glare on the windshield, I saw the tall, lean form of John Doggett waiting on the side of the road.

By the time he climbed into the car beside me, JoHanna, Duncan, and the rooster had settled down a bit, but we were all still white-faced and shaky. I pressed hard on the gas until John touched my hand on the steering wheel. "Ease off, Mattie," he said, looking behind us to make sure we weren't being chased. He patted the sack he carried. "The milk won't spoil in another ten minutes." His words were light, his touch casual, but there was tension in the way he looked behind us every few minutes. As if he expected someone to round the last curve, following.

JoHanna held Duncan in her lap, curled against her more like a child than I'd seen her since the lightning strike. "Did you see Floyd?"

John hesitated. "I couldn't find him, but I couldn't find Mr. Moses either."

"Did you ask his wife?"

"She said they'd gone to get some boards to put over the broken window, but she'd expected them back at lunch today. They took the mule and wagon out to the sawmill, she said. I went over there, but they weren't hanging around. No sign of the mule and wagon either. Maybe they had to go somewhere else."

His words left a strange uneasiness. "Had they been to Leatherwood's?" I asked.

"Nobody would say." John wiped his forehead on his sleeve. He was hot and dirty and tired. "It could be they didn't want to talk to a stranger. The storm has left a lot of folks spooked."

"That's probably it."

As I cast a quick glance in the backseat, JoHanna kissed Duncan's forehead, shielding her against her breasts. It looked like Duncan may have gone to sleep. Or drifted back into that still silence that frightened all of us.

JoHanna spoke again, softly. "Mattie, you tell John what we found."

I gave him the whole story, about how we went down the road because of Duncan's dream, killing time while we waited to pick him up. Just as I got to the part about the bodies hanging in the trees, I pulled

into the McVays' yard. I turned off the motor and told him about the
bodies. Parked in the shade of the chinaberry tree, we all sat in the car
for a while without talking. It was Pecos who broke the spell, flapping
out of the car as if he'd had enough of human foolishness, to sit in a hot
car without going anywhere.

John reached over and touched my cheek where Pecos had drawn
blood. "I swear, Mattie, you look like you've been attacked by wild
Indians."

I burst into tears, which provoked a round of sobs from Jo-
Hanna and Duncan. John, the handkerchief in his hand where he'd
intended to wipe the blood from my face, looked from one of us to
the other.

"What are we going to do?" JoHanna took a ragged breath. "John,
those children have to be cut down. We can't risk going back through
town."

"You're right about that." He got out of the car and leaned into the
back to pull Duncan out of JoHanna's arms and into his. She clutched
his neck and pressed her face into his shirt, now damp and sweat-
covered from the hot, hot sun.

"We can't leave them. . . ." JoHanna put her hand on the back of the
front seat to get out.

"We can and we are." John spoke sharply as he started in the house
with Duncan.

JoHanna nudged me to get out, and she followed as we all walked toward the house, Pecos at our heels. I noticed several of his longest tail
feathers were missing.

"John, something has to be done. . . ."

"We have to stay away from there," I said. "There's nothing we can
do for dead folks." To reveal our knowledge of the deaths would be to
open the door to trouble. Not a single person in that town would believe we happened down that red twisty road. If the sheriff and his
henchmen ever found out JoHanna and Duncan had been at that little
farm, there would be hell to pay. The bad feelings in Jexville would boil
over, and Duncan would be the one to get scalded. There was nothing
we could do for that family now. They were dead. And if we didn't want
trouble, we'd have to keep quiet and keep our distance.

John walked straight through the kitchen and took Duncan to her
room. He eased her down in the bed and brushed away the tears that

clung to her eyelashes as JoHanna stood at the bed and I hovered two feet back. Duncan was too pale, her eyes too large and black.

"Are you okay?" he asked.

Duncan nodded.

"Can you talk?" I asked, afraid she'd gone back into her mute state again.

She nodded.

"Then talk. Say something."

"Are those people dead because of me?" She asked the question of Jo-Hanna.

JoHanna sat on the bed. "They're dead because someone did something horrible. You had nothing to do with it."

"People will think that I did. Mattie's right. If we tell about being there, people will think that we killed them."

"It doesn't matter what people think, Duncan. You know the truth." JoHanna smoothed Duncan's fine, dark hair, concentrating on her daughter.

I caught John's signal and started to ease out of the room, but Jo-Hanna reached out and caught my pants. Her fingers closed over the shape of the gun and I saw the surprise in her eyes, but she hid it from Duncan. "I want all of us to hear this. Back there at that farm, I got scared and I ran. In doing that, I acted like we'd done something wrong. But we hadn't. We *didn't do anything wrong*." She ruffled Duncan's hair in a continuous motion. "Someone killed that family. I don't know who would do such a thing, but it was someone either really sick or really mean. It was our misfortune that we found what they'd done."

"Are we going to leave them?" Duncan's bottom lip trembled. "That little girl . . ."

John leaned down. "Duncan, they're dead. We can't do anything to help them."

"But—"

"No buts. Someone will find them and take care of it. We have to stay clear of this. We didn't do anything wrong, but the people in town may not see it that way. They're already afraid."

"Of me."

"Of you," he conceded.

"They think I'm evil."

"They think a lot of things. That doesn't make it right, but it does make them dangerous." John put his hands on JoHanna's shoulders, but he spoke to Duncan. "In your dream, did you see the man drowning all of them?"

Duncan's eyes grew vague as she concentrated. "I saw them lying in the field beside the house, side by side, the woman and then the children, the two boys beside the mother and the little girl last."

"And the man, what was he doing?"

"He was on his knees by the ditch where the water was running fast, and the rain was coming down. I thought he was praying." She closed her eyes. "But he had drowned them."

"Are you sure?" John asked.

"What difference does it make?" JoHanna said. "They're dead. He's dead."

John straightened up and looked at me. "Because if he didn't kill them, someone else did. And that someone may still be on the loose around here. That's the difference."

"What should we do?" JoHanna asked. The thought of that entire family hanging there was eating away at her. They were dead, certainly, and hanging there couldn't matter to them. But it was another violation to leave them there to swing in the sun like some awful fruit, slowly ripening. The right thing to do would be to notify Sheriff Grissham and let him cut them down. But calling the sheriff put JoHanna square in the middle of some questions that had no reasonable answers.

"Let it go." John signaled me again with his eyes as he left the room.

I met him in the kitchen. He was standing at the sink staring out the window at the chinaberry tree. The yard was covered with leaves blown down by the storm.

"Things are bad in town," he said. "There's lots of talk. After you drove away, they wanted to come out here and burn the house down."

"Why didn't they?"

"Doc Westfall shamed them. Some of the men are truly afraid, Mattie. Someone's got them so worked up they believe JoHanna and Duncan can kill people with a look. Those are the ones Doc shamed. But the ones behind all this . . . They know better, and they're doing this deliberately." He didn't look at me.

"You think it's Elikah, don't you?" My stomach had grown tight, hot.

"Maybe. He stayed in his barbershop, made certain he wasn't part of any crowd. It doesn't make any sense." His hands flexed on the lip of the sink, gripping, then relaxing. "That's what frightens me. It doesn't make a bit of sense, but they're acting like it does."

"Are they going to hurt us?"

His hands tightened on the porcelain, a pulse of frustration. "I want you to help me convince JoHanna to leave tonight. She can get to New Augusta or Hattiesburg. I'll go to Mobile and wait for Will to come in on the train."

"Why can't we go to Mobile?" It didn't make sense for us to go in the opposite direction from Will.

"There was storm damage. I'm not certain how bad, but it may not be safe for you. The roads north will be clearer. Besides, it's hot. There's always sickness after a storm like this."

"Yellow jack." I'd heard the stories of epidemics. Those were wartime epidemics. They didn't happen now, did they?

"If you go on to Hattiesburg, you'll be safer." His hands loosened with a deliberate effort that tensed his shoulders. "It's the best I can do."

"I'll talk to her."

He finally turned around. There was something else he wanted to say. "Mattie, the talk is ugly. About JoHanna. About the past."

"What are they saying?"

"That she takes lovers when Will's out of town. That Duncan isn't his child." He hesitated. "That Floyd is her lover. And yours."

"That's crazy talk. Floyd doesn't even understand—"

"I know." The gentleness of his voice stopped me. "Right now the truth doesn't matter. What matters is that you get out of here."

"What else are they saying?" I saw it in his eyes, something worse than lovers.

"It's Duncan. They say she's wicked. Marked. A child of the devil." He tried to smile, but fear held his lips too rigid.

"That's the stupidest thing I ever heard. One look and you can see Will McVay stamped all over her."

"Mattie, they're afraid. They aren't looking, or thinking. And what I'm afraid of is they're going to come down that road and do something that I can't stop."

"Do they know you're here, with us?"

He walked to the table and put his hands on the back of a chair. He was a man used to action, to moving on, and now he was stuck. Whatever he'd taken from Will, he'd lost his freedom in the bargain. "They're curious about me, but there are other strangers in town, people stranded by the storm. I tried not to ask too many questions, but there was this secretiveness. Wherever I went, I felt it. The hair on the back of my neck tingled. They were watching me, calculating. They're planning something, and they weren't going to let a stranger in on it. They don't trust anyone."

"We can't leave without Floyd." I brushed past him and went to the sink. Evening was falling and it was time to start supper, but I had no appetite and no idea what to make. JoHanna was still in the bedroom with Duncan. I could hear the rise and fall of her voice as she talked on and on, soothing, comforting, mothering.

"I looked everywhere for him."

Something in his voice warned me. I turned around to face him. "You think he's been hurt?"

He spoke slowly. "I think they have him."

"They?" My heart pounded at the thought of Elikah, at the pleasure he'd take in tormenting an innocent like Floyd. "Who's they?"

"Some of the men. Your husband, the sheriff, that Odom man. I don't know all their names."

"And Mr. Moses?"

"I don't know. His wife was very upset. I don't know if she knows where they are and what they're doing and won't say, or if she's worried about her husband."

"They know Floyd isn't right." I felt as if the blood was coagulating in my heart. No matter how hard or fast it beat, the blood had gelled and wouldn't move. Each beat brought a sharp pain.

"That's exactly the reason they took him. Floyd would go along without a fight, never imagining that they would hurt him."

"We have to find him, John." My legs were liquid fire, my breath scorched dust. I couldn't think because the need to act was so powerful. Floyd. They would hurt him. Each second was a notch of pain.

John was across the room before I saw him move, his hands assisting me into a chair.

"I looked everywhere. The livery stable, the jail. I climbed up and looked through the bars. He isn't in there. I went around the back of the barbershop and through the feed store. I don't know where he is." His hands rubbed my shoulders; then he picked up one of my cold hands and rubbed it between his own. "I heard a rumor that they'd taken him somewhere."

"Where?" I turned to look at him, snatching my hand away. "Why didn't you say so? You have no idea what they might do to him."

But I saw in his face that he had a very good idea, and that he was fairly certain we were too late.

"Tommy Ladnier's."

The only thing that came to me was the image of boots. Tall, black leather boots as elegant and slick as a coachwhip snake's hide. Black boots that glistened in the sunlight worn by a snake-slender man with a slow, assessing smile.

"Tommy Ladnier, the bootlegger?"

"I don't know if they meant for me to hear that so I'd go off half-cocked. It could be a setup, but those black boots have disappeared from the boot shop."

"Did they . . . did they act like he was still alive?" Something pressed against the back of my throat, a tumor of fear that threatened to gag me. Fear, for Floyd and for what was happening, had begun to grow inside me like a new and terrible organ, tentacles shooting into my weakened legs, into my brain to stop my thinking.

John caught me by the nape of my neck as I slumped in the chair. He put me back in the chair, then slid his hands down to hold my shoulders. He knelt beside me, shaking me. "Don't faint, Mattie. Don't you dare faint. Not now. I need you. JoHanna needs you." His hand groped at my leg until he found the derringer still in my pants pocket. "God dammit, Mattie, you can't go down on me now." He pressed the gun hard into my flesh, harder than the fear, external and internal pain in conflict, for me.

He made me look at him, see him. His voice reached through the fear and caught at me, drawing me back to the chair, the table, JoHanna's kitchen, the derisive chatter of a big black crow outside the window. It was the hoarse voice of the bird that finally anchored me. The crow had come to pick through the storm debris. They're scavengers, crows, eating dead things, waiting for death.

I almost fell when I tried to stand, but John helped me up and I went to the window. The crow was perched on a fence post, staring in at us. Waiting.

"What is it you want me to do?" I could do what he told me. I couldn't think of anything on my own, but I could do what he said.

"Start packing JoHanna's things. And Duncan's. No matter what she says, we have to get them out of here. North. To Hattiesburg."

"She won't go if she finds out about Floyd."

By the time I heard the creak of the floorboard, it was too late. I looked over John's shoulder to see her standing in the doorway, a hand on either side of the frame as she braced herself.

"Finds out what about Floyd?"

She spoke softly, the ripple of water flowing over the hard clay bottom of a shallow creek. A whisper of sound, but a constant force, one not to be denied.

John said nothing as he got up slowly from his knees and turned to face her. "You have to leave. Tonight. With Mattie and Duncan."

My fear arced across the room and touched her, making her flinch. It occurred to me that JoHanna was not used to governing her life with fear. It was so much more painful for me to see it in her than to feel it in myself. But she fought harder. She struggled against it even as she held herself upright by the door frame.

"What about Floyd?" There was no tremor in her voice. She spoke as calmly as if she were asking if we had eggs in the house.

"JoHanna, they're saying that Duncan is the daughter of Satan. They've lost their minds with fear and vengeance. They're going to hurt Duncan, and you, if you try to stop them." John's voice was raw with helplessness and worry.

"What about Floyd?" JoHanna repeated.

"Floyd can't be helped right now. Not by you or me. Once you're safe, once Will is back, we'll go and find him."

"Then you know something's happened to him?"

"I suspect as much. I know nothing for certain."

"Where is he, John? Where have they taken him? Is he still alive?"

"I don't know, JoHanna."

"And if you did, you wouldn't tell me, now would you?"

He sighed, an admission of defeat. "I can't lie to you, Jo. Not even for your own safety. You choose your own path, and I won't send you down it on lies."

JoHanna nodded, an almost imperceptible movement of her head. "Mattie, would you get some bags out of my closet? Two. Put a few of Duncan's clothes in one. Easy things. Nothing fancy. We'll pack something for us in a minute."

I glanced once again at the post outside the kitchen window. The crow stared back at me, then flapped his wings once and lifted awkwardly into the air, winging away into the purpling sky as night walked softly toward us from the east.

I left them in the kitchen and went to her bedroom, where I could still hear every word they said. They argued, back and forth. John told her what he'd told me. He hadn't wanted to tell her, but he meant what he said about lies. He could not deceive her. Not even for her own safety. The packing of the bags was a hopeful thing for John, until he discovered exactly where it was she meant to go.

Thirty-two

IT was decided. John would go to Jeb Fairley's house and leave an anonymous note reporting the hangings out on Red Licorice Road. JoHanna had recalled the name of the twisty little path that led to the macabre scene, and other than Doc Westfall, Jeb was the only person JoHanna had any faith would contact the authorities on the strength of an unsigned letter describing such a gory scene. Even if Jeb suspected where the information came from, he'd keep his mouth shut. JoHanna was positive of it, and I agreed. Once the note was delivered, John would use the darkness to search the town. Sheriff Grissham was not a man to patrol the streets. There had been no need for such tactics. JoHanna had determined that John might discover more by spying in Axim's windows than by asking questions. If Mr. Moses had returned home to his wife—without Floyd—then John might press for some answers.

Less than certain about the plan, John conceded because he could think of no other. He took the pen and wrote down the information as he and JoHanna concocted it by the light of a single lamp on the kitchen table. "Five people are dead on Red Licorice Road. I don't know what happened, but it's a gruesome sight. About five miles down from the old federal road." John folded the note and put it in his pocket.

By the time they were done, I had packed for all of us, except John, who had already made sure that not a single possession of his was left in the house. He'd come without much, and what he had was in his pockets or the small bundle of clothes he'd tied together, his journal and pen in the middle.

After scouting Jexville, if he discovered nothing, John would take Mable from behind Elikah's house and ride for Mobile, where he would telegraph the facts to us and wait for Will's train. JoHanna wanted him to steal a car, but John pointed out that a horse might make better time if the roads were blocked by trees. Mable was a good horse, steady and willing.

We loaded the car in complete darkness, just in case anyone was watching. JoHanna walked out the back door without a thought of locking it. There was no point. If they came and wanted in, they would get in. JoHanna got behind the wheel with John in the passenger seat and we drove through the sticky heat of the night toward Jexville.

John had convinced JoHanna that the furor of the multiple hangings would buy Floyd a little diversion, and more time, if he was indeed being held at Tommy Ladnier's Biloxi home. JoHanna had promised not to take any rash action, only to watch the house and determine what was happening until John could arrive with Will. They both knew it would do little good to contact the authorities on the coast. Tommy Ladnier did not have the political connections that Will had, but he had more local muscle, and a lot of it included the lawmen of the area. Tommy paid hard coin for the loyalty of the badge.

In short, terse sentences that contained nothing of John's normal speech, he laid out the best possible scenario about Floyd's condition. As the red car pushed through the humid night toward town, John told us that he did not believe Floyd's life was in real danger. They might have beaten him, and undoubtedly humiliated him, but John was certain he was alive. John said that Floyd was helpless, and men like Elikah and Clyde Odom could not pass up a chance to torment a helpless creature. But surely they had not seriously injured him. More likely they were having sport at his expense while they kept him down at Tommy's, a jester for their parties.

Sitting in the backseat with Duncan pressed against me and a much subdued Pecos on her other side, I tried not to think of my husband or Clyde Odom, a man I'd met once in passing on Redemption Road. A man who'd taken grim pleasure in belittling Floyd and putting his hand on my breast because he felt certain that the conditions of my life would not allow me to protest. Like Elikah, Clyde and his brother Boley understood the finest shadings of humiliation, of cruelty. They were capable of things that John had not considered. But how far would Floyd allow it to go? He was an innocent, but he knew the difference between right and wrong. And because he was an innocent, he might try to fight them if they pushed him too far. I closed my eyes tight and let the hot wind whip my hair free of its pins.

Will would get Floyd back. Will, with his deliberating eyes and his broad shoulders. He would make them let Floyd go. For Will, along with his muscle and his brain, knew every senator and congressman in Washington. Tracing his progress homeward, John would catch him on the way and wire him. Will might even stop in Jackson and speak with the Governor. Floyd would be rescued.

The car bumped across the railroad tracks and I opened my eyes as we slowed to a halt. John opened the car door. JoHanna's hand stopped him.

"Be careful," she whispered to him, taking his hand and holding it to her lips with her face turned so that Duncan could not see her tears. "Be careful, John."

"I will." He got out of the car and walked away without turning back. In seconds the darkness swallowed him, and I remembered my first meeting of him. I had always thought he would disappear, and I had a sudden, terrible foreknowledge that we would never see him again. When Will returned, John would seek out the solitude of the riverbank once again. He would go back to his writing, to his pursuit of the past, because he did not have the promise of the future that he wanted. He would not try to take her future with Will. He would not ask for even the chance. What was between him and JoHanna was over, killed by the ugliness of the people in Jexville.

Perhaps it was wrong, forbidden, a sin before God. But it did not seem so terrible a thing.

Duncan had eased into a troubled sleep, and I climbed over the seat into the front even as JoHanna turned the car south toward the coast.

"He's a good man," JoHanna said as the car picked up speed.

"He seems to be."

JoHanna brushed the tears from her cheek. "John will send us a telegram at the Seaview if he finds out anything we need to know. I told him we'd be staying there."

"JoHanna." The word escaped me. "What are we going to do?"

"Whatever we have to, Mattie. Whatever it takes to get Floyd back. Then we'll leave. I never believed they were bad people. Narrow-minded, sanctimonious, hypocritical, all of those things in abundance. But I never even considered the possibility that they would truly hurt me."

"They're afraid."

"Of what?" Her voice rose in frustration. "Of a woman who minds her own business? Of a child who loves life? Yes, we are a terrifying duo."

"You scare them because you wear the britches. Not Will's britches. You don't need to take his because you have your own. Everything you believe goes against the grain of the men." I thought of what she called her religion. "Of the very land they work, the animals and trees they use. The women and children they rule. You want them to consider something other than their own needs, their own desires. They don't like that."

"I never tried to force them to believe the way I did. None of them."

I finally understood it. "No, but you made them think. And that, in a town like Jexville, is unforgivable."

We drove in silence for several minutes. Finally, JoHanna glanced at me. In the pale wash of steamy moonlight, I couldn't tell if she was beaten or tired. "They need to think, Mattie. They're like fat cows, all lined up and following one behind the other. They're so eager to be led, to be told what to do and how to do it. Especially the women." The bit-terness made her voice hard. "Especially the women. I didn't set out on any crusade. I didn't. I just refused to pretend to go along. But I'll tell you one thing. Not a single one of them is worth one of Floyd's smiles. He doesn't have to think his way to goodness. It comes from his heart. We'll find him and we'll leave. We won't even go back for our things. We have enough."

She knew then that we couldn't go back. It wasn't voluntary. Not re-ally. I looked in the backseat at Duncan, so peacefully asleep. So trust-ing that we would take care of her. "They'll kill her, JoHanna."

"Yes. They're capable of such a thing. I finally accept that."

"You should have let John come with us."

"No." She swerved in the road to miss part of a tree that had not been fully removed. "If I could be certain that Elikah wouldn't beat you, I would have made you stay, too. It isn't safe to be my friend. It's because of me that they even thought to hurt Floyd. Because he was my friend."

I remembered the day we walked to the creek to see the baptism. The day Mary Lincoln drowned in her pure white dress, the long sash hanging on the roots of a submerged tree. The creek had shifted the tree slowly, inch by inch, along the deep, sandy bottom. It had taken years, perhaps, for the tree to suddenly appear in a pool where countless other people had been safely immersed. On the way to the baptism, JoHanna had talked to me of trees and nature, of awareness of the value of all living things. In her world, though, there was no reckoning for creatures such as Elikah. Because she could not harm another out of anything except survival, she had not accepted, not truly, that others were capable of such acts. Now she knew it, just as I had learned so long ago at Jojo's hand. I fought back the burn of tears. This was a lesson I would have spared her.

"It wasn't because Floyd is your friend," I told her, finally able to reach across the seat and touch her. "Elikah and Clyde and the others have done this because they are who they are. They would have found some other reason or some other weaker creature to destroy." I squeezed her arm, and she took her hand off the wheel and grasped mine, holding on to me. "This isn't your fault any more than those dead people hanging in a tree are Duncan's fault. Could be that you delayed this, because they were a little bit afraid of you."

"Oh, dear God, Mattie, what if I brought all of this down on us?"

I shook my head. "You told me, JoHanna. We are by nature what we are. Some folks are just mean. You didn't make them that way, and nothing you do or say can change them. Nothing." I gave her a minute to think about that. "We could be smarter than them, and I'm not certain driving to Biloxi is the smartest thing we can do."

JoHanna used her shoulder to brush tears from her cheek. "It's the only thing I know to do, Mattie. We have to find Floyd, before it's too late."

In the backseat Duncan stirred, moaning softly as she opened her eyes. "Mama, I have to pee." Duncan leaned her chin on the back of the seat. "And I'm hungry."

JoHanna squeezed my hand once, briskly, then withdrew it to put it on the wheel. I could almost feel her straightening, drawing up to face the challenge, to meet her daughter's needs.

"We'll stop in a little while, Duncan, but you'll have to wait to eat until we get to the coast. We didn't bring any food."

I grinned into the darkness and leaned over the seat to pull a bag from the back. "Wrong. While you and John were plotting, I got some bread and cheese and that fresh milk. We might as well drink it before it spoils."

Duncan clapped her hands, waking Pecos who demanded a crust of bread. As we ate the coarse bread and cheese and passed the milk bottle around the car, we left behind the worst of our fears, at least for the moment. At Duncan's suggestion, we sang all of the dance songs we knew as we drove through the night toward the Mississippi Sound and the home of a bootlegger.

~ Thirty-three ~

A STRANGE squalling sound and laughter penetrated the layers of deep sleep. My eyes opened slowly and followed the long, red gleam of the car hood to the biggest expanse of water I'd ever seen. It was a landscape of grays. Stranger still was the sight of a woman in a pair of rolled-up men's pants, floppy sun hat on her head in the predawn light, chasing a fussing rooster who pursued a big white and gray bird along the edge of the surf. In the backseat of the car, Duncan McVay was laughing.

"Get him, Mama," she called out, climbing over the seat and starting toward her mother and Pecos. I rubbed my eyes and watched as Duncan ran awkwardly through the waist-high grass toward the water. Past Jo-Hanna, the gray sky met the dark, slick grayness of what had to be the Mississippi Sound. I rolled down my sleeves and pulled up my collar. The hot snap after the hurricane had broken, and fall had returned with its melancholy dawn mists and dampness.

"Head him off, Duncan." JoHanna issued the order as she ran ahead to try and flank Pecos.

Head darting forward and back, wings flapping in some strange ritual, Pecos ran at the white bird, then danced away. The white bird had a big bill. It looked like it could snap Pecos up and swallow him whole. Overhead the sky was filled with strange cries, and I looked up to see more of the white birds, so different in the air than on land. They circled and swooped, graceful, elegant, creatures of the air. For the first time I felt sorry for Pecos. He was such an ungainly creature. He couldn't even fly twenty feet. And now he'd set his heart on courting one of the beautiful sky birds. I got out of the car and went to help round him up. In my pants and lace-up shoes, running was much easier than in a dress. I angled across the grass so that I would intersect the running line of mother, daughter and rooster farther down the beach.

As I trotted along, I tried to recall the events of the night. JoHanna and I had talked until the monotony of the motor, the rhythmic flickering of the headlights along the sides of the road, had spun me into sleep. I had joined Duncan in that haven of forgetfulness. Instead of going to the hotel, apparently JoHanna had stopped the car along the highway and gone to sleep herself. We had all awakened with our first view of the water. Or my first view. Will and JoHanna had been to the coast before. As I'd discovered on the ride, they'd been to some of Tommy Ladnier's parties.

JoHanna knew Tommy far better than she'd ever let on to John, or me. Both she and Will knew him. It was a thought that troubled me.

"Pecos," JoHanna called him gently. "Come here, you fool. It's a seagull you've set your heart on, and she'll have nothing to do with you."

Pecos didn't believe a word JoHanna said. He shook out his wings and danced toward the gull, making ardent little rooster noises as he pranced and strutted. The gull eyed him calmly, as if debating whether to gobble him up or not. Standing on her skinny little legs, she turned her head back to the sea, ignoring his advances. Above us the gulls wheeled, cutting suddenly toward the water, diving headfirst into the rolling waves with an explosion that made me cry out in alarm. Foam breaking around one bird, it struggled back into the air, a small fish captured in its beak.

The other birds circled and cried, winging over the water for another look.

Pecos was oblivious to the water antics of the gulls. He had eyes only for the solitary one that continued to stand on the beach. He eased closer to her, walking around to look at her from another view. Puffing out his chest, he called to her with a lot of fancy cackling thrown in.

"Why doesn't she fly away?" Duncan had caught up with JoHanna. She stood by her mother and asked the question.

"I don't know." JoHanna had given up chasing Pecos. When the gull left, we'd be able to catch him.

"Do you think she knows he's a rooster?" Duncan asked.

"I suspect she knows he isn't a seagull. I'm not certain she knows exactly what he is. But I can tell you, if we don't catch him soon, he's going to be our supper tonight. That bird has been nothing but a torment for the last few days. Aunt Sadie was right. The only place inside a home he deserves to be is inside a pot."

Duncan laughed at her mother. "He can't help himself, Mama. He's fallen in love."

Duncan meant the words in jest, but they went straight to JoHanna's heart. She paled, then forced a smile. "I suppose love is a force that should earn some patience from others," she said, ruffling Duncan's hair. "But I'd like some breakfast and a bath. We should go to the Seaview and check in."

"Why didn't we go last night?" Duncan asked. "You should have gotten me and Mattie up if we were going to camp on the beach."

"I didn't mean to sleep the whole night. I was going to take a nap, but I didn't wake until I felt the dawn mist on my face." JoHanna smiled, then bent to kiss Duncan's cheek. "Catch that nasty bird of yours and let's go get a room."

"Can we have Biloxi bacon and grits?" Duncan licked her lips in anticipation.

"I think that sounds delightful."

In answer to my questioning look, Duncan laughed. "It's fried mullet, Mattie, with a big old plate of hot buttered grits. And maybe biscuits, if we're lucky. You'll love it."

I had walked a little closer to the edge of the water, analyzing the funny feel of the air, the faintest twang that rested on my tongue when I opened my mouth.

"It's salt water, Mattie. You can feel it on your skin, taste it." JoHanna smiled. "It's easier to swim in salt water. It holds you up some."

I looked out to the horizon where I thought I saw something in the distance.

"That's a small barrier island. This water is the Sound. On the other side of the island is the Gulf of Mexico. I remember you telling me once that you dreamed about the blue water and white beaches." JoHanna pointed to where the tantalizing bit of land drifted in and out of visibility. A hint of being there for just a split second, then gone in the haze. "There's a ferryboat that goes out there. An excursion boat, out to Ship

Island. We can take a picnic, and you can see the Gulf. After we find Floyd."

We turned back to the car, and I halted in the dark gray clay that formed the lip of the beach. My attention had been so focused on the water, on Pecos and his romance, that I hadn't thought to look behind me. The biggest, grandest house I'd ever seen was not a hundred yards away. Huge oaks seemed to open their arms to the water, embracing the salty air, inviting everyone who passed to look and admire. I was so taken with the house at first that it took me a while to see the hull of a boat in the front yard. The portico on the right side of the house looked as if it might be falling, and a rocking chair was crashed against one of the trees. Other bits of debris became evident, and as I looked, five men rounded the corner of the house and began putting up ladders on the portico.

"The hurricane," JoHanna said. "But it doesn't look that bad. Not here, at least. That's the DeSalvo House."

"Yancy DeSalvo?" I couldn't believe it. Yancy DeSalvo starred in moving pictures. Callie, who had fallen in love with his movie poster outside the Star Theater in Meridian, had said he was from Mississippi. She was concerned that he wouldn't do well in talkies because of his accent.

"Actually, the house belongs to his parents." JoHanna smiled at my open awe. "But he comes here fairly often."

"You've met him?" I couldn't believe it.

JoHanna's face took on a speculative look as she stared at the house. "At some of Tommy Ladnier's parties. Tommy draws an interesting crowd."

"What are you thinking, JoHanna?" I could see it in the calm stillness of her features. But her eyes weren't still. They were crackling with some internal flame.

"Tommy's house is right on the water. There are brick terraces that lead down into the Sound." She was thinking aloud. "If the DeSalvos have a work crew, surely Tommy does, too. If the DeSalvos have five or ten men cleaning up after the storm, Tommy will have fifty. He has to do everything bigger and grander than anyone else. I told him once that his vanity would be his downfall."

It wasn't possible that I'd caught on to her suggestion. "You don't honestly think that we could pretend to be workers and get away with it?" I looked at her figure. She was wearing pants, that was true. But not from the front, back or side did she look like a man. And I looked like a boy. A skinny, weak boy that no one in his right mind would hire as a laborer.

"Not as workers." JoHanna's smile was pleased. "We could bring sandwiches to sell to the crew. We could pass ourselves off as caterers. And we could do it in such a way that Tommy would never recognize me."

"And what about me?" Duncan had been listening to the conversation with sharp interest.

"You and Pecos are going to have to stay at the Seaview."

"No!" Duncan lifted her chin. "I want to help Floyd."

JoHanna shifted so that she could find Pecos. He was still doing his rooster dance of affection to the gull, who stood unmoved by his attentions. "If you want to help Floyd, catch that damn rooster and let's go to the Seaview. We need to bathe, change, and eat. And then we'll come up with a plan."

Duncan turned away, kicking a clump of sea grass as she did. "I won't be left behind," she said to the Sound. "I won't be."

I looked at JoHanna, who lifted a shoulder. "I've never denied her anything I could get for her. I suppose we all have to learn there are things we simply can't have."

She went and got in the car, and I followed. Fifteen minutes later, an out-of-breath Duncan returned to the car with the rooster wrapped in her shirt. She was bare from the waist up, and shivering, but Pecos was contained. I got the only sweater I'd thought to pack for her and we headed down the highway toward the hotel.

Our progress was slow. The neatness of the DeSalvo house had not prepared us for the fury the storm had wreaked elsewhere. Men with cross-saws were out removing the trees which had been uprooted by the force of the wind. Huge oaks, their root systems as big as houses, had fallen. JoHanna was near tears. "Some of those trees are hundreds of years old," she said. "Some of them survived the storm in 1906, and now they're gone."

"There are lots of trees left, Mama." Duncan patted her shoulders. "Look, there's a bunch."

And we looked at the grove of live oaks that marked the entrance to a large house set back from the road. Men with ladders were headed toward a tree, and I saw the remains of a small boat in the branches. The wind and water must have picked up the boat and hurled it into the oaks.

Roofs had been swept from houses, buildings collapsed by the weight of water and wind. All along the water the piers and wharves that had been built for boats or fishing had been destroyed. In most places only the posts remained, marking where once the wooden piers had stood. Stricken by the scene, JoHanna drove slowly to an enormous white hotel that looked like an old mansion. The sign out front, plastered with leaves that looked as if they'd been embedded into the wood, proclaimed it to be the Seaview.

JoHanna slowed the car in the white shell drive. "Thank goodness," she said. "I was beginning to think the storm might have blown it away."

The massive building, fronting the beach with fifteen enormous white columns, had made a good target for the wind, but the walls were solid. JoHanna said the bricks were handmade by slaves, coated with heavy plaster and then painted white. We pulled up to the front where a man in a red uniform opened the door for me and JoHanna, and then took our bags out.

"The lobby is a little damp," he said, not smiling at all. "But the rooms on the second floor are fine."

JoHanna thanked him and gave him a coin, and he drove the car away while another man took our bags and followed us into the lobby.

My trip to Mobile and New Orleans had given me a glimpse of the splendor of a fine hotel, so I didn't gawk and act like a bumpkin. The hotel, even with maids sopping up water from the carpets and carpenters replacing window frames and panes, was beautiful. And there was an amazing cheerfulness about the clerk and bellboys as they signed us in and took us to a room. Duncan was busy with the suitcase where she'd secreted Pecos. She was terrified the rooster would get in a tizzy and give himself away. She didn't see JoHanna when she signed our names as Martha Lindsey, Jane and Emily Lindsey. The scratch of the pen across the heavy pages of the registry book gave me a chill. I had forgotten, for the moment, why we'd come to Biloxi.

"Will John know how to get us a message?" I whispered to her. As we followed a young man in a smart red jacket to our rooms, she nodded. "John knows the names."

The bellman carried our bags as if they weighed nothing. Unlocking the door, he stowed our luggage, opened the windows, and waited discreetly by the door until JoHanna gave him a coin, too. The Seaview was an expensive place, just getting up to the room.

I went to the window, touching the heavy rose fabric of the draperies. They matched the wallpaper of wild roses and green leaves, which matched the dark rose chaise beside the window. Outside the sun was burning off the gray mist, and though the wind was chill, the day promised to be fine.

"I'll have a bath first," JoHanna said as she watched Duncan free Pecos. "Then Mattie."

"I'm hungry." Duncan looked up from the bird.

"Call room service," JoHanna directed. "Then figure out some way to confine that bird. We can't have him flying out the second-floor window every time he gets a yen for a seagull."

Duncan sighed as she went to the bell pull and tugged it gently. "You act like you wish me and Pecos weren't here."

JoHanna turned in the doorway. "I wish you weren't. Because I love you and I want you safe. If I'd had time to take you to Hattiesburg, I would have. And I'm telling you now, Duncan, if you give me the first bit of trouble, I'll put you on a train to New Orleans. The first one that pulls out. You can stay with Vanessa."

The threat was enough to make Duncan clamp her mouth shut. She waited until her mother closed the bathroom door before she turned to me. "Vanessa is a bitch. I hate her."

"Who is Vanessa?" I asked. I'd never heard JoHanna mention her.

"Daddy's cousin. She disapproves of Mama and me. She thinks Daddy made a mistake in marrying Mama."

"She says so?" I couldn't believe it.

"All the time. In front of Mama and Daddy and me." Duncan grinned. "She calls me a rotten brat. She says Mama bewitched Daddy and he's never gotten out of the spell."

I sank down on the chaise to wait bath or food, whichever came first. "I hope we don't have to meet her."

Duncan went to the window and stood with her hand on Pecos's shifting head. "I guess I'll have to stay here with the rooster while y'all have all the fun."

Thirty-four

WHATEVER else my visit at Tommy Ladnier's house entailed, it was not fun. Even with her hair only an inch long, JoHanna was still very recognizable as JoHanna. Actually, the haircut probably made her more so. She could not mingle among the workers, selling sandwiches and cookies for a nickel. Even though it made my knees knock to consider walking into the place, I was determined to find Floyd.

From one of the maids at the Seaview, JoHanna finagled a plain blue dress and a white pinafore apron for me to wear. Her skillful fingers braided my unruly hair into a neat coronet, and she gave me the basket of sandwiches and oatmeal cookies the kitchen had prepared for our "picnic on the beach." She parked the big red car a quarter mile from the water in a grove of pecan trees that had suffered heavy damage from the storm but that no one was paying any attention to. She said she would wait for me there while I sold the sandwiches and talked with the workmen. She warned me to be careful of any men wearing suits, and not to talk to any of the women who lived in the house at all. She said a whore was a whore and she'd sell pleasure or secrets and it wouldn't matter to her which.

The house was huge, a two-story stucco concoction painted a pale coral with a beautiful green tile roof. Gardens of dark green gardenias surrounded it and in the back, baked brick terraces fell like giant steps down into the Sound. There were workmen everywhere as they began to repair the damage, big and small, inflicted by the storm. I made my way around the estate with my basket of sandwiches and a sickly smile while I sought any trace of Floyd.

The workmen were hungry, and the sandwiches were gone long before I'd covered the gardens. I'd explored a building where three big cars were parked. There was no trace of Floyd there. Another building had tools and supplies, but no sign of Floyd. I was headed back to the terraces that had once been lined and highlighted by beautiful flowers until the storm. The terraces, solid bricks worn smooth by time and salty mist, were gentle giant steps down to the water. Gardeners were busy pulling up dying chrysanthemums and geraniums that had been killed by the salt water and putting in new dirt and new plants. I held the empty basket and walked along, praying that no one would ask me my business.

Outside the big back doors with their dozens of panes of glass, four men in suit pants and white shirts watched over the workmen. They wore suspenders and hats and smoked cigarettes and laughed a lot. One of them spotted me and said something to the others. They laughed, but one of them rose slowly to his feet. I pretended not to notice but started walking in the other direction, my empty basket bumping my thigh.

"Hey, you!" The man was right behind me.

I ignored him and kept walking, forcing my legs not to run. To run now would only make it worse.

"Hey, I'm talking to *you*." His hand on my shoulder turned me around.

I saw his surprise when he looked at me closely. The bruises around my eyes were mostly gone, but up close it was easy to see I'd been beaten. The more recent rooster attack had left a wound on my cheek. "What are you doing here?" he demanded.

"I brought some sandwiches to sell." My voice sounded sheeplike, afraid, manna for a bully boy. I forced the panic from it and lifted my chin. "For the workmen. Sandwiches for their lunch."

He reached down and took the empty basket, shaking it. "Looks like you sold out."

"Yes." My hand went instinctively to my pocket where I'd put the nickels. "They bought them all. I was just getting ready to go home."

"Did Mr. Ladnier say you could sell sandwiches on his property?" The question was a formality. He knew I didn't have permission.

"No. I didn't think he'd care. It saves the workmen from leaving for lunch. They can work harder."

"Oh, so you were serving Tommy's best interests?" The man smiled and he had the biggest teeth I'd ever seen, piano key teeth, but his gray eyes were harder than the brick terrace.

"No, I was trying to make some money. The storm . . ." I didn't want to start too many lies.

"Maybe you'd better talk to Mr. Ladnier. I'm not so sure he'd view your little business as good for him." His breath smelled like cigarettes and his teeth were stained yellow.

"There's no need to trouble Mr. Ladnier. I'll go and won't come back." I tried to pass by him but he caught my arm.

"You act like you were doing something wrong." He held my arm so tight it hurt, but I gritted my teeth and refused to cry out.

"I wasn't doing anything wrong," I ground out the words.

"I'm supposed to believe you?" He put a heavy layer of sarcasm on the last word.

"Listen, Mr. . . ." He ignored my effort to get his name. "I don't want to make trouble. I want to go home."

"Maybe Mr. Ladnier deserves a portion of that money you made. After all, you were selling sandwiches on his property. Maybe he needs a cut."

I swallowed. "I didn't think he'd care. The men were hungry. My mother said I should make the sandwiches and bring them over."

"Maybe he will care, maybe he won't." The man laughed and held my arm as he half-dragged me toward the house. The other men at the back door were laughing, too.

"Caught yourself an en-tre-pre-neur?" one of them called out. "A real dangerous looking criminal. Looks like she's already taken a beating for something." He leaned down and lifted my chin with a finger. "What crime did you commit to get punched around so?"

I was terrified but I didn't say anything. There were four of them, and they were all staring at me, reaching out to touch me. JoHanna was a half mile away, and there was no one who could help me. If Tommy Ladnier found out the real reason I was there, he'd probably have them kill me and dump my body in the Sound. I had to brazen it out.

The glass-paned door swung open and a tall, slender man with a dark mustache stepped out. His hair was groomed back in an elegant, Valentino fashion, and he wore a white shirt open at the throat, black pants. And Floyd's black boots.

He smiled as my gaze lingered on his boots, and he turned his leg so that I could fully admire the workmanship of the boot. "Lovely, aren't they?"

I nodded, unable to look away from them.

"What manner of criminal is this?" Tommy Ladnier asked the man who held me. He smelled of cologne, a fragrance intense and subtle at the same time. Expensive. I didn't have to be sophisticated to recognize that.

"She was selling sandwiches in the gardens to the workers."

Tommy Ladnier walked to me and lifted the cloth of my basket. "Were they good sandwiches?"

"Yes, sir. Roast beef and ham." I looked at the basket, afraid to look into his eyes. He knew Elikah. He knew everyone, everywhere. What if he recognized me?

"Does our little sandwich girl have a name?"

I hadn't expected the question and I didn't have an answer. I couldn't use my real name. I couldn't say the name JoHanna used at the Seaview.

"I think she needs something to drink," Tommy said. "She's so dry she can't get her name out."

He opened the door and before I could cry out for help, the man who held me forced me inside.

JoHanna had told me to see as much of the house as I could. She said that Floyd would probably be in the out buildings, but he wasn't. But Tommy Ladnier had the boots. That was the evidence I needed to believe that Floyd was somewhere nearby. I couldn't help Floyd if I was a coward. He had to be there. Somewhere. And I was getting inside, even if one of Tommy Ladnier's goons was about to pinch my arm off.

"Should I take her to the kitchen?" the man who held me asked.

Tommy's smile was slow. "No, the library. And take your hand off her. She's a sandwich girl, not a killer."

The man snatched his hand away as if my arm had suddenly caught on fire. From the staircase I heard low, throaty laughter.

"Boy, when Tommy says jump, you jump, don't you, Teddy?"

The man who'd held me scowled. "Shut up, Myra."

"I don't have to shut up until Tommy tells me to shut up."

"Shut up, Myra," Tommy said. "Quit baiting Teddy, or I'll have to send you home to Mama."

Undaunted, the girl sat down on the stairs so she could watch us through the balusters. The beautifully carved wood framed her pale face, and her red-gold hair flowed over the wood. "Who's the pretty baby?" she asked.

Tommy laughed, and when he spoke he'd adopted a fake accent. "A young lass come to sell sandwiches to the workers. Just an honest lass, out to make some money to help her poor, starvin' mother." Tommy's voice was filled with fun and laughter, but it gave me a chill.

"Oh, a noble young thing." The girl laughed. "Well, I always wanted to sell *sandwiches* to make a living."

All of the men laughed, and I felt a surge of panic. The entire house was evil. The girl on the steps was wearing some fancy nightclothes and it was past noon. Living with Elikah had taught me a few things about life, and I wasn't the innocent fool I'd been four months before. What I couldn't tell was whether she was Tommy's girlfriend or Teddy's? Or was she there for anyone who wanted her?

"Get us some coffee, Myra," Tommy directed as we followed him into a big room with all four walls filled with books. The fire in the fireplace was dead, but the smell of burning wood persisted, contrasting with the smell of the books. Money. Power. The room reeked of it.

"Who told you to come here?" Tommy turned to confront me with whiplike speed.

I was struck speechless by his transformation from bantering playboy to inquisitor. "N—n—no one." I finally got the words out. "I was going to sell the sandwiches on the beach, but no one was there. The storm." I licked my lips in nervousness. My mouth was parched, but there was no sign of Myra in the door. "There wasn't anyone on the beach, and I heard the hammering. So I thought maybe the men working would be hungry." I shut up because there wasn't anything else I could say.

Tommy Ladnier's eyes were peculiar. They seemed to shift rapidly from side to side. A tiny motion, but one that made me think he never really slept. They would shift beneath his lids, seeing even when his eyes were closed. I had to look away.

"Besides selling sandwiches, what do you do?"

He was toying with me because it amused the men who had all taken casual positions about the room. They were grinning at each other, sending looks that said what a powerhouse Tommy was, and what a pitiable creature I was.

"I clean and cook and sew. Whatever needs to be done." Anger was giving me back my courage, and I wanted to tell him that I plotted to help my friends. But I couldn't do that.

"If you need work so badly that you're in my yard selling sandwiches, I think I'll give you a job."

His performance was for his men, so I didn't know whether to believe him or not. "What kind of job?" Also, I suspected that the jobs he offered to women would not be to my liking.

"In the kitchen." He grinned. "I don't take children upstairs. Not even one who has a taste for a little slap and tickle." So quick I didn't have time to pull away he brought his hand up to my face and traced the bruise beneath my left eye with the gentlest of touches.

The men guffawed and I felt the blood climb my face. I looked at him. Working in the kitchen was perfect, the opportunity of a lifetime. "Can I go to work now?" They could laugh all they wanted.

"What can you cook?" he asked, his gray eyes watching.

"I can cook anything. Breakfast and pies are my specialty."

He picked at the white ruffle of my apron. "I'm particular about the way I like my eggs."

"What man isn't?" I replied.

This time the men laughed with me.

"Dillard, take her to the kitchen and tell Love she's going to be her new help. Love hates to get up to cook breakfast. Maybe the little sandwich girl will be to her liking."

Elation made me want to sing or jump, but I made sure that nothing except gratitude showed on my face. "Thank you," I said and turned to leave the room.

Tommy's hand caught me at the neck, pinching just hard enough to let me know he could hurt me. I closed my eyes to shut out the panic he might see in them when he turned me to face him again.

"You never told us your name."

Opening my eyes, I saw the long, dark eyelashes that framed each gray eye. His features were striking. He was immaculately groomed. "Lola," I whispered. I'd decided to take the name of the woman who'd taken my place in Elikah's bed. She'd made her escape with his money. Maybe I'd be as lucky.

"Little Lola." His hand lifted and caressed the underside of my jaw. "If you're as good in the kitchen as you say, maybe we'll see what your other talents are."

The men laughed, and he nodded for me to leave. The tall man named Dillard waited at the door for me. Without a word he led me into the big kitchen, where a huge black woman bent over an oven full of hot rolls. The sweet smell of hot yeast bread made me realize it was midafternoon and I'd not eaten since breakfast.

"Here's some kitchen help for you, Love. Tommy says she'll make breakfast so you don't have to get up."

Love touched the top of the rolls, eyed them critically, then shoved them back inside the oven before she stood up and turned to look at me. She was the tallest woman I'd ever seen, a deep, chocolate black woman with small eyes and a sharp nose. "You can cook breakfast?"

"Yes."

"Mr. Tommy is a good man to work for, but you mess up his eggs, he gone mess up your face, even more than someone done done."

My finding Floyd depended on staying in that kitchen. "I can cook."

Her gaze slid over my body, resting on my stomach.

"You not gettin' ready to swell up with some bastard young-un, are you?"

The question was unexpected. "No."

"Keep it that way. You get pregnant, you can't work in my kitchen. Never had more trouble with my bread and cakes than when Mr. Tommy sent that pregnant whore to work in here. Nothin' would rise. Not the first thing. I reckon that girl made the wrong thing rise and she got the hoodoo. Wouldn't nothin' lift up around her."

I looked at the door and saw that Dillard was gone. "Can I go home now and come back tomorrow?"

Love took the rolls out of the oven before she answered me.

"Mr. Tommy likes for us to stay here. He don't hold with us running all over the place."

"I have to get my clothes and things."

"Get that loafin' Dillard to go get them. Or ask Mr. Tommy for some new things. He's free with his money."

"I really prefer my own things." I edged toward the door. I had to get back to JoHanna and let her know I was okay. She'd be worried sick. I was half an hour late already. "I'll be back before dawn, ready to go to work. How many do I cook for? What time in the morning does Mr. Ladnier like to eat?"

"They come in shifts, mostly. Fourteen, give or take a few. Them whores don't eat breakfast, so you don't have to mess with them. They'll try to have you runnin' trays of toast and coffee upstairs, but don't let 'em get that foolishness started. They like to ack like they something, but they just whores, and don't you let 'em forget it."

"Will you be here in the morning?" I was suddenly concerned about the job I'd undertaken. I'd never cooked for fourteen men.

She put her hands on her wide hips and waited. Finally she spoke. "What you doin' here?"

"I need a job."

She came around the counter, her arms dusty with flour up to the elbow. "What you really doin' here?"

I didn't know what to say. JoHanna's warning came back to me. She'd told me not to talk to the women in the house. I could feel Love's look boring into me, her small eyes completely dark. I'd never really had a conversation with a colored person before, and I had to make her believe me. "I need the work."

"Say now, child. You gone tell Love the truth or I'll be calling Mr. Tommy in here to ask. You got thievin' on your mind, you put it aside. Nobody steals from Mr. Tommy. Nobody."

"I'm not a thief." I'd never taken a single thing in my whole life. The idea that a colored person would think me a thief made me angry.

"You no cook neither. What's your business here? And this is your las' chance to tell the truth."

She would call Tommy Ladnier and get me fired before I'd even begun. She was a big, shrewd woman. "I'm looking for someone." I whispered the words it seemed, but she heard them clearly.

"One of Mr. Tommy's young men?" She gave me a contemptuous look. "You done give away your freshness to one of those men? More fool you are. You'd best get outta here."

I shook my head. "I'm looking for someone else."

Her eyes halted, not looking or seeing, but thinking. She sucked her full bottom lip into her mouth as she thought. "You lookin' for that stupid boy. That handsome fella, but not all together in the head."

I nodded. "Floyd."

She released her lip and it popped out of her mouth. She shook her head. "You get outta here, and you don't come back." She went back around the counter and picked up a large brush. Without looking up at me she dipped the brush in a bowl of melted butter and began working on the hot rolls. "Get outta here. I'll tell Mr. Tommy you didn't know nothin' about cookin' and I sent you on your way. He won't come lookin' for you if I says I fired you."

"I have to find Floyd." She was sympathetic to me. I could tell. She didn't want to be, but she was.

"He ain't here no more."

Disappointment made me cry out, a soft ah that made her look up at me in sudden concern. "Where is he?" I couldn't keep the desperation out of my voice.

"He ain't been here today." My panic had frightened her, and she wouldn't look at me.

"But he was here yesterday?"

"Get outta here while you can, girl. Don't be asking no more questions." The rolls drank the butter as she passed the brush across them.

"I have to find him. He's not able to take care of himself. Just tell me, was he here yesterday?"

"He was here yesterday," she confirmed. "I made him some French toast. He said it was his favorite." Her hand stopped in midair. "He liked that French toast with the powdered sugar and the syrup. That boy could eat."

My disappointment gave way to a sense of relief. "Then he was okay? He wasn't hurt?"

"He wasn't hurt bad." She started buttering the rolls again. "Little white girl, you get yourself out of this kitchen and this house. You go now before Mr. Tommy fines out what you askin' about. Cause if he fines out, he will make you one sorry little skinny girl." She didn't look at me as she talked. She swept the brush across the warm crust of the rolls.

"Just tell me that Floyd was okay. Can you tell me that?"

She kept on brushing the rolls until the smooth brown tops glistened. "He was okay."

"Do you know where they took him? Did they take him back to Jexville?"

She put the brush down. "They took him somewhere else. Mr. Tommy don't ask Love where he can take folks who make trouble for him. Maybe they took him home. Maybe they took him for a swim. Now you, little girl, you get out!" She clapped her hands hard together and a puff of flour floated up around her. "Get out before you get in big trouble. I'm gone count to ten, and if you ain't gone, I'm callin' Mr. Tommy. I can't risk gettin' myself in trouble to save your skinny white hide. So go!"

∽ Thirty-five ∽

I RAN the whole way back to where JoHanna had parked the car. The grass in the pecan orchard had not been cut all summer, tall bahia that tangled around my feet and clutched at my skirt. Limbs had been blown down all over the orchard, and I dodged them as I cut through the rows and rows of gray, leafless trees, staying clear of the roadway just in case Love wasn't good for her word, or wasn't able to convince Tommy and the boys that she had sent me away. Finding JoHanna and not getting caught were the only thoughts I allowed myself, but beneath that was a steady joy that Floyd had been at Tommy Ladnier's, and that he was okay.

The red car was a flare of color in the gray-green of the orchard. JoHanna paced beside the car. Her long stride took her forward, then she pivoted and went back.

"JoHanna!" I called as soon as I was within yelling distance, and struggled on through the grass.

"Mattie!" She started running toward me. "Oh, Mattie, I thought something terrible had happened to you."

"It almost did." I pulled in air. "It's Floyd." I clasped the hand she held out to me. "He was there, but he's gone now. The cook said he was okay, but they took him someplace else."

"Where?"

I shook my head, still trying to get enough breath to talk. "She didn't know where."

"Are you certain he was gone? She could be lying. She could have made up a story just to get rid of you."

I thought of Love, hands on her big hips, small eyes watching me with neither pity nor compassion. "I don't think she was lying."

JoHanna signaled for me to get in the car. "We have to get back and check on Duncan. I told her to order from room service and to stay in the room."

But—

It was unspoken. Duncan had been raised not to be afraid. She couldn't comprehend the damage she could do by straying out of the room and being seen by the wrong people. She was enough like JoHanna that she wouldn't believe the danger until it was too late.

As we maneuvered onto the main road, we were forced to slow down. Mules and wagons were pulled up on each side of the roadbed. Men with their shirt sleeves rolled and their faces gleaming with sweat loaded debris into the wagons while the mules stood patiently, cowlike tails flicking at the yellow flies and mosquitoes, which seemed to have blown in by the millions.

The afternoon had drawn even more workers out along the beach front. The sky was still gray, but the sun burned hot and angry, heating the clouds into a sticky humidity. Ignoring the stifling heat, the men worked on. Sometimes they paused as they heard our motor and waved or whistled as we drove by. I was taken by the fact that so many were dark haired with deep tans. Olive-skinned people descended from sailors, handsome men who flashed a smile at us as they wiped the sweat from their foreheads. Most of them were working hard, but in a couple of places, where the damage was worst, some stood beside their property and stared at it, as if they did not believe what had occurred.

We passed an empty section of beach where five black wreaths erupted from the sea grass. At first I thought they were thin old women dressed all in black, but JoHanna slowed, and I could see that the wreaths had been hung on sturdy wire stands, the legs planted firmly in the sand. The black ribbons blew lazily on the erratic gulf breeze. JoHanna said that someone had been killed at sea, probably five fishermen, and the wreaths were a symbol of death and mourning. Victims of the sea.

I thought of the dead family on Red Licorice Road, victims of a storm far worse than a hurricane. What madness had come swirling through the rain and wind to stop at that neat little farm? I could not believe that a father, even touched by madness, could systematically drown his wife and children. Especially not a three-year-old girl. I had avoided looking at their contorted faces as much as possible, but I could not forget that child's feet, dark and purpling beneath the folds of her wet gown. The image haunted me, as did that family, left dangling in my imagination.

JoHanna's driving pulled me from my dark thoughts. Once clear of the wagons and mules, JoHanna drove too fast, but no one seemed to notice us as we whizzed toward the Seaview. Turning into the white shell drive, JoHanna relaxed, easing her grip on the wheel. Once again, a young man met us at the door and took the car while we hurried inside.

"Mrs. Lindsey?" The voice of the clerk stopped us halfway across the lobby. "There's a telegram for you." He waved an envelope at us and JoHanna hurried to the desk to get it.

I watched her face as she ripped open the envelope and scanned the thin white page. She looked up at me, her face curiously blank. "Will is on his way here. John is going back to Jexville to search for Floyd there."

"That's all it says?" I had expected more. More detail. Had John been able to find anything out about Floyd? About who had taken him and brought him down to Tommy Ladnier's? About the dead family? When would Will arrive?

JoHanna crumpled the telegram and then held it in her hand as she started toward the room. After seeing the look in her eyes I would have walked through Jexville stark naked rather than ask her another single question about the telegram.

We found Duncan on the hotel room floor with shreds of newspaper all around her. She'd ordered a paper from room service and had been busy with a pair of scissors from the front desk, clipping out every storm story. She had ordered the stories into three piles. One for Florida, one for Alabama, and one for Mississippi. There were thousands dead in Florida, where the storm had swept across from the Atlantic and then regathered her strength in the Gulf of Mexico for an assault on Mobile.

JoHanna sank into a chair as she read the clippings, passing them on to me with a sigh or shake of her head. The devastation in Florida was in the millions of dollars. More gruesome was the front page listing of locations and a count of the dead and injured. "Miami: known dead 194; known injured 75; estimated dead 115; seriously injured 250. More than 10,000 homeless." And the count moved across the state. Miami Beach, Pompano, Hollywood, and on and on.

According to the stories printed in the *Mobile Daily Register*, Mobile had been hit twice by the storm with winds up to ninety-four miles an hour. But there had been no known loss of life. JoHanna shook her head as she handed that article to me. "We were very lucky. The eye must have passed over Mobile."

I started to say that Mobile, sitting right on the Bay, had escaped with no deaths. In Jexville there were at least five. Neither JoHanna nor Duncan needed to be reminded of that, though, so I watched Pecos scratching around in the unread portion of the paper.

With a light breeze fluttering the curtains in the room and Duncan on her stomach, feet crossed behind her back, it didn't seem possible that so much destruction had occurred. I went to the window and looked out at the Sound. The water was choppy, gray tipped with white. The sun broke free of the clouds and gave the water a million sparkles before it disappeared behind the clouds again.

"Is Will coming here?" I asked. I hated to pry, but JoHanna wasn't going to give out any information.

"Yes. Straight here. He won't even go to Mobile. John was able to get word to him."

"When will he arrive?" I noticed that Duncan gave up her pretense of disinterest at news of her father. She was still aggravated at being left behind, but the idea of Will's impending arrival pushed her over her bad mood.

"Tomorrow afternoon." JoHanna's voice registered no emotion.

"Daddy's coming tomorrow?" Duncan dropped the scissors and rolled over so she could sit up. "I can't wait! He'll find Floyd and take care of everything. Then we can go home. Pecos and I hate being cooped up here in the room, hiding."

JoHanna's smile was unsteady. "He'll take care of things, Duncan. I'm sure he will." She got up and paced to the edge of the rug.

"And he'll find Floyd, won't he?"

It did not escape JoHanna or me that Duncan had rephrased her statement, turning it over and into a question. Though she had said nothing until now, Floyd was very much on her mind.

"You haven't had . . ." My voice was strident, and Duncan and Jo-Hanna stared at me. I swallowed and tried again. "You haven't had any dreams about Floyd, have you?"

Duncan shook her head. Then frowned. "I dreamt about the man in the water, and that was the last dream. Mama, you don't think Floyd has drowned, do you? The storm was over before he left us."

JoHanna's voice was sad. "No, I don't think he's drowned." She paced to the window, looking out to sea.

"Then Daddy will find him and everything will be okay again." She lifted her arms and stretched. "What are we going to do until Daddy gets here?" Duncan looked at me. JoHanna slipped from the room and went into the separate bath and closed the door.

"We could get some cards. Maybe play gin or hearts." I could hear Jo-Hanna. She was crying, and I was doing my best to distract Duncan. "Since your mama's here to watch Pecos, maybe you and I could go walking around the grounds. The hotel is pretty."

Duncan tried to feign indifference, but she was sick of the room, and she got up and put on her shoes.

"JoHanna, Duncan and I are going for a walk. Watch Pecos." I spoke through the bathroom door.

"Don't leave the hotel grounds." Her voice was hoarse, raw.

"Mama?" Duncan touched the wood of the door for only an instant. Before JoHanna could reply she fled the room, slamming the door on me and Pecos.

I caught up with her in the hallway. Her legs seemed to heal more and more with each passing hour. She wore a short dress, a dark green smock, and I noticed that even the scars from the burns were beginning to fade. Her hair had taken a sudden growth spurt. Dark and thick, it was lustrous, catching the dim lights of the hallway and holding them deep.

"Let's go to the gardens," she said, leading the way.

Gardeners were hard at work on the rose bushes and the flower beds. The wind had ripped all of the leaves from the huge oaks that marked the grounds. The sound of saws was menacing, but the smell of the fresh wood was familiar, and comforting. Men were cutting back damaged limbs, mending the ravages of the storm. An old man in blue overalls and a blue work shirt took a shine to Duncan. He showed her where some of the old limbs, so heavy and graceful they actually touched the ground, had been braced to prevent severe wind damage. He assured us that by spring the Seaview gardens would once again be the setting for beautiful weddings and parties where wealthy people danced among the trees.

I could see that the hurricane had done heavy damage, but not nearly as extensive as the havoc wreaked by the salt water in Tommy Ladnier's terraced gardens. With a wave the old man went back to his saw, and Duncan and I walked along the white shell paths. Duncan told me of the tons of oysters harvested and eaten to procure the shells for the walkways. The act of walking, the freedom of movement, the bustle of the gardens, and the friendliness of the workers, all combined to bring Duncan out of her moodiness. She ran and talked with the gardeners, asking questions or laughing, teasing the young and old with her impish smile and quick tongue. It was a pleasure to see her as an ordinary child, a nine-year-old girl playing on the grounds of a luxury resort. Yet each time I turned a corner or came upon a new vista, I was struck by the oddness of the scene. Though the day had warmed to a hot summer feel, the grounds were stripped of all greenery. My body registered summer, but my eyes gave me the facts of winter. The perversity touched me in a way that made me afraid. It was a feeling I did not want to acknowledge or explore, so I listened to Duncan's bright chatter and watched the pleasure with which the workmen responded to her. She was a bright and precocious child, and in a place where no one knew her, she was so very easily loved. Perhaps JoHanna and Will would never go back to Jexville. Perhaps we would all go and live somewhere else. New Orleans. Natchez. St. Louis. Towns along a river that JoHanna could learn to love as much as she loved the Pascagoula.

Still in the long blue dress of the sandwich girl, I hunted for the few spots of shade and sweltered and indulged in fantasy as Duncan sported. I wanted to give JoHanna some time alone to pull herself together. The idea of returning to the room and the lash of her naked emotion kept us both outside longer than we otherwise might have remained.

After an hour, though, we were sweaty and itching from the bites of the deer flies and mosquitoes. Even Duncan was ready to return to the screened coolness of the room.

JoHanna met us at the door, all trace of anguish gone. She smiled as she drew Duncan into her arms and hugged her. "We'll get up early tomorrow and take the excursion boat out to Ship Island," she said. "Mattie has been waiting all of her life for a view of the Gulf. Since we're this close, we shouldn't let the opportunity pass."

Duncan clapped with delight, but then her smile darkened. "What about Pecos?"

JoHanna laughed. "I hadn't thought of him." She looked at the rooster, who jumped to the window and pecked at the screen. "I suppose we could take him back to the beach this afternoon and let him hunt his lady love. Tomorrow, though, we'll have to find a chicken yard and board him."

"What about Daddy?"

"We'll be back and packed to leave before he gets here."

Duncan nodded. "And then we'll find Floyd?"

JoHanna's chest rose silently, a long breath. "Yes. Will can find him, Duncan. Your father can do what we can't. If Floyd's back in Jexville, the men will tell Will where he is."

Jexville. How was it possible that a word could strike as painfully as a knife. Jexville. It plunged into my gut and weakened my legs. I knelt on the floor and began picking up the scattered newspaper. We were returning to Jexville, and I felt a rush of fear. Somehow, in the past day, I'd managed to forget that Jexville waited for me. I had become a person who lived only in the present moment.

In the course of the past several days, I had undergone a strange series of transformations. Because JoHanna asked it, I had become the sandwich girl spying on Tommy Ladnier. Walking the grounds, I had sold my cookies and sandwiches to the workers, and they had accepted me for what I said I was. When Teddy gripped my arm, when Tommy Ladnier looked into my eyes, when the wind whipped about my face in the car, or when the deer flies bit the back of my neck—I was those sensations and emotions. There was no connection to things I had felt or thought in the past, no desire to anticipate the future.

As I gathered the newspaper, my fingers brushed the deep burgundy and gray of the rug. Color, texture, the faint odor of time. Weak sunlight broke free of the clouds and slanted across my fingers, changing my skin to a blistered white. Here, at this moment, I was something and someone else, and I resisted the return to Jexville with every ounce of strength I possessed. But reality was so much stronger than I was. Even as I touched the woven wool of the rug, felt the sun, I knew I was a transient in a place of transient comfort. The Seaview was only a momentary respite. I was not a McVay. JoHanna could not absorb me no matter how much I wanted her to do so.

The clippings scattered from my fingers as a sob broke from me.

"Duncan, put Pecos in that bag and take him on down to the car.

We'll be down in a few minutes. And don't let him out of the bag no matter what. If that desk clerk sees him, we'll be put out on our ears." JoHanna knelt on the floor beside me. "You don't have to go back, Mattie. We can keep this room and you can stay here."

Pecos and I cried together. He resisted the snare of Duncan's hands as heartily as I fought against the truth of my situation. JoHanna held my shoulders and said nothing until the rooster was captured, stowed in the bag, and Duncan had hustled out the door with him.

"Mattie, listen to me. You can stay here and file for divorce. Will can set everything up for you. There's no need for you to go back to Jexville. You don't ever have to see Elikah again. I mean except in court, and maybe there's a way to take care of that. I'm not certain, but Will knows these things."

She smoothed my hair and rubbed my back and talked. My tears were spent, and I listened. I didn't doubt what she said, but I couldn't explain to her that the words were draining the marrow out of my bones. If she dissolved the Mattie of Jexville, there would be no one left. I could stay in the Seaview, in this very room. I could bathe and dress and go down to the dining room to eat, but what part of me would that be?

I had let go of the Mattie who'd picked blackberries with two young blond girls named Callie and Lena Rae. Sometimes, I could still catch the sound of their laughter, and I knew it. But it was distant now, released when I chose not to linger in the past. When I thought of myself, alone, at the Seaview, there was only a terrifying blankness. I could visualize myself going through the motions of the day, sleeping, dressing, eating, walking along the beach. Absent, though, were the thoughts and emotions of such a Mattie. That Mattie did not exist. Not yet. Maybe never.

I listened to the sound, sensible words of JoHanna and understood a terrifying thing. I had to go back to Jexville. I could not go forward until I went back.

Thirty-six

RIDING at the front of the big boat, I tasted the salt spray as we bumped through the waves. I kept my eyes focused on the horizon, and what had once been a speck of land grew larger and larger as we slapped and wallowed our way toward Ship Island. During the night the heat wave had truly broken, and the sun had risen on a crisp fall day that made the excursion to see the Gulf of Mexico a magnificent adventure. Or at least that's how JoHanna decided to play it. She had to do something to keep from going insane at our lack of ability to help Floyd. Her skin had taken on a fine white sheen, a papery luster, as if all of the moisture were being burned away behind it. Duncan, on the other hand, had accepted that JoHanna and Will, when he arrived, would be able to make things right. Wherever Floyd had gone, Will would fetch him back. I tried not to think about it, and I took my comfort from the fact that Duncan had not dreamed of Floyd. The bond that linked them was so strong, I felt certain she would know if anything were truly wrong with him. Whenever I felt the gnawing sickness of frustration or the chill of apprehension, I held onto that thought and forced the dark mood away. I could not afford to cater to any unfounded fears. I would confront the future with courage.

In the back of the boat, JoHanna held the basket I'd used to sell sandwiches at Tommy Ladnier's. This time it was packed with a picnic lunch for us. JoHanna said we would walk the white sand of the island, wade in the aqua surf, picnic, and return to Biloxi before Will's train arrived at three. I allowed my mind to go no further than the image of

Will, stepping off the train with his bag in one hand and his hat in the other.

A burst of laughter and applause came from the back of the boat and I turned to see Duncan, without the benefit of any music, on the deck of that lumbering ship, marking off the steps of the Charleston while a tall young man with freckles imitated her every move.

"That's much better, Michael," Duncan said, giving her chin a jerk of satisfaction. "If you could come to the house where we have music, I could teach you in ten minutes flat. You're a natural."

Duncan was the most popular passenger on the boat. The crew and spectators all talked with her, all charmed by the devil-may-care smile that was so much like Will's. JoHanna sat and held the basket, and I could see her continued worry in the stillness of her posture.

"Pecos can dance the Charleston," Duncan told her audience, and then launched into a story about the rooster.

Pecos had been taken in by a farmer several miles from the Seaview who promised to let him have the run of the henyard for the day. That rooster needed something to boost his spirits. The afternoon before he'd encountered another seagull and met with the same disappointing response, and he was so low his comb was about to drag the ground. No matter how he strutted and swaggered, the gulls showed no interest in him. JoHanna had said that a day with some attentive hens would soften the bitterness of the gulls' rejection. As I listened with half an ear to Duncan's story, I couldn't help but smile. Duncan loved that ornery rooster, but I think even she secretly relished the idea of being free from him for a day. Pecos could be very demanding.

The boat crested a larger than normal wave and dropped into the trough, eliciting a few cries of alarm from the other three female passengers. At first the motion of the boat had frightened me and caused me to stagger against the rail, but I'd gotten used to the lurch and roll. I even liked it. My only complaint was that the boat was full, and the sides seemed so close to the water. If we hit a wave wrong, it seemed water would spill over the sides of the ship, pushing us deeper into the Sound, where more water would come into the boat and on and on until we sank. I shook my head at my own morbid fantasies and looked back to JoHanna.

The young man who had been dancing with Duncan was headed my way. There were at least twenty-five passengers, all going out to see what damage the hurricane had done to the barrier island. Some of the passengers were more than sightseers. They carried equipment to chart and mark and document what the high winds and tide had done to the small island. The young man walking toward me was one of those men. He'd spent the first fifteen minutes of the ride telling me how the island was only half a mile in width, a mere spot of land that marked the Gulf from the Sound. He said there were other islands. Petite Bois, Horn. One called Dauphin, off the coast of Alabama. He said they had probably all been one land mass, but that big storms had cut them into smaller pieces that were constantly shifting in size, moving about in the water.

I liked listening to him talk. He spoke softly, but with such intensity about the islands, that I knew he loved them. With his curly auburn hair and freckles, he reminded me of Adam Maxwell, a boy I went to school with for a spell. Even in the first grade he'd talked about learning how to be a doctor for animals. He'd talked in the same softly intense way of the man who now stood beside me. Adam's daddy had been hurt when a log fell on him and Adam had quit school in the fifth grade to go help his ma work the farm. He said he'd come back, but he didn't. I'd heard his daddy was crippled.

"Mattie, Mrs. McVay wanted me to ask if you were warm enough?"

JoHanna had insisted on buying us all thick sweaters, but it was colder at the front of the boat than the back. I knew my cheeks and nose were red from the wind as the boat plowed into it, but I didn't want to go to the back where it was so much more crowded. I liked being up front, more alone.

"I'm fine."

"Do you mind if I keep you company?"

His question startled me, and it shouldn't have. I'd seen him looking at my hands earlier. I had taken Elikah's wedding ring off. Somewhere between the past and the present, I had slipped the thin gold band from my finger and let it go. I could not remember the exact moment of doing it. I didn't care enough to try to remember.

"I'd be delighted for your company," I told him, and meant it. "Tell me more about the island."

His name was Michael Garvi, and he walked with us along the beach, rolling up his pants to stand in the surf and let the waves suck at his toes. We all did it and listened to Duncan scream with delight. I wondered how it was possible that I'd pictured the azure water and the rolling hills of white sand so accurately. I didn't have Duncan's gift of prophecy, but the water and beach were exactly as I had dreamed them. We had walked across the entire island, and it was only as wide as Michael Garvi said. The contrast between Sound and Gulf was magical. We played in the pure white sand, where the water foamed up at us, hissing and laughing. We built castles that the incoming tide knocked down with the dancing waves crested in white. When we were exhausted and the hems of our dresses thoroughly soaked, we spread the red-checked cloth for lunch.

Michael ate our picnic with us, and while I repacked the basket, Jo-Hanna and Duncan went to search for shells in the brief time we had left upon the sand.

"Mattie, would it be okay if I called on you next Sunday? Maybe I could take you to church?"

This time his interest didn't take me by surprise. "I don't think so, Michael." I packed the cloth on top of everything else and looked at him. Why hadn't I met him in May? Why hadn't I met him before Jojo sold me off to Elikah? "I'm married."

The words sounded like a death sentence to me, but it was something that had to be said. No point in dragging another innocent into the mess of my life. I didn't know if I'd ever be rid of Elikah. By law, I was still his wife. I held up my hands. "I threw my wedding ring away, but I'm still married."

He looked down at the picnic basket. "Mrs. McVay told me you were married."

"What else did she tell you?"

He shrugged, then finally looked at me. "That life has some bitter twists. She said it wouldn't hurt for me to ask, that you would make your own decision."

"I don't have a future." I shook my head at the startled look on his face. "Not like that. What I mean is that I can't see one step down the road ahead of me." A vee of brown pelicans burst over us from the Sound side of the island. Their formation was perfect, their ungainly legs tucked up tight and their necks pulled in. When they angled down toward the beach they looked like prehistoric creatures. "I have to go back to where I lost the thread of myself."

"You're going back to your husband?" The light brushing of freckles across his nose darkened with his disapproval. "Mrs. McVay said he wasn't a very nice man."

"I don't know that I'm going back to Elikah, but I am going back to Jexville with the McVays. We have a friend we have to find. Then I'll decide what I'm going to do."

"If you come back to Biloxi, can I call on you?"

I smiled. "I'd like that very much."

Duncan lurched over the top of a small sand dune, screaming and running toward us as she looked back over her shoulder. Behind her Jo-Hanna leaped out of the grass Michael had told me was called sea oats. In her hand she waved a gruesome creature that had huge pinchers for claws. It snapped at Duncan's head, sending her into a new series of high-pitched shrieks. Her legs churned in the sand and sent her sprinting in our direction.

"Save me! It's Crab Mama!"

Panting, JoHanna minced toward us, waving the blue creature which she held tightly by the back. The claws snapped in the air.

"Get that thing away from me." I moved so that Michael was between us, since he seemed to find JoHanna's creature so amusing.

"My little friend is hungry. He wants a bite of Duncan for dessert." JoHanna crept forward, the snapping thing extended.

Duncan shrilled and clung to my back.

In a few moments we were all tumbling in the sand, laughing and trying to get away from the snapping creature that JoHanna held always just out of reach.

The whistle of the boat brought us all to our feet, and JoHanna released the crab, now angry and afraid, back into water.

"How'd you catch him?" Michael asked.

"With some string and a bite of chicken from the picnic. Greed got the better of him and he grabbed it and wouldn't let go." JoHanna was chuckling.

"Mama reeled him in, and then chased me." Duncan shook her finger at JoHanna. "I'll get you back. Just wait. I'll catch a jarful of those big roaches and dump them over in your bed!"

"And I'll cook you *and* that rooster of yours in a pot full of dumplings."

I had stepped a short distance away from them to say good-bye to the

water. I had imagined it for so long, and here it was, just in front of me,
a force that would continue no matter what occurred in my life.
Michael had told me that a few people had built shanties on some of the
barrier islands. He said the houses were little more than shacks, but that
sometimes they could be rented out for a weekend. On Horn Island,
which was larger, there was a small stand of pines and wild deer and rab-
bits that somehow managed to survive the hurricanes.

Even without one of the shanties, a person could camp on the island.
Just pitch a tent and sleep under the stars with the sound of the water
not ten feet away. As I watched the water moving and shifting, never
still, my heart responded to the rhythm of the surf, and I felt a quiet that
I knew I wanted again. No matter what happened with Elikah, I would
come here at least one more time, to spend the night and have a full day
of the water, the sand, and the stars. I would return.

"Ready, Mattie?" Michael touched me lightly on the shoulder. The
boat whistle sounded again, three sharp blasts.

"I'll be back." I whispered the words to the water, and to myself.

Michael carried the picnic basket as we walked across the spit of
sandy island to the boat. On the ride back, he sat beside me and told me
of his childhood growing up on a farm twenty miles north of the beach.
I said little about my past. I had cut it loose in order to survive, but it
was pleasant to hear him recall his love of the water and the barrier islands and his determination to live in Biloxi. Through sheer will, he'd
made his dream come true. In comparison, it might not seem like much
to anyone else, but I had at last realized my dream of seeing the blue,
blue water. I had also made a promise.

The train depot in Biloxi was little more than a narrow room with a few
chairs and a green wooden platform. The big black engine with the fear-
some cow-catcher on the front pulled in from Hattiesburg with a puff of
dark smoke and a hiss. Will was the first passenger to step off, his brown
leather case in one hand, his coat over his arm, and his hat in the other
hand. Like a moving-picture star, he opened his arms and JoHanna ran
into them. Duncan attached herself to his leg and hugged with all her
might. Even in the midst of that welcome, he sent me a wink and a
"Good to see you, Mattie," before JoHanna kissed him. I turned away,
my heart pounding and my face burning.

All around was the general confusion of people leaving town or arriving. A woman with seven small children had gotten off the train behind Will, and the young-uns were running and screaming back and forth on the platform, dodging here and there and generally acting like hellions. The conductor, exasperated at the children, swiped at one boy's head as he shouted "All aboard," and the wheels of the train began to turn, creating such noise that I was able to slip back into the station house and allow the McVays a moment to reunite. Through the dirty station window I watched Will bend to lift Duncan into his arms as the train pulled away.

JoHanna, Will, and Duncan swept into the station on a tide of stampeding children, but they didn't seem to notice. They were a laughing, hugging whirlwind that swept me into it, and we blew out into the yard beside the station and piled into the car. With Will at the wheel and driving slowly, JoHanna and Duncan told him about the storm as we passed sites where trees had been removed and debris gathered. Will had an acute knowledge of the coast and told us who owned what property and how long they had been there and the probability of whether they would rebuild or move on. For a man who spent most of his time in Washington or New York or Natchez or Memphis, Will knew Biloxi.

We arrived at the Seaview to collect our things. JoHanna had packed our bags but left them in the room. She also wanted to "show her appreciation" to the maid who had managed, somehow, not to find Pecos in the room. "I won't be long," she said as she got out of the car.

Duncan ran into the gardens to say good-bye to the workmen she had made friends with while JoHanna hurried upstairs. I didn't want to sit in the car and wait, so I started in to make one last check of the room when Will's hand caught my elbow.

"How are you, Mattie?" he asked, his chocolate eyes void of all humor or teasing. Either JoHanna or John, in his telegram, had told him about my beating and my sickness afterward.

"Better."

"You can stay here. We'll keep the room."

I shook my head. "No, I can't."

"Are you certain?"

I met his gaze, noticing again how the outer rim of his iris was darker than the center. "I'm certain."

He didn't release me. Instead he looked beyond me, making certain that JoHanna was not coming down the steps.

"Who is John Doggett?"

It was the question I dreaded, though I had not expected him to ask it of me. JoHanna was his wife. She held the answer to that question.

"He's a writer. We met him up at Fitler."

"What is he to JoHanna?"

I remembered very clearly the first time I'd ever heard JoHanna lie to Duncan. It was a lie to protect her. I had not expected dishonesty from her, not even to protect her child. But I didn't know the truth of what John was to JoHanna. I could not even confront the truth of my own feelings for Will. I had fallen in love with him, knowing he was the husband of the only person who had been my friend. To admit this, even to myself, was more truth than I wanted to swallow. Who was I to decide the truth of JoHanna's feelings?

"When JoHanna heard that Elikah had beaten me so badly, she got John to come with her to take me away from him. You weren't here, and I think she was afraid that Elikah would hurt me, or her. Or both of us. Then he was stranded by the storm."

Not a single feature of his face changed, but something in his eyes darkened. "Excuse me, Mattie," he said as he walked past me and followed the route his wife had taken up the steps into the hotel.

I got back in the car and waited. Duncan found me there. She wore a crown of coral-colored spider lilies that the old gardener had made as a going away gift for her. She radiated happiness, casting glances at the front door of the hotel as she chatted and waited for her father to come out. As much as she loved her mother, Duncan worshiped Will. I tried not to imagine what was being said in that second-floor hotel room, where the curtains lifted and floated on the breeze that swept across the aqua water of the Gulf of Mexico, over the spit of land known as Ship Island, skimming the top of the dark gray Sound and finally into the window.

"What are they doing? We were already packed. And we have to get Pecos." Duncan got out of the car and slammed the door with impatience. "I'm going to get them."

"Wait here with me, Duncan."

"We have to get to Jexville. It's going to be dark and we won't be able to hunt for Floyd." She started up the drive, shells crunching beneath her determined step.

"Wait, Duncan. Please."

She stopped and turned slowly. "What's going on?"

"I think your folks need some time to talk. Give them a minute."

"About what?"

"Things that have happened. Will has missed a lot. JoHanna has to tell him things so he can figure out the best plan."

"She can tell him on the way." She started toward the hotel again.

"Duncan . . ." I looked up to see JoHanna standing on the front steps, both of our suitcases in her hand. My heart stopped. Will was not coming with us.

The door behind her opened and he came out. Taking the bags he took steps longer even than hers and left her behind as he came to the car and stowed the luggage. "It's time to go home," he said as he cranked the motor and slid behind the wheel.

Will did not object as JoHanna gave him directions to the farm to get Pecos. He said nothing at all. Duncan leaned on the back of the front seat and talked a blue streak to him, but when he answered her only in monosyllables, she settled back and looked at me. "What's wrong?" she whispered.

I shook my head.

We pulled into the farmyard, and Duncan climbed out of the car and went around to the back to call her rooster. Will got out and went to the front door to pay the farmer the amount due for Pecos's board.

Left alone in the car with JoHanna, I wanted to tell her what I had said. I had gone over it again and again in my mind, and I had not said anything that implied JoHanna and John were involved. I had not meant to imply that. Surely I had not. "JoHanna, I didn't say anything about John," I finally blurted.

For a moment she didn't respond. She kept her attention focused on Will's back as he stood at the doorway talking to the farmer. Reaching into his pocket, he drew out money. The screen door opened and the farmer took it, shifting it into his own pocket.

"Have you ever thought about the degrees of absence?" JoHanna asked. "How a person can be physically gone, and still there. Or how he can be sitting right beside you and not be there at all?" Her voice cracked, and she swallowed. "I meant to buy some of those dark glasses they were selling on the beach. Sun protectors. Did you see them?"

Suddenly furious at her flip question, at what she'd done, I got out of the car, intending to go and help Duncan catch her rooster. If Pecos had gotten any encouragement at all from the farmer's hens, he might decide he didn't ever want to be caught again. If JoHanna was so all fired up about things being true to their nature, maybe she'd order Duncan to leave him where he could be a real rooster. I slammed the car door hard as I stalked away.

Duncan met me as I rounded the corner of the house. Pecos was not happy about being captured, and neither was Duncan. Large tears rolled down her cheeks. She held the rooster extended in front of her, and he had his spurs out, as if he meant serious business.

"He doesn't want to come with me." She managed the words between sobs. "He'd rather stay here."

"Oh, Duncan." I wanted to go to her, but I wasn't getting near Pecos and those spurs. I'd come too close twice before and knew how sharply they could slice.

"He pecked me and came at me." She took a breath. "He's never done that to me. Never."

I could hear the chickens gossiping over the latest henyard development. Pecos heard them too and began to struggle in Duncan's hands.

"What should I do, Mattie?"

"Oh, Duncan, I could wring that rooster's neck myself." How was it possible that two McVays had been betrayed in less than twenty minutes? "Do you want him bad enough to hold him all the way back to Jexville? I think once you get him home he'll straighten up. He just got a taste of being king of the roost and it's hard to go from being king back to being someone's pet."

Duncan turned back toward the chicken yard. The hens were frantically running here and there. Maybe they were looking for Pecos, maybe not. Who could tell what a chicken was doing?

"What should I do, Mattie?"

I could see her arms were tired of holding the bird. They were shaking slightly. Pecos had given up struggling, but he kept his attention on the chickens.

"What's wrong, Duncan?" Will had come around the corner of the house and was standing, watching us.

"Pecos doesn't want to be my pet rooster anymore." Duncan managed the words with a show of bravado that made my eyes sting. "He wants to be king of the chickens."

"He does, does he?" Will walked up, tousled her hair, and then lifted

Pecos into his arms. He cradled the rooster against his chest as if he were a baby. With one finger he turned the rooster's head so that Pecos's beady little chicken eyes were staring directly into his. "Are you sure that's what you want, Pecos? Being the rooster isn't all it's cracked up to be."

"He thinks it's terrific."

Will lifted his eyebrows at Duncan. "Perhaps you should tell Pecos that he might last it out the rest of this year, but by next fall, he'll be replaced. Some new cock will come along and Pecos will be fair game for the roasting pan."

Duncan's tears dried. "They'll eat him?"

"Honey, once we drive out of here, do you think Mr. Longeneaux will even try to remember Pecos from the other roosters around here? He may try, but in a week or two, one bird will blend into the other and by next year . . ."

Duncan looked back at the chickens. They had settled down considerably. Pecos, held tightly in Will's arms, had also grown more docile.

Duncan held out her arms to her father. With great care, Will placed Pecos in them, making sure his spurs were relaxed.

"I think we should all go home." Duncan started toward the car, the rooster in her arms. "That storm just got everything messed up. Once we get home, things will get back to normal, won't they, Daddy?"

When Will didn't answer, Duncan stopped and turned back to him. "They will, won't they?"

"Tell me, how bad did the storm hit the house?" he asked as he opened the door for me and Duncan and ushered us into the backseat. Duncan settled with Pecos pressed between her body and the door. The car roared to life, and we were headed for Jexville, headed into the night.

Thirty-seven

THE stars were brighter than I'd ever seen them, and a pale quarter moon hung in the sky as we drove the final few miles to Jexville. It made me think of the legend of Anola and the Hunter's Moon that John Doggett had told us. The legend of a river where the dead sang out at night to those who would listen.

Duncan had fallen asleep in my lap, and I was glad for the solid warmth of her against me. Summer was gone. The creeping cold of night and the air blowing back on me from the motion of the car had chilled me through to the bone. Still, nothing the weather could provide was as cold as the silence in the front seat. Will's hands moved on the steering wheel as he guided the car through the darkness that contained only the hush of hibernating insects. That slight movement of his hands, side to side, adjusting for the bumps and curves, was the only motion in the front seat. JoHanna might have been turned to stone.

I snuggled down with Duncan, Pecos asleep at last between her feet, and tried not to hear the anger.

When the car turned on Peterson Lane, I knew exactly where we were and I sat up straighter, searching for the familiar landmarks in the swift flare of the headlights. There were so many things I wanted to say in the last moments of the ride, before the wheels stopped and life was no longer suspended, things that had no words but were only emotions. I wanted to tell them that whatever had happened, they were meant for one another. They were part of one thing, a union that gave both more substance. I wanted to tell them that the thing that had come between them was not violent or mean or cruel, and was therefore forgivable. I wanted to say these things, but I could not say a word. My feelings were true, but there was another truth, too. JoHanna had betrayed Will. I did not understand how two things so diabolically opposed could both be real. My lack of understanding kept me silent, as silent as the two of them.

In the headlights of the car I saw the large oak trees that framed the front of the house and I felt a measure of relief. We were home. Maybe once they were free of the car, JoHanna and Will would talk. Maybe Duncan, when she awakened, could prevail on them to remember a life that did not include John Doggett or his shadow that now separated them.

I struggled up in the seat and started to wake Duncan as Will turned the car into the drive. "Let her sleep," Will said. Instead of going to the back, he drove to the front steps where he could carry Duncan and the luggage inside with greater ease.

I was looking for my shoe in the floor of the car when I heard Jo-Hanna's small cry. Will had stopped the car, and I heard the air leave his lungs. I looked toward the house, expecting to see that someone had burned it down, but it was there, dark against the starry night. In the beam of the headlights Jeb Fairley sat on the steps. At first he was so still I did not see him. He rose slowly and stood, his tall, thin frame coatless in the cold, hands hanging at his side, as he waited for us to get out of the car.

"Jeb!" JoHanna opened her door as Will killed the motor. Her voice was a cry for help and she stumbled in front of the car.

Getting out on his side, Will left the door open as he hurried forward, catching JoHanna at the front of the car. They began to struggle, Will trying to hold JoHanna and she trying to escape him and get to the porch. The headlights cast their shadows against the front of the house, tall distorted images that joined together in slow motion, blending into one form on the front of the house, creeping across the front door and the windows as they fought in a horrible, silent battle of wills.

"Jeb!" JoHanna almost broke free, but Will held her.

"I didn't know where else to bring him," Jeb said.

It was then I saw the bundle of clothing on the porch. I recognized Jeb's coat on top and wondered why he wasn't wearing it. I slid out from under Duncan's head and eased out of the car, trying hard to move fast, but unable to, cold syrup pooling on a saucer. Too slow.

"Mattie!" Will called out to me, but he could not let go of JoHanna. She had turned into some wild creature, and she fought against him, thrashing with small, harsh noises. Against the front of the house her shadow lunged and twisted against Will's tall form. I kept walking, up to the steps, up to Jeb, who looked down at me.

"I'm sorry, Mattie. I tried to stop them."

I lifted the collar of the coat and found Floyd. "Floyd?" I did not believe what I was seeing. It was impossible that the cold, still features were those of a young man I had come to love. "Floyd?" I asked again. I knew he was dead, but I brushed my fingers across his cheek, hoping for a flush of warmth. He was chill, the texture of his skin no longer human.

Jeb reached down to me and helped me up the steps. Behind him, JoHanna's shadow had ceased its struggle. She leaned against Will, shaking with soundless sobs.

"Duncan is still in the car," Will said. He wanted to go to his daughter, but he held JoHanna against him, giving both restraint and support. Duncan was still asleep. We could not wake her. She could not see Floyd.

Looking at Jeb, I still didn't believe he was there. I slowly dropped my arm that he held and he released me. "We need to take Duncan in the back door," I told him. Without waiting, I went back down the steps and lifted her into my arms. Jeb offered to take her, but I shook my head. Her small body was hot, alive. Real. Duncan was not part of the nightmare, and I clung to her while Jeb got the bags and the sleeping Pecos from the floorboard. Avoiding the front steps, we walked around the house to the back door and went inside.

Duncan weighed nothing in my arms. I took her through the kitchen and into her room, where I tumbled her into the bed and drew the spread over her from the other side. She still wore her shoes and coat, but it didn't matter. What could such things matter now?

Jeb put the rooster at the foot of the bed and backed out of the room. "I tried to stop them," he said again. "There was nothing I could do. They tied me in a chair in the barbershop. A barber's chair." He spoke with sad bitterness.

I watched his lips move, still thin and blue from the cold. I heard what he said and understood the words, but not their meaning. "I think

I'll make some coffee." I started toward the kitchen when I heard Jo-Hanna's wail of anguish. It was a sound I'd never heard before, a cry of fury and pain, a mortal wound. Then came the pounding of feet on the front porch boards, then another cry from JoHanna.

"Easy." Jeb Fairley gripped my elbow. I don't know if he was supporting me or holding me back, but I couldn't have moved had I known where to go. We simply stood, joined by his firm hold, until there was only silence on the front porch.

Will opened the front door and came in. He went to the linen closet at the end of the hall and lifted a stack of white sheets. Turning, he caught sight of me. "Mattie, would you make some coffee? Jeb, if you don't mind, could you give me a hand?"

Before Will turned completely away, I called out to him. "Where's JoHanna? Is she okay?"

"She'll be in in a moment." He looked toward the kitchen. "That coffee sure would be appreciated."

I left the hall and went to the kitchen and lit a lamp. With the same match I lit the stove and waited for the wood to kindle as I drew water and measured the coffee into the metal container of the pot. In my head was the pounding of seconds, time slipping by. Life continuing on. There were other noises, of water heating, wood crackling in the stove. Time passing in the brief respite before I would begin to feel again, when I would have to let myself understand what had happened.

The front door opened and Will came in. He went to his bedroom and came out with a suit, socks, and a pair of polished black shoes. They caught the light from the lamp in the buffed leather.

"Mattie, would you put some water on to heat? Not for the coffee. A big kettle of water." His voice was quiet with shock. "JoHanna's going to wash the body right there on the front porch."

"Does she need some help?" I could help. I could help wash Floyd. He had been my friend.

"I'll ask her. How about that coffee?"

I pointed to the small kettle, which was finally beginning to sing. "In a minute. It has to drip through."

"I'll ask JoHanna what she wants you to do." He went back onto the porch, closing the door very carefully behind him.

It struck me how important the tiniest things become when life has halted. I lifted the kettle and poured the water in the dripolater, hearing each drop of water as it fell through the metal, soaked into the ground coffee and struck the tin bottom of the pot. I'd heard the sound a million times in my life, but I had never really heard it. In the next room, Duncan was breathing with a soft, easy rhythm. It was the sound of promise. Outside, a night bird cried an eerie message.

Will came in for the hot water, pulling clean washcloths from the drawer beside the sink. He and Jeb disappeared back onto the front porch, the door a final click behind them. The coffee had dripped, and I poured four cups, fixing Will's black and JoHanna's with a spoon of sugar. I guessed that Jeb would take his with milk and sugar, so I made the last two cups that way. I had intended to take them out on a tray, but I hesitated. It struck me as bizarre that we would sit out on the porch drinking coffee with Floyd dead at our feet. Yet JoHanna would not come in and leave Floyd alone. I picked up my cup and hers and went down the hall to the front door.

Using my toe, I kicked the wood, and Will opened the door. He was holding a lantern, but he had not killed the headlights of the car. JoHanna stood on the ground beside Floyd. She had unbuttoned his shirt and was washing his face and hair. I hesitated, the coffee steaming in the night.

JoHanna was almost a silhouette, lit so strongly from behind by the headlamps of the car. The light Will held was weak by contrast, filling in only the shallowest planes. Her hands worked with such tenderness that I heard Will swallow a sob.

"You and Jeb go on inside and have your coffee," I told him. "I'll give JoHanna a hand." I was surprised to find that I sounded so reasonable, so strong.

Will put his hand on my shoulder. "I don't think you should do that, Mattie."

His voice was still distant, as if he could not believe what he was seeing. Surely this was a nightmare that would end when the sun came out and we could truly see. It was all a trick of the strange lighting, the contrast of shadow and night.

"I'll help JoHanna." I lifted both cups of coffee. "I brought us some out here."

"Let's get us some coffee," Jeb said. He was still standing on the porch without a coat. He had to be freezing, but he never gave any indication. He reached out to Will and took the lamp, setting it down on the painted gray boards. Putting his hand on Will's back he gently pushed him toward the front door, which was still open. Will stumbled slightly, then stepped through the door and Jeb closed it behind him. Jeb stepped close beside me, his cheek cold against my ear.

"It's awful, Mattie, but JoHanna said she's going to wash him and put him in Will's suit before anyone else sees him. Doc Westfall has pronounced him dead and noted all the injuries. Sheriff Grissham can't be found anywhere in the county, so I guess it's okay to dress out the body."

His words were a babble against my ear. What he said was important, but I couldn't be troubled with such details as Sheriff Grissham. Doc Westfall wasn't any help either. There was nothing they could do for Floyd now. It was JoHanna's hands that he required. Her touch, and as I watched she lifted a soapy cloth to his chest, the steam rising from the warm water like his spirit departing.

I nodded absently to Jeb and walked to the steps. Midway down I stopped, aware that Jeb was still on the porch, waiting. "Go inside, Jeb. It's freezing out here. JoHanna and I will take care of him."

Uncertain what he should do, he hesitated. Turning quickly, he opened the door just enough for his narrow frame and slipped inside. I took the last three steps and moved beside JoHanna. With the car lights behind me, the scene shifted drastically. Floyd's white profile gleamed in the harsh light, bloodless. His fair hair, dampened by JoHanna's washing, looked dark and clung to his scalp. For the first time I felt a twinge of pain so bitter, so intense, I almost dropped the coffee. Floyd! His name fluttered up from my lungs and into my brain. I wanted to call him back, to scream his name so loudly that he would hear me and return.

"JoHanna." I pressed her cup of coffee toward her. "Drink this."

She took the cup and sipped, but her gaze never left Floyd's face.

"How could they?" she asked, as if she expected an answer from me that would explain. "How could they do this?"

I touched his jaw with fingers still warm from holding my coffee cup, but I could bring no heat to him. He had been dead for several hours. JoHanna drank her coffee in large swallows and put the cup on the porch.

"On my life, they are going to pay for this," she said as she bent to unbutton his shirt the rest of the way.

Together we managed to get his shirt off. His chest showed no evidence of the wound that had killed him. It was his back that gaped raw from the gunshot.

It didn't surprise me to learn that they had shot him in the back. In fact, it gave me a measure of comfort that he had not been looking at them as they pulled the trigger. He did not have to confront the cruelty and meet it eye to eye. Floyd would not have understood such total evil. At least shot in the back, he may have thought he had a chance of getting away. He may have died with hope.

JoHanna washed him first, then tore up one sheet and used it to bind his torso, winding the clean white cotton around and around him while I braced my legs and held him up. JoHanna dressed him in one of Will's finely starched shirts and a black vest, and finally the jacket.

Even though the night was cold, JoHanna and I were sweating by the time we moved down to his pants. JoHanna unbuckled his belt and then stopped. "Maybe you should go inside and let Will come out and help me."

"I've seen a man before." It was the first words we'd spoken since we started. I wasn't the innocent JoHanna had met at the birthday party of a chinless wonder. I could help wash Floyd. I wanted to do that for him.

"It isn't that, Mattie. It's . . ." She stopped.

Pushing her hands away I undid the buttons of his fly. The fabric was stiff, awkward. Something inside my head warned me, but I didn't slow down or listen. I unbuttoned his pants and in the harsh arc of the car's headlamps, I saw what they had done to him.

I slowly lifted my hands, and saw the smudges of blood. I did not move or utter a sound. JoHanna turned to me and folded my hands into her own. Against the white frame house, our shadows appeared to pray.

"Mattie, go on in the house. Send Will out to help me."

JoHanna's hands warmed mine, and after what seemed like a thousand years I pulled air into my lungs. There was a scream trapped deep inside me. Far too deep to find its way out. I shook my head. I knew who had done this. And why. I recognized the deft handiwork of a man who loved the idea of a scalpel. That knowledge gave me the strength not to go insane.

I would not give Elikah the pleasure.

"Let's wash him." I felt the tears against my cool cheeks. "I don't want anyone else to see him this way. No one will know what Elikah did to him. No one."

JoHanna began to tug at his pants, sliding them from beneath him. He was heavy, and we struggled. "Oh, they'll know. They'll know and they'll pay because of it. They will pay for this. I swear it."

Even as she talked she removed his pants and together we washed his horrible wound and bound him with clean strips of cotton sheet. At last we managed to get Will's suit pants on him. Together we put on his socks and shoes.

"He would like these shoes," JoHanna said. Her voice broke, but she continued. "They're fine leather. Will got them in New Orleans. Floyd would appreciate the craftsmanship."

"What are we going to do now?" I asked.

JoHanna turned so that she could lean against the porch. "I don't know except they're going to pay. I don't care how. I don't care what it takes. I'm going to find them and make them pay."

"You know it was Elikah."

I thought she would deny it, but she didn't. "I know."

"And probably some of Tommy Ladnier's men, if not Tommy himself."

"He's capable."

"And Sheriff Grissham?" I wasn't certain.

"Up to his eyeballs." JoHanna had no doubts.

Sheriff Grissham and Tommy Ladnier were the most powerful men in the county. What could we do against them? JoHanna stood in the cold night. She rolled down the sleeves of her dress but that didn't still the chattering of her teeth. We needed to go inside, but she lingered against the porch and acted as if we had the power to avenge Floyd.

"We can't make them pay." I saw it clearly if she did not.

"Oh, we can." She spoke softly, as if she knew a secret. "And we will."

The front door creaked open slowly. Will came out onto the porch, his face well lit by the headlights of the car. "JoHanna." His voice sounded ghostly, and I looked up to be sure it was him.

Something in his voice touched her, too. "What? What is it, Will?"

He stepped closer to the edge of the porch, closer to Floyd, and knelt down and touched Floyd's forehead, brushing back a strand of damp hair. "JoHanna, Jeb just told me that they've put John Doggett in prison. They're saying he killed a family of five out on Red Licorice Road."

∾ *Thirty-eight* ∾

DAWN found me sitting on the bank of the creek behind Jo-Hanna's house where Floyd and Duncan and JoHanna and I had gone swimming one hot summer day. Floyd had sat with his back against the tree where I now sat, and the dense green leaves had dappled his blond hair with sun. I could see him clearly. I could hear his voice in the whisper of the bare September trees as they rustled with a chill autumn wind. My tears were spent, and I knew I should go back to the house to be there when Duncan awoke. When JoHanna and Will would have to tell her about Floyd. Somehow, I could not convince my body to move.

While my grief was depleted, my anger had begun to build. Floyd was dead, mutilated and shot in the back. John Doggett had been falsely accused of five gruesome deaths. And the men who had abused and killed Floyd were walking around, free. One of them would soon be snapping a white cloth in the air as he prepared to tuck it around a customer's neck. He would lift up the very same straight-edge he'd used to inflict the ultimate wound on an innocent young man. Stroke by stroke, he'd scrape his customer's whiskers away as he told a joke or repeated a tidbit of gossip. All the time knowing that he would never be punished for what he had done.

The injustice of it all had driven me from the house and into the woods. I could not face JoHanna. I had not been able to witness her helplessness to undo what had been done to Floyd. Her inability to save John Doggett. No one had to tell me that all of the power in Washington that Will might bring to bear could not change a single thing for John.

Five counts of murder. A family hung in a tree. The jury would not think beyond that horrible image. John Doggett would die for it.

Jeb had said that he found the note John left on his door and reported the deaths. Grissham and several men had gone out to Red Licorice Road and found that poor family. By the time they got back to Jexville, they had formulated their plan. John had gone down to the Moseses' house to hunt for news of Floyd, and it was there that they arrested him.

They'd found John's journal in his belongings and matched his handwriting to the note he'd left at Jeb's. It was flimsy evidence, but more than enough for their purposes. John's crime was his relationship with JoHanna, not the murder of five people. Before Grissham, Tommy Ladnier, and Elikah were through, they'd blame what happened to Floyd on John Doggett, too.

And JoHanna was helpless to stop it.

There was only one small flaw in their plan. One thing they had no way of knowing. John Doggett had left his derringer with me. I had it now, in the pocket of the jacket I wore.

Waiting for the dawn to come, I had arrived at my own plan of action. Nothing could bring Floyd back, and John Doggett would surely be executed. But Elikah Mills would not live to enjoy it. There were two shots in that gun. I would do to him what he'd done to Floyd with the first shot, and with the second I would spatter his brains. I did not want to die along with John Doggett, but I had a chance. Everyone in town knew that Elikah had beaten me. Doc Westfall would testify on my behalf. I would claim self-defense. Chances were I'd go to prison, but I didn't think they'd kill me outright.

The birds began to awaken in the trees and shrubs around me. They rustled through the dead leaves and chirped and sang, eager for the end of night and the return of the sun. Eager to start a new day. I turned toward the house and slowly began to walk.

At the edge of the woods I stopped and looked at JoHanna's house. There was a lamp lit in the kitchen, and then I saw Duncan sitting on the back steps, her head in her hands. She didn't make a sound, but her shoulders shook. Pecos, no longer distracted by his lady loves, had resumed his position of sentinel by her right foot. As I approached he gave me a warning shake of his wings.

"Duncan." I spoke softly.

My answer was a sob that sounded as if it had torn her throat.

"Oh, Duncan." I sat down beside her and put my arm around her. She didn't shake me off, but she didn't acknowledge me, either. I rubbed her back the way I'd seen JoHanna do and waited for the end of her tears. I had nothing left to cry. All moisture, all goodness, had turned to stone while I sat on the banks of that small creek and made my plan.

"Mattie?" JoHanna stood at the screen door looking down at us on the steps. "I need to talk with you."

"Duncan, you want to come inside?" I kissed her head.

"Let her cry," JoHanna said. "Just let her cry."

I opened the screen and went inside. It was obvious that JoHanna had been crying. Will, too. Even Jeb looked as if the last drop of emotion had been wrung out of him. They must have stayed up all night talking, trying to figure some way out. I knew from looking at them that they hadn't been able to come up with a thing. Oh, Will would extract his revenge, but it wouldn't save John Doggett. He'd use his political power to punish Sheriff Grissham at a later date, and maybe ruin Tommy Ladnier. He might publicly beat them, and Elikah, to a pulp. But it was too little, too late.

"We need to take Floyd up to the church." JoHanna handed me a cup of coffee. "I'm going to make the arrangements for a funeral, and Will's going to see the sheriff. We have to tell him that we saw that dead family and told John about it. That he wrote the note at my behest."

She had gone completely mad. It didn't matter what she told them. They knew John Doggett was innocent. They didn't care. They were going to try him, find him guilty, and kill him, and nothing she said would make any difference. Unless she confessed to the murders herself. She or Duncan.

"I told her it wouldn't do any good." Will must have read my mind. "Jeb is going to take his car to Hattiesburg and find a lawyer for John. Theodore Isles is my choice, if he'll take the case. We'll fight this with everything we have."

Will's words were bold, but his eyes told me otherwise. He would fight. With every nickel he owned. Even though he knew it was hopeless. At that moment I admired him more than I ever had before.

"Mattie, will you stay here with Duncan?" JoHanna paled even as she asked. "I'm afraid to take her into town, and I'm afraid to leave her here."

"I'll stay with Duncan." I could kill Elikah as good in the evening as the morning. It honestly didn't matter to me.

"Are you okay?" Will got up and came to me, lifting my chin with a crooked finger and staring directly into my eyes.

"What they did to Floyd, the Odoms and the sheriff and all of them, you'll make them pay, won't you?"

"And Elikah?" he asked.

"Him most of all," I answered. It would be better for JoHanna and Will not to have any idea what I intended. "Do whatever you want to him."

"You never have to go back there," JoHanna said.

"She'd better not try," Jeb added drily. "Elikah's gotten it into his head he won't have to pay for what he does. I wouldn't put it past him to try and kill her." He leaned over and blew out the lamp. I noticed that it was full morning, a clear, crisp day. An October morning that promised the best of south Mississippi.

"Mattie, would you pack as many of our clothes as you can?" JoHanna looked around the kitchen. "We'll send someone for the rest."

"Where are you going?"

"*We* . . ." She emphasized the word. "We're going to Fitler to get Aunt Sadie, and then we're moving to Natchez."

"And John Doggett?" I couldn't believe she'd leave him in jail.

JoHanna glanced at Will, then dropped her gaze.

"The best thing for John would be for JoHanna to clear out of town," Will said. "It isn't him they want to hurt; it's her. Maybe, if we can get a good lawyer and delay the trial, folks will forget."

"They'll forget that five people are dead, hanging from an oak tree?" I couldn't believe they were so naive. Not Will and JoHanna. They knew better.

"They may forget how important it is to blame John Doggett."

"Who will they blame? If JoHanna and Duncan are gone, who will they blame?"

Will shook his head. "I don't know, Mattie. But it's best for John if JoHanna isn't here to remind them each day." His dark eyes flashed me a warning. One I read clearly.

Will would pay for the lawyer. He'd even stay in town and defend Doggett if he had to, but he wouldn't sacrifice his wife. That decision had been made. JoHanna and Duncan were leaving Jexville.

"Have you told Duncan?"

JoHanna shook her head. "No. She won't care, though. Floyd was the one thing that tied her heart here. He was her dock at Jexville." She tried to smile and faltered. "Mine, too, I suppose."

"It's best for you to leave." Jeb stood up and drained his coffee. "Now it's time for us to get about our business. They're going to convene a grand jury for John this week. If I'm going to find that big-shot lawyer, I'd better get on the road."

"Yes, the funeral." JoHanna brushed at her hair as if it were still long and tickling her face. "Will, are you ready?"

He stood up, retrieving his jacket. When he put it on he looked as if he were getting ready to step back on the train to return to New York.

"Take care of Duncan," JoHanna said, kissing me on the cheek. For the first time I noticed she was wearing a dark gray dress. It looked more like Aunt Sadie's clothes than hers, though it fit perfectly. She placed a small black hat with a veil on her head, and she took Will's arm as they went down the hall to the front door, Jeb leading the way.

I knew they were going to have to put Floyd in the car, and I didn't want to watch, so I went out the back door and sat beside Duncan on the steps.

"Are you coming with us when we move to Natchez?" Duncan asked. Her voice was blurred by grief.

"I've never thought on living in Natchez." I couldn't tell her I'd probably be in jail.

"Maybe I'll make some friends there. Friends my own age." She glared at me. "Friends who won't get killed."

"Floyd would want you to make new friends," I said as gently as I could.

She stood up and rubbed her eyes with her fists. "I hate this place. I hate everything about it." Her dark eyes were filled with rage. "If I could call down a curse on this place, I'd do it. A real curse, like they're all afraid of. One that would curl their toenails."

She wasn't funny, but I had to smile at her. She was only nine. Her life with Will and JoHanna had not prepared her for such a cruel reality. What they had given her, though, was the will to fight. She would not lie down and be stomped. She would come back swinging.

"Let's go inside. I have to pack."

Together we went into the house, and Duncan sat on her bed while I spread a big sheet on the floor and began to put all of her clothes in the center. Bundled in a sheet, her things would be easier to carry. JoHanna could save the suitcases for Will's suits and her fancy dresses.

When we were done, Duncan patted the bed beside her and I took a seat. "What will it be like in Natchez, Mattie?"

The idea of the change had begun to disturb her. She didn't like Jexville, but Natchez was the unknown. "Well, it's on the Mississippi River. I hear it's a beautiful town. Lots of big, fancy houses. A lot more Negroes, too. They had plantations up around there, so there's lots of coloreds now."

Duncan nodded. She eased back on the bed, maneuvering until her head was on the pillow. "Tell me a story about Natchez."

Tears were welling up beneath her eyelids and oozing down the side of her face. She was remembering Floyd, wanting him to tell a story, not me. I told her the story of a young boy and a colored man who took a raft down the Mississippi River. I'd read the story in a leather-bound book from the library. The parts I couldn't remember, I made up, adding a young girl about nine who was smarter than everyone else.

Duncan liked the story a lot. It made the idea of Natchez and the Mississippi River seem like an adventure just up the road and waiting for her to arrive and set it in motion. Once her fears and grief had been suspended, she drifted into a sound sleep.

I sat beside her for a long time, knowing this might be my last time to do so. I studied her eyelashes against her cheek, so delicate and child-like. Her eyes shifted beneath the lids and I wondered what she might be dreaming. Something beautiful. Maybe she had joined Floyd in that world where life and death can mingle. Her lips twitched in a soft smile before relaxing, and I stood up to leave. The light rise and fall of her chest was a miracle. Duncan McVay was nothing less than a true miracle.

"I love you, Duncan." I kissed her cheek and didn't even jump when Pecos darted in the bedroom window, wings flapping but not making a sound. "Let her sleep," I warned the rooster as I left Duncan's room and went to JoHanna's to continue the packing she had requested.

Accumulating Duncan's things had been an easy task. JoHanna's was much more difficult. There were so many things, all of them delicate or crushable. They could not be bundled into a sheet and tied into submission. I got out the suitcases and packed away the most delicate things first, wondering what exactly JoHanna would need for a new life in Natchez. I held up her enormous hat with the rooster feathers and the now dried out black-eyed Susans. Would she wear this hat in Natchez, attracting the stares she'd ignored in Jexville? Or would the move bring about a more modest JoHanna? I could not decide what part of her she was going to leave behind, so I packed everything.

I had just folded the copper dress she'd worn to Annabelle Lee's birthday party when I heard Duncan moaning. I listened, then started toward her room, goaded by a deep groundswell of terror brought on by her gibbering nonsensical sounds.

The bedroom door was open, and I hurried up to her bed to find her twisting and contorting on the bed. She acted as if someone, or something, had hold of her arm and was pulling at her. She fought and bucked to get away, moaning and crying out in a strange language as she struggled.

It was a nightmare, I could see that plainly.

"Duncan." I grabbed her flailing leg and held it down with one hand while I pinned her shoulder with the other. "Duncan!"

She was deep in the spell of the dream and I could not reach her. Her mouth opened and shut, gulping air, as if she were drowning.

The terror of it galvanized me into action. Without thinking I slapped her right cheek, a crack of noise that startled Pecos into squawking retribution. The rooster flew at me, spurs extended, and I fell across Duncan, landing squarely on her stomach. Knees and elbows gouged at me as I dodged the rooster and tried to get off her. When I finally managed to push away, Duncan suddenly stilled. The change was so sudden that I knew something terrible had happened to her.

"Duncan!" I was breathless. Scrambling away from her, I looked into her face. Her eyes were wide open, the eyeballs rolled back in her head, her mouth working open and shut, open and shut. She was not breathing. She was drowning in her own room.

"Duncan!" Her name was a wail as I bent over her, trying to remember how to push air into someone's lungs. "Duncan!"

Her hand lashed out so quickly I had no time to avoid it, no time to think. Her fingers clutched my throat, a death grip that locked around my windpipe.

"Duncan." Her name was rusty, broken. I could not look away from those blind eye sockets. I could not move. She had me in a grip so tight

I knew she was going to choke me to death if she didn't drown first. I twisted and squirmed, but I could not get away, and I felt my strength ebbing. "Duncan," I pleaded with her.

"Mattie." Her lips formed the word, but it was not Duncan who spoke. The rhythm was different.

"Mattie?" She spoke again, her lips, her voice, but the nightmare speaking.

I staggered, losing strength in my legs, but she held me, her arm rigid, her eyes dead. I had to make one last effort to twist free of her grip. Before I could do anything, Pecos flapped past my face and landed on the pillow beside Duncan's head. He looked into her eyes and squawked once before he began to viciously peck her forehead. The white skin burst into little nicks of blood as he stabbed his sharp beak into the tender white flesh.

Duncan's arm trembled, her fingers loosened, and she closed her mouth. With her free hand she fought the bird away from her.

It was enough for me to wrench free, dragging air into my bruised throat, swallowing the sudden desire to vomit. Pecos easily flapped out of the way of her swinging hands, finding a perch on the bedstead.

"Duncan!" I ran back to her side keeping a wary eye on her hand. Her eyes had closed and her chest rose and fell in shallow, rapid breaths, as if she had been running.

"Duncan." I had to get her out of the dream. I couldn't risk her slipping back so deeply beneath the spell. I had almost lost her. She had almost drowned. Or worse.

"Duncan!" Just as I drew back my hand to slap her again, her eyes opened. Confusion simmered in the brown depths and she slowly lifted a hand to her forehead. When she drew it back it was covered in her own blood. The sight seemed to daze her even more.

"He had me, Mattie." She whispered the words as she stared into my eyes. "He finally caught hold of me good, and he wasn't going to let me go."

I knew who she was talking about, the dead man under the bridge in the Pascagoula River. The man with a gar grinning out of his ribs. "It's okay, Duncan. You're here now."

She pushed up on the pillows and gathered Pecos into her lap. "You pecked the fool out of me, Pecos." She stroked his head. "Pecos was going to drive that dead man right out of my brain."

I sank down on the bed, my hand trembling as I reached out to Duncan. "You almost choked me," I said.

She saw the red marks around my throat and tentatively lifted a hand to them. "It was him," she said. "He had me, but when he saw you he let me go. He reached through me to you."

The old grandfather clock in the hallway struck noon. We stared at each other through the bongs of the hours, counting, listening.

"Why would he want you, Mattie?" she asked.

I did not look at her.

"He called your name, Mattie."

I got up, stopping halfway to the door. "I heard *you* call my name, Duncan. It was you."

When I turned around, Duncan was staring at me with a look on her face that was more adult than I believed her capable of. "Be careful, Mattie," she said. "The river can be very treacherous."

"Duncan, who is that man in the river? How did he drown?"

Duncan swung her legs over the side of the bed and slid to her feet. "He didn't drown by himself, Mattie." She walked past me to the doorway, then turned back. "Not by himself at all." She turned away again and stared straight ahead. "I'm starving. Let's fix something for lunch." She didn't wait for me. She walked out of the room without even looking back.

Thirty-nine

WILL and JoHanna returned late that afternoon. Blood spotted the front of Will's starched white shirt and the knuckles of his right hand were cut. Both hands were badly bruised. JoHanna said only that Floyd's funeral was set for the next morning from the Methodist church. The same minister who had preached Red Lassiter's service was coming back. JoHanna had handled the funeral arrangements while Will took care of other things. JoHanna gave me the broadest outline of Will's agenda. I picked up the details from what she didn't say.

Will's first stop had been the jail. John Doggett was unharmed, and Will said he was holding up better than could be expected. John had been relieved to hear Will was securing a lawyer for him.

From the jail, Will had gone into town. The boot shop was closed and the Moseses were gone out of town. Will had not been able to find out where they'd gone or when they would be back. The Odom brothers were gone, and Sheriff Grissham had gone to Ellisville to retrieve "something very special." Will hadn't been able to find out what, exactly, but he did learn that it pertained to John Doggett's inevitable swift and speedy conviction . . . and execution.

Only Elikah had elected to remain in town. He didn't want to lose the business by closing his shop. It was not a smart decision on his part. Doc Westfall had had to pull Will off. Wiping his bleeding hand on a starched linen handkerchief, Will had climbed in the Auburn with JoHanna at the wheel, and they had driven home.

Neither Duncan nor I mentioned the dream she'd had. The small wounds on her forehead made by Pecos's beak we explained as scratches. I covered my bruised throat with a high collar. We'd had enough of prophecies and death.

JoHanna and I peeled vegetables for a pot of soup while Will sat at the table and watched his wife work. We all listened to Duncan talk. Natchez intrigued her. She was captivated by the idea of living on a river with big boats and a town with antebellum mansions. The romance of it had swept Duncan away, though it was clear from Jo-Hanna's silence that she was not so enthused. Will answered Duncan's hundreds of questions as a strange peace settled over the kitchen. Events had stilled. The steady march to the brink of confrontation had slowed.

Floyd's body was the log in the path.

The funeral loomed ahead of us, one more immediate hurdle. Then the trial. JoHanna and Duncan would not remain for the trial. For John's sake and their own. I had decided to wait until JoHanna left town to kill Elikah. I had begun to plan it out. I'd chosen the bedroom as the perfect place. The scene had taken shape in my head without conscious effort. It would require that I go home to Elikah, but after seeing Will's hands, I didn't think my husband would prove much of a threat to me. I would draw him a bath, getting the water just at the temperature he liked. Once he was naked and immersed in the tub, I would walk in the room with the gun. The first shot would revenge Floyd. The second shot would put an end to his cruelties forever. And then I would go over to the sheriff's office and turn myself in. The last laugh would be that I didn't even have to clean up the mess.

"Mattie?"

I whirled at Will's voice.

"Are you okay?"

My pulse was fast and I could feel the flush of victory on my face as I nodded and swallowed.

"What were you daydreaming about?" Duncan asked. Her dark eyes held a knowing look.

"Natchez," I answered, the lie slipping easily off my tongue. What was a lie from a woman who could contemplate murdering her own husband with a smile?

We set the table and ate the soup and cornbread. When we were done, I sent Will and JoHanna for a walk while Duncan and I cleaned the kitchen and packed. By tomorrow afternoon they would be leaving Jexville forever.

Duncan showed me her mother's favorite pots and pans and we packed those, leaving most things for the movers she said she'd send for her belongings. It was going to be hard for JoHanna, and I wanted her to have some of her own things with her when she set up her new household in Natchez.

"You're not coming with us, are you?" Duncan was wrapping a pitcher with a dishcloth.

I was stacking the plates back on the shelf. "No. But don't tell JoHanna or Will."

"Will you come and stay with us later?"

Tears flooded my eyes, and I wasn't certain if it was the idea of losing JoHanna and Duncan, and Will, or pity for the fate I'd chosen. "I will if I can."

That didn't satisfy Duncan, but she let it go when she heard her parents coming in the front door. JoHanna went in her bedroom and Duncan followed, and Will and I were left in the kitchen.

We stood and stared at each other for what seemed like a long time. Finally I was the one to speak. "I'm staying in Jexville."

Will showed no surprise. "I don't think Elikah will ever lay a hand on you again. I don't know that he'll be able to. I'm afraid most of his fingers are broken."

"Elikah sets a great store by his hands." I remembered how he kept his nails so neat and clean. "Surgeon's hands," he'd called them.

"Well, he should have been more careful what he did with those hands." He walked over to the kitchen window and looked out into the night. "I'd rather you go with JoHanna and Duncan, but if you're going to stay, I could use your help with John's case."

"I'll do what I can." I wasn't certain what good I'd be in the cell next to him, but there wasn't much point in saying that. "Are you staying behind for the trial?"

"I'm staying behind."

It suddenly occurred to me that he might not go with JoHanna ever. I went to him, grabbing his arm before I thought. "You're not leaving her, are you?"

He shook his head. "No. I thought about it, but I'm not." The amusement in his eyes was at his own expense. "Long ago I fell in love with

JoHanna and gave her my heart. To demand it back now would be a foolish thing. What's left wouldn't be worth having."

"Oh, Will." I had never loved him as much. I reached up to touch his cheek, a gesture of comfort. He put his hand over mine, pressing my palm into the stubble of his beard.

"If I were a young man, free and unattached, I would love you, Mattie. Stay in Jexville for John's trial, but then you must leave. You can't throw yourself away on Elikah Mills."

I couldn't speak for the tears. He knew. He knew how much I loved him. I thought my heart would break when he leaned over and kissed the tears from my cheeks and pulled me into his arms.

Will, JoHanna, Duncan, and I were the only people in the church for Floyd's funeral. The minister spoke of innocence lost, of the haven Floyd would find in heaven. The service was short. We all sensed the growing uneasiness outside the church. We followed the casket out into the clear sunshine of October.

Floyd would lie in the Jexville cemetery, on a small rise beneath a cedar tree. We women walked behind the casket, which was carried by Will and three hired gravediggers. They had prepared the grave, and it took only a few moments to say the necessary words as the coffin was lowered. Duncan sobbed as if her heart was broken as the gravediggers began to return the dirt. I focused on the distant fringe of leafless trees that ringed the cemetery. The day was bright, a perfect fall day, but winter was on the way. Several jays and mockingbirds taunted a small cluster of grackles that patiently waited for us to leave so they could pick through the newly turned earth. Even the birds were mostly silent. Waiting. Except for the small funeral party, it was as if the town were deserted.

Will paid the minister, and we walked back to the car.

"Take good care of Pecos," I whispered to Duncan as I kissed the top of her head and then her tear-stained cheeks.

"Come with us," she begged, grabbing hold of my dress. I wore one of JoHanna's dresses, taken in at the waist with a belt. Her tears soaked the gray flannel.

"I'll be along," I lied, rumpling her hair, which was growing out thick and silky.

"Mattie?" JoHanna searched my face. "Don't stay here."

I wanted to throw myself into her arms, to bury my face on her shoulder and cry against the pain that burned my chest and throat. Instead I took her hand and held it, squeezing it tight. "I'll be fine. I'm going to stay and help Will."

"Then you'll come?" she pressed.

"When John is free."

"Maybe I should stay." She looked at Will. He shook his head and she clutched at the keys in her hand. "Natchez isn't that far. I can get back in a matter of hours if you need me."

Oh, I needed her. I needed Duncan and Will. But only I could do what had to be done. And I had to do it alone. "I love you," I whispered as I stood tall to kiss her cheek. "I love you all so very much."

I turned away, catching sight of the gravediggers as they lifted the red earth and shoveled it into the grave. "I love you," I said again as I started to walk the short distance back to town.

If I had looked back once and they had signaled me, I could not have kept walking. So I didn't turn around. I left Will to say his good-byes to his wife and daughter, and I headed for Redemption Road. At the corner of Mercy and Redemption, I went east, to the boot shop. The window had not been replaced after the storm. A large board had been nailed over the broken glass, but through the door I could see that the interior of the shop had not been cleaned up. I pressed my cheek to the door, cool in the October chill, and tried to remember. Try as I might, though, I could not conjure up the picture of Floyd at work. He was gone. Even his memory had departed. The black riding boots he'd worked on with such love were on the feet of Tommy Ladnier, and the other boots, the ones Duncan had helped him design, were also gone from the shelf in the window. They had taken his handiwork, along with his life.

I walked along the street, noticing that Mara was in her shop baking. She waved a floury hand at me as I passed, her smile sad and old. Nodding at her, I turned back and retraced my steps, willing myself to confront the other side of the street.

The barbershop was dark and closed. Elikah had lost a day's business thanks to Will's beating. He would lose more than a day. I would see to that.

I crossed the street and walked by Gordon's. Olivia saw me, hesitated, and bent to straighten some boxes beneath the counter. I walked on, noticing that several wagons waited a block away at the courthouse. Had Will made it to the jail? How long would it be before Jeb arrived with the lawyer? My footsteps echoed softly in the packed dirt and it seemed that all around me time had stopped. The clock ticked only for me. The beating of my heart marked the seconds.

If Elikah wasn't at the shop, he was at home. My feet turned in that direction, but what waited in the back of one of the wagons stopped me with the power of a punch to the stomach. Quincy Grissham was standing beside a wagon that contained a big black box of some type. Two of his henchmen were lifting a chair from the wagon. In the quiet streets, the buckles on the leather straps of the chair clanged and jingled.

I had never seen anything like it, but even at first glance I knew it was sinister.

Grissham's laugh cut through the street as sharp as a slap as he lifted a coil of wire and threw it. The black line snaked out, up to the barred window of a cell, where a hand reached out suddenly and caught it.

I forced my feet to walk, to take the long, sure strides of JoHanna.

As I passed Jeb Fairley's house I heard two mockingbirds argue. Jojo came to mind and I realized I had not thought of him in days. My only regret was that I couldn't kill him when I killed Elikah. It seemed a shame to let him live. Maybe I'd make a desperate getaway and take the train to Meridian to finish my bloody spree.

I was smiling as I walked across the lawn and up the front steps of my house. The front door was open, and I walked in. Elikah sat at the kitchen table, his hands a swathe of bandages and his face a swollen mass of bruises. The skin at the corners of his mouth whitened when he saw me.

"Hello, Elikah." I went to the cabinet and got a glass. From the pitcher on the counter I poured some water and drank half of it before I turned to look at him again.

"What do you want?" His eyes held suspicion, and something far more satisfying. Fear. He glanced out the kitchen window, alert. He thought Will had come with me.

"I've come home." I put the glass in the sink and went to the icebox to see what was inside. "Would you like some stew for supper?"

He didn't say anything. His eyes darted to the window, then to me, then toward the front door.

"How about a nice beef pie? With crust just the way you like it? Since the weather has cooled, a hot meat pie might be just the thing." I got the flour and lard and reached up on the shelf for a mixing bowl.

"What do you think you're doing?"

"I'm home." I couldn't look at him. He would see my hatred and know it was a trick. As I reached up the shelf I could feel John Doggett's derringer pressing against my leg.

"Where's that McVay slut?"

I finally turned, pressing my hands against the counter, holding myself back. "JoHanna's gone," I said softly. "They're moving away."

A smile notched up one side of his mustache. "So, they left you."

I shrugged and turned back to begin making the crust for the pie.

"Once they moved along, they wouldn't take you with them." Satisfaction oozed from him. "Yeah, they left you behind like an old rag dress. Well, her boyfriend is going to get a big surprise. A historic moment for Jexville and the state of Mississippi."

Something in his voice made me turn back to look at him. There was a secret in the quirk of his lips, in his hot eyes.

"Ever heard of 'the chair'?"

I didn't answer because I couldn't. The jangle of the straps and belts on the chair that Sheriff Grissham was unloading came back to me.

"It's a new form of execution. A portable chair with a generator. They'll strap Doggett in that chair and fasten those conductors to his head and heart. When they send that jolt of electricity through him, he'll jump and buck. I've heard it boils a person's blood. Sort of like being struck by lightning, only worse."

I cut the lard into the flour with a fork. I couldn't afford to let him know how he affected me.

My silence allowed him to expand, taking up more of the room. "He won't be such a pretty boy once he's fried. I guess JoHanna made the right decision. Her husband came home, and she cut her losses. Left old John Doggett to take the rap for killing that family. She realized the stakes were too high for her, so she ran."

I glanced up at him. His fear was completely gone. Surrounded by bruises and swollen tissue, his eyes were hard, angry. I couldn't help myself. "You know John Doggett didn't kill those people."

"Do you think that really matters?" He leaned back in his chair. "Doc Westfall said all of their lungs were full of water, except the man. His neck was broken." He scraped his chair back from the table. "The bank was getting ready to foreclose on them. Put me on a pot of coffee."

Pushing back the bowl, I wiped my hands on a towel and checked the wood in the stove before putting the kettle on to heat.

"What was the family's name?"

"Spencer." He slipped his suspender down one shoulder.

"Did you know them?" I got the rolling pin and moved the bowl to the table where I could roll out the dough. Almost as much as beating me, Elikah loved to gossip.

"They weren't from around here. Took over the Dalton place last year. The sheriff said they stayed to themselves. They didn't have any neighbors out on that dead-end road."

Behind me the kettle began to boil, and I poured the hot water into the pot. Elikah liked his coffee strong. Strong and black. I knew exactly how to fix it. When it had dripped through, I poured us both a cup and sat his before him. I couldn't help but look at his hands. "Can you manage?"

He snorted. "I'll manage. And when my hands get well, I'll settle the score with Will McVay, if have to track him down to wherever he's running off to." He looked up at me, knowing without asking that I wouldn't tell him where the McVays were headed. "I've got a score to settle with you, too, Mattie." He spoke softly, but his intention was clear. In the past, it would have been enough to make me cower. I dropped my gaze and went back to my cooking. I got out onions and carrots and potatoes and set them on the table to be peeled and cut.

Holding the cup with both hands, Elikah drank the coffee and watched me work. He signaled for a refill, and I poured him more coffee and finished putting the pie together. After I slid it into the stove, I turned to him. "Would you like me to draw you a bath? I could put some more water on to heat. It might take some of the stiffness out of your muscles if it was good and hot."

"Well, well." He grinned. "The dutiful wife."

I stood completely still, casting my gaze down to the floor. If I looked at him I might shoot him on the spot.

"Look at me, Mattie."

Very slowly I looked up, shifting along the floor to his feet. I made a small sound. Elikah wore the boots Floyd had designed for Sheriff Grissham.

His laugh was soft, cruel. "You like 'em? Floyd did fine work, didn't he? He was nothing but an idiot, but he could make a boot. The sheriff said I should have them for all my skill. Floyd didn't object much. He was too busy trying to stop the flow of blood . . ."

"You cut him, didn't you?" I grabbed the back of a chair to steady myself and looked at him. I wanted to hear him say it. I couldn't look away from Elikah's eyes. They were burning with emotion.

"I always wanted to be a surgeon." He smiled. "Now put that water on for my bath."

"Why did you shoot him in the back?"

Quick as a cobra, Elikah leaned forward and swept the bowl and rolling pin onto the floor. The heavy crockery shattered and little pebbles of dough scattered across the floor.

"Because he tried to run." Elikah stood up. "He couldn't believe I'd cut him. When he finally realized it, when the shock wore off and he started to feel it, he tried to run. None of us wanted to chase him down, so Clyde shot him." He shouldered off his other suspender. "It was a kindness." He stepped toward me where I stood, unable to move, air whistling through my teeth as I tried hard to breathe. "Now put that water on. I need a bath and a shave. Tommy's coming by for me later. We have some business. Now that Will's stepping aside, Tommy sees opportunity in the import-export business." He raised his eyebrows at the look of confusion I wasn't quick enough to hide. I had never thought to question what it was that Will sold on his trips.

Elikah chuckled, his delight an unexpected bonus. "You didn't know Will was a bootlegger. A high-level one, to be sure. Booze opens a lot of doors in real high places, Mattie. With Will out of the way, Tommy's star is going to rise."

No matter the consequences to me or John, I could not wait to kill Elikah. It had to be done now. I needed time to think, so I refilled the kettle and put it on. I had not counted on Tommy Ladnier's presence in the house. Tommy would recognize me as the girl who'd been at his house to sell sandwiches. I couldn't allow Elikah to become suspicious of me. He was cruel, not stupid.

"Mattie, get the tub." He walked into the bedroom. "Then get in here and undress me."

"Yes, Elikah." I gave him my meekest voice.

If I could have willed the water to boil, it would have been bubbling off the stove. I set up the tub and got out his shaving tools. The handle of the razor was crusted with a small, dark stain, and I knew it was Floyd's blood. It was something I couldn't dwell on. I had to turn my mind in another direction. Revenge. That was what I had to focus on. Cool, satisfying revenge. To see Elikah grovel and beg before I blew his brains out. To watch the blood seep up in the water of the tub. The image calmed me and I patted the derringer in my pocket as I put the flat iron on the stove to heat so I could press a shirt for Elikah while another kettle of water heated. The bath was almost ready. Time ticked in my head as I listened to him, naked, walking about the bedroom, waiting for me to serve him.

At last the water boiled and I added the second kettle to the water I'd already drawn. Dipping my wrist into it, I tested the temperature. "Perfect," I said.

"It had better be." He stepped into the tub, easing down into the water with a sigh. "You'll have to shave me." He held up his bandaged hands. "Thanks to you, I'm an invalid."

I lathered the soap in his cup and carefully applied it to his bruised and swollen face with the soft brush. He tilted his head back, eyes closed, confident that I would not dare to inflict the tiniest pain.

When I lifted the razor, I thought how easy it would be to slit his throat. How terribly easy. Would I ever feel any remorse? I couldn't be certain, but I didn't think so. I stroked the razor across his cheek, scraping away the soap and stubble. The blade inched below his chin. The only thing that stopped me was the idea of shooting him in the privates. I wanted that satisfaction. The blade would be too quick. And sitting behind him, I couldn't see his eyes.

I finished shaving him. "Let me get you a hot towel," I said, rising. My intention was to go into the kitchen and come out, gun in hand. To watch him as I walked up to the tub as he realized what I meant to do.

I was halfway across the room when I heard the footsteps in the hall. Panic froze me as I watched Tommy Ladnier walk into the kitchen, white shirt crisp, black boots gleaming.

His eyes brightened with recognition. "Hello, little sandwich girl." He grinned as it all clicked into place. "Well, well, when you buried that idiot today, you forgot the most important part of him. Ah, the missing part." Laughing, he brushed past me and went into the bedroom.

"Tommy." Elikah's greeting was warm. "My wife was just getting me cleaned up."

"Your wife is an interesting woman." While I stood helpless, Tommy started to tell Elikah about my appearance in his house.

My brain finally started to work. Pulling the gun from my pocket, I went to the doorway. Tommy had taken a seat in the chair I'd used to shave Elikah. He was behind Elikah's head, but I could still hit him. And then Elikah. It wasn't what I'd planned, but maybe it was better. Two for the price of one.

Neither of them moved when they saw me in the doorway. Tommy's light eyes looked me over without a hint of emotion. "I think you're going to have to kill her," he said, his voice conversational. The water in the tub sloshed as Elikah started to rise.

I lifted the hand with the gun. The barrel was silver and it caught the light from the bedroom window. "Sit down or I'll shoot." The trigger pressed back against my finger, a slight tension that I liked.

Stunned, Elikah sank back into the water.

"Kill her," Tommy said. He crossed his legs, the black boots soft and beautiful in the light from the window.

Elikah stared at me, his swollen face now slack-jawed by his disbelief at my actions. Then his pride kicked in. "By God I will." He started to rise again, but I cocked the gun, and he settled back into the water, aware that I knew how to use the derringer.

Propped back in his chair, Tommy sighed and gave Elikah a contemptuous look.

"I know Elikah cut Floyd." I spoke to Tommy. "Clyde killed him, but he would have bled to death anyway. How is it, Tommy, that you never do your own dirty work? Elikah may go to prison, but your hands are clean. You put them up to it, didn't you?" It wasn't until he walked into the room that I understood his role.

"You stupid bastard." Tommy grabbed Elikah's hair with a swiftness that almost made me discharge the gun. "You told her, didn't you? You had to brag about it. I told you all to keep your mouths shut, but you had to brag."

Elikah jerked his head free. His grin was ugly. "She can't do a thing. No matter what I told her, she can't speak against me." He smoothed his hair down with his bandaged hand. "She can't do a thing. She's my wife."

I knew the truth of his words. I could not do a thing. As Elikah's wife, my testimony against him would be worthless.

"She can't be *forced* to testify." Tommy was coldly furious. "She can still do it."

"Nobody will listen to her." Elikah's confidence was returning. He squirmed in the water, ready to get out but not certain how to do it without looking foolish.

"It won't matter much when you're dead." I could see that my words held less power. There were two of them and only me. They didn't believe I'd shoot them.

Tommy pushed back the chair, clearing a space between him and the tub. He was going to try to jump me. At the same time, Elikah shifted his legs, getting his feet up under him. They didn't bother to look at each other.

"Seems to me your wife hasn't learned her place." Tommy put both feet on the floor. "I thought you were more man than that, Mills."

"Oh, Mattie's tractable. Now that that McVay woman is gone, me and Mattie are going to come to an understanding." Elikah rose in the tub. The water sloughed from his slick body, spattering into the bath. Even with his bruises and bandages, he was a handsome man. His stomach rippled with muscles, the water making his skin glisten and shine. He was partially aroused, primed by the danger and the idea of making me pay.

"You're right, Elikah." I spoke so softly the sound of the water dripping off him almost drowned me out. "I'm your wife." I held the gun pointed directly at his chest. "Nobody would believe my word against yours."

Elikah's grin was slow, confident. "I told you, Tommy. Mattie won't be a problem."

"She's holding a gun on you, you idiot. And you say she won't be a problem?" Tommy's voice was cruel. "We should kill her and be done with it."

"No." Elikah held out a hand and stopped Tommy as he started to move. "Not now. That's the one thing that would keep McVay and his wife in town. As it is, they're leaving. Once Doggett is dead, they'll be gone." Elikah licked his lips. His mind was clicking away. I always knew he was a cunning man.

Tommy relaxed in his chair. "You'd better make certain she doesn't open her mouth. I don't care how you do it, but I'm telling you to do it. She can make trouble for all of us."

"Give him the gun, Mattie." Elikah's voice cracked like a whip. "Give him the gun, because if I have to come take it from you, Tommy will get to hold you while I beat you." He glanced sideways. "You'd like that, wouldn't you, Tommy?"

I lowered the gun and watched the smiles of victory creep across their faces. In one smooth motion, just as Jojo had taught me, I lifted the gun and pulled the trigger. Blood sprang across the white front of Tommy Ladnier's shirt.

"Mattie! Jesus, Mattie!" Elikah leaped from the tub, almost slipping as he banged his injured hands against the side. "Jesus Christ, Mattie!" He grabbed Tommy just as he fell. The two of them, Elikah slick with soap and water, tumbled to the bedroom floor. Elikah held Tommy in his arms.

Tommy struggled to breathe. His gaze darted around the room as if he hoped to find something that would save him. There was nothing anyone could do. I'd hit his heart, and with each beat, blood pumped out of him. Elikah planted a palm over the wound, but the blood flooded between his fingers. Tommy Ladnier would be dead in a matter of seconds.

"Remember, Elikah, I'm your wife. Your testimony against me is as worthless as mine against you. Tommy Ladnier attacked me. I was defending myself." I lowered the gun and stepped back, thinking of only one thing. I'd done exactly as John Doggett had told me. I'd aimed for the chest.

"I'm going to the jail to get Will and that high-priced lawyer from Hattiesburg. They'll be interested to hear how Tommy Ladnier confessed to killing the Spencer family and then tried to attack you in the bathtub. When I came in to help you, he turned on me."

Elikah held Tommy Ladnier in his arms. The blood had almost stopped. Shifting, Elikah glared up at me. "I'll see you burn in hell first. I won't lie to save your skinny ass."

Elikah would lie. I would make certain of it. "You can lie or you can tell Will McVay the truth. Just remember, Elikah, Tommy Ladnier isn't here to protect you." I hated him with a pureness that was fire in my veins. "Once John Doggett is free, I'm going to divorce you." He started to rise, but I lifted the gun. "I have one shot left. Jojo taught me not to flinch." I lowered the gun to his crotch. "I intended to shoot you right there, and then finish you off after you'd had time to think about Floyd. Tommy Ladnier saved your life. You'd better take it."

He stilled, staring at me as if he were trying to gauge whether I would shoot him or not

"If you doubt what I'm capable of, look at your friend." I waited until he dropped his gaze. "I'll be back shortly."

He rose suddenly. Tommy slid away from him, eyes open but unseeing. "No divorce."

I didn't bother to answer him.

"I'll agree with your story, but no divorce."

There was something in his eyes. "I'd kill you rather than stay married to you."

Elikah shook his head slowly. "If you were going to kill me, you would have."

His confidence was completely insane. I hadn't killed him because only Elikah could clear John Doggett. As he rightly said, no one would take my word.

"It's my bargain." He spoke quickly. "We'll say Tommy came to kill me because I knew he had killed that family. You killed him first. That way Doggett is freed. But you have to stay with me." One corner of his mustache quivered. "As a married couple, we can't testify against each other. It's a draw." His lips twitched again, and then I saw it in the corner of his eyes, the crinkling of skin. He was laughing at me.

"I'd rather burn in hell than live with you."

"It's the only way to get Doggett off. He could be free in an hour. The people in town will believe me if I tell them about Tommy. Sheriff Grissham will have to believe me."

"And Floyd?"

Elikah shrugged, not bothering to hide his grin anymore. "Tommy can take the rap for that one, too, if anybody decides to prosecute."

"I won't stay here."

"Oh, yes you will. That's the bargain. You stay." He stepped over Tommy and went to the bed to pick up the towel I'd put out for him.

"I hate you enough to kill you right on the spot."

He toweled his hair, then began rubbing his arms and shoulders. Supremely confident. "But you won't. Not today. You need me today. And by tomorrow, I'll have a paper drawn up with everything in it so that if anything untoward happens to me, you'll be accused."

He didn't even bother to look at me as he spoke. He'd set a better trap than I had. I could kill him, but that wouldn't free John. Only Elikah could do that, and he had to be alive to do it. John Doggett's life was more important than my freedom. He knew that. He didn't even have to bluff.

"Why are you doing this? I hate you. Why do you want me to stay? You hate me as much as I hate you."

He turned slowly and the grin was gone. In its place was a black hatred that made me step back. "That's exactly why. You'll pay each day. In little ways. I'll have the pleasure of making each day a living hell for you." His cocky grin was back in place. "That McVay bitch is ruined and out of town. She's gone, and you'll stay here as my wife."

"What makes you hate me so?" The question slipped out of my mouth. "I tried to make you a good wife. I honestly tried at first. I wanted to please you, to make you happy. You hated me from the first. Why?"

"You bring out the best in me, Mattie." He picked up the shirt I'd ironed and slipped it on. "Now help me button this up. I need to be dressed when you bring Will over here. Oh, and if you're going to make this believable, I think you should scream and cry a little as you run to the courthouse. You're a little too calm to be an accidental murderess."

❦ *Forty* ❧

JOHN Doggett stood at the train depot in Mobile. He held his ticket to New Orleans in his hand, and everything he owned was packed in a suitcase that rested beside his right leg. Not ten yards away the train puffed and hissed, ready to pull out as soon as all the passengers had loaded. John was the last.

"Is there anything you want me to tell JoHanna?" I asked him. John would not ask me to arrange an assignation or relay his need for her. It was a matter of honor. Will had stepped in to save his life. More important, it was a matter of JoHanna's happiness.

He shook his head, and the look in his eyes told me that he was already gone from the spot where he stood. "We said it all."

"What about Duncan?"

"Tell her not to forget to go back to the Pascagoula on the night of the Hunter's Moon to hear my people. Tell her to grow up strong, and to dance." He looked beyond me.

"You'll like New Orleans, John. It's a good place for a writer."

He stepped toward me, taking my shoulders in his hands. "Take care, Mattie. I don't know how you managed to get me out, but I owe you my life."

"No." I shook my head. "No, you don't owe me anything."

"If you went up to Natchez to visit JoHanna and Duncan, you could ride the riverboat down to New Orleans to see me."

"I won't be traveling for a spell, John."

His mouth tightened. "Why are you staying with that man, Mattie?"

How could I explain? Elikah and I were locked in a death embrace. We were tied together in a pact far more binding than vows of matrimony. "I'm doing what I feel I have to do, John. Just as you are. Just as Will is."

John sighed and nodded. "Then he went on up to Natchez?"

"He left this morning."

He could not bring himself to say that it was good. His love for JoHanna was as hopeless as mine for Will. I believe John suffered even more than I did because he had tasted JoHanna, what it might have been like. I had only fantasies. JoHanna's love was boundless, inclusive. She scattered it among us like pearls. I reached up and put my hand on John's cheek. "Take care, John."

Behind him I saw the conductor waving a final signal. "All aboard!" he cried, waving again.

"Will you write me?" he asked.

I nodded, pleased that he had asked. If we could not have JoHanna, we could share our memories with each other. He picked up his bag and started toward the train.

"You'll send me news of JoHanna and Duncan?"

"Every bit I hear." I was walking fast beside him as he hurried toward the train. He walked like JoHanna. Long, determined strides. He would be okay. I had to believe that, because it gave me hope for myself.

"Oh, Mattie!" He swept me against his side with his free arm. "Remember the days we spent along the river at Fitler, and remember the river is our bond. We'll always go back to her, each of us for our own reasons. You'll find your freedom in that river, Mattie." He kissed my cheek and gave me that clear look that seemed to come from another time, a place long ago. "Duncan told me so."

I squeezed him as hard as I could. "Good-bye," I whispered as I broke away from him and ran in the opposite direction. When I got to the end of the platform, I turned around. He was gone. With a blast and a geyser of smoke, the train began to pull away.

Jeb Fairley waited in the car beside the depot. He'd driven me and John over to make sure no one tried to detain John when he boarded. John's innocence wasn't exactly an established fact around Jexville, and Jeb, Will, the lawyer, and I had decided to put John on the first train to New Orleans we could manage, just in case Elikah decided to go back on his word. Sheriff Grissham had been deeply upset that after going all the way to Ellisville, he had no one to strap in the traveling electric chair.

Jeb shook his head as we both watched the train pull out. "Mattie, girl, you should board that train and go with him. He struck me as a de-cent man. One who cares about you."

I opened the door and got in the car, not even bothering to try and hide my tears. "They'd hunt me down like a rabid dog." I tried to smile, but it was pointless.

Jeb reached into his pocket and brought out a clean handkerchief. He handed it to me and patted me on the arm. "Jexville is no place for you. Elikah may have promised you he'd change, but he won't. Without JoHanna and Will to protect you, he could hurt you bad."

I looked over at Jeb. He was a kind old man. A good man. Other than that big magnolia tree in his yard, what else kept him in town? He had saved his money. He could relocate anywhere he wanted. "Why do *you* stay?"

He shrugged. "I don't know. I just don't know." He put the car in gear, and we headed back to Jexville. "No place I've ever been to seemed much better. I guess I don't have a lot of faith in the human an-imal to rise above his nature. Jexville is as good a place as any, better than some."

"Are you going to marry Aunt Sadie?"

He chuckled. "Now that's just like a woman to think a wedding will patch everything up."

"Are you?"

"I'm going to ask. She may not have me."

"I bet she will."

"Maybe we're too old to get used to each other." He gave me a specu-lative look. "She wouldn't consider going to Natchez with JoHanna, and she won't come to Jexville. I guess I'll have to go to Fitler to live. Then who would keep an eye on you?"

"Elikah won't ever hit me again, Jeb. I can promise you that." I wiped my eyes and settled back in the car.

He put the old Ford in gear, and we bumped over a set of freight tracks and onto a brick street. Jexville was a long ride away, and I wanted to enjoy the cold wind on my face for the few hours of freedom I had. I was not fool enough to think Elikah and I would work things out. We were bound by hatred and a common desire to punish each other as much as possible. Strangely enough, I preferred it this way. I would not try to please him as I once had. I would spend my days inflicting as much suffering as possible. Elikah's life had been touched by the hand of God, and I was the retribution sent down to plague him. Disease, locusts, rivers of blood; I intended to do my worst. It was not the life I'd chosen, but I could stand it.

One thing I knew for certain: He would not beat me down or break me.

"Tell me something, Mattie."

Jeb's voice brought me back to the present. "What's that?"

"Those dreams that Duncan had, the prophecies. Was there anything that caused them?"

I'd given this a lot of thought on and off. "They started the day she was struck by lightning, out dancing the Charleston at Annabelle Lee's birthday party."

"Ansel Wells got struck by lightning, and he went blind."

We had left the smell of the Mobile River behind us, the sweet odor of fruit ripening on the dock and water meeting rich brown soil. We drove down the tree-lined street that would eventually turn into the old federal road that led through Jexville and finally up to Natchez, where the McVays had gone.

When I didn't answer him, Jeb spoke again. "Last year three of Oscar File's cows got struck. He said it fried the blood right inside them."

I looked at the houses to my right, taking in the wide porches and the plantation-style homes set on tiny lots. It seemed to me that folks with enough money to build that kind of house would have bought enough land to sit it on without making it look all crowded and scrunched up. I thought of the barrier islands and the small shacks that had been built facing right into the Gulf. I wanted to live someplace where the wind blew free and fierce, and the waves crashed hard on pure white sand. No matter how fancy the house, living jammed up against someone wasn't for me.

"Mattie, what do you suppose it was that made Duncan dream the future instead of going blind or deaf?"

I couldn't ignore him any longer. He was going to persist. And it wasn't that nosey kind of question that Janelle would ask. "Floyd thought it was a gift."

"What did Duncan think?"

I wasn't certain, but I had a fair idea. "Duncan wasn't afraid of the dreams. She accepted them as fact. Some of them she understood better than others, and when she did, like with Mary Lincoln or Red, she tried to warn the folks involved. It wasn't anything bad or mean. She didn't invite it, but she wasn't afraid of it."

"There were other dreams?" He glanced at me, shocked.

I'd forgotten that we'd told no one about the dead family, the Spencers, driven to madness and desperation by money. It was best to let that one go, but I didn't see any harm in telling him the one about the man at the bridge. "There was one other, the only one that frightened Duncan. We all thought it might have to do with Mr. Senseney, the man who wanted to build the bridge. Duncan kept seeing a body at the base of the bridge in Fitler, a man with boots like JoHanna said Jacob Senseney wore. The man kept trying to talk to Duncan, and it scared her."

"What did he say?"

I shook my head and realized he was watching the road. "I don't know, Jeb. JoHanna was always afraid that it was Duncan, predicting her own death."

"And what did you think, Mattie?"

"That one dream really frightened Duncan, and I think it was because we never could figure it out. But I think we never understood it because it was about the past. Maybe it was old Mr. Senseney trying to tell what had happened to him. I guess some mysteries aren't meant to be solved."

The conversation made me sad. I missed Duncan and JoHanna terribly, with a physical pain far worse than anything I'd suffered at Elikah's hands. I turned my attention to the passing scenery. Though I'd been to Mobile several times now, I kept seeing it anew. We had left the fancy residential section behind and were on the outskirts. Fine homes had turned into smaller houses with more land. Fall gardens of turnips and pumpkins reminded me of JoHanna's garden. Would they sell the house? I hadn't asked. I guess I didn't want to know for sure. I could always pretend they might come back if I didn't know for sure.

Jeb cleared his throat to get my attention. "You reckon Duncan will dream those dreams in Natchez?"

I'd thought about that, too. "I don't know, Jeb."

"It'll make life a lot simpler for the McVays if she doesn't."

I had to smile at that. "Maybe, maybe not. The only thing that would make life easier for JoHanna would be to stop thinking, to fall in line without question." My smiled widened. "I don't believe that will happen. She's beat-up now and suffering hard, but I honestly don't think she can help herself. Not any more than Duncan could help the dreams."

Jeb drove on in silence, pondering what I'd said. JoHanna would survive. She was strong. She was beaten, but she wasn't defeated, not by a long shot. That was the one thing that made it all worthwhile.

Forty-one

"LOCALLY, the Jexville Ladies Club has gathered over five thousand pounds of scrap metal. A truck from Mobile will arrive Saturday to pick it up and take it to the war effort." Janelle nodded and beamed at the polite round of applause from the fifteen women in the room.

"Our bake sale and fund-raiser was an exceptional success last Saturday." Janelle hesitated. The years had not been kind to her. Fat had accumulated on her hips and middle, and her large eyes, once wide with intrigue and gossip, were hooded in disappointment. "We owe a special thanks to Mattie Mills, who arranged the, uh, the theatrics. The troupe was very professional, and we all appreciate the work she did to bring them to us from New Orleans. They were, uh, very dramatic. Mattie's trademark."

The applause was barely a ripple around the room, but I acknowledged it with a gracious smile, then glanced out the window. The storm clouds that had begun to gather about noon now covered the eastern horizon in a gray mass that seemed to draw the evening behind them. April storms were usually intense but brief. I checked my watch and hoped that it would hold off until I could get home. I didn't relish the idea of being stranded in the meeting for an extra half hour.

"Now, on to the plans for the town victory garden. Mr. Elmo has plowed the garden, and we all have our list of plants that we're to bring?" Janelle looked around the room to be sure that everyone nodded in agreement. She had a special talent as an organizer. She didn't do much physical work herself, but she was a master at getting others to work. Everyone except me. As everyone in town knew, other than my job as part-time court reporter, I hadn't hit a lick at a snake in nearly twenty years. I sat on my front porch swing listening to records or reading strange magazines that came in the mail, along with big packages from all over the world. And I wrote letters. Every day at least one, which I saved until I could get to Fitler or Mobile to mail.

"Mrs. Stewart's son left this morning to go to Jackson, where he'll be inducted into the navy. We'll all very proud of our brave boys, going over to fight the Germans and the Japs. . . ." Janelle's voice broke. Her own son was in the Pacific. Janelle had not fully recovered from the shock of his leaving, the day-to-day threat that he would not survive. I felt a moment of pity for her and a fierce delight that I had not left myself open for such anguish.

Janelle recovered herself. "At any rate, we should take a moment to remember Mrs. Stewart. A phone call would be greatly appreciated; I know from personal experience. I vote we also send over a flag with a star for her front window so everyone will know she has a family member in the war." She blinked the tears away. "Now that's all the business, and we'll serve refreshments. Carrie has prepared a delicious dewberry cobbler with berries picked by her own little Carol Beth. And Annabelle Lee Adams, née Leatherwood, has some of her homemade ice cream for us to top it." Janelle stepped away from the podium and fanned herself with her program even though it was not warm at all in the Kittrells' spacious living room. Carrie Kittrell was the newest member of the Jexville Ladies Club. She had recently moved to town with her husband to take over Doc Westfall's practice. I felt her gaze upon me and knew she'd been warned about me.

I smiled at her, forcing her to look away. I felt a pang of remorse. She was about my age and looked nice. Maybe she would have been a friend to me, but I couldn't allow it. The life I'd chosen had no room for friends. If I opened the door to my emotions even one tiny crack, I wouldn't be able to maintain the life I'd built. I wouldn't be able to continue. I had my letters from JoHanna and Duncan and Will and John. My little notes from Callie, who had five children, and Lena Rae, with her two sons. That was the only closeness I could manage, and only that because it was far removed from Jexville.

Mama had died the past spring, and none of us knew if Jojo was still kicking or not. I prayed he'd live to be very, very old. He deserved longevity. I had come to see it as the greatest punishment of all.

"Now everyone take a seat, and we'll serve you," Agnes Leatherwood said. She was a whisper of her former self, a ghost of a person who lost a little more color and substance each year. She lived with her daughter and son-in-law in the same house on Redemption Road where I'd first met JoHanna and Duncan.

Laying my purse and gloves on the sofa, I got up and went into the kitchen to offer to help serve. They wouldn't let me, just as they had no interest in having one of the Tuesday meetings in my home. I was allowed to belong, on the fringes. Never in the center. It was an amusing way of dealing with me. I had taken up where JoHanna left off as the town pariah and agitator, but they did not hate me the way they'd hated her. The element of fear was missing.

They did not fear me because I was no threat. I never had the strength of JoHanna, or the ability to love. I didn't have her joy for life, and there was no need for them to waste their hatred on a dead person.

The bitterness of that sudden knowledge almost made me flinch, but I straightened my shoulders and continued into the kitchen.

"Annabelle Lee, let me help with the ice cream." I reached for the spoon and dasher, and she drew back as if my red fingernails were too hot to touch.

"No. No, you might ruin your dress." She stared at me, the spoon in one hand and her mouth open slightly. Her mother stood behind her.

"That's an interesting dress, Mattie." Janelle walked up to my shoulder. "I didn't realize that with the war effort they were limiting rations to one yard of material per dress."

"Certainly not, Janelle. There are allotments for larger-sized women. But I'm willing to do whatever I can for our boys on the front." JoHanna had sent me the red dress from New York. It was sleeveless, tight, and above the knee. The shortage of fabric was due to the war effort. The bright red color was due to JoHanna. I gave them all a big smile. "I just got the most precious little Dido. The entire thing wraps around like a little playsuit and ties at the waist. The American designers have done a remarkable job of taking the war limitations and using them creatively. I wouldn't want to be one of those women who wasted a zipper on an everyday dress."

Janelle's face had gone a hot, hot red. Sweat beaded her upper lip. She still gripped her program in her hand and waved it in an attempt to cool off. Janelle and Vernell were still good friends with Elikah. They pitied him for having such a hard wife, a woman who would not give him children or cook his meals. A woman who wasted her time reading magazines and dressing in outrageous styles that called attention to herself.

"When Elikah was over at our house for breakfast this morning," Janelle spoke loudly, to be sure everyone heard, "he was saying how he had decided to join up. He said he'd heard where the infantry needed medics. He's always had a talent in that area, and he said he was going to join up to help the war." Janelle's face had cooled, but her blue eyes had not. "He said he'd already packed his things."

Janelle's news silenced me. It was so unexpected, so out of the blue. Elikah was over forty. He was still lean and fit, a handsome man for those who didn't know the core of him. Deep inside, he didn't have a patriotic bone in his body, and he had no intention of risking his hide. He just wanted to sound noble.

"Surely he doesn't mean it?" Agnes Leatherwood stared at me. "He could be killed. Those Nazis will kill a medic as quick as a soldier."

I shrugged. "I think it would be a noble thing. After all, it would be a shame to waste Elikah's talent, when the boys need him so." I slipped my cigarette case out of the one pocket we were allowed on any dress or shirt. The gold case, with inset lighter, had come from London, a gift from Duncan before the war, when she'd gone there to dance.

"You mean he hasn't discussed it with you?" Agnes was on the scent of some clue to my relationship with my husband. When all other gossip ran out in Jexville, there was always the Mattie-Elikah bone to gnaw. "He'd consider signing up without telling you?"

I smiled slowly, exhaling a thin stream of smoke. "Of course. Whatever Elikah does is the exact right thing." I shrugged as I inhaled again. "He never has to discuss anything with me. I agree with everything he says and does. Going to war is exactly the right thing for my husband to do."

"Why don't you put out that cigarette and have some ice cream?" Agnes pushed a bowl at me, but I avoided it. "You're thin as a bamboo sprout. A woman needs a little meat on her bones as she ages." She gave me a meaningful glance.

"You were always too thin." Janelle covered her anger with a look of concern. "I always felt if you'd had a little meat on you, you could have had children. I guess it just wasn't in the Lord's plan for you."

I was used to Janelle's meanness. It didn't even sting anymore.

Before I could zing her back, Nell Anderson stepped into the kitchen. "Do you need some help with that pie and ice cream?" She spoke calmly, but it was clear that she spoke for the women who remained seated in the living room, waiting, while we bickered in the kitchen. Apparently everyone had heard the exchange.

"We've got it," Annabelle Lee said as she bustled away with two heaping bowls in her hand. Exclamations of delight came from the living room as Agnes went out with more bowls.

"How are you, Mattie?" Nell stepped closer. She was ramrod straight with hair completely white. Her oldest son had been killed at Normandy, and the heartbreak had made her suddenly old.

"I'm fine, Nell, and you?"

"Good. I'm good. What's the news from JoHanna?"

"She and Will are in Washington." I thought Nell's interest was sincere, but I'd learned not to ever reveal more than the bare essentials.

"And Duncan? Did she go back to dancing after the baby?"

"She's in New York." I smiled. "She's quite a sensation. They say little Clair is dancing in her diapers. Just like Duncan used to do."

"I miss those McVays. It's been twenty years, and I still miss them." Nell smiled, too, and for a moment the pain was so intense I thought I felt my heart breaking with the memories.

As if she read my mind, Nell continued. "I remember the first day I met you, Mattie. It was at Agnes's house. It was the day Duncan got struck by lightning."

Annabelle Lee stepped to my side and gave Nell a bowl of pie and ice cream and thrust one into my hand before I could resist. "Try it, Mattie," she said as she backed away.

"You were just a child," Nell continued. "We had all gone into the kitchen to serve the ice cream, and Duncan was outside dancing her heart out. You know, I was certain she was dead."

Outside there was a rumble of thunder, a long growl of clouds heavy with rain. The ice cream was cold in my hand, and a sudden gust of cool wind blew through the open kitchen window. I shivered.

"Mattie, are you okay?" Janelle put her bowl down and took my elbow. "You're as white as a ghost."

"I'm fine." My fingers were cramped in the shape of the bowl. I held it out to Nell, and she took it from me, unhooking it from my hand and putting it down on the kitchen table.

"What's wrong?" She held my hand between hers, rubbing it until the fingers relaxed.

I shook my head.

She held on to my hand, and in her eyes I saw that she suspected what my life might really be. It wasn't pity that I saw but sorrow. "What I came in here to tell you was that I read an article recently about those islands off the coast that you're so wild about. You know the government ordered everyone off them."

"Really?" I remembered the wooden shanties that Michael Garvi told me were used as summer homes. In unguarded moments I found myself imagining a life in one of them.

"It's part of the war. They don't want anyone living there for fear the German subs will see the lights and use them as a guide. The entire island chain is in a blackout."

"I always wanted to live on one of those islands." It was the most revealing thing I'd said in twenty years, and I was surprised to hear the words come from my mouth.

"Why, the first good hurricane would blow you away, Mattie." Nell was surprised by my flight of fancy.

"I suppose." I was embarrassed.

"You know, if that's what you really want, you should wait until the war is over and then go down to Mexico. I hear it's beautiful down along the Gulf. Blue water, white sand. My son, Albert, went down there to look at some of those Mayan ruins. You know, he was an archaeologist before the war." Her eyes glistened, but her voice was strong. "He said it was paradise there."

"Mexico?"

"He planned to move there for a year or two, after the war." She picked up her pie and ice cream and held it a moment. "He said it was like being born into someone else's skin." She walked over to the sink and put her bowl in it. "Sometimes, at night when I can't sleep, I pretend that he's in Mexico."

I walked across the kitchen and put my arm around her shoulders. It was the first time I'd voluntarily touched anyone other than JoHanna or Duncan in twenty years. "I'm sorry, Nell."

"Albert had more of his dream than most people get." Nell had regained control. "Albert and Duncan. They both got more than most of us. You're still a good-looking woman, Mattie. Don't wake up to find yourself old and dried-up." She turned away and walked into the living room. I could hear her telling Carrie and the other women good-bye.

Outside the window a fork of lightning streaked the sky, and the sound of thunder rattled the window panes. The storm was upon us. Without bothering to find my gloves or purse, I ran out the back door and into the street that had once been red dirt. I ran just as the first heavy, fat drops of rain began to fall.

More to aggravate Elikah than anything, I'd taken a job as a court reporter. The irony also pleased me. Every time there was a trial in Jexville, I sat beside the judge as an official of the court, the woman who had shot Tommy Ladnier and never been charged with a single crime. The job also gave me the money to buy an old car. I only used the old Ford to drive to Fitler to see Aunt Sadie and Jeb or to go to the post office in Mobile, where JoHanna sometimes sent me letters.

I walked to work, preferring the exercise to the car. I walked to the small café where I took my lunch. Food held little interest for me. I had come to believe that I was afraid to taste anything. One delicious taste, one moment of weakness, and I would crumble. So I walked and hoarded my gas rations.

As I ran through the rain, I thought I had enough gas to get me across the border. Nell Anderson had opened that door. Mexico. I had seen the aqua waters of the Gulf only once. Now they pounded in my head like my footsteps on the road. For years all impulse had been held rigidly in check. All desire. All life. I could not stand it a moment longer.

I ran as hard as I could in the tight, short skirt of the dress. I ran past Elikah's barbershop, not caring if he saw me or not. He would not stop me. Not this time. I was leaving, no matter what he threatened. John Doggett was long gone from New Orleans. He was covering the war for the *Kansas City Star*. He was far from Elikah's reach. Quincy Grissham had been defeated in the election six years before. Will and Johanna were safe and happy. And Duncan. Duncan had danced her way across the stages of the world and into the arms of a young man who wrote songs for a living. They were poor but happy in New York, where Duncan assured me his star would rise with his next musical. Duncan still danced, but she mostly put her long, graceful legs to work chasing Clair around their apartment.

Only I remained trapped. Held captive by my own inability to flee. But that was over. I was going now, and Elikah could not stop me.

I pounded into the house and flung open my closet door, rain dripping from my face and hair. I had suitcases and more clothes than I could ever pack. I grabbed them from the closet by the hangers and shook them free of the wire to push them helter-skelter into the first open piece of luggage. Raking shoes into my arms, I threw them on top.

Everything in my closet had come from Will or JoHanna, extravagant dresses to set the tongues wagging in Jexville. It had been the only thing JoHanna could do to amuse me. Had the clothes not come from her, I would have left them behind.

"What are you doing?"

I turned to find Elikah in the doorway. He had run behind me all the way home. A strand of hair, slicked with rain and a heavy sprinkling of gray, hung in his left eye. His chest heaved slightly with the exertion, and his left hand, the one with two crooked fingers, clutched the doorjamb.

"I'm leaving."

He spread his legs in the doorway. "I don't think you've thought this through."

It was the most civil exchange we'd had in years.

"It's over, Elikah. I've had enough. We've punished each other enough." I slammed the first suitcase shut. "We've punished ourselves enough."

It was the sound of his chuckle that made me turn around. "That's where you're wrong, Mattie. I've only begun to work on you." He stepped toward me.

I thought at first he might hit me, and in that split second I felt the return of a fear I thought I'd left behind forever. In opening the door to Mexico, I had also opened the door on hope. With it came fear and a billion other feelings that I had not allowed for so long I had thought they were dead.

"Let me go, Elikah. We can both have a life." I spoke to him as reasonably as I knew how. In my newfound desire to live, I had forgotten what he was.

He shook his head. "You think you can let twenty years go by and then decide you're going to walk out." He shook his head harder. "You'd better think again."

"Janelle said you were talking about enlisting. We could both go our separate ways. Start over. You can sell the shop and the house and keep all the money. I just want to go. I just . . ."

The shrill of the telephone caught me in midsentence. No one ever called the house. I had no friends. Elikah's friends were the type who met him after dark at the barbershop. They were hard men with pouting faces who drank the whiskey still illegal in Chickasaw County, even though the rest of the nation had long ago conceded that liquor could not be abolished. They sat in the shop and played cards, drinking and talking about the growing "Negro problem."

I walked to the telephone in the small hallway and picked up the black receiver. "Hello."

"Mattie, it's Sadie."

There was trouble in her voice. "What is it?"

"It's Duncan."

There was not a chair to sit on so I eased one hip onto the telephone table to steady myself. "What is it?"

"She's not hurt." Sadie sounded even more worried. "She called me this morning. I've been trying to reach you all day. She was very upset. She said something happened last night. She had a dream. About a man in the river reaching out to her and calling to her. She made me promise that I would call and tell you. She said she knew who it was. She said . . ."

I looked at Elikah. My gaze fell upon his feet, and I saw the boots. They were brand-new. He'd had the bootmaker who'd bought out Mr. Moses when he retired make the boots. They were exactly like the pair Floyd had made for Sheriff Grissham. The pair Elikah had worn every day until they had worn out. He'd just gotten the new pair only a few days before. The beautiful design of the vamp was struck by a slant of weak light from the window. Outside the storm was breaking up, and the sun was shining with a pale yellow light.

"Mattie! Mattie!" Aunt Sadie's voice was tinny and worried. "Did you hear me, Mattie?"

I hadn't heard her, but it didn't matter. "I have to go, Aunt Sadie."

"Duncan said she would call you later tonight. She was frantic, Mattie. Truly afraid. She was talking about trying to catch a train down here, but it's so hard with the war."

"If she calls you, tell her that I'm fine."

"She hasn't had a dream since they moved from Jexville, Mattie. What does this mean? She said she knew the man in the river, and that she had to talk to you."

"Tell her I'm fine." I hung up the telephone before she could continue. Later, much later, I'd explain.

I turned back to face Elikah, my gaze moving from those boots up to his eyes. For a long time now I had not allowed myself to feel even my hatred for him. I was surprised at the power of it. Twenty years had not dimmed it. He had also forgotten what I was capable of.

"I'm going, Elikah, whether you like it or not."

"Not after all this time, Mattie. I've wasted too many years to see you leave now. We're in this together, to the end."

I would never understand why he hated me so. Me and JoHanna. And probably Duncan, had he ever known her as a woman. What had we done that made him willing to spend his life hurting us?

"At least we're talking about this." I went into the kitchen. "I'll make some coffee." The stove was gas now, and the blue flames shot up the minute I turned it on. The old cast-iron kettle had been replaced with a shiny silver one with a whistle.

Elikah took a seat at the table. "You won't leave here alive, Mattie. Get it in your head; you're not going anywhere."

I put coffee in the pot. "I'm going out in the yard to feed the chickens. I'll be back." I pushed open the screen and went out to the barn. Mable had died ten years before, and we had buried her beside the barn. Now our only animals were the chickens I raised for their eggs and in honor of Pecos, who was buried in Natchez beside the Mississippi River.

I walked to the back of the barn where I kept the chicken feed and got a panful before I walked to the back of the yard.

"Chick, chick, chick." I called the birds over to me. None of them had the sense of a flea, but I loved the soft murmuring noises they made as they pecked the dirt for the cracked corn I threw.

I'd covered Mable's grave with some flowers, a weedy-looking plant that would produce, later in the summer, a tiny yellow bloom with a deep purple throat. I'd gotten the plants in Fitler, from the grave of a woman I never knew, Lillith Eckhart. She had been twenty-two years old when she was hanged for poisoning her husband. She had been young, desperate. Impetuous. I had planned better. And waited for a war.

Glancing up at the kitchen window, I made certain Elikah wasn't watching as I plucked a big handful of leaves and stuck them in the one pocket of my dress beside my cigarettes. The juice of the crushed leaves stained my hand, a strong smell, a lot like tobacco.

Halfway back to the house I thought to drop the chicken pan before I walked in. Elikah sat at the table, waiting. His hard eyes calculated how far he'd have to go to stop me.

I braced my hands against the stove. "Maybe I haven't thought this through," I said. "I don't want trouble for JoHanna or John Doggett."

"Or yourself." He grinned, leaning back in his chair.

I patted my pocket and spoke absently as I picked up a potholder to grab the kettle. "I must have left my cigarettes in the bedroom." He hated that I smoked. Without a word he got up and went to the bedroom to find them. He took great pleasure in tearing them apart in front of me.

As soon as he left I opened the kettle and dropped the fresh green leaves inside. When he returned I had a cigarette lit. I blew a ring of smoke in the air.

"Put the cigarette out." His hands were clenched at his sides.

Behind me the kettle screamed. Without looking away from him, I walked slowly across the kitchen to the back door. I took one last drag and flicked the cigarette out into the yard.

"Since we're talking, it's time you stopped that vulgar habit. Smoking makes a woman look cheap." His small victory made him hungry for more.

I ignored him as I went to the stove. I poured the water into the coffeepot and turned off the gas.

"I think a lot of things are going to change around here."

By allowing myself to feel again, I'd signaled to Elikah that I was vulnerable. He'd waited twenty years for that sign from me.

He took his seat at the table and waited for the coffee. My hands were shaking as I poured the cup, strong and black, just as he liked it.

Twenty years had passed, but I hadn't forgotten. He watched my hands, taking pleasure in my fear. I poured another cup for myself and leaned against the counter, holding the hot cup in hands that visibly trembled.

He sipped the coffee and made a face. "Everything you touch smells like cigarettes. That's the last one you're going to smoke, you hear?"

The coffee steamed in front of my face, the smell of tobacco clearly present. Elikah drank again. "I've got to get back up to the shop. It was closing time when you ran by like a scalded cat, but I need to put the combs in the disinfectant and bring the towels back here. I need you to wash them for me." He took another swallow and pushed the cup aside. "I'll be home for supper tonight, and I expect you to cook something."

Fear blocked my throat. Not even a sound could escape. I swallowed repeatedly, but it didn't help.

Elikah stood. The plant had had no effect. I don't know what I had expected, but something. He lifted his cup and drained it, never one to waste expensive coffee. Without looking at me, he started down the hall. It was only at the front door that he staggered.

I think he knew it then, but it was too late. Hoping to get out onto the porch, he slammed into the screen door and lurched outside. I ran after him, grabbing him around the waist and barreling as fast as I could down the steps and to the car parked at the front of the house.

"What's wrong, Elikah?" I asked him. His face was covered with a sheen of sweat and his eyes bulged. "You look sick. I'd better get you over to the new doctor's."

He was barely able to walk, but I got him into the passenger's seat and shut the door. I ran back into the house for my keys and then climbed into the driver's seat. Taking the back road, I headed to Fitler.

Dusk was settling in with a sky swirled pink and gold. The evening had cleared, a cool April twilight that carried the smell of wisteria and honeysuckle on it. A beautiful night as the Ford hummed along the paved road to Hattiesburg. At the turnoff to Fitler, the road changed to rutted gravel, and the car bounced from side to side on the narrow road.

In the twenty years that had passed, Fitler had been left far, far behind in the progress of the state. I pressed the gas harder as we bounced toward the river. Beside me, Elikah was either unconscious or dead. There was something I just had to tell him. One last delicious thing. "You know, Elikah, I never would have thought of this if it hadn't been for you, shooting off your mouth to Janelle. Picture her face when I go up and ask for my flag with a star to hang in the window, when I tell her my man has gone to war." I glanced at his pale profile. "Not a person in the world will suspect me of a thing since you told everyone you had already packed to go."

I passed the turn to Aunt Sadie's house and kept on. Jeb kept a wooden fishing boat chained to a cypress stump in one of the small landings. The chain weighed at least a hundred pounds. Jeb laughed that he'd rather have his boat sunk than stolen. But he'd given me a key for the rare times I wanted to fish. I backed the car down to the landing and then pushed Elikah out the door. He rolled to the edge of the water.

Fear gave me the strength to get him in the boat. Fear and hatred. As the boat drifted out into the current, I wrapped the chain around him as best I could, hauling it around his chest and between his legs and locking it tight with the big padlock. The boat was upriver from the bridge, and just as I finished, the moon broke over the horizon of thick trees and I saw the pilings silhouetted against the moon-shot water of the river.

Using the paddle to guide the boat, I drifted to a piling and grabbed the rope that some fisherman had tied there for a makeshift mooring. Elikah's body was still, motionless, but I knew that he wasn't dead. I knew because Duncan had never predicted anything but drownings.

Using every bit of strength I had, I heaved him over the side at the very base of the piling. There was the rattle of chains and the shush of air trapped in his clothes as he sank. Then, one last bubble of air, as if the river had suddenly swallowed him.

For a long time I sat in the boat, waiting for my heart to quiet and my fear to calm. It was done. There was no going back. For twenty years I had paid the price of this murder. I had done my time, and now I was free. Sitting tied to the piling, I got a cigarette from my pocket and had a smoke.

The butt sizzled in the river, and I untied the boat, guiding her slowly toward the shore. When I was almost to the bank, as far from the treacherous current as I dared to go without stranding the boat in the too-still shallows, I jumped clear of her, kicking her back toward the faster current as I swam to the bank.

The night was chill as I staggered out of the river and turned to watch the boat drifting slowly in the silvered water, drifting down the

Pascagoula toward the Sound and eventually the Gulf. Jeb would report her stolen, chain and all. Some scavenger farther down the river would find her and keep her.

It was a long walk back to the car, and the woods seemed to close down around me. I kept walking, unable to think or plan. The only picture in my mind was a spit of white sand and a small isolated beach house with bright red flowers ruffled by a strong wind. I would keep the house in Jexville. I would need a place to come to each spring, a place to wait for the waters of the river to run high, for the time when secrets were brought up from the murky depths.

One day Elikah's body might surface. One day. But until that time I was free. Truly free.

ACKNOWLEDGMENTS

Thanks, once again, to the Deep South Writers Salon: Rebecca Barrett, Alice Jackson Baughn, Renee Paul, Susan Tanner, Stephanie Vincent, and Jan Zimlich, and a special thanks to Pam Batson. Without their help the book would not be possible.

Janet Smith and the George County Regional Library were invaluable—and always wonderful—in helping me fight through the thicket of time and find material. In keeping with historical accuracy, the traveling electric chair was not used in Mississippi in the 1920s; hanging was the official method of execution. It wasn't until the forties that the portable chair became the legal means of execution. The chair would travel to the county where the conviction had occurred. These, and a million other facts, were found in the library, thanks to the staff.

My agent, Marian Young, offered encouragement and honesty, as she does with every book.

Audrey LaFehr, editor, and Elaine Koster, publisher, gave me the time and encouragement to finish this book—and a little push back to Jexville to find the story. Many thanks.

If a writer can attribute a book to anything except imagination and the desire to write, I have to acknowledge my family. My grandmother and mother taught me by example what it means to be strong, and my father showed me what it means to love. And late at night, while I wrote, it was the soft whisper of my mother's voice that shaped the story.